To Tame a Wild Heart

She was as wild as a mustang caught fresh from the hills—untamed, wary, and spooked. Wolf wanted inexplicably to gentle her.

Suddenly his mouth quirked upward at the absurdity of comparing this lovely, sensuous Rebeccah Rawlings to a horse.

"What're you smiling at?" she demanded, suspicion darkening her eyes.

"I'm thinking about—"

"Liar."

"Now you're hurting my feelings."

His wounded air sent a wave of irritation through her. "Oh, I forgot," she said acidly, yanking free of his arms. "Lawmen don't lie. Lawmen are good, pure, honest, upright—"

"Lawmen are men, Rebeccah," Wolf said tautly, his arms flashing out to snare her tight against him once more. Her glowing, sunlit face upturned toward him sent his blood pounding and turned his voice husky. "Flesh-and-blood men. Don't ever forget that."

How could I? Rebeccah wondered dazedly, when he was kissing her with such succulent, demanding kisses, again and again, holding her so tightly within those corded arms, she might have felt trapped but instead felt oddly, gloriously free. . . .

Also by Jill Gregory

Cherished
Forever After

JILL GREGORY

A Dell Book

Published by
Dell Publishing
a division of
Bantam Doubleday Dell Publishing Group, Inc.
1540 Broadway
New York, New York 10036

ISBN: 0-440-21618-4

Printed in the United States of America

Published simultaneously in Canada

May 1994

10   9   8   7   6   5   4   3   2   1

OPM

For Isadore and Jenny, and Morris and Sophie,
with love

PROLOGUE

Arizona Territory
1866

Stillness gripped the valley but for the hawks wheeling in the hot, merciless air. The run-down outlaw shack hidden among the sage-gray rocks and juniper appeared empty.

But Wolf Bodine knew better than to trust appearances. Though he was only twenty-two, his four-year stint in the U.S. cavalry had taught him shrewdness and caution. As he sidled through the rough-hewn door, his gun was drawn and at the ready, and every muscle in his large, rugged frame was taut.

The reputed hideout of Bear Rawlings's gang was not the place to get careless.

But it seemed his caution was for nothing, Wolf concluded in disappointment after prowling through the main room of the shack and the small, windowless bedroom in back. If Rawlings had ever been here, he was gone now, and there was no sign of him or his gang. The shack contained nothing but a rusting water pail in one corner, a bed, a few pieces of stacked wood near an ancient stove, two chairs, and some tin cups and plates in a cupboard. The place had been cleaned up and cleaned out. But as Wolf moved toward the door, he heard a sound from the bedroom.

His gray eyes grew hard, wary. Stealthily he made his way through the doorway into the bedroom, his boots treading lightly across the hard-packed earthen floor.

A faint film of sweat glistened at the open neck of his blue cambric shirt as he ran his gaze once more over the room. There was only one place to hide—beneath the narrow cot on the far bedroom wall.

Then came another sound, a tiny one, the merest scuff of a heel, but Wolf was on it in a flash. He heaved the cot up with one hand and sent it crashing against the back wall while with his other hand he aimed the pistol at the shape huddled, exposed, beneath.

"Don't move!"

But even as these words rang out, Wolf knew a keen disappointment. He realized at once that the culprit who'd been hiding beneath the cot was not Bear Rawlings or another one of his outlaw pards, after all, but only a scrawny kid, no more than ten or eleven years old.

Wolf swore under his breath. Carefully he holstered his gun and then with one muscle-corded arm hauled the youngster up.

The boy struggled wildly against the iron hands that lifted him clear off the dirt floor, but he was no match for the six foot two, very agile, and very strong Bodine.

"Let me go!" The kid kicked, punched, spat like the devil—missing his aim, however, each time.

"Take it easy, boy." Wolf's lean face relaxed as he pinioned the boy's thin wrists in one fist, and he knelt down to study him at eye level with a steady, appraising glance. "I won't hurt you if you tell me where Bear and his pards are hiding."

And then he stopped. His eyes narrowed on the scrawny, raggedly dressed boy flailing wildly against his grasp. Boy?

Hell and damnation, not by a long shot.

Brilliant violet eyes blazed back at him from within a small, pinched, nut-brown face. Wolf saw the she-cat sizzle in those dazzling eyes, saw that they were fringed by spiky, sooty lashes, and he noted simultaneously the fragile sweep of cheekbone so delicate, it could only be feminine. The dark brows were slim, daintily arched. And as he watched in stunned amazement the youth's flea-bitten sombrero slipped sideways, and a tangle of jaggedly cut long black hair flopped forward.

"Let me go, you dirty, low-down, no-good lawman!"

A girl. Stunned, he rocked back on his heels and let her go.

Instantly she swung her arm at him in a wide, vicious arc that swooshed through the air and narrowly missed his jaw.

"Why, you little hellcat." He grinned. "That wasn't very polite."

As he reached for her wrist again, she lunged at him, her dirt-encrusted nails clawing, her small mouth working contortedly as she spewed out a string of curses that would have done a cavalry-man proud. Wolf grasped her again by both wrists, holding her only as tightly as was necessary to keep her still, trying not to hurt her. "Easy, peanut," he said soothingly. "Take it easy. I only want to talk to you."

She was perhaps eleven, maybe twelve, no more —a dirty, swearing, ragged little beauty, with legs skinny as twigs and tiny breasts only beginning to bud beneath her greasy flannel shirt.

But one day, Wolf guessed, she'd be a stunner. What the hell was she doing here?

"What's your name?" he inquired as she at last ceased struggling and glared at him with unmitigated loathing.

For answer she drew a deep breath and spat square into his face.

Wolf wiped away the spittle with his bandanna, all the while holding both her wrists easily in one large hand, trying to retain his patience. He'd endured all the rigors of war, seen his friends and enemies brutally slain, withstood heat, hunger, fatigue, and despair. He could certainly manage one feisty eleven-year-old girl without losing his temper.

One undoubtedly frightened eleven-year-old girl. Though her face radiated defiance, plain common sense told him that beneath the furious rebellion she must be plenty scared. Her pulse raced beneath his thumb. Her violet eyes shone dark and wild in the shadowy dimness.

Wolf tried to be cool and professional about the situation, but he was touched with pity. The last thing he wanted to do was terrify a child, but he couldn't very well leave without finding out who she was and what her connection was with the Rawlings gang—if there was any connection. He kept his voice quiet, calm, speaking to her the way he would have to his own little sister, if she'd lived past infancy.

"I won't hurt you, honey. I promise. But I'll tell you right now, I'm not letting go of you until you give me some answers. And I'm a real patient man, so I'll wait all day—all night—if I have to."

"Bear'll kill you if you touch me! Say your prayers, mister, you're going straight to hell!"

"Where is Bear? Did he leave you here all alone? You know where he is, don't you, peanut? Are you his daughter?"

Her mouth twisted with contempt. "Who wants to know?"

"Wolf Bodine."

She went very still. Her skin seemed to pale beneath her weathered tan. She stared intently, all quiet and coiled like a rattler.

"You want to kill my father." She breathed at last, hate and loathing throbbing through her voice. "I've heard of you. You cleaned up Medicine Bend. And killed the Foster gang. Well, I won't let you kill Bear. I'll shoot you myself first!"

"Look, sweetheart, I don't want to kill anyone. But Bear Rawlings and his gang stole a very important payroll a few days ago from the stage headed to Tucson, and that money doesn't belong to them. They broke the law—you understand that, don't you?"

"I'm not stupid! But Bear says if you can outsmart folks and get their money away, you've earned it and they don't deserve it! If he catches you here, you'll be real sorry! Bear can't stomach lawmen. Me neither! So let me go and get the hell out of here while you're still breathin', cuz when they come back . . . !"

So they were coming back for her. That was all he needed to know.

"What's your name, honey?"

"None of your damned business."

Wolf shook his head. "You shouldn't be here," he said quietly, releasing her wrists and rising to his full height. "It's no life for a pretty little girl."

Those were the last words he uttered before he saw her eyes flick upward, focusing on someone behind him—someone, he realized instantly, who'd sneaked in while he was intent on her, and who in the next split second hit him from behind—hit him hard with something that sent Wolf Bodine crashing into iron blackness.

Reb sprang forward, her heart skittering like a jackrabbit in her chest. "You've killed him!" she cried. Fearfully she knelt over the handsome young stranger with the chestnut hair and quiet voice and touched his unmoving shoulder. She was crying, she discovered, and she didn't know why.

Russ Gaglin fingered the butt of his gun, which had just slammed Wolf Bodine in the skull. He studied the blood that ran from a gash in the fallen man's temple. "He ain't dead, Reb. See his chest goin' up and down? Should've killed him, though," he grumbled. "Don't know why I didn't. Could've shot him in the back easy as pie. Matter of fact maybe I should finish him off right now—"

"No!"

She was on him in a flash, shoving him backward. "You've done enough! Leave him be!"

Russ snorted in disgust at the way the kid had herself all worked up over Bodine. Bear's girl sure was a strange one—she could be quiet as an ant for days and then suddenly explode in your face like a miniature firecracker. But he slipped his gun into his holster and held up his hands in surrender.

"Okay, Reb, okay. But don't waste your tears on no lawman. Bear's waitin' for us up on the Rim."

"Tears . . . what're you talkin' about?" She swiped at her face with grimy fingers. "Who's crying? Not me!"

"Yeah, sure. Let's go."

He stomped to the door of the cabin and waited for her to scurry out in front of him, but she lingered a moment, biting her lip, gazing down in agitation at the unconscious man bleeding all over the floor.

"Maybe we should do something. . . ."

"You deaf, missy? Bear's waitin'! Let's ride!"

Sorry, Mr. Wolf Bodine, Reb thought as she leaped onto the back of the hardy pinto mustang Russ had kept hidden for her in a remote section of the valley. *But you shouldn't have come after Bear. You shouldn't have tried to track down our gang.*

Still, as she galloped across the blazing Arizona wilderness with Russ in the lead, she couldn't stop thinking about the stranger. He was unlike any man she'd ever encountered before, even Bear.

When she'd looked at him, despite her anger and her fear, something had happened inside. A topsy-turvy feeling. It had been real hard to breathe.

It wasn't only because he was so handsome, she mused, as the pinto galloped up a steep rocky incline bordered by mesquite and scrub. He'd been nice. Decent.

And there had been something kind in his cool, clear eyes.

Don't think about him, a little voice inside instructed. *He's a lawman. He's no good. Think about how he wanted to put Bear in jail.*

But later that night, reunited with Bear and the rest of the gang at the hideout on the Rim, Reb couldn't stop thinking about the tall stranger with the cool gray eyes. She huddled on the ground before the campfire while the men played cards and drank whiskey and argued under the trees, and she found herself gazing up at the wishing star. She wanted to make a wish, but she didn't know exactly what it was—and anyway, she decided, tossing her heavy hair back from her face, wishing was for babies.

And she was no longer a baby.

She didn't understand it. She didn't understand what was happening to her. Her body was changing in strange, unnerving ways. It scared her. It was confusing. All she knew was that everything was different, and she wanted everything to stay the same.

The red flames of the fire danced in the cool, pine-scented night. Reb stared moodily into the glowing heart of the fire and saw a face, a lean, strong-jawed face she knew she should forget.

"Go away," she whispered, and hugged her arms around herself.

But the face in the campfire remained, shimmering and clear, and something ached deep inside her heart.

She was possessed suddenly by a sweet, hard, powerful yearning.

"Wolf Bodine," she whispered in wonder to the dark, empty Arizona night.

It was the first time she ever spoke his name, as the longing and the loneliness welled up in her, but through the years of Rebeccah Rawlings's growing-up it would not be the last.

Powder Creek, Montana
1874

"Stage's late."

Ernest Duke shifted from one foot to the other and peered into the rolling, green distance as if trying to conjure the stagecoach out of thin, crystal-clear Montana air. But there was nothing, no sign, no sound other than the usual town sounds, of horses' hooves and creaky plankboards and children hollering and folks greeting one another in passing. "Stage is mighty late," he reiterated nervously, drawing wrathful stares from the little greeting party of Powder Creek dignitaries who waited uneasily alongside him outside Koppel's General Store.

"We know that, Ernest," snapped Myrtle Lee Anderson, head of the town social committee. Her doughy cheeks flushed a deep, ruddy shade that matched her stiffly pinned-up hair. She plopped her hands on her ample hips and glared at him. "Question is, *why* is it late? You tell me that, or keep your thoughts to yourself."

"My dear Mrs. Anderson," Ernest said with injured dignity, puffing out his spindly chest and casting her a pained look from beneath gray brows that arced in an inverted V over eyes as black as the Montana night sky. "If I knew the reason *why* the stage is late, I could do something about it. I could help Sheriff Bodine round up a posse to ride out and find 'em, in case they've lost a wheel or overturned, or—"

He broke off, not wishing to continue with any of the other possibilities, such as an Indian attack or a holdup by one of the brutal outlaw bands roaming Montana and preying on unprotected citizens. No one wanted to think about that yet. As mayor of Powder Creek it was his responsibility to see that things ran smoothly, properly, according to schedule, plan, and recognized procedure. Late stages were not all that uncommon, he tried to tell himself, but this one was nearly four hours late, and he, Myrtle Lee Anderson, and Waylon Pritchard had been waiting in the hot sun for a good portion of that time ready to welcome Powder Creek's new official schoolteacher—only now they were wondering if this might turn out to be a burying party instead of a welcoming one.

They were wondering it, but no one wanted to say it.

Still, as the late-afternoon sun inched across the sky, and the brilliant August day ambled on toward hazy sunset, each of them knew that something was wrong.

Ernest Duke felt it in his bones. Myrtle Lee Anderson sensed it in the air. And Waylon Pritchard, son of the most prosperous rancher in this part of Montana, detected it in his gut.

Waylon, whose pa had insisted he make up part of the welcoming committee, glanced in disgust at his gold pocket watch, then stuffed it back into his black Sunday-best suit. He scowled out at the lush, emerald-green horizon that dipped and rose and curved in every direction past Powder Creek, at the majestic splendor of the snow-capped Rocky Mountains to the west, and thought yearningly of all the fun he could be having with Coral right now in the little room above the Gold Bar Saloon, 'stead of wasting his entire afternoon waiting for some prissy schoolteacher, like his pa insisted.

"Damn Pa anyway. He'll never let me marry Coral, just because she's a dance-hall girl. Well, I'll be a lizard 'fore I saddle myself with some mousy little schoolmarm for life," Waylon reflected resentfully, and glanced up at the window of the room Coral shared with three other girls. Even as he looked, she appeared magically in the window, lovely in a low-cut crimson gown. She waved to him briefly before disappearing.

"Dad gurn it," Waylon exploded, knowing he didn't have time to visit Coral now and still get home before his ma served supper, "why don't we git Sheriff Bodine to send out a search party? It's been long enough. I'm goin' home. Maybe you have nothing better to do, but I'm not standing here one more blasted minute—"

But Waylon broke off as from a distance came the low rumble of hooves and coach wheels, and a dust cloud billowed up far down the road.

"Here she comes!" Ernest crowed, wiping the sweat from his face. Myrtle Lee gripped her parasol in both hands and squinted down the road.

"Slim's comin' mighty fast," she muttered, and

stepped forward to lean over the boardwalk railing for a better look.

It was true. The stagecoach driver was whipping the team of six horses to a furious lather as the stage roared up with a thunder of hoofbeats, ringing gunshots, and shouts of "Whoa!"

When the dust cleared, the driver hollered down at the welcoming committee: "We was held up! Got a dead man on top!"

Sure enough, a corpse was strapped to the top of the coach, wrapped in a blood-soaked horse blanket beside a pile of baggage.

"That a passenger, Slim?" Waylon asked as Myrtle gasped in horror beside him.

"Nope. One of the varmints who tried to rob us!"

"You shot one?" Ernest gazed approvingly at the sweating, dust-caked face of the driver as he leaped down from the coach and threw open the door. "Good work, Slim—"

" 'Fraid I cain't take credit for it, or Raidy neither," the driver said, interrupting. With one quick motion, he let down the stagecoach steps.

"Well, if *you* didn't shoot him, then who—?"

"She did." He jerked his thumb toward the door of the coach as a bright-eyed young woman gracefully alighted.

Behind her straggled a batch of other passengers: a portly silver-haired man; a matron in black bombazine and high-laced boots, and a gawky young fellow with spectacles perched on his thin, high-bridged nose and carrying a satchel over his arm. But no one in the welcoming committee paid any of them the least heed—they all stared with varying degrees of amazement at the slender, dark-haired girl in the sapphire-blue silk traveling dress who paused in the street and regarded them with quiet appraisal. For a moment there was silence as the sun beat down, the horses tossed their heads, and the wind whistled down from the mountains.

Then the girl straightened her shoulders, pushed back a loose tendril of her heavy hair, and strode across the street with brisk, assured steps. She addressed the welcoming committee curtly.

"Someone kindly send for the sheriff. I would greatly like to finish this business at once and be on my way."

Thus Rebeccah Rawlings arrived in her new hometown of Powder Creek. While the townsfolk looked her over with good old-fashioned curiosity, gaping and whispering among themselves, she gripped her reticule in weary fingers and managed, as she had for the last several hours, to keep from retching.

She'd never killed a man before. She'd shot at some and target-practiced at tin cans, tree stumps, and even coins tossed in the air, but never had she aimed her gun at a man and meant to kill him. Until today.

But that desperado had actually fired inside the coach—he could have killed any one of the passengers, herself included, and no one else had seemed inclined to do anything. So she had done what Bear had taught her to do—shoot back, defend herself. Afterward she'd wanted to scream, moan, and vomit out her guts, but she couldn't. Too many people around. She'd have looked like a weak little fool.

And she was hardly that. She forced her shoulders straighter. She was Bear Rawlings's daughter. She was far too tough to flinch or cry or even ponder about the life she'd snuffed out with the squeeze of a trigger.

And she couldn't ever forget it, even for a moment. She had too many enemies now, she reflected. For a moment her stomach clenched as she remembered the man who had accosted her in Boston before she set out. Neely Stoner had sent him to scare her. As if she were a sniveling coward who would have turned over the papers to the silver mine even if she had them!

But Neely'd tried to get them anyhow. She knew he—and the others—would try again. It was possible, Rebeccah acknowledged with a cold pinprick of fear, that she had even been followed to Montana, that somehow the men who were after those papers had found out about the ranch. And that meant that sooner or later—probably sooner—some mean, greedy hombres would show up to steal them or force her to hand them over.

She couldn't let her guard down even for a moment, couldn't let herself go soft or weak. If she did, Neely and the rest would close in for the kill.

Through her weariness and the bilious waves of nausea, she exerted every effort to appear brisk and unconcerned. She allowed herself a swift glance around the town and drew comfort from what she saw. In all the years she'd been away in Boston, she'd forgotten just how rough and primitive frontier towns were. This one was as rough as any of them. But something inside her lifted at the sight of Koppel's General Store with its large swinging sign and false front, at the apothecary and dry-goods stores alongside it, even at the numerous saloons lining both sides of the narrow street. She gazed quickly about at the rough wooden boardwalk and hitching posts, at the water troughs and the dusty street filled with cowboys, merchants, horses, chickens, and dogs, at the women in homespun calico clutching babies in their arms. Her gaze rose to sweep over the wide-open stunning blue horizon.

The sky was huge as heaven. The towering Rockies loomed majestically in the distance, dotted here and there by tiny crystal lakes that glimmered like miniature sapphires among the high firs and pines. At the feet of the cobalt mountains the valleys were lush and breathtaking with late-summer flowers: poppies, asters, Indian paintbrush, lilies, and white and purple heather.

Montana was a land of glittering beauty—sharp mountains, jade prairies, bluegrass, laurel, red cedar, and spruce.

And space—shining clean, tingly, wide-open space, where she could breathe and ride free and lose herself—and lose her memories, every single one of them.

Her gaze returned almost dazedly to the scene before her—the street with its wandering chickens, the dogs, children, horses, and buggies all part of this raw little town before her—and she took hold of herself with quick effort. But deep inside she felt glad—quietly, joyfully glad.

She was free. Free of Boston. Free of Miss Elizabeth Wright's Academy for Young Ladies, free of that horrid, stuffy brick building trimmed in ivy, free of the cramped little room that she'd called home the past two years. She was free now of the dry, tasteless meals at table, the prim stares of the rest of the teachers, any of whom would have probably fainted away at the sight of this wild western town. No more schedules, prissy gowns buttoned up to the neck, long days teaching literature to girls who never bothered to pick up a book. This was home now. Not this town precisely, or any of these staring people. But once she rode out to the ranch, found it in its lovely little valley, threw open the door of the ranchhouse her father had bequeathed to her, and stepped inside, she would be home. And the moment she unpacked her own belongings, her books, her piano music, her paintings, she'd be free for good.

Weary as she was from her journey, from the violence of what had happened this very afternoon, from the bloodshed in which she had been forced to play a part, she knew a taut pulling of anticipation, of longing as she thought of the ranch. She couldn't wait to get there, to be alone, at peace in her very own home.

"Ma'am, are you telling us that you shot that varmint up there?" Ernest Duke couldn't believe his ears. This elegant, spectacularly lovely female dressed in all that silky, lacy finery, with those feathers sticking out of her little blue velvet hat, and her dress so fine—a little crumpled but rich-looking for all that—this *girl* had killed an outlaw? He peered at her incredulously, unable to conceal his doubt. "With what, may I ask?"

Rebeccah's intense violet eyes skewered him. "Are you the sheriff, sir?"

Ernest took a step back beneath that blistering stare.

"Why, no. I'm Mayor Duke. But—"

"I prefer to tell my story to the sheriff." She turned away from him with a dismissive wave of her gloved hand, let her glance flit over Myrtle Lee's bulky form, and allowed it at last to come to rest upon Waylon Pritchard's sweating one.

"Would you be so kind," she said in slowly distinct accents, as if speaking to a very small child or someone bereft of sense, "to fetch the sheriff to me? I have no wish to stand here in the sun for however many hours remain in the day."

Waylon flushed beneath those large, brilliant, icy eyes. He had never seen a woman like this before. He'd thought Coral was beautiful, with her pale, curly hair and sweet light-green eyes, but this girl took his breath away. Regal as a princess she was and talked every bit as fine. Her face was heart-shaped, as delicately formed as his ma's best china. Beneath that little feathered hat of hers, her skin glowed like fresh cream. He was fascinated by the way those eyes of hers tilted slightly upward at the outer ends. Most appealing. They were a rich, wild violet hue, so deep and brilliant, they put the poor sky to shame. She was tall, willowy—but not too willowy, he noted admiringly. A few wisps of jet-black hair had escaped her heavy chignon during the journey and now sprang rebelliously about her cheeks, adding dark, earthy drama to the beauty before him.

"Ma'am," Waylon stuttered at last as she continued to stare at him with growing impatience, "I'll be glad to fetch the sheriff for you. It'd be an honor. It'd be a privilege. I'd like nothing better than to do you this service."

"Then git goin'!" the driver, Slim, bellowed, tossing baggage down onto the street.

And then someone from the crowd yelled, "Hold yore horses, Waylon! Here comes the sheriff now!"

And Rebeccah sighed with relief. At last. The crowd parted. She braced herself for the explanation ahead of her, for the tough stance she was prepared to take in order to get possession of the reward money. She had exactly forty-seven dollars in her reticule, all the money she possessed in the world, and it wasn't nearly enough to build up and maintain a ranch. She would need every penny to survive on her own out here. The thought of how close she was to poverty frightened her, but she took refuge in knowing that at least she didn't *look* poor. Anyone seeing her fine clothes and the ruby ring winking on her finger, the pearl choker at her throat, would think she was rich as Midas. But appearances, Rebeccah knew well, could be deceiving.

She shaded her eyes with her hand and peered through the opening in the throng. She had a deep-seated distrust and resentment of lawmen and was eager to get this business over with as rapidly as possible. The less she had to do with the sheriff of Powder Creek, the better, but she needed this money, and he was the only one who could get it for her. Rebeccah believed in facing up to difficult tasks immediately instead of putting them off. She'd dispatch matters with this sheriff, she told herself, and then get out to the ranch in time to sleep in her very own bed tonight.

She didn't know precisely what she expected, perhaps a balding, middle-aged lawman with a paunch and red-rimmed eyes, or an ancient oak of a man, leathered and squinty and bow-kneed, but the man coming toward her with easy, purposeful strides was none of those things.

He moved with the grace of an Indian. Something about his height, the way he carried himself seemed oddly familiar.

Rebeccah felt a curious twisting of her heart.

And then it began to hammer. . . .

He was tall, with wide, muscular shoulders beneath his blue shirt and leather vest. He had a lean, taut-muscled body and a flowing, dangerous gait. *Don't mess with me,* his walk said. *I don't look for trouble, but I won't run from it either.*

Like him. . . . she thought on a wave of memory. *Like him.*

The sun glided westward, no longer hampering her vision, and she could see his face as he paused before her.

Rebeccah gasped.

It was *his* face, strong and stern and quiet. And strikingly familiar, even after all these years.

Wolf Bodine.

He was the same—and yet different.

He could be no more than twenty-eight, twenty-nine years old, but there was a grim hardness now in the set of his jaw, a sort of weathered toughness that had matured and intensified over the years. The cool gray eyes had tiny fine lines around their edges now, a hint of sadness or bitterness or perhaps harshness reflected in their clear depths—and they glinted like polished stones, missing nothing.

Oh, God. He was as handsome as she remembered—no, she realized dazedly, more so. The years had chiseled him, hardened him, stamped him with a keen, fine-honed ruggedness. His body was corded with muscle. His stomach was flat, his hips lean beneath his dark trousers.

Wolf Bodine.

How can this be? she thought with a quivering disbelief, her gaze taking in those compelling eyes, the clean-shaven jaw, the burnished chestnut hair that just reached the collar of his shirt. She trembled inwardly at the bronzed toughness of that never-to-be-forgotten face, lost herself in the long-lashed gray eyes that pierced her like tomahawks as she held her ground on the boardwalk. She was all too aware of the sinewy muscularity of his imposing frame, of his steady, quiet manner that was no less dangerous for all its calm. It was *him*.

She had seen him a thousand times in her memories, her dreams, her thoughts. He was the one . . . the one she'd been foolishly, idiotically in love with since she was twelve years old.

Loco. That's what she was. Loco to have thought

all this time about a man she'd met as a child, a man she'd spent only moments with, a man who was her father's enemy.

A man she'd left for dead on the dirt floor of a hideaway cabin in the middle of nowhere.

2 His badge glittered in the late-after-noon sun. Rebeccah clenched the silken strap of her reticule and worked at not letting her feet fidget. Bear always said her feet twitched when she was nervous. And lawmen always made her nervous.

Reflex, probably. She'd spent a good portion of her life running from the law.

But there's no reason to be in such a tizzy over Wolf Bodine, she told herself desperately. *You're a grown woman now, nearly twenty-one years old, not a stupid little girl.*

And you've done nothing wrong.

Besides, he didn't remember her. He was staring at her with a cool detachment that held no trace of recognition.

Well, why should he remember a filthy kid who'd spit in his face and let him get clobbered with a Colt revolver?

Better if he never remembered any of that, she realized hastily. She gulped in a deep breath. She knew she'd scream if the silence went on another moment.

"Sheriff," she blurted out, her words tumbling a shade too fast, "that man up there, the dead one, tried to rob our stagecoach. I shot him in self-defense. The driver says he is a wanted man by the name of Scoop Parmalee—of the Parmalee gang. There is a price on his head. I wish therefore to claim the reward money."

He had his thumbs hooked in his gunbelt, and he was staring at her, staring hard.

"Have we met before?"

"No . . . oo." She went pink. The lie had just jumped out before she even realized it, and now it was too late to take it back.

His cool eyes studied her. "I'm reckoned to be good with faces."

"How nice for you." Sweat dripped down her armpits, dampening her gown.

"Ever been to Tucson?"

Relentless, that's what he was. Typical lawman. Rebeccah's nerves stretched taut. *Think!*

Her mind racing, she dropped her reticule to give herself more time. She wasn't very good at this business of feminine wiles, but if ever there was a time for it, Rebeccah concluded, this must be it. The small bag struck the boardwalk with a thud.

Wolf Bodine moved not a muscle.

"Oh, dear." She tried to sound helpless and dismayed.

Still he made no move to retrieve it for her. Instead he advanced closer. Rebeccah was intensely aware of his size, his strength. She breathed in the scent of him, a clean scent . . . like cake soap and good leather and pine needles. With misgiving she saw the determination in his eyes as they pinned her coldly, ruthlessly.

Suspiciously.

"You didn't answer my question, ma'am," he said in a quiet drawl that was nevertheless purposeful. *"Have you ever been to Tucson?"*

"Never."

Lies ought to come easily to her, but they didn't. She met his gaze with tremendous effort, keeping her stare unflinching. Someone coughed behind her. The stagecoach driver threw down another trunk. Rebeccah's feet itched to fidget. She knew she'd burst if she had to stare into those piercing eyes another moment.

In desperation she stooped to retrieve her own bag. As luck would have it, Waylon Pritchard bent to retrieve it at precisely the same moment.

Their heads banged together.

There was a resounding thump.

"Ouch!" she gasped, wincing and seeing stars as the pain rocked straight through to her skull.

"Dang it," Waylon moaned, sinking onto the boardwalk.

Myrtle Lee Anderson guffawed. Mayor Duke tsked sympathetically, and the stagecoach passengers murmured concern as Waylon went on to curse out a string of colorful oaths. The rest of the onlookers laughed and began drifting away. They had chores to finish, work to do, and plenty of time to hear the gossip about the lady who shot Scoop Parmalee later.

Rebeccah's head smarted from the force of the collision. She straightened with an effort, then a moment later staggered back, dizzy. Instantly Wolf

Bodine's hands shot out to steady her, preventing her from falling.

"Easy, there. You all right? Waylon, you clumsy oaf. Are you trying to help this lady or kill her?"

Pritchard, a bristly-bearded young man with the wit of a longhorn, hunkered down on the boardwalk and cradled his head in his hands.

"Aw, come on, Wolf. I was just *tryin'* to be a gentleman, but this here lady has the hardest head I ever did come up against—"

"How dare you!" Stung out of her own pain, Rebeccah jerked free of Bodine's grasp. The damnable temper she'd inherited from Bear flared up and galvanized her instinct to protect herself—for over the years she'd learned that if she didn't do it, nobody would. "You're the most clumsy, dim-witted fool ever to cross my path, you . . . you obstreperous calamity. And give me back my bag!"

Bodine watched as the girl snatched her reticule from Waylon and smacked him in the shoulder with it. "Sheriff, are you going to give me that reward money or not?"

Bodine had to admire her for sheer orneriness. How could anyone who looked like such an elegant little angel be so full of spice and chili pepper? And this petite, violet-eyed angel was oddly familiar. But he couldn't place her to save his life. Maybe it wasn't Tucson . . . but something nagged at him.

Regardless, she was trouble.

He knew it just by looking at her, by the lush cloud of velvet-black hair framing her dainty cheeks, by the imperious glimmer in those soot-lashed eyes, by the intelligent tilt of her majestic little chin. Trouble. He smelled it as surely as he smelled her fancy French perfume.

He fervently hoped she was just passing through Powder Creek and not coming to visit for any length of time.

With an effort Wolf dragged his eyes from her. He turned his attention to Slim and the shotgun rider, Raidy. "Is this lady right about what happened to-day?"

Slim left the horses to lumber up beside him. The top of the driver's shaggy head nearly reached the lawman's shoulder. "Sure as you're standin' there, Sheriff," he declared. "Four of 'em tried to hold us up—this young lady shot two. Winged one of 'em, but Scoop is shore dead. Nice shootin,' eh? Mebbe you should take her on as a deputy."

The remaining crowd guffawed with laughter. Bodine grinned, his eyes lightening suddenly.

"Maybe I should."

Rebeccah gritted her teeth. *Deputy? Over my dead body.*

Again his gaze burned a hole through her. "Would you like a badge, ma'am?" he drawled with a slow, lazy grin that would have melted her heart if Rebeccah had let it. Instead she steeled herself with every ounce of determination she possessed.

"All I want is my reward, Sheriff," she managed to bite out.

He threw a quick glance at the dead man atop the coach, pulled himself up for a better look, and then nodded grimly to Slim and Raidy. It was Parmalee all right.

Wolf jumped back down and ran a quick glance over the other passengers, who were waiting as if for permission to go on their way. "Anyone hurt?" he inquired.

"Only that awful bandit, Sheriff," the woman in black bombazine piped up. "This young lady saved our lives."

Wolf touched the tip of his hat. "Then I reckon she ought to get her reward," he said. He took Rebeccah's arm. "My office is down the street. Come sign some papers, answer some questions, and this business will be all wrapped up."

"Don't worry, miss, I'll set your bags inside the hotel till you're ready to fetch 'em," Slim called after her as Wolf Bodine drew her along the boardwalk. "All you folks continuing on to Silver Bluff— we'll take supper and head out in an hour's time," he announced, and turned toward the saloon.

Ernest Duke's distressed wail stopped both Slim and Wolf Bodine in their tracks.

"H . . . o . . . ld on! Slim, you can't go yet. Surely there must be more passengers. Where in blazes is she?" Ernest demanded, his black eyes nearly popping out of his head.

"Where's who, mayor?"

"Miss Kellum—the new schoolteacher!" Myrtle Lee snapped.

The driver snorted. "Oh, that one. Why, she caused me more trouble'n a pack of coyotes. She turned tail and ran after the holdup and shootin' and all. Kicked up such a dust like you never did see. Had hysterics till I agreed to take her straight

back to Helena. Reckon she's headed back east
where she come from."

"But . . ." Myrtle sputtered. "That can't be! We
have a contract. Don't we, Ernest?"

The mayor scowled, thinking of the timid little
wren of a schoolmarm he had interviewed a month
ago in Philadelphia. She'd had such excellent cre-
dentials—too bad backbone wasn't one of them.
"What good is a contract without the damned
teacher?" he grumbled in reply, and Waylon Pritchard threw his hat on the ground in fury and
stomped on it.

"Tarnation. Do you mean I wasted my entire afternoon as part of a welcoming committee for a
teacher who ain't comin'? If that don't beat all!"

"Sheriff, what're we going to do now?" Mayor
Duke demanded, as always turning to the one person he could count on to think clearly in a crisis.

Bodine returned to the little group, regarding Ernest, Myrtle, and Waylon thoughtfully. The dark-
haired young woman who'd shot Scoop Parmalee
hung back, though she appeared to be listening intently.

"It seems to me that if your Miss Kellum didn't
have the gumption to stick it out until she reached
Powder Creek, she most likely wouldn't have been
much good for our youngsters anyway. We need
someone with a little starch to them, as Caitlin always says." A rueful smile touched Wolf's lips. He
shook his head. "I reckon we'll have to start all
over again until we find someone else. Maybe we
could take out an advertisement in a newspaper."

"That'll take time—meanwhiles we'll have another winter with no schoolin' for our young 'uns," Myrtle Lee snapped.

Wolf fixed his cool gaze on her flushed, scowling face. "You could always teach 'em yourself, Myrtle," he suggested, another flash of humor lighting his eyes.

"Me?" She shook a stubby finger in his face. "That'll be the day. I raised six children and I don't mind telling you I've had it up to here with every one of 'em. No, thank you, sir! Now, Sheriff, be serious. I'd think you'd want to find someone educated proper, who could teach our kids what they'll need to know to improve themselves, someone with enough patience and spirit to handle a rowdy bunch of young 'uns too frisky for their own good —you, with a boy of your own, should want a proper teacher as much as anyone in this town!"

A boy of your own?

Stunned, Rebeccah felt her mouth drop open. She quickly shut it. Her startled gaze flew to the sheriff's impassive face. *So you're married now, Wolf Bodine. A husband and a father.* She felt something wither inside of her and had a horrible vision of a sweet golden-blond wife with rosy cheeks and a perpetually adoring smile on her face. And babies in her arms. A houseful of children, a perfect little home with pies baking and a crackling fire.

She felt numb. A cherry-colored flush blossomed up from her neck to suffuse her face. All of those stupid daydreams about this man! Those giddy, romantic, heart-stopping melodramas she'd played out in her head. Over and over she'd imagined him coming for her at Miss Wright's Academy, riding right up to the door . . . declaring that he couldn't forget her, even as young as she'd been, that he'd had to find her, to see what kind of a woman she'd grown into.

Miss Rawlings, I haven't been able to stop thinking about you for a single day since we met. You've haunted my thoughts. Oh, yes, I know you were young, but you were so lovely, so incredibly lovely. I think you bewitched me—which is why I never heard Russ Gaglin sneak up and conk me on the head. No, my sweet, don't fret over that. It's done. How could I ever be angry with you? You were only helping to protect your father—a most noble goal. Miss Rawlings, may I tell you this? I sensed from the first something fine and delicate and noble in your soul. I know this sounds strange, but I knew at once you would become a beautiful woman. I waited for you. I'm glad I did. No other woman could ever make me feel the way I do looking at you right this minute. Miss Rawlings, may I have the infinite pleasure of kissing you?

"Myrtle, I want a good schoolteacher to settle in here every bit as much as you," Wolf Bodine was saying evenly to the cross-looking woman in the hideous green bonnet. "But I can't exactly force one to come all the way to Montana—or to stay even if she does."

"That's right, Myrtle. There's no call getting mad at the sheriff," Ernest chided.

Even Waylon, put out as he was by the entire situation, felt compelled to agree. "If it weren't for

Sheriff Bodine, we'd have no decent women who'd even think of comin' to this town, and you know it, Myrtle. Who cleared the Saunders gang out of here, and the Bentley brothers? Wal, don't forget it. If Sheriff Bodine wasn't around, these here streets'd be crawlin' with riffraff, that's what my pa always says, and my ma agrees with him."

"Now, don't start talking about your ma and pa, Waylon," Ernest intervened hastily, "or we'll be jawing all day. I, for one, am in need of sustenance after the events of this afternoon. Anyone who cares to join me in the Gold Bar Saloon is more than welcome."

Rebeccah found herself keeping pace with the long-legged Bodine once more as he headed toward his office and the members of the welcoming committee went their separate ways.

Her thoughts clipped along as rapidly as her kid-booted feet as she tried to sort through a myriad of feelings and information. So the irritating Miss Kellum, who'd moaned complaints all during the journey, had left a teaching position wide open here in Powder Creek, she mused to herself, storing the information away for further consideration. Not that Rebeccah relished the prospect of resuming any teaching duties—two years of snooty and frivolous students at Miss Wright's Academy had been more than enough. But if it turned out she needed to work until the ranch was running at a profit, at least she knew there was a position for which she was qualified.

She said nothing, however, preferring to wait until she had thought the matter over and seen in what condition of prosperity was her ranch.

The sheriff's office was a one-story building at the far end of the street. Wolf Bodine held the door for her, and she glanced inside at a small, tidy room consisting of a cluttered desk and some old leather chairs, green-painted shutters at the windows, neat shelves filled to overflowing with books, and stacks of papers.

And a six-foot-square cell, complete with iron bars, a cot, bucket, and a dingy brown blanket.

Apart from that the cell was empty.

But the sight of it made a knot tighten painfully in her stomach.

"What's the matter?"

"Nothing."

He was staring at her, noting her obvious hesitation to cross the threshold.

"Your feet are fidgeting."

"What . . . ? Oh." In dismay she realized that he was right, she had been tapping her foot, shifting her weight, tapping the other foot.

She clenched her teeth in chagrin and marched into the office. Wolf shut the door behind her. "I'm tired, Sheriff," Rebeccah offered by way of explanation. She kept her eyes averted from the cell. "I'd like to finish this business quickly and be on my way."

"Where're you headed?"

"Not far from here."

"Can you be a mite more specific?"

"Why?"

He came nonchalantly around his desk, eased his long frame into the chair, sat back, and looked up into her face. Seconds ticked by. Rebeccah diligently concentrated on keeping her feet motionless.

"Because you strike me as a lady trying to hide something," he said softly.

And suddenly Rebeccah realized the futility of trying to keep her identity from him—from anyone in Powder Creek. If she was going to live on a ranch just outside of town, everyone in Powder Creek would soon know exactly who she was—Bear Rawlings's daughter. She just hadn't planned on having to deal with it so soon.

But there was no avoiding it.

"I'm the new owner of the Rawlings property." She kept her voice even despite the rapid thrum of her heart. "Perhaps you know it. It used to be the Peastone place."

"The place Bear Rawlings won from old Amos Peastone in a poker game?" His eyes flickered with something, whether it was premonition, intuition, or just plain suspicion, Rebeccah wasn't sure. He leaned forward. "And your name is . . ."

"Rebeccah Rawlings. How nice to see you again, Mr. Bodine."

He was out of the chair in a flash. He reached her with a minimum of movement, his long legs gliding around the desk, his arms snaking out to grasp her. *"Nice* isn't exactly the word I would choose."

Rebeccah flinched. Unthinking, she took a step backward at the cold fury in his face. He must have thought she was going to turn tail and run, because he grasped her even more firmly by the arms and yanked her forward with sudden and overpowering strength, much as he had done in the shack all those years ago.

"You're not going anywhere. I have a score to settle with you, lady."

She twisted wildly, unable to break free. "It wasn't my fault—"

"You set me up. Distracted me so that one of your father's gang could smash my head in."

"No!" Rebeccah stopped struggling, meeting his glittering gaze with consternation. His eyes were the color of molten iron, and the anger in him was hot and potent, blazing between them. "I never meant . . . I didn't know Russ was coming back until he was in the door, signaling me to keep quiet. I never wanted him to hurt you."

"I'm supposed to believe Bear Rawlings's daughter?" He gave a short laugh. "That'll be the day."

Rebeccah went completely still. She turned white with anger. Then, in a frenzy, she tried to push him away, but he only tightened his grip on her, his hands manacling her arms with ruthless ease. "Let me go! I've done nothing wrong. Committed no crime. And you've no right to manhandle me."

"Manhandle?" Wolf suddenly glanced down at his own powerful fingers and realized what he was doing. He drew in his breath and released his grip. *Easy, Bodine,* he told himself. *Where's that famous cool-headedness? Why are you letting her get you so riled up?*

Maybe because his instincts about her had been right all those years ago. She'd grown into a stun-

ner. The same violet eyes, alluringly upturned at
the outer corners, blazed at him, only now they
were the eyes of a gorgeous woman. She had the
same sooty lashes, the same fiery rebelliousness,
but the face and body now belonged to a dazzling
angel of femininity, not a filthy rough-and-tumble
kid.

But there was another reason she was getting
under his skin, a voice inside of him admitted. She
reminded him in some strange way of Clarissa.
Maybe it was the dark hair, the fair, creamy skin—
but the eyes and mouth were completely different.
Clarissa had long, catlike green eyes, the color of
summer grass. And a delicate bow mouth, small
and perfect, while Rebeccah Rawlings's lips were
richly full, downright sensuous.

No, that's not it, Wolf decided hastily, shifting his
gaze from those lush parted lips. *I'm letting her get
to me because I've carried a grudge all these years
against that seemingly innocent little kid in an Arizona hideout shack who set me up to get pistol-
whipped. I was careless and she saw it—hell, she
instigated it.*

No matter what the reason, his blood was boil-
ing, and Wolf knew he had to cool it down.

He moved away from her and stalked over to the
bookcase, regarding her in silence from a distance
of about seven feet. It was hot in the office, breeze-
less and stuffy, and Wolf at that moment badly
wanted a drink. *Not until you've dealt with her,* he
told himself. *Calmly, dispassionately, and decisively.*

She looked like she could use a drink too.

She isn't that same dirty little kid anymore, he reminded himself. *She's a woman. An exquisite
woman.*

And therefore even more dangerous.

He moved toward her, under control now. She
was watching him, her piquant face set afire with
anger, and flushed in the rosy sunlight streaming
through the window. Her fingers unconsciously
rubbed her wrist where he had grabbed her, but
her spine was straight and rigid, her mouth a firm
line. She fairly quivered with outrage. *She looks a
hell of a lot more furious than frightened,* Wolf
thought coldly. *And that's not good.*

He wanted to scare her, to send her packing.

She was trouble.

"What makes you think Bear Rawlings's daughter
is welcome in my town?" he asked softly, stopping
right before her and hooking his thumbs in his gunbelt. "Maybe, Miss Rawlings, you should just get
right back on that stagecoach and keep going."

Rebeccah swallowed back a lump of pain. How
vividly she remembered someone else confronting
her with that same tone, and almost those same
words. The day she'd arrived at Miss Wright's
Academy, Analee Caruthers had stalked into her
room, followed by four other girls, crossed her
arms across her chest, and suggested Rebeccah
"get back on the train that had brought her from
wherever." Analee's hazel eyes had glowed with
malice. "We don't want you here. You're not our
kind. Why don't you simply go somewhere else?"

"You can't force me to leave," she told Wolf Bodine, her mouth dry. Why had she ever expected that anyone would accept her, would let her start over in peace? She repeated the words she had told Analee and the others. "I'm staying."

Sunlight filtered in through the green shutters, burnishing Wolf's hair, casting shadows on the deep coppered bronze of his skin. *He could never trust me, much less like me,* Rebeccah realized with a rush of agonizing insight. *No one here will. I should go, after all.*

But where?

There was no place else. She was alone. And broke. She'd rid herself of everything Bear had given her, all but a few clothes, some keepsakes— and the ranch.

You mustn't cry, she instructed herself fiercely, blinking away the needle sting of unshed tears. *You mustn't let him or anyone see that they can make you bleed.* Bear had warned her how dangerous any sign of weakness before enemies could be.

They'll eat you like vultures, he'd said time and again. *There'll be nothing left but gnawed-up bones.*

Wolf Bodine was watching her closely.

"I'm staying," she said again, her fingers clenching the delicate strap of her reticule.

"I reckon that's your choice. But don't expect folks around here to welcome you with open arms. Your father and his gang robbed the bank a few years back, before I came to town." He paused, seemed about to say something else, then changed his mind and went on quickly, "They got clean away with money belonging to a lot of folks. Maybe you're wearing some of that money right now," he added meaningfully, his eyes fixed on her pearl choker.

"What I'm wearing is none of your business. I'm here in this office to get my reward money, Sheriff Bodine. Now, are you going to give it to me or not?"

I'd like to give it to you, all right, he thought, but aloud he only said, "Take it easy, Miss Rawlings. I intend to give you everything you deserve."

Rebeccah stiffened, but she let the remark pass. All she wanted was to get this entire business over with and to get out of here. And if she never saw Wolf Bodine or this odious sheriff's office again, it would be far too soon.

In silence she filled out the papers he gave her. He in turn signed them without glancing at her.

"I'll have to wire for the money. I'll bring it out to you when I get it."

"See that you do."

She was nearly through the door when his voice stopped her. "You've got a fair distance to travel, Miss Rawlings. Might be a good idea to stay overnight in the hotel and head out for the ranch tomorrow."

"No, thank you, Sheriff," she snapped. All she wanted was to leave this town behind. Not one person here would welcome her when they learned who she was—Bodine was right about that. *Bear, why did you have to rob the bank in this particular town?*

She had no desire to be stared at, sneered at, or accosted. She wanted only to be left alone. *I've already killed a man this afternoon—certainly that's quite enough of defending myself for one day.*

"Your concern is touching, but I've no desire to stay in your flea-bitten little hotel." Somehow she managed a derisive tone. "If it's as small, dirty, and uninviting as the rest of the town, I am much better off on my own property."

"Suit yourself. So long, Miss Rawlings."

His voice followed her—mockingly, she felt—as she sailed out onto the boardwalk.

She slammed the door. Weariness and a pang of aloneness brought tears dangerously close, but she forced them away.

She'd survived too much with her dignity intact to let the fact that Wolf Bodine wanted her out of his town make her weepy. Besides, she thought as she forced one foot before the other, she hated weepy females. The thing to do was to concentrate on getting out to the ranch. *Don't think—do.*

She'd need a horse and buggy. When that was arranged, she would retrieve her baggage, inquire directions at the hotel, and be on her way.

A short time later she emerged from the hotel dragging her trunk, with her velvet-banded hatbox tucked in the crook of her arm. She was trying not to notice the delicious smells emanating from the hotel dining room, or the growling of her stomach. But realizing how hungry she was did remind her of something: She ought to stop at the general store and buy some flour, eggs, beans, and other supplies before going to the ranch. She didn't know what to expect when she reached it, and Bear had always taught her to be prepared for anything.

With that in mind she remembered the derringer

tucked inside the pocket of her traveling gown. It was small but effective, as Mr. Scoop Parmalee had discovered. And it would come in handy in case . . .

But she pushed that thought away as well. She couldn't afford to worry about Neely Stoner or the others who were after the silver mine right now. At the moment her biggest problem was going to be hefting this trunk up into the wagon. It contained everything she had left in the world—which wasn't all that much, but still . . .

She grabbed hold of the trunk's handle, but before she could try to lift it, a powerful hand covered hers.

"I'll do that."

Wolf Bodine met her surprised gaze with his own hard, gray one. "Wouldn't want you to strain anything," he remarked, and as Rebeccah hastily withdrew her hand from beneath his warm, strong palm, he grasped hold of the trunk. He lifted it without any visible effort and plunked it down in the wagon.

"You're very kind," she bit out icily, too surprised by his aid to think of anything else to say. "Now, if you'll excuse me—"

"Not so fast."

"I beg your pardon?"

"I'm escorting you out to the ranch."

"You will do nothing of the sort."

"I hate to argue with a lady," Wolf informed her with a determined glint in his eye, "but it's all settled. It'll be near dark by the time you get there, and you don't know the way. The last thing I need is to have you getting lost out in the foothills."

Her voice was low. "I would think you'd be happy to be rid of me."

"Not like that."

Something in the way he said it made her heart skip a beat. She'd forgotten for a moment that she was dealing with a lawman here, not an outlaw or a gambler or a rustler, like those men who had been such good friends of her father's. Wolf Bodine was of a different ilk. He might despise her and feel contempt for her because she was an outlaw's daughter, but he would feel obligated to see to the protection of any lone woman within his dominion —even Bear Rawlings's brat.

But she couldn't afford to be beholden to him, and besides, she told herself firmly, she didn't need his protection or his chivalry.

"It isn't necessary," she informed him, and set her hatbox into the wagon. "I have an excellent sense of direction, Sheriff Bodine, and Mr. Winstead in the hotel gave me very clear instructions—"

"Are you getting in this wagon or not?" he interrupted irritatedly.

"No, not yet. I'm going into the general store to buy supplies first. You needn't be here when I get back."

She turned on her heel and walked across the street with the assured grace of a debutante, but inwardly she was cursing as colorfully as Waylon Pritchard had earlier. She was weary, parched, and disheveled: her traveling gown was sadly wrinkled, the feathers in her hat must be drooping as tiredly as her shoulders, and she desperately wanted to lie down between cool sheets and go to sleep.

But she wouldn't be sleeping for many hours to come, she knew. She also knew, without understanding how, that Wolf Bodine would be there waiting when she came out of the general store.

He was. He was saddled up on a handsome sorrel gelding that stood restively beside her stocky rented mare and creaky wagon. *Stubborn, insufferable man,* she muttered to herself as she crossed the street carrying a parcel of groceries in each arm, but she couldn't help the rush of pink color that flooded her cheeks as she watched him from beneath her lashes.

This time he made no move to help her, but waited on horseback as she dumped her parcels in the wagon beside the trunk. "I thought I told you to leave me alone. I don't need or want your help."

"Ah-huh."

His laconic calm infuriated her. She scowled at his tall, lean figure, though his face was shadowed by the gray brim of his hat. "Well?"

"Well, let's go," he returned evenly. He glanced pointedly at the darkening lavender sky. "Daylight's almost gone, and we've got a fair-sized ride ahead of us."

There was no getting rid of him now. Rebeccah was uncomfortably aware of his gaze on her as she mounted into the wagon and picked up the reins. "Shouldn't you be going home to your wife and family?" she bit out at last, half turning toward him, and for the first time she saw something in his face besides that cool, steady nonchalance.

Pain flickered sharp as a knife blade behind his eyes for a split second. His whole body went tense. Then, just as suddenly, the signs of strain were gone. That cold distance was back. His mouth was straight, grim, unsmiling, the eyes unexpressive, and he was spurring the gelding forward without a word in response.

Rebeccah didn't know what to make of that. Perhaps he didn't deign to discuss his precious wife and son with Bear Rawlings's daughter. Perhaps she wasn't fit to speak of them.

She urged the mare forward, her shoulders aching with tension. Why did Wolf Bodine have to be the sheriff of Powder Creek? For eight years—eight foolish, unhappy, idiotic years—she'd dreamed of seeing him again, but not like this, not *here*. In her dreams Wolf Bodine had been smitten like a schoolboy when she'd encountered him again. He'd smiled in admiration when he saw her, lost his train of thought, and swept her into his arms. He'd whispered of how beautiful and fascinating she had become, kissed her as if he'd never stop.

He didn't try to run her out of his town, he didn't hold her in contempt, and he didn't ride beside her in steely silence, driven not to passionate action and speech but to icy hostility, looking straight ahead, ignoring her as if she was a piece of driftwood or a rock.

Neither of them said another word as the sun crawled across the rosy-purple sky and a pair of eagles soared overhead, their calls echoing shrilly through the twilight.

They left Powder Creek behind and disappeared into the waving golden sea of buffalo grass.

3 The last rays of a blood-red sunset bathed the river valley as the wagon rounded a bend and the ranch came into view.

Ranch? Rebeccah stared in disbelief at the sprawling, one-story log cabin squatting a few hundred yards ahead. She swallowed hard, trying not to feel dismayed. The place stood between a dark clump of cedar and several small, unpainted wooden sheds. It was built of logs, with a sturdy clapboard roof, and though it was fair-sized, long, rambling, and probably roomy, its windows were gray with grime, the front-porch steps were crumbling, and there was no sign of bunkhouse, stables, corrals, pastures, or gardens . . . no sign of prosperity, ranch hands, horses, chickens, or cattle.

Not much of a ranch. A log cabin and a small, unpainted cedar barn behind it. *Bear, did you even live on this place? Were you ever here?*

Douglas fir, spruce, and ponderosa pine darkened the surrounding hills. Beyond, the Rockies loomed—amethyst mountains outlined sharply against the fiery sky. There was the sharp tang of pine in the air, a stream ran nearby, and there was a lake, Wolf Bodine had told her, Snow Lake. So the land must be fertile and lovely by day, Rebeccah tried to reassure herself, but now it looked bleak and dark and dangerous—and lonely.

"Want to head back to town?" Wolf Bodine asked with satisfaction.

Rebeccah gritted her teeth against disappointment and a twist of fear.

"Certainly not."

"Fine. Welcome home, Miss Rawlings."

He cantered up a dirt lane to the weed-strewn yard and swung down from the saddle. "Place's been empty these past five years. Amos Peastone drank too much. He never could make a go of it. When he lost the land in a poker game in Virginia City, he just moved on to California to try his luck there. But he never outright said who he lost the ranch to, and no one ever showed up to claim it— at least, not that I knew about." He studied her a moment from beneath the rim of his sombrero. "You do have ownership papers, don't you, Miss Rawlings?"

No, I'm Bear Rawlings's daughter, so of course I'm a thief, trying to steal this run-down, good-for-nothing snake pit of a shack.

Rebeccah glared at him and, without answering, began to clamber down from the wagon. But the hem of her gown caught on the splintered old wagon seat, and she pitched forward with a panicked yelp. She would have fallen flat on her face in the dirt, but Wolf Bodine instantly spurred his horse forward and grabbed her as she toppled out. He scooped her up alongside him so that she sprawled across his saddle.

"If you aren't the *clumsiest* woman," he muttered, shaking his head in wonder. "You probably fall out of your bed every night."

"I do not!" she snapped, strangely distracted by his nearness, by the sensation of being held in rocklike arms. "And what goes on in my bed is hardly your concern!" she flashed. Then, as her own words echoed in her ears, she turned scarlet.

The bright flush traveled up her neck, suffused her cheeks, nose, and forehead, and burned her ears.

"I didn't say it was," he replied softly, but his eyes were brimming with gentle amusement. "Unless you want to give me firsthand evidence. . . ."

"You . . . oh!" She shoved hard against his massive chest, which only made his grin deepen. Dimples appeared within his bronzed cheeks.

Rebeccah pushed him again. "You're the most vile-minded, insufferable man. I'm damned if I need your help! Set me down this minute!"

"Yes, ma'am."

He lowered her to the ground, still grinning. As she straightened her hat and twitched at the hem of her skirt, he shook his head. "Can't see what you're so all-fired upset about," he commented mildly, just to irritate her.

"You! And this . . . place. I expected this ranch to be a *bit* more prosperous-looking, that's all. It's a shock."

He dismounted, then reached into the wagon for her trunk and lifted it down with ease. He set it beside her in the darkening yard. Her parcels and hatbox followed. "Maybe you should think about selling," he said slowly. "It'll take a lot of work and a lot of money to make a go of this place. I'm sure Jed Turner over at the land office would be glad to put it on the market for you. You could get a good price."

So he was still trying to get rid of her. Rebeccah squared her shoulders and turned toward him. "Let's get something straight right now, Sheriff Bodine," she said quietly. "I'm not selling this property. I'm not leaving Powder Creek. This is my home, my ranch, and it's going to be the biggest, grandest, most prosperous ranch in the territory before I get through with it, so you can save your long faces and dire threats for some stupid little ninny, which you obviously mistake me for, because I am neither stupid nor a ninny, and nobody tells me what to do."

Now it was his turn to be angry. Even in the gathering dusk she could see it. He scowled at her from beneath his hat, and she sensed the tension in his tall frame. He reached out a hand, tilted up her chin, forced her to meet his gaze. "Let me give you a little warning, Miss Rawlings." He took a step closer, and leaned down, his face very close to hers. "You'd better not be as low-down and crooked as your father was because we don't put up with lawbreakers in Powder Creek. And being a woman won't save you from getting plunked in jail if I get even a hint that you're mixed up in any dirty dealings. If anyone shady shows up in town, I'll be breathing down your neck so fast, you won't even see me coming. I'll lock you up in that nice little cell in my office and throw the key in the river, so help me God, I will. You understand? Because it's easy to see you're as stubborn and as bad-tempered as your father, but if you take after him in any other way—"

"Damn you," Rebeccah cried. Her fingers balled into fists. "My father was *not* bad-tempered!"

"What?"

She was quivering with rage. She wanted to hit him so badly, her fingers smarted at her sides. "Bear was *good-natured,* do you hear me, Sheriff Bodine, as good-natured as any man you'll ever meet —unless he was crossed. Unless someone did something really bad to him or to me—" Her voice broke, only for a moment, then gained steam again. "You didn't know him, so don't you dare speak to me about him. He may not have been honest, and he may have been stubborn and full of himself and a few other things, but he was *kind,* and good-natured, and gentle deep down, and as true a friend as any man could want to find, and I won't stand here and listen to you speak ill of him!"

Wolf didn't know what to make of her. She was obviously loyal to her father, and passionate in his defense, and it occurred to him suddenly that she must have loved Bear a great deal. Bodine found it difficult to believe that anyone could love the huge, barrel-chested, irascible outlaw known for his cunning and greed, but looking at Rawlings's daughter, it was impossible to believe anything else. Those violet eyes shone with it, and beneath the love and obvious devotion he saw something else: loss. It seared through her as hot and painful as a brand-ing iron. The girl was glaring at him, fearless as could be, and quivering with an unspoken agony. Bear had been dead a little more than four months now—shot down by a posse outside Laramie after a bank robbery. For decent, law-abiding citizens of the West it was hardly a loss—it was cause for cele-bration. For this strange, proud, unpleasant girl, Wolf realized grimly, it was hell.

Rebeccah Rawlings was grieving for her father.

"Fair enough," he said at last in response to her tirade. "Guess I should know better than to speak ill of the dead."

She nodded, her mouth trembling a little.

If she ever discovers the full extent of what Bear did in Powder Creek and how he was hated here, Wolf reflected, *she'll be devastated.* He had a feeling it was only a matter of time before she did find out. But somehow he didn't think she should have to make that unpleasant discovery tonight. She looked tired enough, weary enough—he almost hated leaving her here at this cabin alone—the place was scarcely habitable.

But she's not your concern, he told himself. *Why are you worrying about her?*

"I'm leaving," he said abruptly, deciding that the brief contact he'd had with Rebeccah Rawlings was somehow scrambling his brains. "One last time—you're sure you want to stay out here all alone?"

"Sheriff, I can't *wait* to be here all alone."

Wolf's eyes narrowed at her withering tone. She sounded so tough. It would serve her right if she got spooked out here tonight, with only the coyotes, wolves, and snakes for company. It sure was none of his concern.

He mounted Dusty, turned the horse toward his own property, which adjoined this one, and gave Rebeccah Rawlings one last glance. Silhouetted against the cabin that way, with the darkness settling down about her like a thick cloak over the land, she looked touchingly alone and vulnerable— yet somehow staunch, with her head held high and her lovely face set with cold determination.

"Stay out of trouble, Miss Rawlings," he warned by way of farewell. "I'll be watching."

"Get me my money!" she shouted after him as he spurred the gelding into a gallop. She watched, biting her lip, until he had disappeared over a rise.

Miss Rawlings, may I have the infinite pleasure of kissing you?

Her own wishful dreams clamored in her head, mocking her, as the man who had played such a central role in every one of them rode away without a backward glance.

With a pang that seemed to puncture her heart, she turned slowly back to study the dilapidated cabin. Her shoulders drooped. Her temples throbbed. Her new home was nothing but a dreary eyesore.

And Wolf Bodine hadn't even been gentleman enough to carry her bags inside for her.

Well, she didn't need him, she told herself coldly. She didn't need anyone.

A coyote howled nearby. The wind rattled through the trees. From behind her an animal skittered noisily through the brush.

Rebeccah glanced around, on edge now, then quickly hoisted her trunk with an unladylike grunt and dragged it as swiftly as she could toward the door.

4 There was a kerosene lamp on a counter in the kitchen. Thankfully Rebeccah had bought matches and candles, and she rummaged for them among her store-bought parcels. As she lit the lamp and turned up the wick, she took comfort in the cozy amber glow that flooded across the room. Somehow the light seemed a weapon against the gathering darkness outside. And so were the sturdy log walls of the cabin, she reminded herself, as she picked up the lamp and began an inspection of her new home.

The cabin's interior was no better, but not much worse, than she had expected after viewing it from outside.

Dust four inches thick coated everything: the floor, the crude wooden counters and shelves in the kitchen, the window ledges, the battered, camel-backed horsehair sofa that was the only real piece of furniture in the cabin. And a musty odor pervaded each room. The place had not been aired in ages.

Rebeccah took careful stock, trying not to be daunted by the tasks looming before her. Grimy, yellowed gingham curtains drooped at the win-

dows. In the kitchen there was a scarred wooden
bench, several three-legged stools, and a long
wooden table. She was relieved to see the cast-iron
stove in the corner. Chipped and old though it appeared, it was a welcome sight, as was the large
fireplace and chimney. Old Amos Peastone had
lived a Spartan existence, it seemed, for the cabin
lacked much in the way of beauty and comfort, but
to Rebeccah's relief he had possessed at least the
basic kitchen essentials: iron pots and pans, a skillet and coffeepot, as well as dishes and eating utensils stacked on the dusty shelves. Rebeccah took a
swift inventory and found a voluminous yellow
slicker folded inside a box on the pantry floor,
alongside a bucket, a box of safety matches, and
coils of rope. Not exactly a treasure trove of luxury,
but in terms of usefulness they would certainly do.

She made her way carefully to the bedroom at
the rear of the cabin. It was nearly as large as the
parlor and almost as barren, but it did boast a
faded red-and-blue rag rug on the floor. There was
an iron bedstead, a straw mattress, and a worn
blue eiderdown quilt. Across from the bed was a
chest of pine drawers, with another kerosene lamp
on top of it, as well as a pair of brass candlesticks
and a cracked enamel pitcher and bowl.

Welcome home, Miss Rawlings.

The walls seemed mockingly to echo the words
around her.

Grimly Rebeccah rolled up her sleeves.

It was several hours later before she felt the
house was habitable for the night. Exhausted, but
oddly satisfied, Rebeccah surveyed her accom-

plishments. The floors were now swept and
scrubbed, as were the countertops—and the musty
odor in the cabin had been banished by blustery
fresh air from the opened windows, as well as the
pungent aroma of lye soap and vinegar.

Much better. There was still a great deal to do,
but as Rebeccah carried her bucket and rags from
the bedroom into the kitchen, she reminded herself
not to be persnickety. She had slept in far worse
places than this when she was on the run with Bear
and the gang. They'd camped under trees in pouring rain, in open fields beneath blizzarding snow, in
abandoned mines and damp caves. They'd holed
up in flea-bitten hotels; burned-out, rat-infested
shacks half the size of this cabin—and twice as
filthy—in smoky backrooms of saloons and broth-
els.

At least this place is mine, she thought, setting
down her bucket near the stove and regarding the
scrubbed-down kitchen with satisfaction. All it
needed was a little more elbow grease, some new
slipcovers and needlework pillows, her paintings to
brighten up the walls, perhaps some fresh curtains
—white lace ones would be wonderful—and a few
feminine touches: a tea table with a lacy doily
tossed across it, her books displayed on a painted
shelf, some pretty china knickknacks set about
here and there, maybe some wildflowers blooming
in a vase. . . .

Her mind raced with possibilities. Oh, yes, this
little cabin would be her haven, far preferable to
the anesthetic little room in Miss Wright's Academy that she'd shared with two other teachers.

Rebeccah shuddered, remembering the dull-green walls; stiff, dark curtains; and rigid, narrow beds with their ugly maroon coverlets.

How she'd dreamed of leaving, of having her own home. When a solicitor had shown up at the Academy more than a month after she'd been rocked by news of Bear's death, Rebeccah had been stunned to learn of how carefully her father had arranged for her future. He had left her wonderfully provided for, with hefty bank accounts in her name in both Denver and Tucson. There were even some shares in railroad stock. And the ranch in Powder Creek.

She was a very wealthy young woman, the solicitor had informed her expansively, as if expecting her to clap her hands in delight. But Rebeccah had received the news in grim silence. She could not keep the money. Bear had meant the best for her, but all of it, each green-backed dollar, was tainted. She had withdrawn the funds from both bank accounts, sold the railroad stock, and donated the entire amount to the Boston Widows and Orphans Society. Her conscience had demanded it. Yet she had held on to the deed for the ranch, remembering clearly how Bear had told her during one of his visits of winning it fair and square in a poker game.

So the ranch was not ill-gotten gains. Bear had not lied or stolen to acquire it. She could keep it if she wished. Live on it. Realize her dream of escaping Miss Wright's Academy and having a home of her own.

Looking around, tired but pleased with the results of her efforts, Rebeccah felt a trickle of pride. She had already begun to make this place hers—

she had put her mark on it. She had braved the
chilly darkness outside to fetch water from the
stream, set her muscles to aching by scouring
the floors on her hands and knees, worked until
her gown was no more than a limp rag and her face
glistened with sweat. But the cabin was cleaner
and more homelike, and she felt as if it belonged to
her now.

Fortunately she had discovered towels and lin-
ens in the chest of drawers, and rags, liniment,
salve, soap, and some odd tools in a box under the
bed. There had even been a barrel filled with kin-
dling in a tiny shed she discovered behind the
kitchen, along with another barrel for storing water. All began to seem like precious treasures. She
hummed a little tune as she rinsed and dried the
skillet, plates, and utensils, then prepared herself a
quick supper of hardtack biscuits, beans, and jerky.
At last she popped a penny candy from the general
store into her mouth for dessert. She leaned her
elbows on the kitchen table and closed her eyes,
for the first time in hours allowing herself a moment in which to think.

She would certainly have her work cut out for
her here. What was it she had told Wolf Bodine?
She would turn this place into the grandest ranch
in Montana?

She groaned and rubbed her eyes. He must think
her a complete fool. Well, she would show him—
she would show them all.

But it would take time.

She'd start small, selling the last of the jewels
she'd kept, all gifts from her father over the years.

With the money, she might be able to buy some
cattle. And if she took the teaching position in
town, she'd have a salary to live on and to save. If
she was frugal there would be something to put
toward building her herd, hiring some ranch hands,
adding outbuildings, a corral. . . .

No one in town need know she was penniless,
that she'd given away all of the money Bear had left
her. She could let them think she was doing them a
favor by taking the teaching position. She could
build the ranch slowly, living carefully all the while,
taking her time.

Maybe it wouldn't become the biggest ranch in
the territory, she conceded, rising from the table to
carry her plate to the sink, but at least it could
become a working ranch, a ranch that would eventually allow her to be self-supporting and independent.

The wind outside had turned briskly cool. Even
though autumn was only just approaching, winter
seemed to be threatening already. No doubt it will
be here sooner than expected, Rebeccah thought
with a shiver, for Montana's winters were known to
be fierce and deadly. She hastened to the only window still open—the one in the parlor—and tugged
it shut, then made a careful check of the cabin once
more, assuring herself that all the doors and windows were secure. The cabin looked almost cozy,
she thought, with its polished floors and gleaming
shelves and counters. She'd made a dent, at least,
in what needed to be done. A start. It was enough
for tonight.

By the time she'd washed the grime from her

face, neck, and body with a cake of lilac-scented soap she'd brought from Boston, stripped off her crumpled dress to don a lace-trimmed pink cotton nightgown, and crawled into bed, every muscle longed for sleep. Yet lying there in the darkened bedroom with a single stubby candle flickering faintly in its brass holder, she found that sleep would not come. Her thoughts kept returning, stubbornly, to the man whom she'd been trying to block from her mind.

Wolf Bodine.

For the first time it dawned on her that there was an odd similarity between his name and that of her father. Wolf . . . Bear—they were both derived from animals. Her father had earned his because of his size and often menacing demeanor—he'd been Bear since he was sixteen, he'd told her once proudly, though his real name was John Lucas Rawlings.

She wondered fleetingly how Wolf Bodine had come by his name.

Never mind. She decided she didn't want to know. She didn't want to know anything more about him. Her encounters with Wolf Bodine today had destroyed whatever romantic daydreams she had once entertained about him. The man was rude, insufferable, judgmental, and altogether loathsome.

And married.

She'd stay out of town as much as possible and hope she wouldn't run into him very often.

"I'll be watching," he had said before riding off.

Rebeccah shivered beneath the faded blue quilt and stared at the dark-shadowed ceiling. Someone else had said something similar to her recently. And though she'd tried to shrug it off, now that she was here alone on the ranch, with no one else around for miles, it was hard not to think about that other, more menacing warning.

We'll be watching. That's how Neely Stoner's hireling had put it before she'd sent him scurrying from the garden at Miss Wright's Academy, dodging bullets from the derringer she kept on her person at all times. She couldn't help wondering if Stoner would show up himself next time.

Please God, no.

A tight knot of fear twisted inside of her. The memories brought on by thoughts of Neely Stoner turned her skin clammy. Her heart began to beat like the wings of a frenzied bird, and she felt the familiar icy terror building in her chest. She sat up in the bed and hugged her arms around her knees. *Fight it,* she commanded herself. *Don't let him have this power over you.* Yet it was a struggle to drive away the terror. She had spent too many nights trying to stop the trembling, forcing away the sick nausea, the bouts of panic.

Damn you, Neely Stoner.

If Stoner thought he could get away with frightening her, he was dead wrong, she told herself. She'd already had practice killing a man today, and it would give her satisfaction to shoot a bullet through Neely Stoner's evil heart. He deserved it. Her father had nearly killed him that night eight

years ago when he found out what Neely'd done—
Bear had certainly beat him within an inch of his
life and then run him off permanently from the
gang. Rebeccah knew that if Bear had believed for
one minute that Neely Stoner would have the
gumption to show up years later and harass her
over some rumors of a silver mine, he would have
killed him on the spot, Rebeccah was certain of it.
Well, now she might have to do the job herself.

A heavy Montana wind groaned at the window
shutters. Rebeccah burrowed deeper beneath the
threadbare eiderdown quilt. She had a derringer
under her pillow, another one stuffed beneath the
mattress, a third in her reticule. And she'd buy a
shotgun in Powder Creek next time she went into
town.

What would Sheriff Bodine say about that?

"Who cares?" she whispered into the lonely
darkness.

But she fell asleep remembering the expression
on his face when she'd asked about his wife and
son, wondering what exactly in her question had
struck such a tender nerve.

"The teachers in this here school and those
other gals—they're treating you right?" Bear asked,
the first time he came to visit Rebeccah when she
was thirteen years old.

"Yep—yes," she'd amended quickly, remembering the grammar Miss Lindly had been drilling into
her.

Bear seemed to fill the garden where stone-bor-
dered beds of roses and white-and-blue violets nes-

tled among stately oaks and maples, and water splashed in a marble fountain nearby. He paced back and forth, all spruced up in his black suit and starched shirt, his new black bowler set squarely on his head. "You sure, Reb? You were sitting all by yourself when I found you in that library. The other gals, they were all sitting at tables together."

"My particular friends are on an outing today. They went to the museum," she lied.

Bear peered shrewdly at her and sat down beside her on the bench. He took her slender hand in his great big one, holding her fingers gently. "Ah-huh. Tell me, Reb, you know what to do if anyone gives you any trouble? Put up your fists and give 'em their due. You remember how?"

"I remember, Bear." She remembered so well, she'd given Analee Caruthers a black eye only last week—and received a month's worth of demerits for it. "Honest, don't worry about me," she urged, reaching up to hug him, inhaling the powerful sweat and tobacco scent of him. "I'm fine."

But Rebeccah knew he *did* worry about her. He worried a great deal. And she loved him for it. His visits, limited to only two or three a year, were precious to her—even though the whispers, laughter, and pointed fingers were worse after he'd been there.

She was glad he wasn't like the other fathers, so formal and stern, respectable and dull. So what if he looked like an outlaw, a big, striding dangerous man with a booming voice and a harsh, gutteral laugh?

He was hers, all she had, and he loved her more than life itself. That meant everything to Rebeccah.

So she lied to him (after all, he had taught her how) and pretended everything was fine at Miss Wright's, even though she was a pariah among the rich, snippy girls who came from such fine Boston homes, even though her teachers frowned at her for squirming in her seat, throwing spitballs at Analee, and drawing rude caricatures of the vice principal. It didn't seem to matter that she was first in her class, that she learned all of her lessons quickly and with ease, that she was gifted in music and literature and Latin. She'd have been in danger of being called a bluestocking if she wasn't such a rowdy, disrespectful tomboy.

Instead they called her things far worse—troublesome, quarrelsome, ungainly, disrespectful, incorrigible.

But Rebeccah never complained to Bear. It would have troubled him so. He wanted a safe place for her, a place where she could better herself, could learn to be a lady and how to go on in a world without guns, posses, dynamite, and men like Neely Stoner. She instinctively understood all that and was moved by his concerns, and never once told him that she was lonely and friendless and utterly miserable.

She would dream at night that she was back with the gang, galloping like the wind across the Arizona desert, free and wild and safe from all the watching, critical eyes. In her dream Bear was riding beside her, grinning at her, racing her, and she was happy —but then all too often the dream would change.

Bear was gone, everyone was gone, and she was all alone on the banks of a high, raging river. There were weeds tangled around her legs and knees, and she couldn't move. Suddenly Neely Stoner's cruel face would loom over her. His hands would reach out for her, and she couldn't get away, couldn't breathe, couldn't escape those grasping weeds . . . or his hands . . . and she'd wake up screaming.

"Don't scream."

The man's sweaty hand was clamped over her nose and mouth so tightly, she could scarcely breathe, much less scream. But Rebeccah tried anyway. It was reflex born of sheer panic.

He cursed. His fingers dug harder into her cheeks, his knobby palm jamming cruelly against her lips.

"Don't scream!" he barked. "I told you. Not that anyone can hear, but I hate the sound of a woman's screams. I'd as soon kill you as listen to your squawks, understand?"

Rebeccah nodded helplessly, drenched in a sweat of terror. She remained perfectly still, peering up at the stranger pinning her to her bed, praying he would remove his hand so she could breathe freely again.

Darkness smothered the room, but for the thin bars of silver moonlight squeezing in through the drooping curtains. In the dimness she could only just make out an unshaven moon-shaped face; small, dark, glittering eyes; long, greasy hair.

No. Please, no. Don't let this happen. Don't let him touch me.

"You gonna keep quiet?"

She nodded again, as best she could.

He gave a satisfied grunt. His hand slid away from her mouth, and Rebeccah breathed in the fetid stink of him. She fought back the urge to retch. He smelled even worse than he looked.

"Who are you?" she whispered hoarsely, aware that he was shifting his weight from her, leaning back.

"I'll ask the questions, girlie."

From somewhere deep inside, beneath the agonizing fear and the vise of dreadful memories, a burst of defiance made her demand, "What are you waiting for, then?"

"Uppity little cuss, ain't you?" the man said softly. He drew back his hand and struck her hard across the jaw.

Triangles of red blinding light stung her eyes. Her vision blurred—the round, grimy face above her swam in a gray mist.

"There's more where that came from if you don't keep quiet and pay attention. Neely Stoner sent me. I'm Fess Jones. You've heard of me, I'll wager."

She'd heard of him. Fess Jones—cold-blooded murderer, outlaw, gunslinger. He'd killed eight men, two women, maybe more. He was infamous back east. The newspapers screamed of his exploits as one of the Wild West's most brutal outlaws, dubbing him Savage Fess.

"Stoner wants that silver mine your pa left you. So do I. See, him and me are pards, girlie. We're goin' to split everything from that there mine fifty-fifty. All you have to do is hand over the papers and the map. Then, little girl, you get to stay alive."

He was after the mine. The mine. He isn't here to rape, Rebeccah told herself, struggling against the squeezing terror.

Think!

Rebeccah knew she couldn't reach the derringer under her pillow. Not before he could stop her. Her lips felt cracked and dry. She tried to figure out a plan, though the pain in her jaw and head hurt so badly, it dulled her senses.

"Well?" Jones prodded, poking her side with a finger. "You kin talk now. Where's them papers?"

Rebeccah met his squinting, feral gaze, trying to sound more calm and assured than she felt while flat on her back with a slimy killer kneeling over her. "I already told the other man Stoner sent—I don't have any papers to any mine. And I know nothing about a map." She forced herself to stare earnestly, innocently into those cold, vicious eyes, forced herself to speak slowly, though her heart was thumping. "Mr. Jones, if I had what you want, I'd give it to you. I would. But Bear never mentioned any mine to me. Neither did his solicitor. Don't you see? It's all rumor. There's nothing to it. So, please—go away and leave me alone."

He hit her again, even harder than the first time. The room exploded into prisms of red and black and dazzling white. Pain rocked through her jaw, sharp as a sledgehammer. There was a buzzing in her ears.

"You're lying." She heard Fess Jones's snarl as if from a great distance. "I'm counting to ten!"

Little whimpers of pain tore from her lips.

"One! Two! Three . . ."

Rebeccah fought to clear her throbbing head. *Think . . . damn it . . . think. He's stronger and meaner than you are, but for God's sake, he isn't smarter.*

"Eight, nine . . ."

With effort she moved her lips. Her jaw splintered with pain. "The papers . . . are in a strong-box," she whispered. "It's . . . hidden under the floorboards. I have the key . . . in my reticule. I'll get it."

"Don't you move, girlie. None of your tricks. I'll get it myself." He eased off the bed and circled the room with his eyes until he made out her reticule propped on the chest of drawers. "You'd better be tellin' the truth."

When he reached the chest, she lunged, diving under the pillow for the gun, but he threw himself back on her before she could draw it out to fire. Though she kicked at him, he wrenched the gun from her fingers and slapped her backhanded, sending her tumbling off the bed.

"You were lyin' to me, weren't you? You greedy little slut! I'll teach you to lie to ol' Fess Jones."

The knife came from nowhere, glittering in his hand. On her knees on the floor, Rebeccah drew in her breath. Fear gut-punched her. She shinnied away, against the wall, and staggered unsteadily to her feet.

Jones laughed at the terror on her face and the

trembling of her body. He whipped the knife back and forth in a zigzag motion. "You're goin' to be real sorry you didn't tell me the truth, Reb Rawlings," he chuckled. "I'm goin' to cut up that purty face of yours first, and then you're going to hand over them papers."

He moved toward her, grinning. Rebeccah, trapped like a rabbit in her corner, began to scream.

A scream.

Wolf's blood turned to ice as the horrible sound tore from the cabin and through the chill air of the yard. He was inside the darkened cabin in an instant, and following the sound of the second scream. He burst through the bedroom door like a cannonball.

Then two things happened at once.

Fess Jones threw his knife, Bodine drew his Colt, and gunfire thundered through the Rawlings ranch house.

When the explosion died away and the gunsmoke cleared, Fess Jones lay crumpled on the floor, emitting a horrible gurgling gasp. His body twitched from the bullet lodged in his heart, his chest gushed blood, his eyes stared in unseeing agony. And then the twitching stopped, and Jones went still.

Rebeccah slumped against the wall, her palms clinging to it. She dragged her gaze from Jones's body and looked at Wolf Bodine. He nonchalantly pulled the knife from his shoulder and tossed it to the ground, seemingly oblivious of the blood spurting from his wound. In the faint, silvery moonlight she saw the calmness of his expression as he trained his Colt .45 on her.

"Talk."

5 "You're bleeding!"

She started forward, but the harshness of his voice stopped her. "Stay where you are."

"You need help—"

"You're wrong. I need answers, Miss Rawlings. What the hell were you and this hombre up to? Were you double-crossing him in some kind of dirty scheme? You'll answer my questions either here or in a jail cell. It's up to you."

Rebeccah refused to look at the hideous thing on the floor. If she did, she might get sick, and she'd be damned before she let Bodine see her retch her guts out. "You're loco!" she cried, shooting him a look of disgust. "Go ahead and shoot me, Bodine, but I'm not going to let you bleed all over my rug. It's the only one in the cabin, and I happen to like the color, so do you mind? It's bad enough I'll have to scrub *his* blood from the floor."

Bodine's eyes narrowed as she strode across the room, muttering all the while.

"Come sit on the sofa, for God's sake, and let me bind up that shoulder for you. And put your silly gun away. I'm not armed, you know. If I was, do you think I'd have let that snake get near me?"

When she reached his side, moonlight caught her face, and Wolf saw for the first time the ugly welt swelling red and tender across her cheek.

"Looks like you're the one who needs some help," he said sharply. "How badly did he hurt you?"

She put a finger to her cheek, remembering, and then winced. "He only hit me a few times. But he was going to use that knife on me when you came in."

Something fierce and gut-wrenching slammed tight inside of him at the thought of what might have happened if not for his son Billy's sharp eyes. A stroke of luck had brought him here tonight—nothing more. He glanced with contempt at Jones's corpse.

"The filthy coward. You ought to put some liniment on that bruise."

"You're the one who needs doctoring, Sheriff," she reminded him coldly, tugging on his good arm as she led him out to the parlor. "Sit right there while I heat some water and get the salve. And don't ask me any questions, because I can't answer them and minister to you at the same time," she threw over her shoulder as she disappeared into the kitchen.

He didn't know what to make of her. The ragged little wildcat who'd spit in his face in that Arizona shack had grown into a startlingly beautiful and amazingly self-possessed woman. As she boiled water, sponged at the two-inch gash the knife had slashed in his shoulder—a gash no more serious than a flesh wound—gingerly applied salve, and then cut up strips of a clean, thick towel to wrap it, he had an opportunity to study her. He was struck by her delicate, serious face, by the solemn concentration in her eyes as she worked, and by the way the thin pink nightgown hugged the delectable curves of her body. His shoulder throbbed a little, but he ignored it, focusing instead on the soft, flowery scent of her (was it lilacs?) as she sat beside him on the old sofa; on the luxuriant tumble of her midnight hair, glistening in the lamp light; on the gentle way her fingers slid across his injured arm.

What business did this woman have with the likes of Fess Jones?

Wolf couldn't help being suspicious of her. He had learned to be suspicious of women, especially beautiful and clever ones, and from his own observations Rebeccah Rawlings possessed both of those qualities.

Yet he sensed something in her, something that didn't quite fit. He frowned as she finished binding the wound and sat back to study her own handiwork.

"Got any whiskey?"

"Whiskey? Why? Do you feel faint?"

"No, ma'am," he drawled patiently. "Thirsty."

"Well," she said doubtfully, studying his calm, bronzed face as he leaned against the horsehair sofa, looking the picture of strong, manly health, "I haven't come across any whiskey. I could make coffee," she offered.

"I wouldn't want to put you to any trouble."

"Oh, it's no trouble, Sheriff Bodine," she replied, rising and staring down at him as he lounged on

her sofa, "as long as in return you get rid of that
. . . thing in my bedroom for me."

He nodded. "Deal."

Suddenly she noticed his gaze was no longer
trained upon her face but was traveling slowly
along her body, across her breasts, shifting down
to her hips.

With a cry of chagrin Rebeccah suddenly remembered she was still wearing only her nightgown.
Somehow being beaten and nearly cut into little
pieces by Fess Jones had made her completely forget that she was wearing little more than a thin
gown of cotton and lace that barely skimmed her
ankles, while Wolf Bodine wore boots, pants, shirt,
vest, guns, badge, and a Stetson.

"My, God," she breathed in dismay, and backed
away toward the bedroom. A vermilion flush
spread upward from her neck, setting her cheeks
aflame in the lantern light. "How dare you . . .
you despicable . . . why didn't you *say* something?"

"Do you think I'm loco?" he asked softly, but his
eyes held approval along with the amusement. "I
was only admiring how handsomely you've grown
up."

"Don't you dare ogle me or laugh at me," Rebeccah warned, fleeing toward the bedroom door. She
paused at the threshold, clearly steeling herself to
enter the room containing the dead body, but after
throwing one indignant glance back at the tall man
on her sofa, she dashed inside.

It took only a moment to discard her nightgown
and pull on the man's breeches and blue-and-green

flannel shirt she had purchased at one of the larger towns along the stagecoach route, figuring that if she was going to work on the ranch, she'd need something besides dresses. She fastened the shirt's buttons with shaking fingers and didn't look once at Jones's body. Tying her hair back severely with a green ribbon, she stalked back to the parlor once more, leaving the long ends of her shirttail hanging out.

Funny, in her daydreams she had imagined herself reunited with Wolf Bodine in a confection of lavender silk and lace, all frills and beads and ribbons, and now here she was, deliberately dressing like a man, hoping to make him forget about her embarrassing state of near undress a few moments ago.

Life never seems to go according to plan, she decided grimly, as her small, bare feet padded across the floor. She refused to look at Wolf Bodine as she crossed directly to the kitchen, but she could feel his gaze on her.

It seemed to be burning into her backside.

Well, there is nothing the least bit indiscreet about what I'm wearing now, so let him look all he wants, she thought rebelliously.

She has no idea how adorable she looks, Wolf decided as Rebeccah Rawlings stamped past him without a glance. She must have inherited her mother's looks, he concluded, because there was nothing of Bear's heavy jowled face, stocky, powerful build, or shrewd black eyes in his daughter. Only his stubborness and orneriness, Wolf guessed —and possibly his lawlessness.

He had to find out what Fess Jones had been doing here with her, besides beating her and trying to kill her. Wolf had a feeling deep in his gut that Jones wasn't the only outlaw about to descend on his peaceful little neck of the woods, thanks to Miss Rebeccah Rawlings.

He tried to ignore the fiery pain in his shoulder as he mused on the circumstances that had brought him back here tonight. He'd gone home as usual, trying to think of nothing but enjoying his supper with Caitlin and Billy. He'd tried his damndest to avoid thinking about the irritating Miss Rawlings, until Billy had come tearing out the door the moment Wolf had reached the gate.

"Pa, Gramma wouldn't let me come get you—she said I had to stay right here—but I saw him. . . . I saw him, Pa! That fellow on the Wanted poster you got last week from Dodge City—Fess Jones!"

Wolf had swung down from Dusty and knelt beside Caitlin's flower garden to stare intently into his son's excited face. "Slow down, Billy. Are you sure about this?"

"Sure as anything. You know I've got a good eye, Pa," Billy reminded him, his gray eyes shining with excitement.

It was true. Billy frequently visited Wolf at the sheriff's office, where he was fascinated by the collection of rifles, the locked box of ammunition, the big brass ring of keys to the cell, the safe, and all the locked cupboards. But he was most intrigued by the Wanted posters tacked to the corkboard beside the window. He had an amazing memory for a child, and he could recite the mathematical tables and how to spell *hippopotamus,* and he could name the states in which an outlaw was wanted and for what offenses faster than most folks could remember what they'd eaten for breakfast.

"Tell me where you saw him, then," Wolf ordered, and Billy took a deep breath.

"I was fishing in the creek, sitting there real quiet like, and all of a sudden I saw someone riding right through the trees on the other side. Well, he stopped when he saw me. Pa, for a minute there I was mighty scared. The way he stared at me—he looked about as mean as a hungry coyote in an open chicken coop."

Wolf glanced up and saw his mother standing in the doorway, her work-worn hands motionless at her sides. Caitlin's iron-gray hair was bound up as neatly as usual, and her nearly sightless blue eyes gave no hint of her feelings, but her mouth was set and grim within her lined face, providing the one visible sign of her concern.

"Go on," Wolf told the boy quietly, setting a hand on his bony young shoulder. "Did he hurt you, son? Scare you? What did he say?"

"Nothing, Pa. He just looked at me, real long and slow, like he'd like to roast me over a campfire and eat me for dinner—that kind of a look. I was too scared to move. But Sam started growling deep in his throat, and he looked ready to spring. For a moment I thought Fess Jones was going to shoot him."

As if understanding, Billy's big red dog, Sam, nosed his way into the conversation, wriggling between Wolf and his son and resting his nose on the lawman's broad shoulder.

"Good boy, Sam," Wolf said, and stroked the dog's head. "Billy, are you going to finish this story, or do I have to expire with suspense?"

The boy laughed. He enjoyed being the center of attention—in that way, and no other, Wolf decided, he was like his ma.

"He stared at us real long and slow, like I said, and then dug his spurs into his horse and kept riding. Never said a word."

"Which way did he go?"

"That way, toward the Peastone place. Think he's planning to hole up there and wait for some pards to come join him? Maybe he's going to rob the bank in Powder Creek like he did in Lucasville. Maybe—"

"Maybe you should go wash up for supper. Gramma's looking mighty hungry to me."

"Aren't you coming in, Pa?"

"No. But save me some of your gramma's pie." Wolf had stopped the boy with a tug on his sleeve. "You did good, Billy. Real good. I'm proud of you."

And Billy had flushed with pleasure.

If he hadn't run into Fess Jones and recognized him, I wouldn't be here right now, Wolf reflected, wincing as he flexed his shoulder. *And Miss Rebeccah Rawlings would probably be dead.*

It had been too dark to pick up Jones's trail at the creek, but he'd headed back to the Peastone property, taking the less-used route from the borders of his own land, creeping up toward the house from the rear, hiding in the trees and brush, waiting and watching.

He'd seen Rebeccah Rawlings venture out—stupid woman—to fetch water from the stream, had watched her lug it back to the cabin in the dark. He'd caught glimpses of her through the rear cabin window, whisking a broom around. But no sign of Fess Jones. And then about an hour ago a figure had skulked up to the cabin on foot. From his hiding place Wolf surmised that Jones must have left his horse hidden in the brush up the road. He'd made his way noiselessly toward the cabin, opened one of the windows, and crawled in.

Wolf had crept closer, but waited. Waited and wondered—until he heard that scream.

"Do you like milk or sugar in your coffee, Sheriff?"

"Neither one."

He watched her as she handed him the cup, so ladylike, so distant, then settled herself down on the sofa as far away from him as she could get. That suited him just fine. The only thing that had brought him back to this cabin tonight was business. He had no desire to pursue even remotely friendly relations with Bear Rawlings's daughter.

She was up to her pretty little nose in something crooked, Wolf knew it. He just hadn't figured out what her scheme was—yet.

The coffee was good, hot and strong. He drank deeply, then set the cup down and leaned back against the creaking springs of the sofa. "It's time for our little talk, Miss Rawlings. We've gone through all the motions of civility. Now I want some answers."

"We can't always get what we want, Sheriff Bodine, can we?" she replied, her hands clenched tightly in her lap. Her coffee sat on a crate beside her, untouched, ribbons of steam still rising from the tin cup. "I wanted a good night's sleep, peace and quiet, a chance to acclimate myself to my new home. But I didn't get it. That man broke in here in the middle of the night and attacked me. What kind of a town do you run, Sheriff Bodine, where a vicious person like that can accost innocent women in their homes?"

Wolf came to his feet in a surprisingly fluid motion for such a big man. He stalked toward her and yanked her up off the sofa with his one good arm. Ignoring her gasp, he pulled her close, so close he could feel the pounding of her heart and could see the quiver of her lips as she reacted to his nearness and the strength of his hold on her. He let her feel his strength, not hurting her but making sure she recognized that he could do so if he wanted to.

"No more games, Miss Rawlings. No more stalling. You're not an innocent woman. Fess Jones didn't just happen to pick on you. He came here because of you—and I want to know why. What low-down dealings are you up to, and who else can I expect to turn up in my town hatching some dark and dirty business?"

Rebeccah knew she couldn't break free. Even using only one arm, he was far too strong for her. But she would be damned before she'd tell some lawman the kind of trouble she was in and ask him for help. Let him think the worst of her! She didn't care. She'd rather fight off a wagonload of desperadoes than come bawling to Wolf Bodine for help.

"You're making a pile of accusations for a man without any evidence to back them up!" she retorted, lifting her chin. "The last I heard, proof is required in order to lock someone up. Proof of some crime, or intent to commit a crime. The way I see it, Sheriff Bodine, you've got nothing! And you're trespassing on my property. Get out."

Anger tightened his grip on her. Every muscle coiled with tension as he fought to control the wrath that surged through him. Yet through his anger he had to hand it to her. She was tough. As tough as her father. And no doubt every bit as unscrupulous.

"Get out!" she repeated when he didn't say anything or release her. Only the slightest trembling in her voice betrayed her agitation. "And take that dead man with you."

Wolf glared into her diamond-hard eyes; his own narrowed with menace. He thought she flinched as she gazed back, but only for a moment, then the lashes fluttered wide again and she was regarding him with icy rage every bit as determined as his own.

"I'll take him, Miss Rawlings," Wolf drawled. An unpleasant smile just barely touched the edges of his lips. He released her so suddenly, she slumped and ended up sitting down hard on the sofa. Wolf nodded coldly.

"Tomorrow."

He turned on his heel and strode toward the door.

"Tomorrow? But you—"

"Made a deal—and I'll keep it fair and square. I'll get rid of Fess Jones's body for you—tomorrow. You can spend the night with him meantime and think about what might have happened if I hadn't been around. Folks who stray outside the law in these parts have a way of ending up dead. Like your father. Like that hombre in there. Like many more I've seen—and killed. Think about it."

And without another glance he was gone, striding from the cabin with a lithe grace that was no less flowing for the wound in his shoulder, a wound that must be paining him, she knew, though he gave no sign of it.

Rebeccah jumped up as the door slammed behind him. She had to struggle to keep from running outside and hurling the coffee cups after him. Leaving her here alone with that . . . thing. How could he? What if Jones wasn't really dead? What if he got up after she fell asleep and came after her, dripping a trail of blood. . . .

Stop it, she told herself sternly, and paced around the room in an effort to gain control of her emotions. *Check on him, you fool. Then bring your blanket and pillow in here and sleep on this sofa. Don't be a ninny. Show Wolf Bodine you can't be scared by the likes of him or Fess Jones—dead or alive.*

But she scarcely slept a wink all night and awoke on the horsehair sofa shortly after dawn feeling heavy-eyed and haggard. Beyond the parlor window pale sunlight and beautiful country beckoned. But a dead man lay in her bedroom, and Neely Stoner knew where she was. It was only a matter of time before he showed up personally, looking for the deed to that mine.

Her troubles seemed to be growing instead of dwindling. And to top it off, she'd have to face Wolf Bodine again today.

Sighing, Rebeccah put up coffee in the kitchen and nibbled hardtack. Somehow she'd have to find a way to get herself that teacher's job, or she'd be out of both food and money within a month. Chewing hardtack, trying not to think about the flapjacks and sausage and buttermilk biscuits with raspberry preserves her stomach longed for, she wondered bleakly how soon Wolf Bodine would tell everybody in Powder Creek exactly who she was.

6

"Bear Rawlings's daughter! Living on the Peastone place?"

Billy Bodine's gray eyes widened in excitement as he set down his glass of milk and regarded Wolf across the kitchen table. He knew nothing of his father's wound, since it was bandaged under his flannel shirt and vest, and Wolf had been moving about without any visible sign of pain or discomfort, but Billy had asked first thing this morning, while washing up at the pump, if Wolf had caught Fess Jones.

"I did. And we won't have to worry about him anymore," Wolf had responded shortly, then had turned on his heel and gone into the kitchen. But Billy hadn't been satisfied with such meager information. He'd followed his father upstairs, pressed him while he shaved in the brass-framed mirror, and demanded to know everything that had happened after Wolf had ridden off the previous night in search of the outlaw.

Naturally Wolf didn't tell him.

All he said was that Fess Jones was dead and that Jones had been trying to kill the new owner of the Peastone place. When Caitlin had inquired in surprise who that might be, Wolf had set down his coffee.

"Rebeccah Rawlings."

Billy, with his keen memory, had instantly re-called the rumors that Amos Peastone had lost his ranch to the outlaw Bear Rawlings. Of course no one was ever sure, since Bear Rawlings hadn't shown up to lay claim to it. But when Billy heard Rebeccah's name, he put two and two together with amazing speed.

"Is she an outlaw, too, Pa? Are you going to ar-rest her?"

"She could be. And I might."

"Wait till I tell Joey. He says there's no such thing as a lady outlaw. I told him that a lady was just as likely as a man to be dishonest, but he said that—"

"Whoa." Wolf's long arm reached across the ta-ble to grasp the boy's shoulder. Billy met his frown-ing gaze. "You can't go around calling this lady an outlaw, son. She hasn't done anything wrong. And we don't know that she will. We don't know any-thing about her, so until we do, we have to give her the benefit of the doubt. It wouldn't be right to go around spreading tales."

Wolf heard in his own words the echo of what Rebeccah Rawlings had said to him the previous night. Damned if she hadn't made sense, much as it irked him to admit it.

His mother agreed. "Every person deserves a chance, Billy, a chance to be judged on their own merits," she said in her brisk, no-nonsense way. As always Caitlin Bodine had come down to breakfast impeccably dressed in a crisp yellow-and-white everyday gingham, the buttons fastened up to her throat, her gray hair tidily pinned into a topknot, and her sleeves rolled up, ready to work. Though her vision was dim and blurry at best due to the cataracts that had robbed her of clear sight over her fifty-odd years, she could still make out shapes, and she worked fiercely each morning at her toiletry, determined to look neat, clean, and precise, the way a lady ought, even if she couldn't see very well what she was doing.

"Don't you ever be one to start calling folks names for no reason," she warned her grandson, peering at him with effort, seeing only the shape of him, his small frame and dark head, none of the features that only a few years ago she had still been able to make out. "That's no way to be going on. Maybe the young lady is perfectly honest and respectable. She could be hurt from being misjudged."

"Aw, Gramma . . . how can it possibly hurt—" Billy began to argue, but a stern look from his father made him duck his head obediently. "Yes, ma'am," he muttered.

Wolf refilled the boy's milk glass from the blue china pitcher Caitlin had used for nearly forty years. "Eat some of your Gramma's sausage now, and take one of these sourdough biscuits before you see to your chores," he said. "And stay away from Rebeccah Rawlings."

As Wolf swallowed a forkful of the delicious sausage and washed it down with fresh-brewed coffee, he tried not to think about Rebeccah Rawlings spending the night in that godforsaken cabin with

Fess Jones's corpse. Regret had lashed at him the moment he'd ridden off and left her like that—it had been a low-down thing to do—but something about her refusal to answer his questions had goaded him into it. Why did she have to be so stubborn? Why couldn't she be sweet and respectful and good-natured like most other women?

He was sorry he'd done it, though. He'd almost turned right around and gone back and dragged the body out for her right then, but that would have been like giving in, and he'd be damned if he'd give in to Rebeccah Rawlings, ever, on anything. But he'd lain awake in bed all night, feeling bad. At least now it was morning and he could go to the cabin and take care of it. Matthew Crimmons, the undertaker, would be in his office by the time he hauled Jones's body to town.

The talk at the breakfast table turned to the desertion of Miss Kellum, the new schoolteacher, and Wolf dragged his thoughts on to this topic. Billy, reflecting the spirit of the other children of the town, cackled gleefully at the prospect of no school for the entire winter. But Caitlin shook her head.

"Wolf, one way or the other, we *must* find a teacher for these children. It's essential. What are you going to do?"

Wolf sighed as he met the interrogating gaze of this hardy little woman with the tiny hooked nose and wrinkled brown skin. Caitlin Bodine had always felt her oldest son could do anything. She had implicit faith in him and was fond of reminding him of this fact. She had firmly believed that he could raise Billy just fine after the boy's mother was gone and she had been confident that he could clean up Powder Creek when they'd first arrived and found it run by the Saunders gang. Caitlin had always believed he could solve any problem, conquer any obstacle.

Now she wanted him to produce a genuine certified and willing schoolteacher immediately, and out of thin air.

"Any suggestions, Ma?" he inquired with the ghost of a grin.

"As a matter of fact, yes," she returned promptly. She wiped her mouth daintily on her napkin and set it down beside her plate. "Hold a town meeting. Ask if anyone has a relative with a teaching certificate, someone who wants to come west, to settle in a decent, respectable town where the law runs things regular and safe and people take care of their own. *Someone* in Powder Creek must have a nephew or sister or cousin with a hankering for a job."

"No, Caitlin, there's no need for that. I've got a much better idea," Myrtle Lee Anderson declared from the open kitchen doorway. Wolf stood up, regarding her with raised brows.

"Come right on in, Myrtle," he drawled, holding out a chair. "Help yourself to a biscuit."

"Don't mind if I do. Caitlin, I have to talk to you. You've got good sense. Tell me what you think of my scheme. I say we ask that young lady who came to town yesterday—the one who shot Scoop Parmalee—to take over as the new schoolteacher. Word is she didn't take the stage out of town with the other passengers, though I don't know where she is precisely this morning. Maybe at the hotel. Anyhow," Myrtle rushed on, barely pausing for breath as Wolf's eyes narrowed on her, "Rusty at the hotel overheard one of the other passengers say she was a right fine shot for a schoolteacher. A schoolteacher! Seems she told the other folks on the stagecoach she taught at some fancy private academy back east. Well, you could have knocked me over with a feather when I heard that! If it isn't a stroke of luck, I don't know what is!"

"Pa! Is she talking about Rebeccah Rawlings? The outlaw's daughter is going to be our new school-teacher?" Billy burst out, then clapped his hand over his mouth as Wolf shot him a thunderous glance.

"Outlaw's daughter!" Myrtle cried, wheeling to stare at the boy.

It was Caitlin who interjected calmly, "Why, I think it could be a fine idea, Myrtle. You and Waylon and the mayor ought to ask her about it right away."

"But . . . but . . ." Myrtle, like everyone else in the town, was aware of the stories a few years back that Bear Rawlings had won Amos Peastone's ranch. But she had never put much stock in it. "That girl . . . the one who shot Scoop Parmalee —she's Bear Rawlings's daughter? Is she taking over the Peastone place? Good Lord, Sheriff, do you know that for a fact?"

Wolf had no choice but to answer curtly, "I do."

"Well, dear me. Caitlin, how can you even think such a thing would be a fine idea? I never would have suggested it if I'd known who she was."

"According to what my son told me, she's a young woman with great presence of mind and mighty good aim with a pistol," Caitlin said crisply. "Aside from that, Myrtle, we know nothing more about her."

"Except she was mixed up somehow with that hombre Fess Jones," Billy piped in.

Myrtle's mouth dropped open. "Fess Jones!"

Wolf glowered at his son. "Billy, see to your chores."

"But, I—"

"Now."

Billy knew better than to argue with his father when he got that quelling look in his eye. He realized too late that his brash tongue had seriously angered not only his grandmother but his father as well. He pushed back his chair, glanced around the table in some consternation, and mumbled, "Sorry."

"There's only one thing to do," Myrtle said the moment the door swung shut behind the boy.

"And what might that be?" Wolf inquired dryly, though he had a feeling he knew exactly what was coming.

"Run the hussy out of town."

"Myrtle Lee Anderson!" Caitlin's lips clamped together reprovingly. "I'm surprised at you."

"Bear Rawlings was a murdering thief with no conscience—and any kin of his must be just the same." Myrtle's voice throbbed with emotion. *"You* know what he did when he robbed our bank. You both know what happened that day. . . ." Her voice broke, but before either Caitlin or Wolf could say anything, she banged her stout fist on the kitchen table so that the spoons rattled in the saucers, and rushed on with trembling emotion: "We can't have her here in Powder Creek, attracting vermin like Fess Jones. What's he got to do with her anyway, Sheriff?"

"Nothing. He's dead."

"Well, thank goodness for small favors."

Wolf decided he'd had enough. He left the table, lifted his hat from the hook by the door, and regarded the head of the town's social committee with a warning glance. "Sorry I can't oblige you, Myrtle Lee, by running Miss Rawlings out of town on a rail, or maybe lynching her in your backyard, but you see, the lady hasn't done anything wrong. Until she does, she can stay in Powder Creek, she can live on the Peastone ranch, and she can dance down Main Street in her drawers if she wants. It's my sworn duty to see that she's treated as decently as every other citizen. So no one's going to be running anyone out of town, do you understand? Or that someone will have to answer to me."

The door slammed behind him. Silence settled over the bright, tidy Bodine kitchen while he mounted Dusty and headed for town.

Cowed momentarily into speechlessness, Myrtle only stared at the untouched biscuit on her plate. But she wasn't seeing it at all. She was seeing an elegant young woman in a fine blue traveling dress, a woman gazing up at Powder Creek's sheriff with big pansy-blue eyes. Her brows knit together in a dark line. Then she banged her fist on the table again.

"What's got him all riled up?" she demanded.

Caitlin took a sip of coffee. "My son is a fair man. He doesn't like to see folks hastening to judgment against someone—anyone—even if she *is* an outlaw's daughter," she added coolly.

"Maybe it's more than that," Myrtle said, a sly look entering her eyes. "I've seen that girl, Caitlin. She's a beaut. You'd better watch out for Wolf. Oh, I know half the town thinks he's going to get hitched one day soon to that Westerly girl, but that there Rebeccah Rawlings, she's quite a looker. Why, she could turn his head in an instant."

"Not Wolf's head," Caitlin said.

"Don't be so sure. Why, I'll wager that blackhaired hussy could make any man go loco, if she put her mind to it. Waylon Pritchard sure made a fool out of himself. Wait until he finds out who she is."

Caitlin sighed. In a few minutes the youngest Adams girl would be arriving to help her with the day's cooking, cleaning, and household chores. Maybe then Myrtle would leave. Caitlin had heard more than enough nonsense for one morning. Besides, she had several things to think about now: whether Rebeccah Rawlings really might be qualified to become the schoolteacher the town so desperately needed and what kind of a woman she really was. As far as what Myrtle had said about Wolf getting riled because of some attraction toward her, Caitlin felt only skepticism. It had been ten years since Clarissa, and she oftentimes wondered if Wolf would ever get over it. She knew everyone was waiting for him to marry Nel Westerly or possibly even the pretty young widow, Lorelie Simpson, but she also knew he cared not a whit more for them than he did for Molly Duke, the tall, buxom owner of the Silk Drawers Brothel. Wolf was in no more danger of losing his heart than Caitlin herself was of falling into the Pacific Ocean. Yet she made up her mind to meet this Rawlings girl and find out for herself what kind of a woman she was.

And the sooner the better.

Caitlin heard Mary Adams trudging up to the door before she made out the shape of the four-teen-year-old girl's sturdy figure. "Myrtle," she said, rising from the table with what she hoped was a dismissive air, "now that Mary's here, you'll have to excuse me. I'm behind on all my chores, and much as I'd like to do it, I simply can't sit here all day chatting. But do come over for Sunday dinner," she added, fearing she'd been too abrupt and therefore rude. "We'd be happy to have you join us." Wolf would be furious, Caitlin knew, but there was no help for it.

She waited until Myrtle had gone before putting into motion the idea in her head—an idea too irre-sistible to ignore. "Mary, dear, pack up a lunch hamper with a side of beef and the rest of these sourdough biscuits and some of my special pre-serves while I see to these dishes. Oh, and bring a jug of lemonade along. Then get the buggy ready quick as you can. We're going on a little neighborly drive."

7 "Did you sleep well?"

Wolf knew the answer even before he swung down from the saddle. Rebeccah Rawlings, busily sweeping her front porch, glanced over at him, and her weariness was plain to see.

Guilt stabbed at him. Leaving her here all night with that dead body had been a low-down trick. Today he saw the results of it. There were dark circles under her eyes, she was pale, and her shoulders sagged as though they were sore. Yet for all that she looked as pretty as ever in the bright splash of Montana sunshine. Her high-necked blue gingham dress molded becomingly to the curves of her figure, her dark satin hair shone as it fell loosely about her shoulders, and her generous mouth looked all too kissable.

But the bruise on her cheek looked raw and painful.

He was immediately sorry for the sarcastic way he'd begun the conversation. He moved toward her as she paused, broom in hand, and wished he could start this visit over.

"As a matter of fact," Rebeccah said defiantly,

staring at him as he stepped onto the porch to face her, "I slept beautifully."

She straightened her aching shoulders with an effort. All her muscles hurt. Her head throbbed. But at that moment she would rather have died at the stake than appear weak before him.

Why did he have to look so fit, so strong and rested and smug, coming up the walk with that easy lope, with his guns glittering in the sunlight, his hair glinting beneath his hat? She wanted to hit him.

Instead she managed a frosty smile reminiscent of Althea Oxford, vice principal of Miss Wright's academy, and the coldest iceberg of a woman Rebeccah had ever met.

"Why shouldn't I sleep?" she continued, adding an airy wave of her hand for effect. "I was comfortably ensconced in my own home, smack in the middle of this beautiful and spacious country, and there was no one around to bother me."

"So you weren't afraid?"

"Of what?" she managed to sneer. "Ghosts? Dead men? It takes more than that to frighten me, Sheriff Bodine."

He had to hand it to her. She might almost have convinced him—if not for the dark lavender smudges beneath her eyes. And he knew those smudges were all his fault.

"I'll get rid of Jones for you right now," he said. He started toward the cabin door. "You might want to wait in the kitchen while I—"

"Don't bother. He's not in there."

He stopped, then turned slowly, his gaze riveted on her.

"What did you say?"

"He's not in there," Rebeccah repeated, and began sweeping again, forcing him to move quickly aside as the broom danced over and around his boots. Whisk, whisk, whisk, back and forth went the broom. She didn't glance at him. "I didn't like the idea of waiting for you, Sheriff, so I took care of Jones myself. Dragged him outside, that is. I'm quite strong. And not the least bit squeamish, you know. I killed a man yesterday, as I hope you remember. Besides," she rushed on as casually as she could despite the gruesome memory of the body's disgusting appearance and stench, "it was starting to smell, you see, and I won't have a foul odor in my house."

Wolf gripped her by the shoulders, fighting the urge to shake her. Mulish, obstinate woman!

Her head flew up defiantly, and he saw at once that beneath her air of casual indifference she was deeply shaken. Her skin was drawn tight over her cheekbones, and her eyes looked utterly weary.

"Why didn't you wait for me?" he demanded. His own guilt over not having gotten rid of Jones the previous night made his voice come out harsher than he'd intended. "I said I'd do it."

Rebeccah clenched and unclenched her fingers. The dazzling August sun was hurting her eyes, making it even harder to fight back tears. It had been awful getting Fess Jones out of her house, truly awful, but what she'd said to Wolf Bodine was true. She couldn't tolerate Jones fouling up her home one more minute. And she *wouldn't* allow herself to be dependent on Wolf Bodine—wouldn't give him the satisfaction of knowing that she needed his help—or anyone else's.

After the back-breaking effort of dragging the body out back, she'd spent the better part of an hour on her knees scrubbing blood out of the floor. It was all gone now, every drop, and she'd even had a bath in the stream before she'd returned to work in the kitchen.

I think I'm doing very well, she told herself, but all such thoughts faded as she saw the hot anger flare in Wolf Bodine's eyes.

"You are the stupidest, most prideful, high-handed, *damndest* woman I ever met in my life." His fingers singed her flesh, and she nearly gasped aloud at the violent electricity flashing from his powerful hands and pouring from every muscle in his tall, lean frame. "I would have removed that body for you—I said I would—but you were too bullheaded to wait!"

"It wasn't necessary. I didn't want to be dependent on you—or on anyone. It's not my way. So I just did it, that's all. And if you don't want to bury him for me, Sheriff Bodine, I'll do that too. As a matter of fact there's a shovel in the shed. I'll do it right now."

She tried to wrench away from him, but he held her back, fury blasting through him like dynamite. "The hell you will. You're staying right here on this porch. For once you're going to do as you're told, even if I have to turn you over my knee. Which is not a bad idea."

Rage brought vivid color flooding her cheeks.
"How dare you!"

"I'd dare, all right. In fact . . ."

Rebeccah gasped as she saw him warm to the
idea. His eyes suddenly seemed to light with the
devil's own fire, his hands closed around her arms
with ominous purpose.

"Seems to me, Miss Rawlings, that you could
benefit from a good spanking more than anyone
I've ever known."

"Wolf Bodine, you let go of me right this minute!"

"Why should I?"

"Because you have no right to . . . ah!"

She broke away from him with a sudden, furious
yank and fled into the cabin like a jackrabbit pursued by hounds. To her dismay he followed, his
boots stomping purposefully behind her.

"Sheriff Bodine, get out of my house!" she
shrieked, flinging an enraged glance over her shoulder. That glance proved to be her undoing, for she
promptly tripped over the bucket of water she'd
used when scrubbing the floor, overturning it and
sloshing water all over, and then pitched headfirst
onto the sofa. Wolf, charging after her, slipped on
the spilled water and, with arms akimbo, slid forward and tumbled down on top of her.

He managed somehow at the last moment to
brace his arms so as not to hurt her, but for a moment they were wildly entangled. His hard thighs
pressed against her slim legs, his powerful chest
was jammed against her breasts, and his lean face
was only inches above hers.

"You *are* the clumsiest woman I ever met," he

exclaimed, and then stopped, staring in amazement at the terror stamped on her face.

She wasn't breathing. In her eyes was utter panic and a genuine, horrified fear.

"What the hell . . ." he muttered and instinctively reached out a hand to smooth the tumble of hair from her cheek.

"Don't!" she pleaded, flinching. In her eyes was panic and utter fear. "Please, no! Please, don't!"

His hand froze, then dropped. "I won't," he said instantly, his voice softening, though he had no idea what he was not supposed to do. But the sight of Rebeccah Rawlings, who had faced up to all the challenges in the past day with such feisty courage and self-reliance, now pale and trembling in child-like fear stunned him. What was she so upset about?

"I'm not really going to spank you," he said, feeling somewhat foolish. "Or hurt you," he added, and shifted his weight to let her up.

Like lightning she darted from beneath his arm and was off the sofa, not pausing until she had put a distance of a good eight feet between them. Her breathing was labored, her face sickly pale as she faced him.

"I'll thank you to leave now," she managed to order, though he could see that even keeping her voice level was costing her a great deal of effort.

"Why are you afraid of me all of a sudden?" he asked, rising from the sofa, sticking his hat back on his head. A short time ago he'd have sworn Rebeccah Rawlings wasn't afraid of anything. He made no quick moves, so as not to alarm her, and kept his voice quiet as though he were speaking to a wounded animal that needed his care. "Don't tell me you thought I was going to rape you just now."

"Get out."

"That's what you thought, Rebeccah, isn't it?" he asked softly, incredulously.

She said nothing, but only stared at him through dark, lost eyes.

Someone has hurt her, hurt her badly. Wolf was shaken by a violent surge of fury.

Then they both heard the sounds of footsteps and women's voices approaching the open cabin door.

"What in heaven's name are you doing here, Wolf?" Caitlin Bodine demanded, halting at the threshold. "Mary recognized Dusty in the yard, but I could scarcely believe it. I thought you were headed to town. Miss Rawlings?" Caitlin squinted at the dark shape of the slender young woman, who appeared to be frozen in the center of the parlor. "I'm Caitlin Bodine, and this is Mary Adams. We've brought you a housewarming present."

Rebeccah fought quickly to recover her composure. The reflexive terror was fading. Her heartbeat slowed. Wolf Bodine was no longer a terrifying figure, but only a tall, rugged, handsome man with eyes that seared straight through her like a branding poker crashing through glass. She didn't look at him, though. She studied Caitlin Bodine as Wolf performed stiff introductions, and slowly she felt the color returning to her cheeks.

Caitlin was perhaps in her late fifties, no more than five feet tall, yet embodying an air of forcefulness that made her seem somehow indomitable. A trim little woman, she had a tiny beak nose, milky blue eyes, and a daintily pointed chin, which gave her nut-brown, seamed face a sturdy character. Beside her, Mary Adams, a freckle-faced girl of about fourteen, regarded Rebeccah with frank curiosity. She carried a large wicker hamper with a red-and-white-checked cloth across it.

A housewarming present.

"How do you do, Mrs. Bodine," Rebeccah managed, despite her surprise. "It's very kind of you to visit. But please don't come in any farther just yet. I overturned the bucket, and there's water all over the floor. Let me wipe it up so you can come in and sit down."

"Mary will help you," Caitlin said. "That's what we came for—to welcome you to Powder Creek and help you get settled in. You're our nearest neighbor —did my son tell you that? No one's lived on this property since heaven knows when, so it must need quite a bit of work. Far too much for one young lady to handle all alone."

"Not our Miss Rawlings. She can handle everything alone," Wolf commented drily, thinking of the corpse outside.

"Wolf." His mother half turned toward him. "Don't you have some work to do in town?"

"I might."

"Well, shoo, then. We don't need you here—at least not today. Maybe you can chop some wood for Miss Rawlings later," she added thoughtfully. "But right now it's best if you leave us women to our chores."

Rebeccah gazed suspiciously from Wolf to Caitlin and back again. It was difficult to believe that Wolf Bodine's mother—that anyone—wanted to help her settle in. No one in her life had ever welcomed her anywhere. Yet the old woman didn't appear the type to lie. There was a forthrightness about her, something plain and simple and honest, which Rebeccah recognized even through her doubts.

"I appreciate the offer of help, Mrs. Bodine," Rebeccah said slowly, wonderingly. She directed Mary to set the hamper down near the door. Then she looked coolly at Wolf, trying not to think of the fluttering, hot sensations inside her when he'd lain across her on the sofa, an instant before the panic had set in.

"Was there anything else, Sheriff?" she inquired.

"Nothing at all. Except a little matter to see to out back. It won't take long."

Rebeccah skirted the puddle seeping across the floor and followed him quickly to the door. "Please —bury him at the edge of the property," she said in a low tone. "As far away from the house as you can. I don't really want to think about Fess Jones in his final resting-place every time I step outside my kitchen door."

"And I thought you weren't afraid of ghosts or dead men."

"It has nothing to do with fear!"

Wolf stared into those flashing violet eyes, so filled with anger and rebellion. This was the Rebeccah Rawlings he knew—not the terrified woman of a few moments ago. He held up a hand before she could bite out a stinging reproof. "Hold on to your horses, Miss Rawlings. I'm not planning to bury anyone outside your kitchen door. Jones is going to the undertaker, and then he'll be laid to rest proper in Boot Hill. You won't have to think about him or his final resting-place at all."

She forced the next words. "Thank you."

Wolf Bodine touched his fingers to the brim of his hat. His eyes gleamed. "There, that wasn't so difficult, was it?" he said so softly that the others couldn't hear. "You're very welcome, Miss Rawlings."

It was a strange morning. Mary Adams and Caitlin worked side by side with Rebeccah, washing the curtains, hanging them out to dry, beating out the old rag rug, and carrying water from the stream to fill the barrel. Caitlin, whose vision was apparently strong enough to enable her to make her way around unassisted and to do chores not requiring precise sight, had amazing energy and didn't pause for a breath until noon. By then Rebeccah had prepared a simple meal from the hamper the others had brought: succulent meat pies and biscuits and beans and a jug of lemonade.

"And here's some of my peach preserves for your pantry," Caitlin said, handing her a jar. "Sort of an extra welcome present."

Rebeccah's fingers closed tightly around the jar. No one besides Bear had ever given her a present before. And this—a welcome present. Her throat ached. Here she stood in her very own spotless kitchen, surrounded by the savory aromas of a hearty meal, with sunlight slanting in, the sharp blue mountains filling the horizon, and a neighbor smiling pleasantly at her, a smile of pure friendliness, with no guile or smirks attached.

She suddenly felt a long way from Miss Wright's Academy, from Althea Oxford and Analee Caruthers.

"I thank you very much for everything," she said quietly, and setting the jar carefully on the countertop, she turned to grasp Caitlin's work-roughened hand. "You're very kind. In fact"—she took a deep breath—"I've never met anyone half as kind as you."

Caitlin squeezed her hand. "Mary, dear, will you wash up these lunch dishes for Miss Rawlings? Then we'll have to be going. But in the meantime, Miss Rawlings—"

"Call me Rebeccah, please."

"Rebeccah, then. Let's sit on that sofa of yours and talk a bit. There's something I want to ask you."

There wasn't much resemblance between Caitlin Bodine and her son, Rebeccah thought as she seated herself beside the older woman. Caitlin's face was small, her features neat and tiny. Wolf's features were lean, long-jawed, strong. She was aware of a disturbing jittery feeling inside as she thought of him, and pushed his image away. Instead she focused on how odd it seemed to be sitting here with this formidable little woman, feeling not at all uncomfortable but strangely accepted.

"Now," Caitlin began in her brisk, direct manner, "what's this about your being a schoolteacher?"

Rebeccah stared at her in surprise. "How did you know about that?"

"Dear, word gets around quickly in our little western towns. Apparently some of your fellow passengers were overheard mentioning it at the hotel, and the long and the short of it is, Myrtle Lee Anderson came to my door this morning with the news. All excited about it, she was. You know, we desperately *need* a schoolteacher here in town. Haven't had a real teacher in nearly a year now. Last one we had couldn't take our Montana winters and up and left. You strike me as a hardier sort."

"Oh, I'm as hardy as they come." Rebeccah gazed down at her fingers, clasped in her lap. "Bad weather doesn't scare me. As a matter of fact nothing does." Rebeccah had told herself this so many times, she nearly believed it to be true, and spoke the words with conviction. "But I'm not certain I care to go on teaching. I came out here to build myself a ranch. And just because I'm going to have to build a little more than I originally planned, Mrs. Bodine, doesn't mean I'm giving up on my ideas. So I'm afraid Powder Creek will have to find another teacher."

There, she'd said it. She hated to deceive Caitlin in any way, but Rebeccah couldn't bring herself to accept the teacher's position too eagerly. If the town knew she wanted it, they might take their offer away. And she didn't want all of Powder Creek knowing how desperate she was now that she'd rid herself of all of Bear's ill-gotten gains. It was nobody's business, and besides, it would seem disloyal: a public admission of shame over what he had done. She owed Bear more than that, even if privately she did lament his thieving ways. And she knew she stood a much better chance of actually getting the position if she seemed disinterested in it. Sheriff Bodine's warnings about the town's likely attitude toward her had not left her undisturbed. Maybe some wouldn't want to hire her, maybe others would consider it—but if she seemed anxious for the position, they might be more inclined to deny it to her. Let them come to *her,* let them persuade her.

Perhaps she was too proud for her own good, but Rebeccah hated the thought of giving these townspeople, most of whom she hadn't even met yet, the opportunity to hurt her.

Caitlin had accepted her words with nary a flicker in those milky, near-sightless eyes. After a moment, when the only sound they could hear was the buzz of bees outside the parlor window, and the fragrant scent of heather and pine drifted in as light as a caress, she continued slowly. "Seems a shame, you being so well educated and all. But then I reckon your father left you enough money so you don't need to earn a living or anything like that."

"The problem, Mrs. Bodine, is that I didn't care for teaching very much," Rebeccah responded honestly enough. "And I'm reluctant to get involved with the children of everyone in this town." Rebeccah took a deep breath. "I moved out here for peace and quiet. Montana is big country, beautiful country. There's room to breathe here, to just *be.* I don't want to have to answer to anyone, to be beholden to anyone, to be involved with anything other than my own place, my own plans. Of course," she said hurriedly, seeing the disappointment flit across Caitlin's seamed face, "you've been very kind, and I hope we'll stay friends, but . . . others in Powder Creek might not be as friendly, as your son warned me, and I'm sure they wouldn't want me to teach their children, even if I decided to do it."

"Oh, so that's what you're worried about, is it?" Caitlin seized on this statement. She patted Rebeccah's hand. "Well, we'll just see about that. You know, dear, I can't see much with these old eyes, but I can still tell a whole lot more about people than some folks with two good eyes in their heads. You may be an outlaw's daughter, Rebeccah Rawlings, but you're no more disreputable than I am. Now, I had an idea this morning and I think it's a good one. Want to hear it?"

"Go on."

"A town meeting. Will you come? Meet everyone —talk about your qualifications. We heard you've taught for several years at some fancy private school back east."

"Miss Wright's Academy for Young Ladies." Rebeccah grimaced. Her voice took on a dry tone. "I possess a fine education, a teaching certificate, and a number of excellent books—which I have yet to unpack," she added with a smile, "but I don't think I possess the desire to stand up before a town meeting and present myself to your citizens—and their judgment. No, thank you, Mrs. Bodine. I'd rather not."

"What if Wolf and I can persuade the town to give

you the job? Without your going on display at the meeting. Will you agree then?"

Rebeccah doubted very much that Wolf Bodine would persuade the townsfolk to do anything but tar and feather her. But she knew Caitlin would speak earnestly on her behalf, and felt an irresistible warming toward this woman. Yet her feelings were in a tangle. Part of her wanted to accept the teaching position, because she needed the money. And part of her wanted to refuse it, because of the very real reasons she had given Caitlin before. But practicality won out. *And besides,* she told herself, as Mary came in from the kitchen and Caitlin thrust herself to her feet, *maybe the children of Powder Creek won't be quite as unpleasant as those spoiled girls at the Academy. Maybe I can actually do some good for them.* She would see.

"Do what you wish," she said, her voice casual. She rose with an air of finality. "If an offer is made, I will consider it."

She was proud, Caitlin observed with approval. And for some reason eager to appear indifferent, but as Caitlin and Mary drove home in silence, the older woman's thoughts clicked along as rapidly as the horses' hooves. She may have lost most of her vision over the years, but she hadn't lost her wits or her instincts. From Rebeccah's smooth, pleasantly low-timbred voice Caitlin knew the girl was cultured, educated, and intelligent. From what Rebeccah didn't say more than what she did, Caitlin realized that the girl was also vulnerable and very much alone.

An outlaw? By no means.

Caitlin dismissed such suspicions with a certainty born of instinct. But why had Fess Jones gone to her cabin last night?

For no good reason.

The girl must be in some sort of trouble. And she was too proud to ask for help.

It's up to Wolf to see that she's all right, she decided. *And I'm going to tell him so myself.*

She liked Rebeccah Rawlings. And, to her surprise, she had a feeling Wolf did too. He hadn't been immune to her, that was for sure. Caitlin had heard something in his voice when he'd spoken with the girl, something she hadn't heard in a long time.

She smiled to herself as Mary guided the team toward home.

Not once during the entire conversation did Caitlin Bodine mention Wolf, his wife, or his family, Rebeccah reflected as she stood at her kitchen window and gazed out at the turqoise sky dotted with lacy clouds. The fragrance of bluebells drifted into the kitchen, but she scarcely noticed the delicate sweetness of their perfume.

She closed her eyes, her fingertips resting on the sun-warmed window ledge. Why hadn't she asked about Wolf?

Then she opened her eyes and shook off the cobwebs of her own curiosity. "Why should I?" she demanded crossly, and smoothed damp tendrils of hair back from her perspiring brow.

Because you're dying to know, a voice inside told her. Some silly part of her still clung to the foolish

dreams of her girlhood, to the romanticized fantasies she'd engaged in over a tall cowboy with keen
eyes and a kind grin.

"Foolishness!" she muttered to herself, and
turned her back on the majestic, mountain-studded
view. There was plenty of work yet to do in and
around this cabin. And not a minute to waste day-
dreaming about Wolf Bodine.

Wolf had his hands full all the rest of the day.
After bringing Jones's body to the undertaker for
burial at Boot Hill, he was summoned to break up a
fistfight in the Gold Bar Saloon, another at Coyote
Kate's, had to ride to Helena to serve as a witness
at a trial, then back to Powder Creek to tend to the
paperwork that was the scourge of his job, and finally he had the wearisome duty of locking up a
drunken cowboy named Shorty McCall from the
Broken Tree Ranch for disturbing the peace after
Shorty pistol-whipped a gambler in the Silk Drawers Brothel and then shot up all Molly Duke's handsome downstairs windows and mirrors.

Just another quiet day in Powder Creek.

He was about to lock up for the night and go
home for supper when Mayor Duke barreled in,
holding up a pudgy hand as Wolf glanced up from
his desk.

"Won't take up more than a minute of your time,
Sheriff. Don't mind me. Just wanted to tell you.
Myrtle Lee Anderson has called a town meeting.
It's set for tomorrow night at the hotel. She's con-
cerned about that young lady who arrived in town

yesterday. Is it true she's Bear Rawlings's daughter?"

"What if it is?"

Ernest Duke shook his gray head. "Myrtle's been stirring folks up. Most everyone in these parts remembers that bank holdup Bear Rawlings's gang pulled here six, maybe seven years ago, when the teller was killed and Ed Mason's little girl was run down in the street during their getaway. Folks won't take kindly to having the ringleader's daughter living here—much less teaching their kids. Oh, yes," Duke went on, his black eyes fixed unblinkingly on the sheriff, "Myrtle told me Caitlin had some idea about that. But it won't do, Wolf. We'll be lucky if folks don't try to tar and feather that little missy right out of town."

"There'll be no tarring and feathering under my jurisdiction." Wolf stood to his full height. The hard glance he sent the mayor held a quiet yet perceptible warning. "Get a hold of yourself, Ernest. Don't get hysterical like Myrtle Lee."

"Oh, I'm not in favor of it. I just know that folks still get pretty riled up over the mention of Bear Rawlings's name, and the fact that his kin is here, well. . . . Rumor has it over in the hotel and at Coyote Kate's that she's up to her pretty white neck in no good. Some think she's masterminding a future bank job, working with no-good varmints like Fess Jones. Heard you shot that hombre yesterday up at her place. What was he doing there? Were they in cahoots?"

"Ernest, there's no evidence that Miss Rawlings is up to anything other than making a go of the

Peastone place. Last I heard, Bear won it fair and square from old Amos—maybe the only honest possession he ever came by in his life. She has every right to live there, so long as she doesn't bother anybody. And by the same token, nobody has the right to bother her. You savvy?"

Ernest Duke flinched at the ominous look in Bodine's cold gray eyes. Wolf wasn't a man to tangle with, no sir, not if you valued your hide. He was easygoing and soft-spoken most of the time, and courteous to all the citizens of the town, but Ernest suspected that beneath all that a deep, slow anger burned within him, and, once ignited, it would rage like a hell-born fire.

Ernest Duke didn't want to be the one to fan those flames.

"No need to worry about me, Sheriff," he said soothingly, and fingered the lapels of his well-cut dark suit. "I'm just keeping you posted about what's going on. I don't have a thing to do with it personally, but I thought you ought to know."

"What time is the meeting?"

"Seven o'clock. Planning to come?"

Wolf nodded.

"Fine, then, that's real fine. See you there." The mayor bobbed his head and smiled jovially, but Wolf sensed his uneasiness. *Myrtle has already stirred folks up more than he's saying,* Wolf concluded.

He watched Ernest Duke leave his office and cross Main Street, then closed the shutters. Shorty McCall was snoring in his cell, probably passed out for the night. Wolf's deputy, Ace Johnson, would be in later to keep an eye on him. As Wolf left the office and stepped out onto the boardwalk, he pondered the mayor's words and wondered darkly why folks always had to think the worst of strangers. Of course he himself had been suspicious of Rebeccah Rawlings—hell, he still was, up to a point—but that was his job. He'd be damned if he'd let law and order in Powder Creek deteriorate into some hysterical mob out to drive a lone woman from the town.

Even if she was Bear Rawlings's daughter.

8 The whole town was there.

Myrtle Lee Anderson had her red-faced sons and daughters-in-law perched in the front row. Right behind them were Doc Wilson, the mayor and his gossipy chipmunk of a wife, Lillian, and Waylon Pritchard, along with his parents and two older brothers. Wolf's scanning eye noted each citizen crowded into the hotel dining room, where the town meeting was taking place. There was the pretty widow, Lorelie Simpson; Dan Butterick, who owned the sawmill; every rancher whose property came within a thirty-mile radius, prominent among them the Bradys, the Adamses, and the Westerlys, as well as most of the storekeepers and merchants, even some gamblers and saloon girls from Coyote Kate's and the Gold Bar, who had come to hear about the dangerous and undesirable Miss Rawlings.

As thunder rumbled down from the Big Belt Mountains and a late-summer storm hurried its way toward the valleys, Caitlin sat with Wolf near the back of the room, holding her temper in check with great effort. Myrtle Lee Anderson took the podium first.

"That woman's got no more brains than a grouse," Caitlin whispered to Wolf as Myrtle Lee went on and on about the upstanding town they lived in and demanded to know what would happen to them all if riffraff outlaws began to take up residence in Powder Creek?

Abigail Pritchard, Waylon's thickset, eagle-eyed mother, came to her feet when Myrtle paused for breath. "And how will it make poor Emily Brady feel having to see that Rawlings woman in town every week, knowing that she's living high off the hog on money left her by the very man responsible for running down Emily's little niece? It's a mercy the poor Masons have moved away, that's what it is. But we haven't forgotten what Bear Rawlings and his gang did to them. Why should Rebeccah Rawlings be welcome in this town, when little Lottie Mason is buried under six feet of earth because the Rawlings gang ran her down without so much as a backward glance?"

At this, Emily Brady, the child's aunt, sank her head into her hands and wept silent tears of rage. Her husband, Cal, stared down at the floor and patted his wife's knee.

Griff Westerly came to his feet. Beside him his daughter, Nel, scanned the room to see if Wolf Bodine was present. She noted Wolf in the back just as her father started to speak, and her eyes brightened.

"Who needs trouble in Powder Creek?" Westerly demanded, facing the crowd. "We've built ourselves a good, decent town here and we don't need the likes of Bear Rawlings or his kin invading it and planning hell-knows-what the first moment our backs are turned."

"You're right, Griff!" Myrtle Lee nodded vigorously from the podium.

Wolf's mouth tightened. He stood at last, looking out over the assembled crowd, and the frown deepened between his eyes. While thunder rumbled closer and the air seemed to crackle with the violence of the approaching storm, he walked up to the podium, past all the nodding, muttering citizens, past the Bradys and Doc Wilson, past Nel Westerly, Abigail Pritchard, and Abigail's sharp-eyed husband, Culley, the most influential rancher in Powder Creek.

"Let's hear what the sheriff has to say," the whisper began. It raced around the stuffy room like a spark of heat lightning.

"Sheriff?" Myrtle eyed him cautiously. "You want to say something about all this?"

"Well, I don't reckon I'm up here just to take my evening promenade," Wolf replied lazily.

Purple splotches popped onto Myrtle's cheeks as the hotel dining room exploded with laughter. Some of the tension eased.

"Maybe you think this is funny, Sheriff, but it isn't," she harumphed, goaded by his infuriating air of nonchalance.

"Let me show you how far from funny I think it is," Wolf drawled, and in one quick motion he removed his badge from his vest and tossed it onto the table beside the podium.

Immediately a roar went up from the crowd.

"What're you doing, Wolf?"

"What's going on?"

"He's quittin', can't you see?"

"But he can't quit!"

"Wolf, put that thing back on where it belongs!"

Something like panic fluttered among the more longtime residents of Powder Creek, those who remembered when Sheriff Bodine had come, nearly six years ago, with his little boy and his sprightly mother, those who remembered how efficiently he had cleaned the Saunders gang out of their town. When it was over, eight men were dead, all of them brutal murderers, rustlers, or stage robbers.

Bodine had killed the trigger-happy Bentley brothers, too, not more than a year later. After that things had been pretty peaceful—for Montana.

No one in that long, lantern-lit room lined with chairs could imagine Powder Creek without Wolf Bodine as sheriff. He had a reputation that would scare even the roughest of badmen, and more importantly he had the shrewd eye and the deadly aim with a gun that backed it up. Moreover Wolf had courage. He never balked, stalled, or hid from any fight.

And he was honest, incorruptible. That was not always the case with lawmen. In previous years the gold strikes at Alder Gulch, Last Chance Gulch, and Silver Bow Creek had brought thousands of honest prospectors swarming to the territory, men who had built booming, prosperous towns, but they had also drawn in brutal outlaws, who sometimes worked in tandem with crooked lawmen. In Bannack, in the early sixties, Sheriff Henry Plummer's gang of highwaymen had killed over one hundred people as they terrorized stagecoaches and men traveling between Bannack and Alder Gulch, until locally organized vigilantes began capturing and hanging the outlaws—Sheriff Plummer, the ringleader, among them. Plummer was by no means the only lawman to throw his lot in with the criminals. It was a common enough occurrence. Every person in the main dining room of the hotel knew the worth of an honest lawman, and they knew they had one in Wolf Bodine. Without ever having spoken much about it before, they all recognized that they would never find a better man to protect Powder Creek, its citizens, and its property.

Ernest Duke knew it, too, despite his sympathies for Myrtle Lee's point of view. "Now, now, folks, there's no reason to get so riled up, I'm sure," the mayor interjected into the simmering pandemonium, but the perspiration beading on his round face did nothing to reassure the townsfolk, and they quickly shouted him down.

"Let Wolf talk," Culley Pritchard ordered, and the babble in the room subsided.

Outside, the wind blasted down from the mountains, smelling of rain and earth and ponderosa pine. Autumn would be coming soon. And then winter. Winter would be hard enough without having to worry about who was going to keep the law.

Every citizen in the room knew that. So they hunkered down in their seats, clapped their gazes intently on the tall figure at the podium, and listened.

"Seems like some people at this meeting—maybe most people—have made up their minds about our newest citizen already," Wolf said, his cool glance sweeping the room as he spoke, resting for a moment on each sober face. "If it were up to some folks here," he went on, with a purposeful glance at Myrtle, "we'd just take a vote about running Miss Rebeccah Rawlings out of town, and then do it. Right?"

"Better safe than sorry, don't you think, Wolf?" Waylon Pritchard called out, still smarting from the set-down the arrogant Miss Rawlings had delivered to him after her arrival in town.

Wolf studied him, his expression unreadable.

"If you really want to be safe rather than sorry, Waylon, I reckon I have a suggestion for you. Why don't we just string the lady up right now, tonight, and be done with it? That way we'll be sure as sure can be that she can't cause any trouble for us, the good, law-abiding citizens of Powder Creek."

Waylon swallowed, his thick Adam's apple bobbing up and down. "I didn't say we ought to do that," he protested.

Across the room Coral sat beside Molly Duke, listening intently. When Waylon glanced uncertainly over to catch her eye, she threw him a look of disgust.

"Hold on, now, Wolf," Ernest Duke broke in again, getting laboriously to his feet. He strode up to the podium, unable to keep silent a moment longer. "No one said anything about stringing anyone up. We all know there's no cause for that—leastways not yet—"

"Maybe this town isn't looking for a sheriff to uphold the law. Maybe what folks want is a vigilante leader," Wolf interrupted. "Someone who'll stand by whenever the good people of Powder Creek feel like taking the law into their own hands. Someone who'll do whatever is popular. If that's the case, you folks had better find yourself another man. I'm stepping down and moving on. Because that's not the kind of town I want to live in, or raise my son in, or serve."

"Don't be hasty, there, Wolf," the mayor exclaimed as frantic conversation sprang up throughout the assembly. "No one said anything about vigilantes—"

"Mayor," Caitlin broke in from the back row, "this meeting is all about vigilante justice, and you know it. I thought the Montana Territory—and especially Powder Creek—had moved beyond those days. What do we have a sheriff for, and a jail, and a judge coming through once a month regular, if every time some nincompoop feels worried about a stranger, the whole town turns into a lynching party? Stuff and nonsense! No wonder Wolf is ready to resign."

Doc Wilson waved his hand in the air. "I agree with Wolf and Caitlin. Do we want vigilante groups running our town, or do we want the law? Wolf Bodine is the law. And until this Rawlings woman does something wrong, it seems to me, the law can't touch her. And neither can we."

"Are you saying that we should just sit around and wait for her to rob the bank or the mill payroll or the stage? Or to run down some innocent child while fleeing the law—just like her pa and his gang did?" Myrtle countered, stamping her foot.

"I say we wait and see what's going to happen—

and trust our sheriff to look out for keeping the
peace and preserving law and order in this town,"
Doc Wilson responded, glaring at her, his eyes
fierce brown specks above his handlebar mustache. "So far as I know, the woman has done nothing wrong."

"You're right, Doc," Caitlin answered, wagging a
finger in the air. "And if having a disreputable par-
ent is cause for being branded dishonest, then a lot
of folks in this town could be in a heap of trouble."
She popped to her feet. "Why, Simon Jones, wasn't
your father thrown in jail about three times every
week for being drunk and disturbing the peace?"
she demanded of a short, bandy-legged rancher,
who flushed a deep crimson. "Well, you turned out
just the opposite, didn't you? No one here's ever
seen you touch a drop or step a peep out of line.
And that's sure to your credit. And you, Myrtle,
didn't we hear tell that your pa was accused of
jumping a claim over at Last Chance Gulch in 'sixty-
four?"

"Nothing was ever proved!"

"No, it wasn't, but I hear folks sure whispered a
lot. Still, that didn't stop you from becoming one of
our leading citizens. Why, you're head of the town
social committee and a very important member of
the school board. Which reminds me, I think you
should be spending more time thinking about
who's going to teach our children this winter than
worrying your head over some young woman all
alone in the world who so far ain't caused a peep of
trouble—except to kill that no-good Scoop Parmalee, who was trying to rob the stagecoach. Only

yesterday folks were admiring her, but today, because we know her name, half the town wants to run her out of the Territory. Makes me ashamed to be a citizen of Powder Creek!"

Everyone started talking at once, arguing, gesturing, raising their voices to be heard over the growing din. Myrtle Lee Anderson, furious at the turn of events and the shift in mood begun by the sheriff's comments, not to mention the low blow Caitlin had inflicted by bringing up the despicable and completely ridiculous charges against her very own father, grabbed up the gavel and began to pound on the podium.

"Well, maybe we've got no call *yet* to be sending that outlaw's daughter hightailing it out of town, but I'll eat a rattlesnake before I consent to considering her for the schoolteacher's position, which Caitlin Bodine wants to do!"

At this another silence fell over the room.

"That true, Caitlin?" Abigail Pritchard inquired, her wide brow puckered with concern. "I've got nothing personal against the girl, you understand, not so far as anything I've heard here tonight, but to consider her as the new teacher . . ."

Wolf took command of the meeting once more, holding up a hand for silence, and getting it. "I telegraphed some inquiries back east about Miss Rawlings, and I think you folks might be interested in hearing what I found out. Are you?"

A chorus of voices shouting "Hell, yes" followed. Wolf nodded and waited until the room had quietened again. Surveying the faces fixed expectantly upon him, most of them frowning or thoughtful, all of them concerned, he noticed a stranger seated on the far right of the back row. A young man, perhaps in his twenties, black-haired and clean-shaved, dressed in a finely cut dark suit and handsome derby. Briefly Wolf wondered what the man was doing here at the meeting. Being a stranger, not a citizen, he therefore had no stake in the discussion.

Taking in the man's neat attire and quiet demeanor, Wolf surmised that perhaps he had heard talk of it in the saloon and decided to see what all the commotion was about.

He could be a gambler, Wolf decided. But the dark-haired young man didn't have the typical slick oiliness and darting eyes of many frontier gamblers Wolf had met. Still, though he watched the proceedings quietly, his hands folded in his lap, Wolf's shrewd gaze detected something bright and exuberant gleaming in his eyes, something that would bear watching.

The room had grown as quiet as it ever would. Rain began to pelt the hotel windows. The storm in all its fury would be here soon.

Wolf raised his voice so that he could be heard over the rain and wind. "It is a fact that there's nothing known about Rebeccah Rawlings to make anyone suspect she's dishonest—setting aside the name of her father. But there are a few more facts I've learned about her, folks—facts which might make some think she could be a damned fine schoolteacher, just what Powder Creek needs. She attended a fancy private school called Miss Elizabeth Wright's Academy for Young Ladies. It's in Boston. And she graduated with honors and earned a teaching certificate. According to the school's records, Miss Rawlings excelled at literature, history, and music, and she is more than competent in mathematics and geography. Moreover she's had two years' teaching experience at the academy, and that's two more years than that brand-new untried teacher we last hired had—the one who turned tail and ran after the holdup attempt."

"But can she be trusted with our children?" Emily Brady asked, worrying at her lower lip. Her son, Joey, was Billy Bodine's best friend, and she wanted to support Wolf and Caitlin, but it was her niece, Lottie Mason, who'd been run down by the Rawlings gang, and Emily Brady was still deeply affected by that tragedy. "We don't know what kind of a young woman she is, after all. A teacher must set an example of high moral values, as well as educate the youngsters. She must have a trustworthy character."

"I spent the better part of a day with her yesterday, and she struck me as a fine young lady," Caitlin responded, meeting Emily's worried gaze directly. "Of course that's just my opinion. For heaven's sake, why doesn't the school-board committee interview her and see for themselves? Then they can make a recommendation."

Nods all around followed this suggestion. Some doubters still shook their heads, but Culley Pritchard said, "Makes sense. Personally I say give the girl a chance. Why don't we take a vote?"

Wolf banged the gavel. "All in favor of the school-board committee interviewing Miss Rebeccah Rawlings for the teacher's position, say Aye!"

"Aye!" came a resounding chorus, immediately followed by a clap of thunder.

"All against, say No!"

"No!" shouted out fewer than a dozen voices, Myrtle Lee Anderson's strident one chief among them.

The slim stranger in the back row slipped out of the room.

Wolf noted his departure, then returned his gaze to the assembly. "Motion passed. Let's everyone get home to our families before this storm takes hold."

In less time than it takes to hitch a wagon the room was emptied. Only Wolf and Caitlin remained.

"Nice work, son. I'm proud of you."

Wolf stared a moment at the silver badge on the table before pinning it back onto his vest. "You're the one who swayed them," he told her. "I don't think Miss Rawlings will have any trouble convincing the board that she'd make a fine teacher—if she chooses to do it."

Wolf saw again that sensuous, fine-boned face with the upturned violet eyes and wide, generous mouth. He remembered her graceful carriage, her sweeping black hair, and the full, rounded breasts, which had been so temptingly outlined by her nightgown. And he again heard her voice, low-timbred and velvety, a voice that heated a man's blood. He had a hunch that Rebeccah Rawlings could be quite sweetly persuasive if she chose to be. Misgivings ate at him as he led Caitlin out of the hotel and into the wagon beneath a tumbling silver rain.

He only hoped that they both hadn't made a big mistake in defending Rebeccah Rawlings so strenuously to the town.

What did they really know about her? She was pretty, a damn good shot, independent, and close-mouthed. He frowned. And damn stubborn to boot.

But remembering that stoic pride, the rigid insistence on not being beholden to anyone, and the pain in her eyes when he'd told her some folks might not want her in Powder Creek, Wolf sensed there was a great deal more going on inside Miss Rebeccah Rawlings than she let on.

But it was none of his business, he reminded himself. He couldn't afford to waste his time thinking about a woman who was no good for him, or for Billy, a woman who seemed to carry along her own special parcel of trouble. He'd had one like that before, and lived to regret it. No matter how attractive or intriguing Rebeccah Rawlings might be, Wolf had no intention of allowing himself to fall into the same she-trap twice. Whatever it took, he would steer clear of any woman marked Trouble.

Billy Bodine glanced apprehensively at the ominous sky. It was thick with clouds and growing blacker by the moment. Anyone could see that a bad storm was brewing, and the sudden slash of blue-white lightning, followed closely by an explosion of thunder, almost made him turn back.

Guilt stabbed at him, as well as trepidation. Pa and Gramma thought he was at home tonight. They had warned him about the storm and instructed him to keep an eye on the house and barn and to do the spelling lesson Caitlin had asked Mary Adams to write up for him. Gramma was particular about education, and it was driving her plumb crazy that there was no teacher in Powder Creek, so she made up lessons for him now and again, just to keep his brain sharp, she said.

But Joey had dared him to come along spying on the lady outlaw living on the Peastone place. Joey'd said that if Billy didn't come with him, he was a yellow-livered chicken.

He'd had no choice!

Still Billy had waited a while, done his spelling, wrestled briefly with his conscience, and then at last saddled up Blue. He'd called Sam to heel and ridden off in the direction of the Peastone ranch, determined to find out what that Rebeccah Rawlings was really up to. Then he could tell his father all about it and show Joey that he was no chicken.

But Billy hadn't counted on the storm, at least not on it blowing up quite so quickly and ferociously as it did.

He met Joey near a rise covered with bluestem, less than a quarter of a mile from the Peastone cabin. Spruce trees and tamaracks shook all around them beneath the gathering wind and eerie gray-yellow light. Tumbleweed and dust blew every which way.

"You ready?" the other boy challenged. Joey Brady was a year older than Billy, taller and stockier, with curly, carrot-colored hair, a good-natured, freckled face, and ears that stuck out like an elf's.

"I sure am," Billy answered with more assurance than he felt. They'd picked a bad night for this job —if they didn't hurry up and get this spying business over with fast they'd both get drenched.

"Let's go," Billy said as Sam gazed inquiringly up at him and whined. "Maybe we should leave the horses here and walk the rest of the way—"

At that moment gold lightning streaked across the sky. It hit the spruce tree nearest to Joey with an earsplitting crackle. The boys yelped in fright, and Sam let out a blood-chilling howl.

But it was the horses that truly panicked. Spooked, Blue reared straight up. Billy used every trick he knew, and somehow managed to stay seated, but Joey's mare bolted forward so suddenly that the boy was whipped right off his saddle by a low-hanging branch. He hit the ground with a thud as the mare disappeared into the darkness.

"Joey!"

Billy jumped from his saddle as the rain began to pound down. A boom of thunder drowned out his frantic cries as he tried to rouse his friend, and the next thing he knew, Blue ran off. In dismay he watched the horse race toward home with nostrils flaring and a scream of terror that echoed through the wild night.

Don't panic, Billy said to himself with a gulp. He knelt beside Joey as lightning again split the sky and wind and rain assaulted them. *At least Sam's here,* he thought, fighting back tears of anxiety. The dog crouched beside Joey, whimpering, his red fur streaming with water. Through the sickly gray-green darkness of the storm, Billy saw that Sam's eyes glowed with fear.

"Joey, wake up. Please, wake up," Billy begged, but as he peered into his friend's freckled face and saw the blood oozing from his temple, Billy knew that something was very wrong.

I have to get help, he thought, glancing dazedly around as the night exploded in storm. "It's up to us, Sam, you and me," he whispered, his lips trembling.

Billy shoved himself to his feet. Without Blue he couldn't ride to town for the doctor. It would take too long even to run to the Adams place, which was the next nearest neighbor, after the Peastone ranch. . . .

The Peastone ranch. It was right over the rise, less than a quarter of a mile ahead.

Billy remembered what his father had said: *Stay away from her.*

But this was an emergency. He needed help, and he needed it fast. Even a lady outlaw would help an injured kid, Billy reasoned, and tried to dismiss the scary voice inside him suggesting that she might have other company, bad company, someone like Fess Jones, sitting in her parlor right now.

But that was a chance he had to take. Billy took one final, frantic look at Joey's bloody face and started forward.

"Come on, Sam," he shouted, stumbling through the wind and rain toward the top of the rise. "We've got to hurry!"

9 It was the barking that captured her attention. Over the rushing wind and the thunder and the whoosh of tree branches it came, incessant and strangely urgent, startling her as she lit the lanterns, stoked up the hearth fire, and prepared to last out the storm.

Barking . . .

Rebeccah hurried to the window and peered out. She saw nothing but greenish darkness, slashing rain, and furiously swaying prairie grasses. The mountains were shadowy monsters looming in the distance.

But the barking persisted.

And then she saw the small figure hurtling through the night and the large red dog bounding at its side.

What in the world? she wondered, her hand at her throat. She ran to open the door.

A huge gust of wind shook the trees to their roots and nearly knocked the boy over, but though he stumbled, he kept running, and the dog beside him barked more frantically.

Rebeccah had the door flung wide by the time he reached the steps. A great rush of rain and wind flew at her, but she clung to the doorframe and watched the small figure dart toward her.

Why, he was no more than ten or eleven. He was soaked to the skin, his red flannel shirt plastered to his bony chest, his hair streaming water into his eyes.

"We need help," he gasped, skidding to a stop on the porch before her, and as if for emphasis the dog gave two short yaps.

"Come in! What's happened?"

She reached for his arm, to draw him safely out of the violent night, but he flinched back, shaking his head.

"It's not me, it's Joey." The boy, who was thin and dark, with huge, intense gray eyes, stared up at her pleadingly. He seemed unaware of his own soaked and muddy condition, of the cold that was turning his lips blue. His face wore a pinched, desperate look that alarmed her more than his startling appearance out of the storm. "Please, I think he's hurt bad. He fell off his horse when the lightning struck. Please, ma'am, he's out there, just over the rise, and he won't wake up. You have to help him."

"Just a minute," Rebeccah said crisply. She spun back across the parlor, through the kitchen, and dashed into the pantry. She grabbed the slicker folded inside the wooden box. Donning it as she ran, she cast a swift glance over the boy and the dog.

"You wait here and take off those wet clothes. There's a blanket in the bedroom—you can wrap yourself in that. I'll find your friend."

He shook his head. His mouth was set with a strangely familiar, determined expression she couldn't quite place, and then he said emphatically, "No. It'll be quicker if I show you."

He was right. Rebeccah nodded. "Let's go."

They found the injured boy a short while later. He had come to and was moaning as he lay in the grassy mud, rivulets of blood and earth streaking his face. Rebeccah never knew how, but somehow she lifted him in her arms and staggered back in the direction of the cabin. The dark-haired boy and the dog ran beside her as the storm lashed out its fury.

It seemed an eternity until they reached the shelter of the cabin.

"He'll be all right," she gasped as she laid the injured boy upon the sofa. She fired off rapid directions to the other youth as she examined the gash from which blood still trickled. "Get out of those wet clothes before you catch your death. There's some long flannel shirts in the chest of drawers in the bedroom—put one on and bring him the other. And take the quilt from the bed. You can both share it." Seeing his anxious expression, she shot him a reassuring smile. "Don't worry, the gash isn't deep. I'm going to bandage it for him, and he'll be fine. What's his name?"

"Joey."

"Joey," she said, rubbing the boy's icy palms between her own. "Joey, can you hear me?"

He stopped moaning and looked dazedly at her. Rebeccah squeezed his hand. "It's all right, Joey. Don't try to move. You're going to be fine."

She worked feverishly for the better part of an hour, stripping off his soaked garments, buttoning him in two layers of flannel shirts so long, they reached his knees. While the other boy warmed his hands and his dog before the fire and watched her, she deftly cleaned the cut and dabbed on salve.

When Joey cried "Ouch!" as she ministered to him, the boy near the fire grinned.

"I reckon he'll live," he said, much more cheerfully, and stroked the dog's damp head.

"I reckon," Rebeccah responded calmly, and reached for a bandage. "How would you boys like a nice hot cup of tea?"

Moments later she handed each child a steaming cup of tea flavored with a peppermint stick from Koppel's General Store.

The two were huddled on the sofa together now, beneath the quilt.

"Well, let's see. I've met Joey. Maybe you should tell me *your* name," she suggested to the dark-haired youngster, who clutched his cup between small, sturdy fingers. Outside, the storm raged unabated, but the cabin seemed positively cozy, Rebeccah reflected with a little lift of the heart. She pondered this as she settled in a straight-back chair. It was surprising how much homier the house appeared with two children snuggled near a blazing fire, their hands clutching teacups.

The dark-haired boy took one tentative sip from the steaming cup, licked his lips with a gusty sigh, and replied, "My name's Billy Bodine."

Rebeccah froze on her chair, her fingers clenched around her cup. *This* boy was Wolf's son?

Of course he was. The eyes were the same. Only younger, more innocent. But the intensity and intelligence in them was the same, as was the sharp, observant way of looking at the world.

She managed to nod casually. "I'm Rebeccah Rawlings."

"I know."

"Oh. How?" Had Wolf talked about her at home, with his wife and child? Or perhaps Caitlin had mentioned something. . . .

"Everyone knows," Billy grinned, and his small, handsome face lit up. Oh, he would be a heartbreaker when he grew up, just like his fath—Rebeccah blocked the rest of that thought.

"How?" she asked again.

"Easy. The whole town's talking about you."

"Because of your pa," Joey piped in. He appeared to be recovering rapidly; there was color in his freckled cheeks, and his eyes held a cheery gleam. "Bear Rawlings did some mighty awful things in these parts. My ma says he—"

"Shush, Joey!" Billy suddenly realized that Rebeccah would be hurt if she knew the purpose of the meeting in town tonight, and about Myrtle Lee Anderson's idea to run her out of Powder Creek. He glanced at her face and decided she looked a little more pale than she had a few moments before, and he knew that it would be wrong of him and Joey to upset her by repeating such talk. He was suddenly ashamed of what he'd done tonight, coming here to spy on her. It was wrong too. And mean-spirited, though they hadn't meant any harm.

"Joey, there's no need to go into all that right

now," he said quickly. "I'm sure Miss Rawlings isn't interested in gossip."

"Oh, but I am. It's all right, Billy, I can take it, whatever it is. Tell me why everyone is talking."

He hesitated. But her eyes were calm, her expression pleasant as she set her teacup on a crate that served as a table. And something very even and determined in her voice compelled him to go on.

"Well . . ."

No. He couldn't.

"It's because of the bank robbery," Joey burst out. Having finished his cup of tea, he leaned back against the horsehair cushions and nodded importantly. "The one where my little cousin Lottie was killed."

Rebeccah's heart stopped. *Dear Lord.*

Something in her face must have alerted even Joey to her shock, for he faltered, glanced at Billy for guidance, and then snapped his mouth shut.

But Rebeccah had to know. "Go on. *I want to hear about it.*"

So Joey told her about the bank robbery six years back, about the teller who'd been shot and killed, and about how during the gang's getaway little Lottie Mason, Joey's cousin, had been run down by someone's horse, trampled in the dust while her ma looked on.

"Oh, God," Rebeccah whispered. She covered her face with her hands.

Grief and guilt tore at her. *Bear, Bear, what did you do?* Yet a part of her knew that her father could not have been the one to run down the little girl. Bear was too good a rider, too strong and skilled not to have found a way to avoid her, even if she had been directly in his path. Bear would never have been able to live with himself if he had harmed a child, and in the past six years of visiting Rebeccah he had never shown any sign of the kind of guilt he would have felt had he run the girl down. But one of the others—Russ Gaglin, Homer Bell, Fred Baker—any of them might have done it and been able to live with themselves.

And Bear had been partly responsible, a small, cold voice told her. He had planned the robbery, ordered it, led it every step of the way. He always had.

Billy Bodine broke into her thoughts. "Sorry, Miss Rawlings. We shouldn't have told you."

Rebeccah swallowed. "I needed to know. Th-thank you."

What was it Wolf Bodine had said to her?

Don't expect folks around here to welcome Bear's daughter with open arms.

Now she knew why, the whole reason, the real reason.

Maybe she should follow Wolf's advice: get on the stagecoach and leave.

But where will I go? She glanced slowly around the small, polished parlor with its crackling fire and thought of the plans she'd had for this ranch, of purchasing Texas longhorns to fill the rangeland, of building a bunkhouse and corrals. She thought of her dreams for the cabin, of the new curtains she'd imagined fluttering at the windows, of the piano she would someday have, with music and flowers filling the house. . . .

"Miss Rawlings—are you okay?"

Both boys were staring at her in dismay, and Rebeccah realized there were tears on her cheeks. She brushed them impatiently aside.

"Of course I am. It's just occurred to me that someone is going to be worried about the two of you. Do your families have any idea you were out in this storm?"

They looked at each other. "No, ma'am." Billy's cheeks reddened. "And please don't ask *why* we were out in it."

"That's really not my concern," she assured him briskly, though she was puzzled over what they were doing on her property. "Your horses are probably home by now, and your families must be searching for you. I'd better find your folks and tell them that you're all right—"

Before the sentence was completed there was a pounding at the door. Sam sprang, growling, from the sofa, where he'd been resting his head on Billy's lap. He stared at the door and growled again low in his throat. More pounding followed.

"Miss Rawlings! Open the door. Quick!"

She pulled it wide to find Wolf Bodine clad in a yellow slicker. Water streamed from it like a cascade of silver bullets. Behind him stood a burly, leather-skinned man with reddish hair and a hawk nose, also clad in a dripping slicker.

"They're in here. They're both safe and sound," she said before either man could say a word. "Come in. How did you know—?"

"Joey bragged to his little brother that he was coming here tonight," the burly man muttered as he stomped after her into the cabin. He stopped and stared at the two boys huddled on the sofa. "Joey, I ought to whomp you," he exclaimed. "What happened to your head?"

"A tree branch hit me when Pepper bolted. Miss Rawlings took care of it just fine, though. It don't even hurt, Pa. Honest."

Wolf Bodine, his slicker streaming water onto Miss Rawlings's clean floor, gazed quietly at his son. Billy returned the gaze, flushing, then dropped his eyes.

"You have something to say to me, son?"

"Sorry, Pa."

"And to Miss Rawlings?"

"Sorry, ma'am."

"What is he sorry for?" Rebeccah asked, mystified.

Wolf said tautly, "I'll let these two boys explain."

Joey hung his head. "We didn't mean nothin', Sheriff Bodine—"

"Billy."

"We came here tonight to spy on you, ma'am," Billy confessed miserably. He stared hard at the floor, unable to meet Rebeccah's eyes. "We wanted to see if you were a lady outlaw. It was wrong. I know that now—"

"You knew it when you set out, Billy, didn't you?" Wolf cut in swiftly. Rebeccah could sense his anger. "I had told you to leave Miss Rawlings alone. And to stay home tonight because a storm was brewing."

"Yes, sir."

"And the same for Joey," Cal Brady agreed, regarding his son with a stern frown. "My boy disobeyed too." He turned to Rebeccah and nodded. "I reckon we owe you, ma'am. I'm much obliged. Though I'd best be taking the boy home now, his ma will call tomorrow to give you her thanks. Maybe you can join us for Sunday dinner this week. We'd be most pleased to have you."

Stunned by the invitation, Rebeccah nodded. "I'd like that. Thank you."

Rebeccah wouldn't allow herself to look at Wolf Bodine, and kept her gaze fixed on Mr. Brady as he withdrew another slicker from the cavernous pocket of his own and held it out to Joey.

"Fetch your clothes, son," he told him gruffly. "And put this on. You've caused this lady enough trouble for one night."

"Oh, it wasn't any trouble," she assured him. "I was worried of course, until I saw Joey was all right, but after that, well . . ." She kept her tone light and brisk. "The boys were good company."

She didn't think Mr. Brady believed her. Fearing that he would be harsh with Joey after they'd left, she followed them to the door and called out as they departed into the wet night. "Come back tomorrow with your ma, Joey! I'll give you some candy—I have lots more peppermint, and licorice too!"

There, maybe that will prove that I'm not angry with Joey about what happened. Perhaps Mr. Brady will go easier on him.

Wolf Bodine was another matter. His anger simmered below the surface, but it was there. While she'd seen the Bradys off, Wolf had been speaking quietly to his son.

Billy was donning a yellow slicker similar to the one Joey had put on. "Sorry to have caused you so much trouble, ma'am," he mumbled, head down as he fastened the buttons, and Sam waited by his side, head hanging as though he, too, had done something terrible.

Rebeccah looked at the pair of them and laughed. Yet something in their forlorn expressions wrenched at her heart. She moved forward, gathering teacups with a casual air.

"Such glum faces, the two of you. And there's no cause for it. Sheriff Bodine, whatever boys' mischief Billy and Joey were up to, they've already been punished quite enough. They had an awful scare in the storm. Yet Billy was very brave and quick-witted to come and find me as he did. He showed me exactly where Joey had fallen and he helped me bring him back here. If I were you, I'd be very proud of him."

"You're not me."

Wolf's expression could have scalded milk, but Billy shot her a grateful smile, and Rebeccah was glad she'd said what she had. As the boy headed toward the bedroom to gather his clothes, he stopped beside her a moment.

"Don't worry too much, Miss Rawlings," he whispered. "Pa won't give me a licking—that's not his way. But he'll find some other punishment that's even worse—like two weeks without a bite of Gramma's blackberry pie. Or extra chores for a month without any time for fishing or riding Blue."

With that glum pronouncement and a roll of his eyes, he disappeared into the bedroom. She glanced at Wolf. She couldn't tell if he had heard the boy's words. His expression was grim and unreadable. How different he was as a father from Bear, she reflected, studying his cool, stern features from beneath her lashes. When Bear had been angry with her when she was a child, he'd exploded with oaths, yelling, cursing, shaking his finger. But after a few moments of hollering, he'd been done. The anger was gone, the air cleared. And the instant she said she was sorry, Bear was ready to forgive and forget.

Wolf was a different story. He obviously planned to deal with Billy's disobedience in a private way, but she had a feeling he would certainly make his point.

He followed her into the kitchen as she carried the cups to the sink, and she was aware of his steady gaze burning into her. She wanted to ask him about the town meeting. Was she to be run out of Powder Creek? Should she prepare herself for armed vigilantes to attack her cabin in the middle of the night? A cold dread wrapped around her like a snake as she thought of what must have occurred at that meeting, of the things people had said, of how they must hate her. She couldn't bring herself to broach the subject, though. If she did, she would undoubtedly be told, "Folks want you out of town —pronto."

And she couldn't bear that. Not now, not when she was finally starting to feel that this cabin and this lovely mountain-studded land was home.

There was another reason why she didn't want to leave, but Rebeccah wouldn't allow herself to dwell on that one. Being close to Wolf Bodine was not a reason to stay in a town that didn't want her. He was married! He had a family. What possible difference could it make if she lived ten miles or ten thousand miles from him? There was no hope of anything between them other than an exchange of words now and then, words bitten out with contemptuous civility. The man held her in dislike, to say the least. And he felt nothing for her but disapproval.

You are an idiotic little fool, she told herself furiously. *You should have left Powder Creek the moment you saw him here.*

Glancing over her shoulder at him, she felt her stomach twist into knots. She braced herself. Wolf Bodine looked like he was in the mood to pick a fight with *someone. Why shouldn't he target me?* she wondered wearily. But his next words came as a surprise.

"It looks like I'm the one who's beholden to you, Miss Rawlings."

His tone was soft. Downright pleasant.

Caught off guard, she nearly dropped the cups. Hastily she set them in the sink and spun to face him, suspicion darkening her violet eyes. What was he up to now? "Not at all," she said warily. "It was nothing."

"You're wrong." Wolf had been trying hard not to notice how pretty she looked in her yellow-and-white calico dress, her cheeks flushed from the excitement of the night, her eyes overbright in her lovely, pale face. Every instinct told him to stop thinking so much about Rebeccah Rawlings. But she seemed to be haunting him these days, and he couldn't figure out why. Frustrated by his own weakness, he nevertheless couldn't keep his mind off how fresh and angelic she looked, how like summer flowers she smelled, how her slim eyebrows drew adorably together when she was thinking hard about something. And about how her feet fidgeted when she was nervous. They were fidgeting right now, Wolf noticed, and wondered with half amusement, half consternation if *he* made her nervous.

Lightning flashed beyond the window. Wolf stepped closer to her and saw her foot wiggle.

"You went out into the storm to rescue Joey, and you kept Billy from catching pneumonia," he said, keeping his voice even and dispassionate, even when she turned those intoxicating eyes on him. "You took care of them both. You kept them warm and dry. I'd say that's something."

"Well—"

"Don't argue with me. I'm trying to thank you."

"It isn't necess—"

"Rebeccah," he cut her off. "Just say, 'You're welcome.'"

Confused, Rebeccah only gazed at him, feeling ridiculous. But it was hard to think when he was staring at her like that, hard to protect herself against his steady, powerful brand of charm.

Suddenly he grinned. Rebeccah's heart turned over. He closed the distance between them with one stride, and before either of them seemed quite aware of what he was doing, he seized her with a firmness that would not be deterred and stared intently down into her face.

"It's easy," he continued, his tone more patient now, his vivid gray eyes glinting into hers with hypnotic warmth. She noted that his chestnut hair was damp, and this made it look even darker in the lamplight. He smelled of autumn rain and crisp leaves and good polished leather. His dimples deepened as he smiled, and he looked almost boyish, Rebeccah thought, her heart melting—yet not like a little boy at all.

"You're . . . welcome," he prodded her gently. He sounded amused. His mouth curled in a slow smile. His face was only inches from hers. "Say it, Miss Rawlings."

"You're . . . welcome, Sheriff."

"Wolf," he corrected swiftly.

"Wolf," she murmured. A dizzy sense of unreality gripped her.

He leaned toward her. *What the hell am I doing?* Wolf wondered at the last moment, and paused. He told himself to pull away. But a force stronger than his own common sense kept him rooted to the spot, holding Miss Rebeccah Rawlings firmly by the arms, gazing directly into those brilliant eyes.

Then his lips touched hers. Lightly, tentatively.

"Wolf," she breathed again, and her hands crept shyly against his chest.

That slight movement, the softness of her touch, was his undoing. Casting reservation aside, he deepened the kiss, and his warm, rough mouth captured hers. His powerful arms locked around her

slender form before either of them realized what
was happening. He inhaled the fresh, flower scent
of her as he drew her close. Held her tight. Tasted
deeply.

Rebeccah felt her senses swooning. Her full
mouth clung eagerly to his. From her temples to
her toenails she suddenly quivered all over with
hot, glowing pleasure. Was this a dream—one of
her many thousands of dreams since that night
years ago when she'd stared into the jeweled heart
of a campfire and hungered for him?

No, it was real. *Real.* His hands at her waist were
strong, hot even through the fabric of her gown.
His lips deliciously imprisoned hers, and she clung
to the warmth of his mouth as if to sweet life itself.

"Sheriff . . ." she gasped when he stopped for
breath.

"Wolf," he corrected her roughly, and kissed her
again.

Swimming, swimming through pounding seas,
she gave herself up to the pleasures he was awak-
ening in her. When his hard, calloused hands slid
along the fabric of her yellow-and-white calico to
cup and stroke her bottom, a tremble ran through
her, and she gasped against his lips. He kissed her
harder. Gathered her closer. Rebeccah, breathless,
felt herself catching fire, burning up.

Wolf touched his tongue to hers, sending a darting flame through her that seared straight down to
her most private parts. Rebeccah's tongue responded like a sword swinging into battle. She
molded her curves against his muscles without

thinking, only feeling. *Hold me,* she pleaded in blissful, silent need. *Wolf, don't ever let me go.*

Shivery heat sizzled through her. Even her kneecaps tingled. She buried her fingers in the thick softness of his damp hair. So gentle was he as he cradled the nape of her neck in one hand and encircled her waist with the other that she never once thought about Neely Stoner, never felt the icy stab of panic, knew only that Wolf was holding her close and kissing her, breathing life into her, doing mysterious, wonderful things to her body and her heart, and she knew that she felt safe, warm, desired, loved.

"Wolf," she whispered shakily at last, clinging to his shoulders as they both came up for air.

"Rebeccah," he murmured. "Such a pretty name."

The sound of her name on his lips filled her with a potent joy she couldn't contain. But suddenly, as his head came down toward hers again, a memory struck at her, and her joy exploded, shattering into a thousand shards.

"My God!" she gasped, and pushed him away.

"What's wrong?" he asked sharply.

She shook her head, too stunned and sick to speak. She touched shaking fingers to her lips as if to blot the burning imprint of his kiss.

"Rebeccah, what is it?"

"How could you . . ." she choked out.

Puzzled, he regarded her for a moment in silence. "Easy, Rebeccah. I don't know what's wrong, but I'll try to make it right," he offered, reaching for her again.

She jumped back as if he'd lunged at her with a branding iron. "Don't you dare touch me!"

Wolf's eyes narrowed. "What the hell is the matter with you, woman? I'm beginning to think you're just plain loco. Am I wrong, or were you just kissing me—and damn well enjoying it?"

Rebeccah felt as low and dirty as a common lightskirt. He must certainly think her no better than one. Her cheeks burned with shame. "It's obvious just what kind of a woman you think I am. Easy pickings. One so disreputable and so desperate for a man's affections that I don't give a damn if he's married!"

A stunned look entered his eyes.

Rebeccah lost all control of her temper and slapped him. "How dare you look so surprised. You think I have *no* scruples, that I'm the commonest, loosest, most despicable kind of female—"

"Hold on a minute and listen to me—"

"A minute? *No,*" she flashed, her face ablaze with mortification and fury. "I've wasted too many minutes on you. You and your son, Sheriff Bodine, had best be on your way immediately. I'm certain Billy's mother is waiting for word of him! Poor woman," she added, her voice trembling with scorn and fury. "I feel only pity for her!"

"That's enough!"

Wolf gripped her wrist so tightly, she cried out. "For your information, Miss Rawlings—" he began, but Billy's voice, sounding very small and sad, interrupted him from the doorway.

"My ma is dead."

Wolf released her and spun to face the boy.

Rebeccah gasped, and rubbed instinctively at her tender wrist. For a moment she was speechless. Billy's young eyes were filled with sorrow. He looked very small, very thin, and very alone. And Wolf had suddenly become a wall of solid granite—hard, cold, and impenetrable.

"Oh, Billy, I'm sorry," she whispered, knowing even as she said them that the words were woefully inadequate. "I didn't know. Billy, I didn't mean to hurt you."

"It's all right." He was trying hard to sound matter-of-fact. But he bit his lip and looked down at the floor. Rebeccah felt as if a rusty knife were twisting inside of her.

What have I done? What have I said?

She wanted to beg Wolf to forgive her stupidity, to look into his eyes and let him see how dreadful she felt, but before she could say or do anything else, he had a hand on Billy's shoulder and was leading him out of the kitchen.

"Billy, let's go."

She wanted to call after them, to explain, to make everything better, but the words choked in her throat.

Then they were outside, riding off together into the inky, vile night, disappearing almost immediately into the streaming darkness.

His wife was dead. *Dead.*

And she had accused him of such terrible things.

Rebeccah stood in the open doorway, staring off in the direction they had gone, letting the chill rain slash against her hot cheeks and her trembling, burning body, still on fire from Wolf's touch.

Oh, God. He truly hates me now. I've hurt him and hurt his son.

She closed her eyes and struggled against the bitter tears. But they came anyway. They mingled with the rain pelting her face, ran down her cheeks, and watered the ache deep in her soul.

10 Four days later on a cool, cloudy September afternoon, Rebeccah perched in a wing chair in the modest Brady parlor and faced questions from Mayor Ernest Duke, Culley Pritchard, Caitlin Bodine, Emily Brady, and Myrtle Lee Anderson, who comprised the school-board committee of Powder Creek.

The formal invitation for the interview had come from Mayor Duke himself, who had explained that Caitlin Bodine had recommended her for the schoolteacher's position at a town meeting and the citizens had approved the suggestion that she be interviewed. That in itself had astounded Rebeccah —how had Caitlin managed to convince them?

The interview lasted more than an hour, and during the course of it she realized that she was being judged not only on how knowledgeably and eloquently she answered their questions relating to her education and training but also on how she conducted herself, how she spoke, moved, whether or not she smacked her lips over her lemonade or ate strawberry pie with her fingers.

She didn't. She wasn't entirely sure she wanted the teacher's position, but she knew she needed it.

So she was careful to smile politely when she answered the questions, to sip her lemonade delicately, to nibble at her pie with exactly the right degree of well-bred enjoyment. The way she had been taught at Miss Elizabeth Wright's Academy for Young Ladies. The way Analee Caruthers would have eaten her strawberry pie.

And it worked. Whether it was the demure chignon into which she'd pinioned her heavy hair or the quiet gray serge gown left over from her teaching days, serviceable and plain, with only a wisp of white lace at the throat, she impressed them enough and overcame their trepidations enough so that they glanced at each other, reached an agreement through some silent signal, and offered her the position.

"The salary is small, but you will be compensated in other ways as well," Ernest Duke informed her with his usual pomposity. "If you take sick, Doc Wilson will treat you at no charge. The town will furnish you with a buckboard and team. Koppel's General Store will provide you with all the eggs, canned milk, and vegetable seed you need at no cost, and the blacksmith will shoe your horses and fix your wagon wheels with nothing asked in return."

"And twice a week," Culley Pritchard told her, "I'll send one of my ranch hands around to help out with chores and wood chopping and repairs— whatever you need. We look after our own, young lady."

Our own. Rebeccah found herself smiling tentatively at him. Besides Caitlin and the Bradys, both of whom had treated her with great kindness since the night of the storm, Culley Pritchard seemed the most friendly member of the board, the one regarding her with real interest and, well, almost approval. He was a broad, powerfully built man who spoke bluntly and with a shrewd, brisk intelligence. And she sensed that unlike Myrtle Lee Anderson and Mayor Duke, he didn't hold her father's misdeeds against her.

"Well," Myrtle Lee said with a sniff, leaning forward in her straight-backed chair to peer crossly at Rebeccah. "Speak up, Miss Rawlings. We don't have all day. Do you accept the position or not?"

"I accept." Rebeccah kept her tone as calm as Culley Pritchard's had been. "When would you like me to start?"

Emily Brady and Caitlin Bodine burst into wide smiles.

"Next Monday will be just fine," Caitlin assured her, and glanced around the sunlit parlor for confirmation. "We'll have time to get the schoolhouse in order by then and pass the word around that Powder Creek has itself a brand-new teacher."

Rebeccah, who considered herself far above sentimentality or excessive emotion, suddenly found herself feeling almost overwhelmed as she realized the responsibility and the trust being placed in her. This was very different from being offered the teaching position at Miss Wright's Academy. Because she was a graduate of the academy, the school had been almost duty-bound to hire her, for she was one of their own, and not to do so would have suggested a lack of confidence in the training they had provided her. But this school board, needy as they were for a teacher, was overcoming strong prejudice against her to give her the job. It demonstrated great faith, she realized, and she couldn't help but be moved.

She rose and glanced around the room, gaining confidence from Emily Brady's reassuring nod and Caitlin's smile. "I appreciate the board's confidence in me, and I will try to do my best for the children," she said crisply, and forced herself to meet the gaze of each member of the school board, even Myrtle Lee Anderson's doubtful frown and Mayor Duke's worried pucker.

"Of course you will," Emily Brady said warmly and came forward to grasp Rebeccah's hand. "I know Joey will be *very* happy. He might not even balk each morning about going to school. Matter of fact I know he won't."

"My younger boy won't either," Culley Pritchard added, looming before her, rugged in his rancher's shirt, vest, and trousers, his spurs jingling as he walked. "But if he ever gives you any trouble, Miss Rawlings—any trouble at all—you be sure to let me know about it right off."

They were kind, Rebeccah thought wonderingly a short time later as she drove herself home in her rented wagon. Genuinely kind. At least the Bradys were, and Culley Pritchard, and Caitlin. After what Bear had done in this town, it was a miracle that anyone would even speak to her, much less give her a job and make her feel welcome.

Maybe Caitlin was too kind, she thought, guiding the horses along the rutted trail with a frown creasing her brow. Confident of the interview's outcome, Caitlin had earlier invited her to have supper with the Bodines afterward, in celebration of Rebeccah's new position, and not knowing what excuse to give, Rebeccah had accepted. But now that the hurdle of the interview was over and she had the job, she was uncertain if Caitlin's kindness was a blessing or a curse. Because of it, in a few short hours Rebeccah would have to face Wolf Bodine again.

She hadn't seen him once since that awful night of the storm, when she'd said such terrible things to him and behaved so . . . ridiculously. That was the only word for it, Rebeccah admitted in shame. *Ridiculous.*

He's sent his deputy, a laconic man named Ace Johnson, out to the ranch to deliver her reward money for shooting Scoop Parmalee. The man had handed over the money without any message, not even one businesslike word, from Wolf Bodine.

Why, oh why, had she let him kiss her? And why had she let it go on for as long as she had?

No man had ever kissed her like that. She hadn't even had time to panic, to feel the familiar cold sweat or the nausea, for Wolf Bodine had taken her completely by surprise, and by the time she realized what was happening, she'd been swept away by inexplicable feelings she'd been powerless to fight.

It had been wonderful. Even more wonderful than her dreams, her fruitless imaginings all those years—because it had been real. Wolf Bodine the man was even more dangerously compelling and irresistible than Wolf Bodine the memory. His knowing touches, his urgent kisses, the rugged, sensuous whole of him, was far more powerful than dream images of such things.

Yet Rebeccah felt dismayed with her own weakness in succumbing to them.

True, Wolf was not married, as she had first thought. His wife was dead—but what difference did that make? He would never care about her. He would never take her seriously or regard her as anything other than an amusing diversion. After all, what more could there be with Bear Rawlings's daughter?

The late-afternoon wind blew autumn leaves across the trail and cooled her burning skin. The memories of that night stung. Considering the contempt in which he held her, a contempt he'd made all too clear from the moment he discovered who she was, Wolf's advances were insulting, painful. She couldn't bear to think about them, and yet she could think about little else.

What was worse, she'd hurt Billy when he'd overheard her comment about his mother. Now he probably despised her as well.

For a fleeting moment as she guided the horses over the rise toward the trail that led to her own yard, she wondered about the woman who had been Wolf's wife. No doubt he still loved her and mourned her. He would probably never get over her and only assuaged his physical needs with loose women and whores who meant nothing to him, while still holding onto his love for . . . what's her name.

Don't think about him, she instructed herself when she reached home and began unhitching the wagon. *Think about Caitlin and Billy. Reach out to them, let them be your friends (if Billy still will). Forget about Wolf Bodine.*

Yet as she sponged herself clean in the icy river, sudsed and rinsed her hair, and then later in the bedroom brushed it until it shone, and slipped on a fresh gown—a sprightly cherry-and-white calico with tight sleeves—she studied herself in her hand mirror and wondered if Wolf Bodine thought her the tiniest bit attractive—or if he had only kissed her because she was an outlaw's daughter and therefore an easy woman, someone unworthy of his respect.

She examined her features in the mirror, each one of them, then made a face. Her mouth was too large, her nose too ordinary. And her hair never seemed to stay contained, no matter how many pins she thrust into it.

The bruise on her cheek had faded, but she brushed on a dusting of rice powder to conceal it further. And a tiny, daring fluff of rouge. If she was to be considered a loose woman, she may as well play the part!

I don't care what he thinks, Rebeccah decided rebelliously as she picked up her good ivory lace shawl. It was time to hitch up the wagon again and start for the Double B.

But she turned and hurried back into the bedroom to dab on the fancy French perfume Bear had sent all the way from San Francisco for her last birthday. *There,* she thought. *That's for me, because*

I like to smell pretty, not for him. Not one little bit for him.

She arranged the shawl around her shoulders and hurried for the door. Worried that she was late, she opened it quickly and started to rush outside.

A man loomed on the threshold, one powerful arm raised.

Rebeccah screamed. She shrank back so abruptly, she nearly stumbled, but he caught her arm just in time.

"What are you screaming about, you clumsy woman? You scared the wits out of me," Wolf Bodine growled at her.

"You! *I* scared *you?*" Rebeccah's heart was racing triple its usual speed. She yanked her arm free of his grasp. "What are you doing here?"

He scowled. Even with the scowl he looked extremely handsome in his dark blue shirt, which hugged his finely molded shoulders and forearms. He wore a silk neckerchief knotted loosely around his neck, and snug-fitting, well-pressed black trousers that emphasized the solid, muscular thickness of his long legs. His boots gleamed as if they'd been freshly polished. In the amber glow of the lantern behind her, Rebeccah saw that his hat only partially concealed the springy locks of his chestnut hair and narrowly shadowed his eyes. But from what she could see below the brim, there was no glint of warmth or even civil friendliness in those eyes. Only a tight coolness.

"Came to drive you over for dinner. I was just about to knock when you yanked the door open.

What's the matter with you, anyway, Miss Rawlings? Why are you so jumpy?"

Miss Rawlings. So they were back to that again. Well, fine. "Nothing." Rebeccah shrugged, matching his cool nonchalance. "I was in a hurry, that's all. Do I look like something's the matter with me?"

He stared hard at her as if determined to give her a brutally honest answer to her question. Rebeccah gritted her teeth under his piercing inspection.

"Are you finished?" she bit off at last, disappointed when she detected not the slightest softening in his eyes, not the least hint of admiration or—*admit it, Rebeccah!*—desire as his gaze raked her from head to toe and every place in between.

"You'll do, I reckon." He shrugged indifferently and turned on his heel. "Let's go."

She found herself taking two quick strides for every one of his long, loping ones, and by the time she reached the wagon, she would have bet her buttons he would not even help her in.

But here she was wrong. He turned, so suddenly she nearly ran into him, put two strong hands around her waist, and hoisted her up with no apparent effort and no excessive gentleness. Rebeccah found herself plopped unceremoniously onto the hard seat.

"I think I'd rather have driven myself," she muttered under her breath as he came around and climbed up beside her, releasing the brake lever in a deft motion.

"Caitlin wouldn't hear of it," he said, staring straight ahead as he set the horses trotting forward. "Otherwise I wouldn't be here."

"How charming." Rebeccah's anger boiled within her, but at the same time her heart was heavy. He hated her now. That much was clear. He hated her even more than he had that first day in town when he'd learned who she was. He despised her. Well, good. Then he would never try to kiss her again or press his unwanted attentions on her just because he felt he could get away with it. She was safe.

Chill air whistled around them as the wagon crossed the sloping land, passed beneath the shadowy spruce, and encountered blowing tumbleweed and numerous ruts and boulders. A low moon sailed the satin sky, a sky studded with a thousand diamond stars. Stealing a quick glance at the man beside her, Rebeccah could make out the unflinching set of his features. She decided that he was the most infuriating and unpleasant man she'd ever encountered. How had she ever, even as a child, thought him kind? He said nothing to her during the entire drive, didn't glance at her once, and made her feel about as welcome as a queen ant at a picnic.

She made up her mind that she hated him too. And that was a welcome relief. The burden of all those idiotic daydreams was gone. Lifted forever. She had been a foolish simpleton, a dreamer, but now she was over him, so very much over him, it was as if she'd been set free from some terrible bondage, from prison, and so light were her spirits at this newfound freedom that she jumped down from the wagon the moment it pulled up at the Double B ranch house, without waiting for Wolf to help her.

The door opened, light poured forth across the spotlessly painted porch and from the windows of the neat, white-frame house, and Caitlin appeared in the glowing doorway, wiping her hands on her apron and smiling with cheery pleasure.

"Come in, Rebeccah! Don't you look pretty! My, I didn't realize it had grown so cold. You must make yourself comfortable by the fire."

Rebeccah ran lightly up the steps and across the porch, without so much as a backward glance at Wolf Bodine.

The ranch house was charmingly appointed, its furnishings at once simple, comfortable, and hardy. A pleasant chintz-covered sofa was flanked by matching wing chairs in the same swirly blue-and-rose pattern. A roaring hearth fire stretched out its warmth to every corner of the high-beamed parlor, illuminating the oak tea table, the glass-enclosed curio cabinets against the wall beneath the stairs, the braided rug on the highly polished floor. Rose muslin draperies were tied back with blue tassels at the windows, and set before the large front window was a claw-footed writing desk with a small brass lamp atop it. Numerous wall sconces glowed with fluttering candles. A narrow varnished staircase led up to a second story, which no doubt was as homey and delightful as this parlor.

What drew Rebeccah's attention almost at once was the piano. It was in the corner near the hearth, a lovely, delicate little spinet with gleaming keys and a glossy rosewood finish.

"It's beautiful," Rebeccah murmured, moving at once to stroke the polished wood. The bench was rosewood, too, with an embroidered seatcover. She stretched out a hand to touch the keyboard with a gentle finger.

"Will you play something for us, Miss Rawlings?" Billy asked out of nowhere, and, startled, Rebeccah glanced up to see him at the bottom of the stair-case, his dark hair damply slicked back, his face scrubbed and shiny in the bright light from the fire, the candles, and the lamp. It was obvious from the eager expression on his face that he did not hate her, and Rebeccah felt a surge of relief. Unlike his father, this bright little eagle of a boy did not hold a grudge because of the sadness her careless words had dredged up. He looked pleased to see her, friendly and open and excited to have company for supper. Rebeccah was surprised by how nice that made her feel.

"Not now," she demurred with a little wave of her hand. "We're going to have supper soon. I'm sure your grandmother can use my help."

"Of course I can, but first play us a little tune," Caitlin invited earnestly. "That piano has been in my family for as long as I can remember. It was my mother's. My sister, Julia, learned to play, but I never had the patience for it. Needlepoint is what I was good at. But Julia died of cholera years back, and the piano came to me after my mother was gone. Once in a while Mary Adams picks out a little tune on it, and now and again Billy pounds on those keys, but if you know any real songs, Rebec-cah, please go ahead. We'd all love to hear some music in this old house, wouldn't we, Wolf?"

Wolf made a sound halfway between a grunt and a cough.

"Pa, wouldn't we like to hear music?" Billy prodded. He tugged Rebeccah toward the bench. "Play something lively," he urged, his eyes dancing. "I'll clap along."

She was self-conscious, what with Wolf glaring at her like that, looking as if he'd just swallowed a whole lemon, including the skin; but there was nothing else for her to do except oblige Caitlin and Billy. She seated herself at the piano and stared down at the keys, her slender fingers poised hesitantly above them. What should she play?

Something lively.

" 'Turkey in the Straw'?" she asked, biting her lip, and Billy nodded emphatically.

"Oh, yes! And then 'Home on the Range'!"

She began to play, and as her fingers danced over the keys, she felt herself becoming engrossed as always in the music. Whether playing Chopin or a country reel, the music never failed to capture her, body and soul. Her fingers raced and pranced, her heart lifted, and she smiled into Billy's rapt face as the boy sang along enthusiastically. When she had finished both songs, Caitlin and Billy burst into applause.

"That was wonderful. You're quite accomplished," Caitlin exclaimed, and a beaming expression suddenly lit her seamed little face. "Perhaps in addition to your regular teaching duties you might want to give the youngsters of Powder Creek—those who want it, that is—music lessons."

"But I'm afraid I don't have a piano." Rebeccah

rose, her cheeks faintly flushed as she moved away from the bench.

"You could give the lessons here, couldn't she, Wolf? This old piano might as well be put to good use. And if Billy'd like, he could be her first pupil."

"Sure." The boy glanced hopefully up at her and tilted his head to one side like an inquisitive bird. "Would you teach me, Miss Rawlings?"

Rebeccah hesitated, unsure whether to laugh or to groan in frustration. She had come to Montana in search of peace and quiet—isolation, really—and here she was caught up in schoolteaching, music lessons, and suppers with friends.

It wasn't exactly unpleasant, however, especially since she'd never before had a friend, except Bear —but it was different from what she'd planned. And things just seemed to keep happening, rolling her life right out of her control.

"Well, yes, I'll teach you to play if you'd like," she heard herself promising Billy as she followed Caitlin to the kitchen.

She saw Wolf Bodine's expression as she said the words, and an aching chill pierced her. She stopped in her tracks and turned. "Unless your father has an objection."

"No objection." But his cold gray eyes were the color of a storm-tossed ocean, and they sparked with anger. He turned suddenly on the heel of his boot and stalked toward the door. "I forgot something I have to do in town," he curtly threw over his shoulder. "Sorry, Ma, but it can't be helped. Reckon you'd best go ahead and start supper without me."

And he was gone, tugging the door shut behind him with a soft but definite thud.

Rebeccah's heart sank like a sack of potatoes tossed down a dark well. He had left—because of her. He couldn't even bear being in the same room with her—even though she was his mother's guest.

The insult stung as if a great wasp had punctured her lungs with its venom. Rebeccah felt her chest constricting as anger lanced through her. And hurt. A deep, slicing hurt that seemed to cut her heart to bloody pieces.

Caitlin plopped her hands on her tiny rounded hips. Her mouth worked in consternation. "I'm going to scalp that boy," she declared.

"What's eating Pa?" Billy demanded, looking from one to the other in bafflement. "He never goes to town at suppertime!"

"Hush." Caitlin threw him a vexed glance. "You go upstairs now and comb your hair. I'll call you when supper's ready."

"I already combed it, Gramma."

"Comb it again," she ordered.

In silence Rebeccah followed Caitlin into the kitchen. It was every bit as homey and tidy as the parlor, and it smelled deliciously of cooked beef with brown gravy, white beans simmering in a skillet alongside sliced potatoes, and fresh buttermilk biscuits.

"Rebeccah, dear, why don't you set the table while I stir these beans. That'll take your mind off of my son's rudeness."

"Will it?" Rebeccah gave a short, bitter laugh. "I shouldn't have come tonight, Caitlin. I suppose I knew all along that it was a mistake. Your son doesn't want me here."

"Don't be so sure." Caitlin pursed her lips as she stirred the beans. She studied the dark-haired girl in the cherry-and-white calico, who was grimly setting plates about the table with its blue-and-white-checkered cloth. "I think my son doesn't know what he wants. And that's why he's acting like a man with a burr under his saddle."

"What ever would make you think that?" Rebeccah paused, one of the pretty blue china plates clenched in her hand.

"A mother knows. Don't ask me how, but it's true. Wolf is all torn up inside about something. Can't make up his mind. I haven't seen him this way in a long time. But you should know that he stood up for you at that town meeting a few days back. He put his job on the line to settle folks down and force them to give you a chance."

"He did that for me?"

"He sure did."

Rebeccah could scarcely believe it. And yet something had influenced the people of Powder Creek who had such strong reasons to resent her. Otherwise she wouldn't have had an opportunity at the teaching position, and she'd probably have been accosted by angry townsfolk by now.

She finished setting the table in silence. Finally she gathered her courage to ask the question that had been gnawing at her for days. "His wife." She forced her voice to sound cool, matter-of-fact. "How did she die? When?"

Caitlin froze. Very deliberately she set down the

wooden fork with which she'd been stirring the beans. "Clarissa was caught in a cross-fire," she answered slowly. She cleared her throat. There was absolutely no expression on her firm, nut-brown face. "She died of a gunshot wound. It happened nine years ago. Billy had just turned one."

"How terrible," Rebeccah whispered. She stared down at the dishes arranged around the table. There was a tiny triangular chip in one.

"Wolf has raised Billy alone—with my help—ever since."

"I see."

"Do you?" Caitlin sighed, and removed the skillet with the beans and potatoes from the fire, pouring them into a scalloped china serving bowl.

"It's not quite as simple as it sounds, Rebeccah. Nothing ever is. Remember that, dear. If I've learned one thing in all my years, it's that."

Rebeccah concentrated on arranging knives, forks, and spoons at each place setting. "He must miss her terribly," she said in a low tone. "He is mourning her still, isn't he? Wolf, I mean. When I mentioned his wife one time, an expression of awful pain entered his eyes. And then, a moment later, it was gone—he had covered it up. I didn't understand at the time."

"You still don't."

Caitlin opened her mouth to say more, but at that moment Billy darted into the kitchen. "I'm starving, Gramma. When can we eat? We're not waiting for Pa, are we?"

"No, we won't wait for Wolf. He'll come back

when he's good and ready. Wash your hands at the pump and then take your seat."

Rebeccah forced herself to smile at Billy and Caitlin as they took their places at the table, but she was all too aware of the empty chair at the head of the table. Damn Wolf Bodine. He had spoiled the dinner for everyone, acting like a spoiled child, running away.

He must truly hate me, she thought yet again. *He can't bear even the briefest time spent in my company. No doubt after hearing me play the piano he completely lost his appetite.*

She bowed her head as Caitlin said grace and then obediently helped herself to a portion of the tender, succulent beef. But her heart was heavy, and she boiled with rage as she thought about the insulting, childish, and oafishly rude manner in which Wolf Bodine had been treating her.

Wolf went straight to the Silk Drawers Brothel, plunked himself down at a small table in the darkest corner, and ordered whiskey. He drank it down in one gulp and ordered another. Molly Duke, wandering toward the stairs from behind the bar, spotted him at once. She sauntered over, her ample breasts swelling above the daringly low-cut décolletage of her black-and-violet-striped gown. A statuesque woman, she enjoyed styling her bright russet hair in a high pompadour held in place by rhinestone or imitation-ruby combs. She favored black silk stockings and a cheap perfume some peddler had once sold her called "Red-Hot Kisses," and she had a long, sultry face that was comely even without the layers of paint she artfully applied.

"Want some company?" she inquired with a faint smile.

Wolf shook his head. "More whiskey," he called to Lil, who nodded and hurried off to the bar.

Molly hesitated. She'd known Wolf Bodine since he'd first come to Powder Creek. In her opinion he was the best thing that had ever happened to the town. She'd drunk whiskey with him, slept with him, broken her heart over him, and ultimately become friends with him. She'd tried to make him fall in love with her, but it hadn't worked, and now she was wise enough and practical enough to settle for mutual friendship with the only man who'd ever treated her like a lady despite the fact that she'd always made her living as a whore.

For the past few years she'd owned the Silk Drawers, and now she was retired from her former profession—she didn't have to sleep with any other man unless she wanted him, but to most of the people in the town, once a whore, always a whore. Molly accepted that. But Wolf Bodine was different. He had never looked down on her, never been rude to her, never hurt her or shouted at her. He was a gentleman. She respected him more than any other man she'd ever known.

And she knew when something was wrong with him. Wolf never drank this much unless something was bothering him. "What's the trouble?" Molly asked bluntly, pulling up a chair and sliding her long, supple body into it, despite the glare of resentment he shot her way.

"I'm not in a talking mood, Molly."

"I can see that. You're in a drinking mood. I just thought you might need a friend."

"Not tonight."

"You sure?"

"Sure as hell."

"Okay, Wolf." Defeated by the cold, hard way he stared down into the amber liquid in his glass, then downed it like a man dying of thirst in the desert, without even sparing her a glance, Molly rose and strolled away. She knew enough about men to recognize when they needed time alone. For Wolf this was one of those times.

Maybe he was thinking about his wife. About Clarissa. She shrugged to herself as she headed to the backroom to begin counting up the day's receipts. She'd probably never know for sure. Though Wolf was her friend, and on occasion spoke frankly to her after one of their passionate sessions in the big velvet-canopied bed upstairs, he didn't confide much about his personal life. Once in a while he talked about his son, and when he did, she could see how proud he was of Billy, of the hopes he had for him. And occasionally he talked to her about his work, or sometimes even about his childhood escapades with his brother. But never about Clarissa, or any other woman. Not Nel Westerly, nor Lorelie Simpson, both of whom had done all in their power to win the tall, handsome sheriff's heart.

But he probably doesn't talk a mite to them either, Molly reflected with a small degree of spite as she sank into the chair behind her desk. Wolf Bodine was a man of action, not of words.

Outside her small floral-carpeted office, Wolf stared at his third glass of whiskey and pushed it away. Getting drunk wouldn't help what ailed him. Hell, he wasn't even sure what it was that did ail him. But he'd learned long ago that liquor only made things worse.

Why did Bear Rawlings have to win property in this town, my town? And why did his daughter, with all her money and fancy jewels and whatever other ill-gotten riches Bear gave her, have to move out here and turn my life upside down?

Caitlin liked her. Billy liked her. Hell, before long, the whole damn town would probably like her. *But I won't,* he told himself coldly, studying the scars and scratches in the knobby table before him. She's stubborn, ill-tempered, and damned secretive —and she had twice now brought up the subject of Clarissa. Of course she did it out of ignorance, but she was plainly nosy, and that was irritating in a woman.

So why do you keep thinking about her—remembering how soft she felt in your arms, remembering the soulful way she kissed you, as if she could never get enough?

Wolf sat up straighter in his chair and scowled at nothing in particular. It had just hit him that it really wasn't Rebeccah Rawlings he was mad at—it was himself.

He never should have kissed her in the first place. He should have walked out of that cabin with his son and just steered clear of her. Unlike the other women he knew, she grabbed hold of a man's attention and didn't let go. Her face, framed by that cloud of midnight hair, kept popping into his mind. Her beautiful eyes seemed to beseech him, even when she was yelling at him. Damn! His fingers itched for that third glass of whiskey, but he forced them to grip the edge of the table instead.

He had to go back. However he felt about Rebeccah, he'd been downright rude to Caitlin, he had probably spoiled the dinner she'd worked so hard to make festive and special, and he'd set a poor example for his son.

Fine, I'll go home and sit there in the same room with her and then drive her home when everyone's had enough of each other, but I won't give her a chance to get under my skin again. No matter what she says, how pretty she looks, how sweet she smells. I've survived the War Between the States, army food, gunfights, ambushes, rattlers, and encounters with desperadoes from here to the Rio Grande. I can sure survive Rebeccah Rawlings.

Two men met on the shallow banks of Deer Run Creek, not far from the Missouri River. In the darkness of the starlit night they dismounted, left their horses to graze, and stood together among the pussy willows and cottonwoods. The taller man, heavier and wearing a wide-brimmed black Stetson, spoke first.

"What did you find out?"

"He's dead." The slimmer man with the clean-shaved face spoke matter-of-factly and smoked a hand-rolled cigarette. "Seems the local sheriff shot him."

"Naw! You're loco! Fess is too damn good for that! No small-town sheriff could plug him."

"This hombre's no ordinary sheriff."

Something in the slimmer man's tone made the other snap his mouth shut. For a moment there was only the hiss and gurgle of the creek, the screech of an owl diving in for the kill, the anguished final cry of his prey dying somewhere in the brush.

Then the big man let out a stream of oaths, followed by a question. "Who is he?"

"Wolf Bodine."

"Damn! Son of a bitch!"

In the starry darkness the clean-shaved man studied the glowing tip of his cigarette. "He won't be a problem."

"He'd better not be. Wolf Bodine. Of all the rotten luck. What about the girl?"

"What about her?" The slimmer man, whose eyes gleamed brightly in the dimness, regarded his companion with something very like a sneer.

"What'd she do, go running to Bodine for protection?"

"I don't think so. She may not have said anything about the mine yet to anyone. At least I haven't heard anything, and I've been listening closely."

"I'd like to get my hands around her stubborn little neck for jest five minutes," the big man growled.

"Leave her to me."

"You seen her yet?"

"You ask too many questions, my friend. Let me handle this my own way. I want that deed as much as you do."

"Then get to work," the large man snapped. "Remember, she's Bear's daughter, so she's tough. She's got all his orneriness, as I remember."

The other man laughed. "I like them ornery."

His companion studied him a moment. "Is it true, that story they tell about you?" he asked slowly, almost in awe. "You strangled a woman down in New Mexico over a bottle of tequila? And then set her house on fire?"

"What difference does it make?" the man replied softly, throwing his cigarette into the swirling waters of the creek. His eyes glistened from beneath his hat as he glanced toward his horse.

"None, none at all. I was jest wonderin' . . ."

"Start wondering how you're going to spend the money from that silver mine, my friend. We'll meet back here in one week, same time."

"I'll be here." The large man sprang into his saddle with remarkable ease for someone of his height and breadth. He turned the horse toward Helena and called over his shoulder, "You watch out for that girl. She 'pears to have the devil's own luck!"

"So do I," the other murmured, smiling to himself as he gently stroked his horse's muzzle. "So do I."

11

He was back.

Rebeccah nearly choked on her raspberry cobbler as she heard the hoofbeats outside, and then Billy, racing to the window, cried out, "It's Pa!"

She didn't glance at him when he strode through the kitchen door, nor when he leaned down to give Caitlin a quick peck on the cheek, nor when he hung his hat on a hook and then slid his long, rugged frame into his chair.

"I'm starved," he declared, as innocently robust as any man who's just come in from a day's hard labor. "Any grub left over for me?"

"Plenty—not that you deserve it," Caitlin zipped back at him, but though she tried to maintain her starched demeanor, it wilted at his grin and disappeared completely when he reached out to nonchalantly pinch her lined cheek.

"Ma, will it help if I apologize?"

"Only if you apologize to Rebeccah."

He turned to Rebeccah, the grin still locked in place, but stiffer now and obviously forced. His eyes had lost the playful glint he'd had when he'd addressed his mother. "Miss Rawlings, I beg your pardon."

Like hell he did. "There's no need, Sheriff Bodine," she murmured dutifully, and stabbed viciously at the hapless raspberries oozing from beneath a wedge of golden crust.

Sensing his eyes boring into her, she peered up and met his glance with a steely gaze of her own. A gaze, Wolf thought, that could freeze a man to death in the height of summer.

"Glad to hear it," he returned shortly, and reached out across the table to tousle Billy's hair.

"Where'd you go, Pa? Why'd you have to leave right at suppertime?"

"I told you, I went to town. It couldn't be avoided. But I'm back now, so pass me some of that beef, son, and a handful of those biscuits. With all that riding, I've worked up quite an appetite."

"I've lost mine," Rebeccah announced coolly, and pushed her plate away. It was all she could do not to hurl the cobbler at Wolf Bodine's smug face as he proceeded to stuff himself with huge amounts of food, packing it all away with relish and precision, as if everything was jim-dandy in his world. *He's the most infuriating, arrogant, insufferable man I've ever met,* Rebeccah thought for perhaps the hundredth time since she'd reencountered Wolf Bodine. As she helped Caitlin clear the table a short while later, she made up her mind that the less she had to see him after tonight, the better.

"You going to the dance?" Caitlin asked as she washed the chipped plate with a soapy dishrag and Rebeccah dried the spoons.

"Dance?"

"Oh, heavens, didn't anyone mention it? It's to be held at the schoolhouse, matter of fact. Two weeks from this Saturday. Everyone will be there. You've got to come, Rebeccah. It'll be a good chance for you to meet folks."

"I don't think so."

"Wolf is going."

Rebeccah rubbed furiously with a towel at the dripping plate Caitlin thrust into her hand. She said nothing.

"He's taking Miss Westerly."

Who was Miss Westerly? For some odd reason a knot like cat's twine balled up tight in her stomach.

"You haven't met her yet, have you?" Caitlin went on. "A right nice and pretty young lady, but a little too sure of herself for my taste. Of course some folks thought sure Wolf would ask Lorelie Simpson—she's only twenty-four and already a widow, poor thing—her husband got killed on a cattle drive two years ago. But Wolf asked the Westerly girl instead. Do you have a dress to wear?"

"I won't be needing one. I'm not going."

"Oh, but . . ."

Rebeccah gave her head a firm shake as she set the dry plate on the countertop and took another wet one from Caitlin. "I don't care for dances," she said airily.

Since it seemed Caitlin was loathe to drop the subject, Rebeccah changed it by asking the first question that sprang to mind. "I've been meaning to ask you," she blurted out, rushing her words. "How did Wolf get his name?" She flushed a little as she spoke the words, and hurried on as Caitlin gave a short chuckle. "I mean, as a baby, surely you didn't call him *Wolf?*" she finished doubtfully.

"No, as a baby I called him Joseph Adam Bodine, after his father, as fine and handsome a man as any woman would ever care to meet." Caitlin's expression grew warm and misty, even her faded, near-sightless eyes seemed to brim with soft emotion. "My husband was a Texas Ranger, a good man, Rebeccah, as strong and decent and honest as a man should be—like Wolf," she said proudly. "He died when Wolf was only a little older than Billy—but I'm straying from my story," she said, straightening her shoulders and giving her gray head a tiny shake. "Wolf was very young—oh, six or seven, I reckon—when he wandered off one morning when I had my hands full with laundry and gardening and the like, and to make a long story short, he got himself lost in the hills. We searched for him, Joseph and me, and our ranch hands, and even his little brother, Jimmy, came along, calling—but we couldn't find him. Not that day, not all through the night. Finally, early next morning, Joseph found him—guess where! Sleeping near some mesquite, curled up on the ground with a great, mangy wolf, of all things. Do you know, that animal actually seemed to be guarding him? Strangest sight Joseph ever saw, or so he said. Well, the nickname Wolf stuck after that. No one's called him anything else in all the years since that morning."

"It suits him," Rebeccah murmured, almost to herself, and marveled at the image of the young boy, Joseph Adam, sleeping in the open hills with a wolf.

Caitlin interrupted her thoughts. "Yes, it does suit him. And he's amazingly similar in character to that wild wolf that guarded him that night, if you think about it," she said firmly. "Fierce and tough and somewhat frightening when you first look at him, but underneath it all, shrewd and smart and . . . a protector. Not easy to know and understand, but a strong friend to have when you're alone in the dark." She broke off and smiled at Rebeccah, a bright, reassuring smile. "Don't mind me, dear, I'm quite sentimental and even foolish when it comes to my boy. But I'm right fond of him."

"Yes, I'm sure you are."

"And I think you'll be fond of him, too, when you've had a chance to get better acquainted," Caitlin finished quickly. Before Rebeccah could protest, she shooed the girl into the parlor.

"Enough chores for now. Let's visit with the menfolk."

Wolf and Billy were engrossed in a game of checkers on the floor. Wolf glanced up and observed her entrance into the parlor with a hint of tightening in his expression. Rebeccah squared her shoulders and turned away, strolling to the mantelpiece with as much casualness as she could muster, trying not to think about Miss Westerly and Mrs. Simpson fluttering over that tall, lean man watching her from the floor.

Her gaze was drawn to the collection of framed photographs displayed upon the mantel. For a moment her heart skittered as she realized she would no doubt see a photograph of Wolf's dead wife. She braced herself to see the woman whom he had loved so much and now mourned so deeply. But there was no young woman, only an old silver-framed daguerreotype of a wedding couple, taken perhaps thirty years earlier. *The woman in the photo is Caitlin,* Rebeccah realized suddenly, and the man with her must be Wolf's father, a tall, imposing man with a lean, strong face remarkably like his son's. The eyes, too, were strikingly similar, clear and keen and compelling. They wore wedding clothes and stiff smiles, but looking at the photograph, Rebeccah fancied she could feel the strong love flowing between them. After a moment her glance shifted to the photograph beside it, the one in the brass frame.

This one was of Wolf. His face, relaxed and handsome, stared out at her with a stark familiarity—identical to the young man who had come to the Arizona hideout shack so many years ago tracking her father. He wore a Union cavalry uniform: a snug-fitting dark woolen coat piped with yellow braid, silk neckerchief, and trousers with the traditional cavalry stripe on the outer seam. The trousers were tucked into straight boots, and to complete his uniform he wore brass spurs secured to the boots with a single spur strap, heavy brass epaulettes decorating his shoulders, and a large Kossuth hat set upon his head. He had his foot propped on a chair and was staring with a slightly bemused smile into the camera, looking so like the young man who had come to the hideout cabin in Arizona and captured her imagination that Rebeccah's throat tightened with memory. She yearned to stare at the photograph, to memorize it, touch it —but feared someone would notice her absorption. So she moved hastily on and forced herself to peer at the one beside it, a small, brass-framed picture of a young man no more than sixteen or seventeen years old, holding his hat in his hand and grinning eagerly from ear to ear.

"That's Uncle Jimmy," Billy announced, glancing up for a moment from the checkerboard to follow her glance. "He was Pa's brother."

Caitlin, seated complacently on the sofa darning a pile of Billy's socks without once glancing down at them, offered up a misty smile. "He was a fine-looking boy, my Jimmy, don't you think so, Rebeccah? That photograph was taken in Carson City, when Jimmy was seventeen. He went to visit cousins in Nevada. It was his first and last trip away from home. . . ." Her voice trailed off.

A solemn tension settled over the parlor. The checkers game over, Billy began putting the pieces away. Wolf went to the window and gazed out toward the infinite glitter of stars. As the fire crackled and popped, Caitlin wearily closed her eyes.

Rebeccah longed to ask what had happened to Jimmy but bit back the question, sensing the answer would be a painful one.

Yet Caitlin opened her eyes and began to speak, responding quietly to her unasked question.

"The town was full of gamblers, outlaws, and thieves, you see, men drawn to the lure of all that silver and gold. It was a rough place, but Jimmy and his cousins wanted that, they wanted, as young men often do, to experience the excitement and adventure of the rawest part of the frontier. There was a sheriff in town, a man by the name of Luke Davis." Caitlin's lip curled over the words. "But he was a coward," she told Rebeccah bitterly, and her fingers clenched on the socks in her lap. "Davis was in cahoots with a group of outlaws planning to steal some poor miner's claim to a rich silver deposit. Jimmy and my nephews saw them drag the old man into an alley and start to beat him. They rushed over and tried to save that man." Caitlin took a deep breath. "Jimmy always hated an unfair fight, and he loathed bullies. Same as Wolf."

Suddenly, in the quiet of the parlor, silent but for the logs popping in the hearth, an anguished sound choked from her throat. Tears brimmed in her faded eyes. Wolf had not turned from the window, but Billy was listening to every word, and watching his grandmother's sturdy, sorrow-wracked face, his own expression somber.

"What happened?" Rebeccah asked, suddenly aware that her palms were damp.

Caitlin picked up the socks and held them tightly between her small, strong fingers. "They killed my Jimmy," she said in a low tone. "And my nephew Roy. Shot them both. Neither boy was armed. My younger nephew, Walt, was left for dead, but a passerby found him and sent for a doctor. He survived to tell us what had happened."

"And that crooked sheriff was the one who shot Uncle Jimmy!" Billy piped up suddenly. Rebeccah realized that he must have heard and contemplated this story many times. "That's why my pa hates crooked lawmen even more than outlaws—'cause they're charged with a solemn duty to uphold the law and protect people, and there's nothing worse than when a lawman goes bad. When he heard what happened to Uncle Jimmy, he tracked that sheriff all the way to Abilene."

"You killed him?" Rebeccah asked softly as Wolf turned from the window at last and met her gaze with stone-hard eyes.

"No." He stuck his thumbs in his pockets and spoke slowly. "I brought Luke Davis back to Carson City and put him in jail to stand trial, along with the other two who shot Roy and Walt in cold blood. I let the law mete out punishment for them. And after they were convicted," he said with grim satisfaction, "I watched them hang."

Caitlin stirred on the sofa. She turned proud, tear-filled eyes in Rebeccah's direction. "Wasn't Jimmy a handsome boy?" she asked softly.

"Yes, Caitlin, I can see he was."

"And he had the kindest soul. I've been blessed with both of my sons—and with my grandson." She smiled stoutly then through her tears and wiped them away with a lace hankie tugged from her pocket. "Who else would take such good care of a useless, blind old lady?"

"Useless?" Wolf and Billy demanded in unison.

"You're about as useless as a rope at a rodeo, and you know it," Wolf commented drily, and Billy grinned. The heavy mood lifted. Rebeccah left the mantel and the collection of photographs and seated herself on the sofa with Caitlin.

"Well, I do manage to find my way around this

house fairly well," the gray-haired woman admitted, twinkling.

"And you prepared the most delicious meal I've ever tasted," Rebeccah exclaimed. "I was wondering . . . perhaps you'd teach me how to prepare that raspberry cobbler sometime?"

"I'd be pleased to do that. Why, you've probably never had the chance to get much practice cooking, have you?"

"No, my mother died when I was two. I don't remember her at all, so I've mostly known only campfire cooking, which I learned when I was very young and rode with my father and his—" She broke off.

"Gang," Billy supplied helpfully.

"Yes, Billy, his gang," Rebeccah said, shooting a defiant glance at Wolf. He lifted his brows but made no comment.

"Anyway, the 'gang's' cook, Old Red, taught me how to fix beans, biscuits, coffee, and a few other staples over a campfire, and occasionally I saw him use a stove, but after I went to Miss Wright's Academy, my meals were all prepared by a kitchen staff, and I never had a chance to learn any more."

"Did you like that school?" Billy inquired.

She met his gaze with dancing eyes. "I hated it. The teachers were stuffy and strict and boring. But the books were interesting. I brought some of them with me—you'll get a chance to see them when school starts next week. And don't you or your pards try any tricks on me, Billy, like spitballs or spiders on my desk, because I know them all," she warned him with a grin, waggling her finger in his face with mock sternness. "I invented them—or at least I thought I did when I was pulling all those pranks at Miss Wright's Academy."

Gazing admiringly at her, Billy spoke with ingenuous innocence. "I never thought I'd look forward to school, but I do now. I think it's going to be downright fun."

"I wouldn't go that far," Wolf said drily. He pulled out his pocket watch. "Time for bed, son."

Billy threw him a disappointed glance and edged closer to Rebeccah. "Will you play one more song for us, Miss Rawlings?"

"Only with your father's permission."

"Pa?"

Wolf studied her darkly as if deciding whether or not she had somehow instigated this small rebellion. "All right," he said at last. "One song."

As Rebeccah took her place at the piano, Wolf tossed another log onto the dwindling fire. The night chill had begun to permeate the ranch house, and Caitlin had pulled a sweater around her thin shoulders as she worked.

The melancholy strains of "Aura Lee" poured forth from the piano to resound with bittersweet valor through every corner of the cozy room. This time Rebeccah sang along with Billy and Caitlin. Her voice was huskily mellifluous, as lightly sensual as the silky lashes sweeping down over her brilliant eyes, and Wolf found himself fighting the overpowering urge to take her in his arms and kiss the lips from which those sweet sounds were tumbling.

Of course Billy called for another song after she

had finished, but Wolf, taut with a tension from which he could find no relief, adamantly shook his head.

"When it's time to get up and do your chores in the morning, you'll thank me," he informed his son, and abruptly took Rebeccah by the arm to lead her to the door.

Caitlin, following, urged Rebeccah to join them for supper again soon.

"And *do* think about changing your mind about the dance," she urged Rebeccah as Wolf held open the front door. "It's a fine opportunity for you to meet folks here and get to know them at their best. I hope you'll come, after all."

Rebeccah flushed with embarrassment as Wolf glanced at her following these words. She felt exposed, as if he could somehow see that part of the reason she didn't want to go to the dance at the schoolhouse was because *he* would be there with that Miss Westerly, and she would have to watch them together. She let him help her onto the wagon seat, and twisted her hands together, praying he would not continue the conversation where Caitlin had left off.

She needn't have worried, she reflected bitterly a short time later. Wolf didn't continue the conversation at all. Silence reigned between them as he drove her home, a taut, tension-filled silence punctuated by the rapid clip-clop of the horses' hooves, the chirp of crickets, the faint rustle of animals in the unseen brush.

The September air had grown quite chilly, though thankfully the wind was still. The moon rode low in the star-filled sky, now and then disappearing behind the peaks of the mountains. Rebeccah pulled her shawl close around her shoulders and tried not to shiver with cold as Wolf guided the horses along the grassy, rutted trail. Shivering was a sign of weakness, and she refused to appear weak before him. But Wolf must have noticed something, for he suddenly yanked a woven Navajo blanket out from under the seat and thrust it at her, not saying a word, and never taking his eyes from the road ahead.

It stopped the shivering, but for some reason her feet began to fidget. Rebeccah concentrated all during the rest of the drive on keeping them still and on keeping at bay the lonely, painful yearning growing ever more strongly inside her.

There was silence in the wagon until Wolf at last halted the horses in front of Rebeccah's front porch. The song of crickets filled the starry night, and the fragrance of autumn leaves and pine air drifted with intoxicating sweetness about them. A mosquito swooped before her nose, and she swatted it away, so intensely aware of Wolf's large, wide-shouldered frame beside her, of his clean, invigorating smell, and of his strong hands holding the reins, that it was all she could do not to tremble with the longing that rose unbidden in the deepest places of her being.

"Why'd you take the teaching position?" Wolf Bodine asked abruptly, so abruptly, she jerked her head toward him in surprise.

"It was offered to me," she replied, her heart

thumping at the unusually intent darkness of his eyes.

Wolf leaned back thoughtfully. He was about to violate all the codes of polite behavior Caitlin had drilled into him for years. But his lawman's suspicious nature and his curiosity drove him to understand why the daughter of a wealthy and successful outlaw would want to earn a pitiful salary teaching school in a town where folks were leery of her. From outward appearances, and from every reasonable expectation, Rebeccah Rawlings should be rolling in money. Unless . . .

"Did your father gamble away all his loot? Is that it?" Wolf demanded, keeping his tone level, studying her with cold, probing eyes that missed nothing. "Miss Rawlings, do you *need* this job?"

Shock whistled through her. He had hit too close to the truth. She couldn't bear to think about what else he might discover, or about how her own feelings might betray her and make her vulnerable to him, more vulnerable than she was already. She threw the blanket off her lap and crouched to face him, drawing on anger and pride to get her through this.

"How dare you." Her shoulders trembled, but no longer from the cold. "You have *no right* to ask me questions of such a personal nature. Or is this an official investigation, Sheriff? Are you going to lock me up now for wanting to teach school? Are you afraid of what I'll teach Billy?"

Wolf's muscles coiled with tension. Moonglow illuminated her heart-shaped face, bringing alive the passionate anger flaring in her magnificent violet eyes, revealing her dainty cheeks flushed the shade of wild roses. He couldn't help noticing the rapid rise and fall of her breasts beneath the clinging calico gown. "Hold on," he growled, almost more to himself than to her. "I only asked a simple question—"

"Maybe I'll teach him to rob stagecoaches," Rebeccah rushed on, too incensed to stop now. Her emotions were galloping away with her, and her voice took on a taunting note. "Is that what you're afraid of? Or maybe you're worried that I'll teach him how to blow open a bank vault with a stick or two of dynamite, or how to lose a posse by covering his tracks so well, not even an Apache scout could find him, or—?"

Wolf grabbed her. Her shoulders felt narrow and vulnerable beneath his taut fingers. "Didn't anyone ever teach you when to shut up?" he exploded.

And suddenly his mouth crushed down on hers with a violent heat that seared away all the words and thoughts that had been bubbling inside of her. Wolf's arms snaked around her, pinioning her against him with brute force, and a rush of jangling feelings tore through her, feelings that overwhelmed her as powerfully as the physical sensations of his ravishing mouth and knowing, gliding hands.

Wolf didn't understand why in hell he was kissing her. It sure wasn't the way he kissed Nel Westerly or Lorelie Simpson—or even Molly Duke. He'd been banging heads and tempers with Rebeccah Rawlings for long enough now and he ought to be staying away from her—she was trouble—but instead of keeping his distance he just kept grabbing her and pulling her close . . . closer. . . .

She tasted sweet as daisies and every bit as wild as one. Wolf's insides seemed to be crunching up like twigs on fire. His hand slid up her back, cupped the delicate nape of her neck, and brushed the tightly coiled fluff of her hair. Then his tongue found its way inside her honey-warm mouth, and Wolf felt his loins grow heavy with a fierce yearning. He groaned and held her tighter, kissed her harder.

Rebeccah's senses surrendered to the onslaught of kissing and touching. A light-as-a-butterfly joy winged through her, and instinctively her hands slid up his broad shoulders and around his neck. It was so strong, corded with muscle. She kissed him back, welcoming his tongue, savoring his taste, and the groaning need she sensed in him. Fire and musk consumed her. He was bringing out all those feelings in her, feelings she had kept hidden and secret for so long, making her whole, aware, alive.

She gave a low moan as his hand cupped the nipple of her breast beneath her gown, rubbing it until tears ached at her eyes. His lips grazed her soft neck, burned along the hollow of her cheek, and nibbled at the seashell curve of her ear, drawing forth sensations of delight.

But then, as Wolf pressed her back against the wagon seat and his powerful body leaned against hers, the panic came.

It cut her like an old rusty razor. It drove away the pleasure and the sweetness and the fire. It roused her like a bucket of stinging cold water. "No!" she begged, tearing her mouth from his.

In terror she pulled back, flailing wildly at his massive strength.

Wolf stopped, his brain struggling to take in her cries and the blows she was raining futilely at his chest. "Rebeccah," he said sharply, his voice hoarse, and then he saw that same look of panic in her eyes that he had seen before.

He straightened, pulling back. His hands fell away. He let her pummel him, saying nothing, until the fear died out of her eyes and she realized he was no longer holding her, no longer even touching her. Her breath came in ragged gasps. Both hands flew to her throat.

"Don't!" she said tremblingly, and started to hurl herself miserably out of the wagon. "Don't ever touch me again!"

He caught her before she could get out. His fingers closed around her arm and yanked her back. Rebeccah gave a startled scream.

"It's all right, Rebeccah. I'm not going to hurt you."

"I want to go inside."

"That's fine. But let me help you down. It's dark, and you could lose your footing. And let me scout out your cabin and make sure there's no unwelcome visitors waiting for you."

His quiet words penetrated the anguished confusion in her brain. Suddenly she glanced at the cabin in trepidation. "Do you really think . . . ?"

"You would know more about that than I would.

But after Fess Jones, I reckon we can't be too careful."

His hands felt so protectively strong and comforting around her waist that the last shreds of Rebeccah's panic faded as he set her down on the ground as carefully as a china doll. She looked into his handsome face, so intent, so serious. *He's a lawman, he won't rape you,* she told herself and her mind knew it was true. There was no resemblance at all between Wolf Bodine and Neely Stoner—he would never do such awful things, but when he'd leaned across her that way, the memories had taken over, as they always did, and she had slipped into that deep, black well of fear.

Looking at Wolf now, standing tall and quiet beside her, her insides turned into a puddle of jelly. She fought the very strong urge to slide her fingers through the burnished curls falling lankly across his forehead, to touch that wonderful, sensuous mouth that had done such indecent things to her own. . . .

"Come in, then—for a moment," Rebeccah Rawlings said with all the composure she could muster under the circumstances—and turned away before she lost what little was left of her resolve and her dignity.

No one was hiding in the cabin. She followed Wolf through the parlor, the kitchen, and finally the bedroom. All was as she had left it, down to the camisole and lace drawers she had left tumbled anyhow on the bed when she had changed into fresh clothes earlier. She noticed his gaze fix on the wispy lace garments, and immediately color seeped into her cheeks.

"Do you mind," she snapped, recovering her composure. She slammed the bedroom door. "I think you should leave now before you overstay your welcome—Sheriff!"

He shot her a look full of amusement, but obediently followed her back to the cabin door, admiring the gentle sway of her hips and rounded bottom beneath that soft cherry-and-white gown.

"You never answered my question," he said as she held open the door for him and left no doubt that she wanted him to leave.

"I don't intend to."

"Then I'll try another. Do you intend to go to the schoolhouse dance?"

Rebeccah's blood tingled. "Absolutely not."

"Why?"

"As I already told your mother earlier this evening, I don't care for dances."

"Ah-huh."

"What does that mean?"

"I never met a woman who didn't care to dance."

"You have now. And besides, it's my understanding you already have a companion for that evening, so I can't imagine why you care about my plans. Good night, Sheriff Bodine."

She banged the door in his face and leaned against it, eyes closed, breathing hard.

Wolf turned slowly away, his expression thoughtful in the pale glint of moonlight. Rebeccah Rawlings changed moods quicker than any female he'd ever met, he decided. One minute she was flinty as stone, the next she was like melting candle wax in his arms—and then the next moment she was as terrified as a beaten pup, and then, quick as the gleam of a firefly, a stone princess in a thorny girdle once more.

She wasn't at all like Clarissa, he realized suddenly as he got back into the wagon and turned the horses for home. Clarissa had a one-track mind: *Clarissa.* Clarissa's pleasure, Clarissa's schemes.

This woman was a jumble of complicated thoughts and emotions. Hard to read, impossible to figure out. But Wolf was coming to understand something about her: She wasn't anywhere near as tough as she tried to appear. Every once in a while that rawhide veneer of hers slipped. It had with Billy and Joey, the night she'd saved their skins and fixed them tea with peppermint and kept them warm and dry by her fire. It had slipped tonight when she'd chatted with Caitlin and Billy, and played the piano, and sang, with a thousand emotions flitting over her face. And again tonight when he'd kissed her and for a time she'd responded with such red-hot passionate need.

Hell, that stubborn, dark-haired angel was simmering right full of passion. But every time he caught a glimpse of the tender woman beneath the surface, she yanked that tough coat of rawhide back over her shoulders again.

She's probably loco. And possibly dishonest. And definitely the wrong woman for you, he told himself, but something made him glance back as the wagon neared the rise, and he saw her slender silhouette framed in the window of the cabin for a brief moment, and it looked like her face was pressed against the glass. When she saw him look back, she moved quickly away, leaving a dark, blank square in her place.

He grinned to himself. Loco. Trouble. Think about Nel Westerly and her delicious blueberry pies. Think about Lorelie Simpson and that brandy-laced chocolate cake specialty of hers. Rebeccah Rawlings can't even cook! Unless you call heating beans and brewing coffee cooking.

Wolf made up his mind. He would stay away from Rebeccah Rawlings. Being around her stirred up feelings that were just plain uncomfortable, and he couldn't be bothered with them or with her. If Caitlin and Billy wanted to be her friends, that was fine. Of course Billy was fast developing a case of calf love for her, but that was harmless so long as Rebeccah didn't laugh at him over it.

Wolf sensed that she wouldn't. Rebeccah Rawlings had dealt with Billy naturally, effortlessly. Something told him she would handle the boy's sensitive feelings with care.

She'd better, he thought, his mouth thinning as the wagon lurched toward home. *Or I'll have to step in and set her straight.* The thought of anyone hurting Billy the way Clarissa had hurt him made his eyes narrow and the anger deep inside him start to flare.

His life was finally in order again, he told himself. The last thing he needed was an ornery, loco woman. The last thing he needed was to get tangled up in any way with Miss Rebeccah Rawlings.

* * *

No photograph of his dead wife, Rebeccah mused as she sat on her bed a few moments later brushing her hair. *I wonder why.*

Perhaps the memories were too painful. Perhaps she was so beautiful, so sweet and beloved, that even looking at her face brought grief freshly to the surface.

She sighed. Well, perhaps Wolf Bodine was finally getting over his grief. After all, he was squiring that Westerly woman to that damned dance. And she gathered from what Caitlin had said that he had the young Widow Simpson dangling on a string as well.

So why does he keep kissing me?

More to the point, she asked herself as she tossed the brush down, blew out the candle, and crawled beneath the soft eiderdown quilt, *why do I keep letting him?*

12 During the next weeks Rebeccah's life in Powder Creek settled into a surprisingly pleasant routine. She began teaching school at the clapboard-roofed schoolhouse, learning the children's names gradually and their ways more quickly. Her students ranged in age from tiny five-year-old Laura Adams to strapping sixteen-year-old Toby Pritchard, Waylon's younger brother. Some could read and count, others could do neither well enough to mention. Some were friendly and eager to please her, others stared at her rebelliously as if waiting for the new teacher to do or say something wrong so they could try to get her fired.

Rebeccah found that teaching the young people of Powder Creek was completely different from teaching the arrogant young women at Miss Wright's Academy. She actually enjoyed it.

She quickly became fond of the little ones with their trusting baby faces and eagerness to learn, the way they chanted out the alphabet and brought her shiny apples and cut-out paper hearts. She also took a fancy to the middle children, like Billy and Joey, and young Mary Adams, who was one of six children and worked at the Bodine house before and after school helping Caitlin. At this age the youngsters had a great many questions about the world outside of Powder Creek, and their minds were still young enough to imagine great adventures. And the older ones were strangely dear to her too—serious and uncertain about the lives awaiting them as they reached the threshold of adulthood. They absorbed her enthusiasm for the novels of Dickens and Cooper, for Byron's poems, and for the fascinating picture book she had found at a Boston book shop containing photographs from all over the world. She planned spelling bees and geography bees; she had every student writing stories about their hopes for the future and the places they'd like to visit; she told about the cities and rivers and lakes she pointed to on the large map of the United States at the front of the classroom, listened to endless recitations of multiplication tables, and answered every question as thoroughly as she could.

Her days were full and busy and stimulating. And at night she returned alone to the cabin, fixed herself a simple supper, and prepared the next day's lessons, always keeping her guns loaded and handy in case another desperado after the silver mine paid her a visit.

She had accomplished much to make the cabin homier, but there was still more to do. With the help of the Pritchards' hired hand she had weeded out her yard and prepared the way for a spring flower and vegetable garden. Everything was swept and scoured and spotless. The porch steps had been repaired and painted, as well as the barn, and

Rebeccah had used a portion of her first week's teacher's salary to buy fabric from Koppel's General Store. She'd sewn new curtains for all the windows, lovely blue lace curtains to match the blue rag rug she'd splurged on for the parlor floor. And she was working on a pretty blue-and-white floral slipcover for that old horsehair sofa—when that was completed, the parlor would have an entirely fresh, new look. With her watercolors brightening the walls, her piano music and a bowl of wildflowers displayed on a crate she'd covered with a doily and was using as a tea table, and a few other homey touches, she had actually made the bleak little cabin quite comfortable.

She had almost managed to put out of her mind the danger from Neely Stoner and others like him who believed Bear had left her the deed to a rich silver mine. Almost. But sometimes, in the blackest soul of night, she would waken and feel cold, pounding fear at some creak of a floorboard or the moan of the wind. It was lonely out at the cabin with only the meadowlarks and an occasional bobolink for company. Yet she was content. She found herself growing strangely peaceful, quietly happy in her teaching work, and deriving satisfaction from fluffing and feathering her own little nest.

Yet as the first week passed and the second week drew to a close, a certain restlessness came over her. She found herself thinking about Caitlin Bodine and her many kindnesses. Not wishing to neglect the budding friendship Caitlin had tried so hard to nurture, Rebeccah thought of paying a call on her one evening before sunset, but one thing held her back.

She had no desire to chance a meeting with Wolf. It had taken days of serenity here at the cabin all alone to drive away the chaos in which his kisses had left her—she had no wish to stir up all those feelings again. Besides, she told herself, Wolf Bodine was completely different now from that young man with the kind eyes whom she'd met in Arizona, the one who had prompted a thousand sweet imaginings. He was older, ruder, meaner, and far more dangerous to her heart than she could ever have dreamed. Before, his image had haunted her sweetly, gently, unforgettably, but now, not only his image, but his words, his voice, and the sharp male electricity of his touch stayed with her—biting at her, she decided irritatedly, like a pesky mosquito who won't go away.

So she stayed clear of the Double B, though she wrote Caitlin a friendly little thank-you note for the fine dinner and asked Billy to deliver it for her. Billy was the only Bodine male she felt confident to handle. Because of the obvious crush he had on her, she recognized the importance of treading lightly with him. Hadn't she, too, been smitten at an impressionable age, on the verge of adolescence? And with Billy's own father! Perhaps if she would have seen Wolf every day, she would have outgrown her romantic illusions about him, just as she expected Billy would about her. Instead she'd had her romantic illusions dashed by the present-day Wolf Bodine, who bore absolutely no resemblance to the tender, ardently smitten suitor who had pursued her through a girlhood of fantasies.

Pursued her? Hah! She hadn't seen hide nor hair of him in nearly two weeks—and that was just fine with Rebeccah. Who needed a lawman bothering her with his questions and insinuations when she could have blessed isolation and quiet?

She had deliberately pushed away all thoughts of the town dance, despite the fact that it was fast approaching. But when she left the schoolhouse Friday afternoon, she did stand in the doorway for a moment and picture how it would look with the desks all pushed up against the walls, with people dancing and stomping and clapping, with fiddlers on the dais and music filling every corner of the room all the way up to the rafters.

Just so they put everything back when they're done and we don't have to waste time moving furniture on Monday morning, she thought grumpily.

On Saturday she drove to town in the new buckboard the town was providing her. The autumn weather was turning cooler, there had been frost on her windowpane yesterday morning, and she would need to stock up on food and provisions before snow and wind and freezing temperatures prohibited regular trips to town. This was only her second visit since her arrival—the first time, when she'd bought fabric and a few more staples, she'd come bright and early, before many shoppers were about, and had only encountered the store clerks. Rebeccah tried not to feel nervous as she guided the team onto Main Street beneath a pale, lemony sun.

The citizens of Powder Creek had accepted her as their schoolteacher, so perhaps there would be no further hostility over who her father was and what his gang had done in this town. But if there was, Rebeccah tried to reassure herself, she would deal with it. The same way she had always dealt with people who didn't want her.

The gentle sense of peacefulness that had enveloped her over the past weeks faded away as she entered the bustling general store, bracing herself for whatever slings and arrows might come her way. With her shoulders squared, her spine straightened, and her eyes flashing cold fire, she marched beneath the wooden archway.

"And when I told Emmy Lou Boswell that her son's dog had torn up my yard and dug up all my potatoes and completely muddied a whole day's wash that was hung up to dry—"

The woman speaking, a birdlike matron attired in starched blue gingham, broke off abruptly and snapped her lips shut as Rebeccah sailed into the store's brightly lit interior. As a matter of fact all conversation in the store ceased. The short, apple-cheeked clerk and the half dozen women gossiping and selecting goods all paused to stare at the dark-haired young beauty in the ruffled gingham dress who swept in while a tiny little bell tinkled above her head.

They all knew who she was. That was why they were so keenly interested.

Rebeccah pretended not to notice the stares. She began to browse the crowded countertops, studying the shelves crammed full of goods, the yards of sateen and woolens and muslins, the cooking utensils and frying pans, the fragrant coffee tins and barrels of cheeses and flour and pickles and potatoes, the open-mouthed jars of penny candies with their delightful flavors: peppermint, cinnamon, orange, and licorice. No candy had been permitted at Miss Wright's Academy, but Bear had secretly sent her parcels of it from time to time, stuffed into the fingers of a pair of kid gloves or inside a fancy new reticule some shopkeeper or other told him was the latest rage in New York or Chicago.

"Excuse me," a firm voice boomed as she reached for a tin of canned milk.

Rebeccah turned to see an imposing woman with broad shoulders; stern, ruddy features; and swooping eyebrows above piercing toffee-colored eyes. "I'm Abigail Pritchard and I believe you are Miss Rawlings. There's something I would like to say to you, young woman. My boy, Toby, has come home lately with all sorts of notions about going to college in a year or two—to study medicine, he says—and I think you are the reason behind it, Miss Rawlings."

Rebeccah braced herself for the tongue-lashing to follow. The riveted gazes of the other women who were crowded into the store seared into her from all sides.

"Well, I can't thank you enough, Miss Rawlings," Abigail Pritchard continued, beaming. Her broad, handsome face creased into a hearty smile. "Toby's always been good at patching up cuts and bruises and using herbs for poultices, and when folks around here can't reach Doc Wilson, Toby's the next one they call on, but he never thought of actually becoming a real doctor before. He says you told him about that college in Boston, and now he's got a hankering that maybe he could go there and become a regular doctor himself. I'm right proud of him. Before, he was afraid of the thought of leaving the Montana Territory, but now all he talks about is saving up money to go east and take entrance exams for medical school."

Rebeccah blinked, so stunned by this turn of the conversation that for a moment she thought the floor beneath her feet was shifting like a seesaw. "I didn't realize," she managed at last.

Yes, she had talked to Toby Pritchard about Harvard's Medical School, but she had never realized that her words had had such an effect. "That's wonderful," she murmured.

Abigail Pritchard bobbed her head. "Yes, it certainly is. My husband, Culley, and I are great believers in higher education and in bettering oneself. We own the Triple Star Ranch, you know—it's the largest spread in the territory. That's not bragging, either, Miss Rawlings, for all these ladies will tell you, it's just the plain, simple truth. Culley's ambitious, and he works hard, and he's earned every penny we've put into that ranch. And we did it so our children could prosper and make the most of themselves. Well, it's just plagued me to death that we've gone so long without a proper schoolteacher, and that's why my Culley stood up at that town meeting when Sheriff Bodine spoke on your behalf, and my Culley said, 'Give the girl a chance.'

And I'm so glad folks did. Do you have an escort for the dance tonight?" she asked suddenly.

Rebeccah wondered if all those women's heads really craned closer in order to better hear her reply or if it was just her imagination.

"No, I—"

"Good. My oldest boy, Waylon, whom I believe you've met, will come by to pick you up. We can't have our pretty new schoolteacher dashing around the dark countryside herself, now, can we? You look out for him about seven o'clock."

"But I'm not planning to attend the dance, Mrs. Pritchard," Rebeccah spoke up firmly, as firmly as one could before this forceful tornado of a woman. "It's nice of you to offer your son's time but—"

"Oh, Waylon will be pleased as punch. He told me himself that first day you came to town that you were pretty as all get out, except you had the devil of a temp—well, never mind that. Of course you'll come to the dance now that you have an escort. Have you met Lillian Duke, the mayor's wife? And this is Gussy Hamilton—her husband owns the feed store. And my neighbor's daughter from the Crooked Bar Ranch, Nel Westerly. . . ."

She droned on with other names attached to other faces, but Rebecca's attention focused solely on Nel Westerly. And Nel Westerly locked upon her with equal intentness.

She's quite beautiful, Rebeccah admitted with a pitiful sinking of the heart. She fought to keep a smile pasted on her face. Nel Westerly reminded her of a painting she'd once seen of the goddess Aphrodite emerging from the sea. She was tall and

slim and graceful, with pale, silvery hair that
flowed loosely over her shoulders. Her features
were lovely: wide-set hazel eyes, a small, daintily
uptilted nose, the slightest dusting of freckles
across smooth cheeks, and perfectly proportioned
lips. Her well-endowed figure was attractively displayed in a dark-green serge riding skirt, white
blouse, and dark-green vest fastened with jet buttons.

No wonder Wolf Bodine is taking her to the
dance tonight, Rebeccah thought in dismay. She
must be the most sought-after young woman in the
territory.

Well, fine. They will make a charming couple.

And I am going with that oaf, Waylon Pritchard.

She suppressed a sudden urge to both laugh and
cry at the same time. How did she come to this
perfectly abominable state of affairs?

It took her nearly an hour to complete all of her
purchases, what with people talking to her, asking
her questions, advising her about how to deal with
this pupil or that one, and informing her about who
was preparing which refreshments to be served at
the dance that evening, and on and on until at last
she made her escape, lugging her parcels out to the
buckboard. She could not stop reflecting on the
friendliness with which she'd been treated. After all
the warnings Wolf Bodine had thrown at her about
what to expect, she had never dreamed of this kind
of acceptance.

Then she remembered something Abigail Pritchard had said: Wolf Bodine had spoken on her behalf. Caitlin had told her the same thing. Between

his backing and Caitlin's, and Abigail Pritchard's vocal approval in the store today, the citizens of Powder Creek were responding with warmth and welcome.

After being alone at boarding school nearly all her life, accustomed to lonely isolation, Rebeccah hadn't quite known how to respond to all their questions and remarks and advice, but she had smiled and nodded and tried to listen to everyone at once. Her head was spinning by the time she set out for home, but there was a curious warm spot in the center of her heart.

At precisely seven o'clock that evening Waylon Pritchard drove into her front yard in a fancy buck-board drawn by two high-stepping matched gray mares. Rebeccah watched from behind her new blue lace curtains as he clambered out and the wind blew his hat off his head. He reclaimed it from the grass and, scowling, dusted it off on his pants leg. His expensive Sunday-best suit, derby, and polished shoes could not disguise the burly oafishness of his appearance, nor the obvious reluctance with which he stomped up to her front door. Rebeccah drew back from the window, stifling a giggle.

If ever a man looked like he wanted to be anywhere else on earth but *here,* Waylon Pritchard looked that way right now.

She couldn't help but feel sorry for him. His mother had obviously compelled him to be her escort tonight, no doubt much against his will. *I'll try to be gentle with you, Mr. Pritchard,* she promised silently as she patted her upswept hair.

The delicate muslin of her peach skirt rustled as she opened the door in response to his one short knock. For a moment as he took in her elegant appearance, the grim look faded from his large, slack-jawed face. His eyes actually widened with appreciation, and he swept off his hat in a hasty gesture.

"You look right pretty, ma'am," he said, and then his eyebrows swooped down, and he peered out anxiously at her, as though expecting her to make some viciously unkind remark in response.

Rebeccah remembered the tongue-lashing she'd given him in town that first day and decided it would be cruel to intimidate him any further. He was obviously a victim of his parents' strong wills as it was. "Well, thank you, Mr. Pritchard," she replied in her mildest tone. "You look quite presentable too."

He smiled tentatively at this promising beginning. "We'd best go, or we'll be late and miss the Virginia Reel," he said, and once more peered at her suspiciously, in anticipation of some stinging retort.

Rebeccah nodded. "Dear me, we wouldn't want to miss that."

It was a misty night, with no moon or stars visible, and a light breeze, which tickled the back of Rebeccah's neck as they drove along. She had pinned her hair up in a high chignon, leaving only a few dark tendrils curling daintily about her face, and the cool breeze felt good above the soft lace of her shawl. She and Waylon made polite conversation, mostly about his brother's medical ambitions, his family's ranch, and the rigors of shipping cattle to the eastern marketplace, but as the rig pulled up before the schoolhouse, alongside dozens of wagons and buckboards and buggies, he suddenly leaned forward with an anguished moan, stared hard at a couple walking across the open grass, and then cried, "I don't want to go!"

Startled, Rebeccah gaped at him. Then she followed the direction of his glance and saw a young woman with pale hair and a bright red dress sashaying into the schoolhouse on the arm of a red-headed cowboy.

"Who is she?"

"Coral." He bit the name out tragically. "Coral Mae Taggett. My sweetheart." Waylon groaned and snatched his derby off his head in a furious motion. He began squashing it in his big, calloused hands and grinding his teeth at the same time. "Why is she doing this to me? She no more wants to be here with that pompous weasel, Clyde Tyler, than I do with y—" Here he broke off, coloring furiously.

"You are by far the rudest, most addle-brained lout of a simpleton—" Rebeccah shouted, but as an abjectly miserable expression settled into every crease of his bristly face, she stopped herself.

"Oh, never mind!"

To her disgust Waylon Pritchard still appeared ready to burst into tears. "Don't give it another thought." She sighed, and without thinking, reached out to pat his hand. "I know perfectly well that your mother forced you to escort me to this stupid dance. But why in heaven's name didn't you just stand up to her and say no? And why didn't you ask Coral in the first place, if she means that much to you?"

Waylon's head drooped. He covered his face with his hands and spoke through thick fingers. "You don't understand."

"Then explain it to me," she ordered, curbing her impatience with an effort.

"My ma and pa both think Coral is beneath me. Because she works as a dance-hall girl at the Gold Bar Saloon." He tore his fingers away from his face and peered at Rebeccah with earnest, miserable eyes. "But she's not bad or indecent, as Ma always says. She's not! She'd like to quit, but she makes more money serving drinks and dancing with the men than she could working as a clerk in the feed mill or a maid at the hotel, and she needs money because she has a little sister living with relatives back in Missouri, and if she doesn't keep sending money, they won't be able to afford to keep her, and . . . and I'd like to marry Coral and have her little sister come live with us so I could take care of both of them but . . . but . . ."

"Yes?" Rebeccah prodded, her eyes intent. "Why don't you do it, then?"

"Because Ma and Pa won't let me!" he burst out.

She sat back and slowly shook her head. "Waylon Pritchard," she said softly, "you are by far the most . . ." She drew in a deep breath. A tongue-lashing wouldn't do. He was weak and timid and wholly browbeaten by his parents. What he needed was to be bucked up, not torn down. "Waylon," she continued more mildly, "you're a grown man. How old are you?"

"Twenty-four."

"Then you're old enough to do what you think is best. If you love Coral and you want to marry her, just go ahead and do it. No one can stop you."

"They'll be mad at me."

"So? They'll get over it when they see that it's not going to make you change your mind. And if they don't . . . well, would you rather live at the Triple Star all your life with your ma and pa? Or worse, marry some woman *they* select for you, someone you don't care a plug nickel for? Or would you rather be with Coral?"

"Coral says the same things," he muttered heavily. "But it wouldn't be easy. I'd have to move out and find work as a hand on someone else's ranch. I wouldn't be able to buy Coral any of those fancy fripperies she likes or pretty baubles like I always bring her."

"Do you think that's what Coral cares about? More than being with you?"

"Why, no, I didn't think that. At least not until now." He scowled bitterly in the direction of the schoolhouse, from which boisterous music poured out into the pine-scented night. "But if she's willing to come to this dance with Clyde Tyler, maybe she doesn't really love me at all."

Rebeccah sighed. "I'll wager she's mad at you for bringing me and not her. Did you tell her you were going to?"

He nodded, still scowling.

"Was she furious?"

"She threw all them pretty wildflowers I brought her straight at my head."

"Waylon Pritchard, what you need to do is march straight into that schoolhouse and ask Coral Mae Taggett to dance."

"Right in front of everyone?"

"Right in front of everyone."

"But Ma and Pa will be there!"

She gritted her teeth in frustration. One glance at his shocked face and darting, anxious eyes destroyed the rest of her patience. "Fine," she snapped, and hitched her shawl across her shoulders. She didn't wait for him to assist her from the buckboard, but jumped lightly down by herself. "Then I suggest you go stand in a corner somewhere and wring your hands all evening while you watch Coral dance with Clyde Tyler. Don't expect me to dance with you, either, because I won't stand up with a man who's too scared to stand up for himself," she flung at him, and began stalking toward the schoolhouse.

Waylon hurried to catch up with her. "You've got a danged ugly temper for such a pretty gal," he sputtered as he pulled open the schoolhouse door for her.

"Thank you!" she shot over her shoulder, and Waylon wasn't sure if she was thanking him for his comment or for holding open the door.

The long, solemn room with its desks, stools, maps, blackboard, and teacher's desk had been transformed into a gaily festooned dance hall rollicking with festivity. A table draped with a checkered cloth had been set up along one wall, and it held platters of cakes and pies and cookies, pitchers of lemonade, homemade cherry brandy, and huckleberry wine. Brightly colored ginghams and calicos spun in a dazzling blur as the floor vibrated with dancers. The whirling, stomping couples in their Sunday best cavorted with more spirit than grace to the fiddlers' soaring tune, and amid laughter and shouts and the buzz of excited talk, everyone looked happy, busy, and lighthearted.

Rebeccah at once spotted Coral and Clyde Tyler spinning across the crowded floor. She studied the girl closely. Beneath Coral's vibrant smile and the determined batting of her eyelashes, she detected pallor, and an air of forced gaiety.

Waylon Pritchard, you couldn't see the Mississippi River if it was coursing up over your knees, she thought in disgust. And then she heard Waylon's voice at her elbow.

"All right, I'm going to do it. Just like you said, Miss Rawlings. I'm going to ask her to dance in front of everyone."

Before she could offer a word of encouragement (and before he could lose his nerve), Waylon darted across the room, shouldering his way through the dancers, and pounded the red-haired cowboy's shoulder with his fist. Then suddenly Clyde was searching for a new partner, and Waylon and Coral twirled by, holding tightly to each other. Their gazes were locked on each other's faces with such rapt expressions that suddenly, unexpectedly, Rebeccah felt her throat tighten with emotion.

Then someone was tapping her on the shoulder, and she spun around, startled into a reaction of instinctive fear.

"Whoa, sweet thing, don't look so scared," a slender, dark-haired man said, catching her chin in his hand. He swept his wide-brimmed Stetson off his head with his other hand and grinned at her. "A lady as lovely as you should never be without a dancing partner," he continued gaily. "Won't you let me fix that right now?"

He had wavy black hair, magnetic, solidly handsome features, and incredibly beautiful eyes of a clear moss-green hue. Over his right shoulder she saw Wolf Bodine near the window, looking relaxed, nonchalant, and vividly handsome as he leaned forward to listen intently to something Nel Westerly was saying to him.

"I'd be delighted," she heard herself muttering grimly, and then she was whisked into a strong grip and swept across the floor to the tune of "Turkey in the Straw," and she had no more time to dwell on the tight pain that squeezed her heart.

13 Images rushed by in a blur: Caitlin Bodine, seated on a ladder-back chair, clapping in time to the music; Billy Bodine, Joey Brady, and some other boys playing a wild game of tag among the chattering onlookers; Culley and Abigail Pritchard eyeing the dance floor in frozen displeasure; Myrtle Lee Anderson stuffing a wedge of pie into her mouth. Dozens of other faces swirled by, but she didn't see and didn't want to see Wolf Bodine and Nel Westerly side by side together.

She was out of breath when the dance ended, her cheeks glowing above the white lace collar of her peach gown. Her dancing partner—she didn't even know his name—lightly held her elbow and guided her off the crowded dance floor and over to the table where refreshments were served.

"For you, the prettiest lady here," he said, handing her a glass of huckleberry wine.

"You're too kind, Mr. . . ."

"Call me Chance."

"Chance?"

He nodded, took a deep drink of the wine, and grinned at her, his teeth flashing very white and straight in his sun-bronzed, boyish face. The green eyes danced. "Chance Navarro."

"An unusual name."

He was watching her sip her wine, smiling a little. "Yup. I made it up. Like the sound of it, I reckon."

"What was wrong with your real name, Mr. Navarro?"

"You ask a lot of questions for such a pretty lady, Miss Rawlings," he drawled.

Now Rebeccah lowered the empty wineglass and stared at him for a long moment. "How did you know my name?"

Chance Navarro set his glass down on the refreshment table and put both of his hands on her shoulders. He turned her around toward the sea of people watching the fiddlers and the dancing. "That lady there . . . in the blue dress?"

"Mrs. Brady," Rebeccah murmured, half to herself.

"Well, Mrs. Brady said to Mr. Brady the moment you and that big fellow walked in the door: 'Caitlin told me Miss Rawlings wasn't coming to the dance tonight, and here she is with Waylon Pritchard. I'm sure glad she changed her mind, aren't you?' And Mr. Pritchard said . . ."

"Do you always eavesdrop on other people's conversations?" Rebeccah demanded, her eyes narrowing as she inspected his wickedly smiling face.

"Only when they're discussing the most beautiful lady in the Territory."

"You're a flatterer, Mr. Navarro."

"No, I'm a gambler, Miss Rawlings. And tonight

I'm gambling everything on making you fall in love with me, ma'am."

"Now, why would you want to do that?" Rebeccah found herself smiling in spite of herself. Chance Navarro had charm, looks, and . . . something else. A happy-go-lucky, mischievous, carefree air that intrigued her. She turned her head slightly as he gave his lighthearted reply and pretended to watch the dancers, but her gaze was really observing the cluster of bright-gowned women fluttering around Sheriff Wolf Bodine.

They were gathered behind a group of chairs where some onlookers sat holding glasses of lemonade or cups of coffee. Nel Westerly, charmingly attired in a pink-sprigged gown and pink kid slippers, with pink and white ribbons fetchingly arranged in her pale upswept hair, laughed the loudest. Rebeccah didn't know the others, but guessed that the slim, auburn-haired woman in the sea-green muslin might be Lorelie Simpson. It was bad enough that two women fawned over him, but four? Rebeccah had no idea who they all were, but Wolf Bodine looked positively surrounded by adoring feminine faces and trills of enthusiastic laughter. So much for mourning his dead wife. The man looked as calmly content, at ease, and good-spirited as she had ever seen him. His blue shirt fit snugly over his broad shoulders and wide chest, accentuating the corded muscles and revealing, just beneath the throat, a thatch of dark, curly chest hair. Dark trousers encased his strong, powerful legs and were tucked into handsomely polished boots. He had hung his hat on a hook near

the schoolroom door and was bare-headed, showing off the neatly combed locks of silky chestnut
hair. And even from this distance Rebeccah could
see the dusk-gray glint of his eyes as he regarded
first one of those fawning women and then another,
his glance moving easily around the attentive
group. And then he saw her.

Their gazes locked, and held. The keen gray eyes
sharpened. He said something to the women, and
they parted to let him pass.

He was coming toward her.

"Let's dance," she said breathlessly to Chance
Navarro, and seized his hand.

"My pleasure, ma'am," he responded gaily, and
let himself be dragged onto the floor.

From the corner of her eyes Rebeccah saw Wolf
stop dead and scowl. She pasted a sunshine-bril-
liant smile on her face and directed every dazzling
ray of it at Chance. He whirled her faster, held her
tighter, and laughed at her delighted gasp. Then
Rebeccah let the music and the wine and the dizzying motion swallow her up so that she noticed
nothing but her own feet flying across the floorboards and the giddy sensation of light-headed-
ness, induced, she told herself, by having such a
great deal of fun.

Wolf watched her dance in the stranger's arms.
She looked so damned happy. She never looked
like that when she was with him.

Gloom settled over him. For a woman who was
always stumbling over buckets or falling out of
wagons, she danced like the most graceful creature
on earth. And what was worse, he'd never seen her

look more beautiful. Whether it was the luscious peach color of her gown or the way her cheeks were flushed a radiant pink or the way her eyes sparkled like sunlit pansies in the bright lantern light, Rebeccah Rawlings outshone every other woman here.

He waited until the country reel was over and then he strode toward her again. She was still talking to that damned stranger, the one who'd sat in the back at the town meeting. Chance Navarro, that was his name. He was a gambler, Wolf had learned from Molly. One with plenty of money and a barrelful of nerve.

Wolf kept his gaze fixed on Rebeccah as he advanced straight toward her. She was thirstily drinking a glass of wine. But before he could reach her, Waylon Pritchard suddenly appeared at her side and led her onto the dance floor.

Wolf froze in his tracks. "Son of a bitch!"

"I beg your pardon?" Lorelie Simpson came out of nowhere and laid a slender hand upon his sleeve. As he glanced distractedly down at her, she slanted him a winsome smile. "It looks like you're on your way to the refreshment table. Mind if I join you? I haven't had a chance to taste Caitlin's strawberry pie yet, and everyone knows it's the best in the Territory."

"It is. Reckon you'll enjoy it. But if you'll excuse me, Lorelie, there's something important I have to do."

Wolf vaguely heard her disappointed sigh as he stalked away, but he immediately forgot all about her. Bearing down on Waylon and Rebeccah pa-

thetically trying to waltz, he caught Rebeccah's
eye. She at once averted her gaze and fixed it upon
Waylon's broad face as Wolf closed in on them.

"And Ma and Pa probably won't speak to me for
days, but I don't care because Coral says I'm the
only man she ever wants to marry, and I owe it all
to you, Miss Rawlings . . . What . . . Oh, Sheriff . . ."

"Mind if I cut in, Waylon?"

Wolf didn't even spare a glance at Pritchard,
however; he was staring determinedly at the slender dark-haired vixen with the sweetest mouth
he'd ever tasted. Without bothering to listen for
the other man's reply, he seized Rebeccah in his
arms. The music blared as he swung her out among
the throng of dancers.

Rebeccah felt light as a daisy. Wolf's arm was so
tight and hard around her waist, it seemed as if all
the breath was squeezed right out of her.

"I thought you weren't coming to the dance, Miss
Rawlings."

"Don't believe everything you hear, Sheriff."

"Wolf."

She tilted her head to one side as if baffled.

"I'm not certain we know each other well enough
to go by given names, Sher—"

He stepped on her toe. On purpose, she was certain.

"Ouch!" Violet fire shot from her eyes.

Wolf drew her even nearer against him, holding
her so tightly, she thought her ribs would crack.
Yet his nearness was warmly delicious, and the
hardness of his body crushing against hers caused

tingles from her shoulder blades to the delicate arches of her kid-slippered feet.

"You had no trouble calling me by my given name the other night," he reminded her, his breath rustling against her cheek. The cool gleam in his eyes was at odds with the vibrant warmth of his body. "In your kitchen. Before Billy walked in."

"I don't recall."

"Liar. Do you remember the night I drove you home from supper?"

"The night you walked out just as Caitlin was about to serve the meal? Oh, yes, I remember that."

Wolf's eyes darkened to opaque charcoals. "That's not the part I'm talking about, Rebeccah. As you know damn well."

"Some things are best left forgotten," she replied tartly. But she was having difficulty keeping up the conversation and reminding herself not to simply melt against him. His nearness, the soap and spice and leather scent of his skin, the sexual heat of his glance, were all having an effect on her senses. She had dreamed of dancing with Wolf Bodine, she had imagined it while gazing into campfires and while peering out the window of Miss Wright's Academy at the wishing star. Now here she was, warm and flushed and dizzy from wine, with the most virilely handsome man she'd ever met waltzing her around a crowded room, and she had to fight the hazardous impulse to clasp her arms around his neck and brazenly kiss him, here in front of everyone.

Imagine Myrtle Lee Anderson's face. And Mayor Duke's. And Waylon Pritchard's.

She giggled.

"What's so funny?"

"Nothing. Everything." A peal of laughter broke from her, and Wolf studied her closely.

"You're drunk, Rebeccah."

Still laughing, she shook her head. Then she blinked as the room swam. Colors ran crazily one into the other.

"I'm . . . dizzy," she whispered in surprise. Putting a hand to her head, she closed her eyes.

He stopped dancing and tugged her toward the door, adroitly steering past the people gathered in bunches, many of whom called out greetings. He pulled her out into the cool mist of the night and around the corner of the schoolhouse, where there were no windows or doors, only an old tree stump set in the midst of the buffalo grass.

"Sit down. Breathe."

He stood over her as she perched on the tree stump and obediently took great gulps of air. "Better?"

For answer she giggled. "Bear used to say that no one could get drunk by drinking wine. It had to be whiskey or bourbon or Tarantula Juice . . . but not wine. Well, he must've been wrong, because I only had two glasses of huckleberry wine and I'm ridiculously drunk and—"

"Haven't you ever had wine before, Rebeccah?"

She gave a peal of laughter and then hiccuped and giggled again. "No. We weren't allowed spirits at Miss Wright's Academy for Young Ladies. Miss Wright wouldn't have heard of it, and Miss Althea—that's the vice principal—wouldn't have heard of it, and Miss Youngston—that's the headmistress—she wouldn't have heard of it, and—"

"I get the picture."

She peeped up at him, and a dreamy smile came over her face.

"Oh, *Wolf,*" she murmured with a great, gusty, longing sigh.

He regarded her suspiciously. "What?"

"Nothing. Just *Wolf.*" There was a beatific glow in her eyes. "Do you know how many times I've *dreamed* of dancing with you? Millions. Millions and millions. And do you know how many times I've positively ached to hear you say, 'Miss Rawlings, may I have the infinite pleasure of kissing you?' She lifted beseeching eyes to his startled face. "Oh, come here and give me one little teensy kiss," she begged.

He was looking at her as if she'd gone loco. Which she had. My, being drunk felt so strange. And yet, it was rather pleasant—foggy and silly and pleasant. And here she was with Wolf, and he looked so handsome, she just couldn't resist him anymore, and she held out her arms and surged to her feet. And would have fallen, but he grabbed her up like he always did and held her close. His arms were supporting her because her knees had buckled like paper, and he wore the most adorable worried expression on his face. Rebeccah gazed blissfully into his eyes.

"One kiss," she pleaded. "Come on, Mr. Lawman Bodine, one teensy kiss right here," and she pointed to her full, pouting lips.

"You're more than drunk, you're rip-roaring

drunk," he accused her ruefully, but his eyes were warm with laughter. "Who would ever expect to see the stiff-necked Miss Rebeccah Rawlings in such condition," he mused, one hand sliding up to grip her delicate nape as she tilted her head back to stare at him. "I could take advantage of you right now, Rebeccah," he continued softly as her eyes rested earnestly, longingly on his face. "Did you really dream about dancing with me? Since when?"

"Since that time in the cabin when you found me hiding under the cot. I've thought and thought about you . . . oh, a thousand times. Wolf, don't you *want* to kiss me? At first I thought you did and then I thought you didn't and now I think you do, but perhaps you don't—and if you want to, you can, but if you don't want to, I'm going to die, and if you want to—"

He kissed her. Just to shut her up. He felt her soft, delicious mouth pulse to life beneath his, and his arms swept around her, hauling her up against him. He kissed her hard, to quieten her. She kissed him back. Clingingly. Her breasts were crushed against his chest, he could feel the soft, full mounds burning through the fabric of his shirt. He kissed her again, his mouth plundering hers, thinking he would shock her and snap her out of this giddy mood, but she only gave a whimper of pleasure and snuggled closer against him. Her fingers slid gentle as feathers through his hair.

"Oh, God, Rebeccah," he groaned, and then he was lowering her to the ground beside the tree stump, lying with her in the crisp gold-brown buffalo grass, and her hair was somehow unpinned from its ladylike chignon and fanned about her on the earth, and her moist, bright lips were parted, inviting him, and her arms stretched out to gather him close, and only then did Wolf remember that she was not herself.

"I can't . . . do this," he muttered in a tortured rasp, and pulled back even as Rebeccah tugged him close.

"What's wrong?" Her eyes filled with tears. Beautiful crystal tears that glistened in the night. "Oh, Wolf, you do hate me, don't you? I thought you did, and then I thought you didn't, and then I thought that, well, maybe you did, but I hoped you didn't, and I knew that *I* didn't hate you, even though I might have *said* I did, or maybe I just *pretended* that I did, but that's because I thought *you* did . . . and . . ."

"Oh, hell," Wolf crushed his mouth to hers. She tasted like wine and honey and sweet, summer flowers. He wanted to drown himself in her taste, her scent, her softness. At last he dragged himself away with an effort, every muscle in his body straining. "Rebeccah, will you shut up? If you remember any of this, you're going to hate yourself tomorrow morning. And I think too highly of you to go ahead and take advantage of your . . . condition, but it sure isn't easy to resist you, not ever, and especially when you're . . . like this. But I'll be damned if I'm going to just sit here and listen to you babble on about a pack of nonsense."

Rebeccah traced a finger along his rugged jaw. Smiling up at him, she wished he would lean down and kiss her again, and touch her all over and take off all of her clothes and let her take off all of his. . . .

"Wolf," she began, rubbing the tip of her finger down his jaw, along his neck, letting it lightly caress the mat of chest hair above his open shirt collar, "I would be so happy if you would take off all my—"

"What in tarnation is going on out here?"

Lying on the grass, they both jumped. Above them towered Waylon Pritchard. And coming up behind him was Coral Mae Taggett, with Myrtle Lee Anderson, Nel Westerly, and Chance Navarro following right behind.

Like a buzzing horde of mosquitoes, Wolf reflected in no small irritation.

"Goodness," Rebeccah remarked, letting her head flop back into the grass so that she was staring straight up at the sky. "Who invited all of these people?"

"What's goin' on here, Wolf?" Waylon demanded. "Is Miss Rawlings sick or something?"

"I'm drunk, you fool," Rebeccah shouted before Wolf could say a word.

Coral Mae Taggett's pretty green eyes widened, and then she covered her smiling mouth with her hand. "Can I get you anything, Miss Rawlings?" she asked solicitously, though her voice quivered.

"This is a fine kettle of fish," Myrtle Lee proclaimed. "Our schoolmarm is inebriated!"

"It's all my fault, ma'am," Chance Navarro spoke up quickly. He flashed his disarming smile at Myrtle Lee, who, to everyone's surprise, smiled uncertainly back. "I kept the lady so busy dancing, she was exceedingly thirsty, and I reckon I supplied her with wine when it should have been lemonade. Anyone can see she's not the type who's used to liquor. All she had was two glasses, but I reckon since she's not used to drinking, it was too much for her."

"Maybe you should arrest her, Wolf, for drunken misconduct," Nel Westerly said lightly, but there was a taut undercurrent to her voice, and in the look she threw at him.

"No!" Rebeccah bolted to a sitting position at this, panic flooding her face. "Don't arrest me, Wolf. Promise me you won't lock me in that jail cell! I've always been terrified of jails! Bear used to talk about what it was like all the time, after he spent some time in a New Mexico jail. Wolf, please, you can't arrest me!"

"Nobody's going to arrest you, Rebeccah!" Wolf told her harshly. But one look at the sheer desperation on her lovely face and his tone softened. "I'm taking you home, that's all."

"What about me?" Nel asked, her eyes narrowing as the lawman scooped the limp Miss Rawlings into his arms.

"I'll be back directly. Soon as I get Miss Rawlings safely into bed."

"Maybe I ought to come with you. With Miss Rawlings in this condition, you might need a woman's help."

"Waylon and I can see her home," Coral Mae Taggett interrupted, stepping forward with a shy smile. "Waylon was her escort tonight, so it's only right.

And besides, I'd like to help you, Miss Rawlings," she added quietly.

But Chance Navarro gently eased her aside and came up to plant himself before Wolf and Rebeccah. "I feel responsible for this situation," he said ruefully. He tilted his head and smiled beguilingly into Rebeccah's overflushed face. "Ma'am, it would be my pleasure, and my duty as a gentleman, to see you safely to your home."

Rebeccah smiled mistily back at him.

A little silence fell over the crowd gathered near the tree stump. Then Nel smoothed her skirt.

"You see, Wolf," she said, with a sweet, careful smile, "Miss Rawlings has so very many friends. Why don't you let Waylon take her home, or this nice gentleman here—"

"Wolf!" Rebeccah announced in a clear, firm tone. "I want Wolf Bodine to take me home. No one else!"

Myrtle Lee Anderson drew in her breath. "Hussy!" she gasped.

"Ma'am?" Wolf turned on her coldly, and she withered a little beneath his steely glance.

"I said Gussy—Gussy Hamilton. She's waiting for me inside. If you'll excuse me . . ."

Wolf started toward the buckboard on the other side of the school building with Rebeccah in his arms. Waylon and Coral made way for him to pass while Chance Navarro and Nel watched in silence.

Suddenly Nel gathered her ruffly skirts and ran after Wolf.

"Don't bother your head over *me,*" she cried as he lifted Rebeccah into the rig. "I know Caitlin and

Billy are going home with the Bradys, so you needn't bother about them. And I'm certain Clyde Tyler or Mr. Navarro or *some* other gentleman will see me home, so there's no need at all for you to hurry back. I certainly wouldn't want you to drive all the way back here out of a mere sense of obligation."

"Nel, I'm sorry," Wolf began quietly, but she gave her head a quick shake and then flashed him the famous Westerly smile that could light up a desert.

"Sure you are. And you'll be even sorrier next time you come to call when my pa runs you clear off our land!"

And she was gone, dashing back inside the schoolhouse, with Chance Navarro holding open the door.

"Well, I reckon she told *you*," Rebeccah commented sagely as she slumped against him in the buckboard. Her fingers curled around the soft fabric of his shirt. Warmth and strength emanated from his body. She gave a deep, contented sigh.

Wolf found he had to keep one arm around her while he was driving the team to keep her from falling.

"Did anyone ever tell you you're more trouble than a skunk in a barnyard?" he asked as the horses ambled down the uneven road.

"Nope. But Bear used to tell me that I had more mischief in me than a litter of kittens. I think I'd rather be compared to a kitten than a skunk, Wolf. Couldn't you think of me more as a kitten?"

"I reckon."

"Well, then?" she persisted, her head nestled against his shoulder.

He could feel her hair softly tickling his neck.

"Please don't ever call me a skunk again. Skunks smell. It's a terrible thing to say to a lady. In all my daydreams about you, you never ever once said I smelled like a skunk . . ."

"I didn't say it now, either, Rebeccah. I said . . . oh, never mind."

"Wolf?"

"What is it?"

"Do you really think I smell like a skunk?"

The buckboard jolted over a rut. His arm tightened around her as she bounced against him in the seat. He breathed in the light, tantalizing flower scent of her and felt his loins growing heavy and hard. "I think you smell like lilacs and rosewater and the wild violets that grow in the river valleys in summer."

"You do?"

"I do. Rebeccah?"

"Hmmm?" Her voice was dreamy.

"What was Fess Jones doing at your cabin?"

Rebeccah yawned. She felt so comfortable here in the buckboard with Wolf holding her tight. It was almost as nice, in a different way, as when he kissed her, but not quite the same. . . .

"What was he doing there, Rebeccah?"

"Trying to kill me."

"Why?"

"Because I wouldn't tell him anything about the deed to the silver mine . . . or give him the map . . . or . . . anything."

"Why not?"

"There isn't any mine. Or any deed. Or any map." She snuggled closer. "But he doesn't believe me. None of them believe me. You believe me, don't you, Wolf? I would know if there was a silver mine. Bear would have told me. It doesn't exist. Wolf . . ."

"What?"

"I'm sleepy."

"Then go to sleep."

"Will you wake me when we get home? I have to check . . . everything. Make sure no one's there. . . ."

"I'll check for you, Rebeccah," he said, a strange tenderness echoing quietly beneath the simple words. "You don't have to worry."

I don't have to worry. Wolf will check everything for me. I can sleep . . . just this once . . . and not worry. . . .

Wolf glanced down at the lovely woman curled trustingly against him. She was sound asleep, looking as peaceful and innocent as a child. Or a kitten. *Damn.* He did not like feeling the way he was feeling right now about Rebeccah Rawlings.

It was the last thing in the world he wanted.

He scowled to himself as the narrow road leading to the cabin came into view. A short time later the team drew up before the darkened house. The scudding clouds overhead parted for a moment, revealing a fuzzy shimmer of moon. In the feeble light Wolf studied her fine-boned face, noting the sweep of her eyelashes above delicate cheeks, the spill of midnight hair as soft as satin, the way her slender fingers curled against his arm.

Something twisted painfully inside him.

He gathered her in his arms and carried her to the house.

14 Rebeccah roused herself when he set her down across the bed. As Wolf lit the candle on the bureau, she struggled up on her elbows, trying to get her bearings. A little glow of light, and then shadows flickered softly in the room, and she could make out his commanding form only a few feet away. She blinked. Her brain was still fuzzy. A light, giddy feeling still floated through her. The blue lace curtains fluttered at the window, anchoring her somehow despite the shifting haze.

"You're home." His strong, calm voice came to her with a ring of quiet comfort, and she relaxed.

"Home, home on the range," she began to sing softly, off-key.

"What am I going to do with you?" he growled.

That stopped her. She threw him a dazzling smile. "Wolf," she said. Her voice was low, soft, eager.

He stood over her, every bit as tense as she was dreamy.

"Yeah?"

"Don't leave me."

"You're perfectly safe, Rebeccah. I've checked

the cabin. You've got a derringer under your pillow, loaded, but I suppose you know that."

"Mmm-hmm. But . . . I'm still dizzy. I couldn't hit a barn with a peashooter," she whispered, reaching for his hand.

He hesitated. Her slim fingers clutching his triggered a sharp reaction deep in his gut. "I'll bring you some coffee."

"No!" She gripped his hand tighter and sat up so quickly, the room leaped wildly before her giddy eyes. "Don't leave me," she said breathily, her voice catching in her throat. "Not yet. Just sit here for a little while so I can sleep and feel . . . safe. It's been so long since I felt safe."

"Why, Rebeccah?" He sat down on the bed, enclosing her hand in his. With his other hand he stroked her hair. Each little movement of his fingers seemed to calm her, and that realization played havoc with his insides. "Because of the men who are after the silver mine?"

"Yes. But they can't get to me when you're here. Not even Neely Stoner. . . ."

"Who's he?"

Her eyes were wide. "A very bad man. One of Bear's gang—until Bear kicked him out."

"Why did he do that?"

This question penetrated her haze. He saw those enchanting violet eyes struggle to focus. She peered into his face as if wondering how much she could tell him, how much she could trust him, and her fingers clung to his with a frantic need.

"Because of what he did to me," she whispered. Suddenly she sat up and gripped his shoulders in her slender hands. "Don't ask me any more, Wolf," she begged. "I can't talk about it. Just promise that you'll stay tonight, just stay with me."

"Hush, Rebeccah, I'm staying."

A glorious smile was his reward. She moved shyly against him and nestled her head upon his broad chest. "Thank . . . you," she said with a sigh.

Wolf sat there a long time, holding her, feeling her womanly softness against him, listening to the hushed rhythm of her breathing. She felt so fragile and vulnerable in his arms.

What had Neely Stoner done to her?

He knew the answer, knew it instinctively, without her putting it into words. He remembered her panic when he'd fallen on top of her that day the water had spilled, remembered the stark terror in her eyes.

Rape.

He stroked her hair, trying to take in the brutality she'd known, trying to obliterate it from her with the gentleness of his touch. And all the while a deadly rage took hold within him. The thought that she had been hurt, not only hurt but viciously brutalized, made him feel as if he'd been pummeled in the stomach until all the breath was knocked out of him. And it made him want to kill. Wolf hadn't felt that way in a long time. He killed in his line of work now and then, when it was necessary, when there was no other way, but he took no pleasure from it and never had. There was no meanness in Wolf Bodine, not an ounce of cruelty. He valued life and respected death. He took neither lightly. But if he ever got his hands on Neely Stoner . . .

As Rebeccah gave a little whimper, Wolf realized that he'd unconsciously dug his fingers into her flesh. He forced himself to relax, ran his hands soothingly over her back, and turned his thoughts away from what had been done to her.

When he realized she had fallen asleep, he lowered her down upon her pillow. She curled innocently on her side, one knee drawn up beneath the peach gown. He thought about removing the dress for her, but figured he'd better not. It was twisted around her long legs and her hips, fully revealing the sumptuous curves of her body. His gaze lingered on the provocative swell of her breasts beneath the thin fabric, then shifted to the rounded curve of her buttocks.

Wolf smiled appreciatively. Beneath that cold, thorny go-to-hell exterior Rebeccah Rawlings was a hungrily passionate, adorably romantic woman. Whatever Neely Stoner had done to her miraculously had not destroyed her feminine instincts or desires. Having kissed her thoroughly, he knew that for a fact. She was passionate all right—not to mention delectably lovely. She'd come a long way from that scrawny kid in Arizona who'd spit in his face and tried to claw his eyes out.

Hell, he wondered suddenly, had she really thought about him—what did she say—a thousand times since that first day?

She'd been just a bratty kid then. No, he realized with a jolt, she'd been a young, impressionable girl. He'd never thought about it that way. But, looking

back, he could see how it had been. He'd been
barely twenty at the time and must have cut a romantic enough figure to her eyes, romantic enough
to inspire a budding young woman's silly fancy.

And she'd nourished it all these years. Only to
come face-to-face with him here in Powder Creek—
and then what? She'd found sharp disillusionment,
that's what. The object of her dreams and memories was ten years older and considerably tough-
ened by life. He had nearly thrown her out of his
town. She'd discovered that he'd married someone
else and had a kid.

So her girlish dreams had died a quick death,
right?

But then he remembered all those things she had
said in the cool, misty darkness behind the schoolhouse, when she was too tipsy from huckleberry
wine to think about what was pouring out of her.
Rebeccah Rawlings still had feelings for him, however she behaved outwardly. Were they just cold
leftovers of those feelings of long ago, those girlish
imaginings, or was it something more? Something
deeper, truer?

It didn't matter. He had to stay away from her, as
of right now. Or at least as of the morning. He
wouldn't leave her here alone tonight—he had
given his word. But come morning he'd have to put
a stop to seeing her, and kissing her. Why the hell
had he been doing all that kissing anyway, he wondered angrily. He'd known from the moment she'd
landed in town that she was nothing but trouble—
and he was right. Now she was luring every two-bit
outlaw this side of the Mississippi to Montana be-

cause of some deed to a silver mine she may or may not have.

Rebeccah Rawlings was pure, unadulterated trouble. Wolf frowned at her sleeping form as she curled a hand beneath her cheek. Clarissa had caused him enough trouble to last a lifetime. Now he needed someone steady and uncomplicated and kind, someone who would help him give his son a calm, happy home. Rebeccah Rawlings, with her wild past and starchy airs and mysterious enemies, was the last woman he needed in his life—or in Billy's.

But now the hell of it was he'd have to find a way to protect her—and stay away from her at the same time. He couldn't afford to encourage any schoolgirlish fancies she might still be clinging to. But he couldn't leave her to stand alone against those low-down buzzards who were swarming down on her either.

Give her no encouragement, he told himself, slipping his hand free of hers. She murmured in her sleep and rolled onto her back, throwing an arm carelessly above her head, an innocent, defenseless posture.

Wolf reached out and smoothed a lock of hair from across her eyes. How could anyone who looked so sweet, so utterly, angelically beautiful when she was asleep, be so disagreeably tart-tongued and difficult when she was awake?

It doesn't matter, he told himself. *You're steering clear of her, remember? There's Nel you've got to patch things up with, and don't forget about Lorelie.* Yet, though he enjoyed the company of both women, and found them each in their own way attractive, intelligent, and warm, neither excited him the way Rebeccah Rawlings did. Neither had her wit, her stinging tongue, her stubbornness, her furious independence. Or her courage, Wolf realized slowly. She's been terrorized by outlaws over this silver mine for a while now, but she's never asked for help. Never even spoken of it to a soul.

"Brave girl," he said softly, touching her cheek with a tentative finger. She was soft and smooth as silk, and his loins suddenly ached as he gazed at her.

Not since Clarissa had any woman stirred such powerful feelings in him. *Damn it, I don't want this,* something in him shouted. But part of him couldn't stop looking at her there in that candlelit room, in a cabin in the middle of nowhere as the night crawled by and a bullfrog croaked outside the window, and Rebeccah Rawlings reached out in her sleep to needily clasp his hand.

15 Morning sun sparkled through the window and splashed honeyed light across the floor, the rug, and the bed. The air was fragrant with pine. Fresh and invigorating, it pranced in, blowing through the window on a boisterous autumn breeze, while a magpie chattered noisily in the spruce tree, and from the yard came the sounds of someone chopping wood.

Rebeccah pushed herself from the murk of sleep and groaned. Her head hurt. Her temples throbbed. And her mouth felt as if she'd been chewing wet sand. *What's happened? What's wrong with me? And who's outside, chopping wood?*

She tried to sit up, grunted, and fell back. Gritting her teeth, Rebeccah tried again and this time managed to swing her legs to the floor. She stayed there a moment, getting her bearings, and trying to sort through the layers of gauze clogging her brain.

The dance. The schoolhouse. The wine. A man named Chance. And Wolf Bodine.

The last thing she remembered was dancing the waltz with Wolf Bodine.

Oh, God, what did I do? Did I get drunk?

Somehow she tottered across the room to the

window, stumbling over the rag rug along the way and stubbing her toe on the floor.

Moaning as the sunlight assaulted her eyes, she squinted out at the large figure chopping wood behind the cabin.

It was *him*.

He was bare-chested, wearing only boots, the tight-fitting trousers he'd worn to the dance last night, and his gunbelt. A faint sheen of sweat glistened across his wide, dark-bronzed chest and midriff as he hefted the ax over the logs again and again. Muscles rippled in that magnificently honed body. Oh, Lord. Rebeccah gripped the window ledge and swallowed hard. He was as beautiful as pure sculpted rock.

He had already accumulated a hefty stack of wood, enough to last a fair portion of the winter, Rebeccah guessed dazedly, but her racing thoughts immediately shifted from the wood to a more pressing question: Why was he here? And why couldn't she remember anything past the moment when he was twirling her around the schoolhouse floor?

Rebeccah had an uneasy feeling about all this. She stiffened when Wolf glanced over, saw her at the window, and set down the ax. To her consternation he began strolling toward her.

"You look like hell," he remarked, pausing outside the window to regard her through narrowed eyes.

She fought not to stare at that sturdy chest lightly matted with crisp, coppery hair. "What are you doing on my property, Sheriff Bodine?"

She thought she detected a glint of rich amusement in his eyes, but all he said was, "You invited me. Matter of fact you insisted I stay on your property last night—all night."

"I . . . did?"

"Yep."

Dismay filled her lovely face. Wolf couldn't help the grin that twitched at the stern lines of his mouth.

"I figure that after playing nursemaid, guard, and wood chopper, you at least owe me breakfast," he informed her casually.

Now, why the hell did I say that? Get the hell out of here. Ride away while you still can. But he couldn't. Looking at her, talking with her, was destroying all his good intentions.

Even with a hangover she looked like an angel. Her hair tumbled softly around her face and drifted anyhow across her shoulders, giving her a sexily mussed-up look that made him itch to run his hands over her. Her eyes looked larger than ever in the paleness of her face, and her lips trembled ever so slightly with the aftereffects of the wine. But she was now drawing herself up straight and tall, fastening her dignity around her like an iron corset, and her words bit out at him like springing vipers.

"You have a number of things to answer for, Sheriff Bodine, and I expect you to explain yourself fully at breakfast. But you'll have to clean yourself up and dress decently if you're going to sit down to a meal at my table." And she yanked the window shut and then the curtains with a vicious tug, leaving him to stare at nothing but crisp blue lace.

"Fair enough, Miss Rawlings," Wolf muttered to himself as he headed toward the stream. "But don't expect me to answer any more of your questions than you did of mine."

By the time Rebeccah had performed a hasty toilette, tugged on a denim skirt and scoop-necked Mexican blouse, and brushed the tangles from her hair, the sun was riding well up in the sky and Wolf Bodine had disappeared. As she threw bacon and eggs in a pan and cut thick slices of bread, she wondered if he had gone home.

"I hope so," she said out loud, but knew that she was lying to herself. She wanted to confront Wolf Bodine face-to-face and to question him about what had happened last night. But that's all she wanted. Just the answers to some questions. Then he could leave and, as far as she was concerned, never come back.

Rebeccah had a queasy feeling she had disgraced herself at the dance. Now the townsfolk would really talk about Bear Rawlings's daughter—they'd probably call her a no-good drunk.

And Wolf? Heaven only knew what cause she had given him, as well as the others, to scorn her.

Why had she ever gone to that stupid dance? Why had she ever come to this lonesome, run-down cabin in Powder Creek?

Just in case Wolf was still there lurking around the premises somewhere, she set two places at the table. She brewed coffee, set out a bowl of wild strawberries, and snatched the pan of sizzling eggs and bacon from the stove just as the kitchen door opened and Wolf looked in at her.

"Am I presentable enough, ma'am?" he drawled, with a quick grin that made his dimples deepen.

"You'll do, I suppose."

In truth he would more than do, but she could barely risk a peek at him. His skin glowed from the cold waters of the stream, his burnished hair was slicked back off his face, and he was wearing the snug-fitting shirt he'd worn to the dance last night. If she'd thought he was handsome in her memories, based on that one fleeting incident in the hideout in Arizona, the reality of Wolf Bodine's appeal was far more devastating. An electric magnetism seemed to draw her gaze to him anytime they were within a hundred yards of each other, and now to have him here in her kitchen, sitting down to breakfast with his hard, gray gaze studying her, his long legs stretched out beneath her table, took its toll on her composure.

She bustled around the kitchen, serving the food, pouring the coffee, delaying the moment when she sat down next to him. Her knee bumped his as she slipped into her chair. She jerked away as if scalded by hot coffee.

"Take it easy." Wolf nonchalantly picked up his fork. "There's no need to be jumpy."

"Who says I'm jumpy? I'm just curious. How . . . did you happen to spend the night . . . here?"

"I told you. You invited me, Rebeccah."

"Why would I do a thing like that? It doesn't make sense. Where did you sleep?"

He shook his head mockingly. "Don't you remember?"

"If I remembered, I wouldn't be asking!"

To her fury, he calmly forked some eggs and bacon into his mouth, swallowed, and reached for his coffee.

"Well?" she demanded at last, and nervously gulped down half a cup of black coffee, forgetting to add sugar.

"Well, what?"

"Aren't you going to tell me what happened last night? I want to know everything, from the moment we were waltzing until I woke up this morning. *Everything.*"

"Too bad, sweet Rebeccah."

"I beg your pardon?"

"I have questions too. Questions you've refused all along to answer. Maybe it's about time we worked out a deal."

She gaped at him. A deal. "Why, you low-down, conniving, snake-in-the-grass—"

His hand shot out across the table to grip her wrist, silencing her. Outside the window birds twittered loudly, but inside there was only the sound of their breathing.

"Rebeccah, tell me about the silver mine."

She drew in her breath. "It sounds like you already know about it."

"Not enough. Look, the time for you and me playing games about this is past. Fess Jones showing up here trying to cut you up like a butchered steer was no game. And this hombre Neely Stoner"—he paused as pain flitted across her face—"It sounds like he's planning to come after you too. I want to help you, Rebeccah. But I can't, not unless you give me the lowdown on these hombres and that mine they're after."

"Why do you want to help me?" she countered, aware that his fingers were scorching her wrist. She couldn't tear her gaze from those long-lashed eyes that were fixed on her with such determination.

"Because I care about you." Damn, why had he said that? Her face lit with something—hope, happiness, warmth—and a ruby blush of color stained her cheeks. Wolf could have kicked himself. "You're a part of this community," he went on quickly, keeping his tone cool. "You're my mother's friend, my son's teacher, and it's my duty to protect every citizen in Powder Creek."

Duty? His mother's friend? His son's teacher?

Something died in her, something she hadn't even realized had been alive. But it had—for one brief, glorious moment a wildly joyous hope had quivered to life. But it was dead now. As it should be. She felt deflated, empty, flat and colorless as the plains of Kansas.

"I see," she said.

"Then tell me about the silver mine," he urged relentlessly, and she could no more read the expression in his eyes than she could touch the moon.

But she told him. She pulled free of his grip, leaned back in her chair, and as the eggs and bacon grew cold on her plate, she related the tale of how Neely Stoner's hired ruffian had accosted her in Boston, demanding the deed and the map to the silver mine. It was the first she had ever heard of such a thing, but the man had made it clear that Bear Rawlings was reputed to have acquired, through fair means or foul, a vast silver mine with deposits as rich as the Comstock Lode in Virginia City. No one knew where it was located or where the deed was, but Bear Rawlings had possession of both, had been keeping them secret for years, and was rumored to be saving the mine as a gift for his daughter.

"That true?" Wolf asked.

Rebeccah pushed back her chair. She rose and paced back and forth across the sunlit kitchen. "Bear never mentioned anything about a silver mine to me. His solicitor made no mention of it either. I've already disposed of everything he left me, except this ranch—and you can see how much that's worth. But if Bear had a rich silver mine tucked away somewhere, he didn't leave a bit of it to me."

"What do you mean, you've disposed of everything but the ranch?"

She stopped in her tracks, then turned slowly to face him. Maybe it was time to be honest. Maybe if she told him the truth, he would tell her the truth about last night, about everything that had happened at the dance—and after. She had to know.

"I donated the proceeds from Bear's bank accounts and stock holdings to charitable institutions," she said quietly. "I kept only the ranch— which he won fair and square at poker. I didn't want any ill-gotten riches or anything tainted by bloodshed," she rushed on, suddenly eager to explain. "This ranch is my chance to make a clean start, to live a decent, independent life. I loved my father, you see, but I didn't love his thieving and shooting and running away. I made up my mind while I was at school that I wouldn't profit by it. Whatever I make of this ranch will be mine—the product of good, solid, honest labor. And no one can take it away from me or say a word against it. Now," she finished, meeting his gaze with a defiant tilt of her chin, "I've said all I intend to say about Bear, about the silver mine, and about this ranch. I know nothing, I have no deed, no map, and no reason at all to believe that any of them exist. They cannot exist! Bear would have told me or left them for me. He was good at planning things out, and he would have planned for me to inherit that mine. But the problem is"—and here she took a deep breath and stared out at the purple haze crowning the distant mountains—"how do I convince Neely Stoner and the others of that? They're not inclined to believe me."

Wolf was out of his chair and at her side in two long strides. He turned her to face him. "Maybe I can convince them."

"How?"

"Let me worry about that, Rebeccah."

"This is my problem, not yours, and I will not allow myself to be beholden—"

"Shut up, Rebeccah," he said impatiently, pulling her to him before he even realized what he was doing.

As he tilted her chin up, she was forced to meet his eyes. He could feel her trembling within the circle of his arms, but she didn't try to break away.

"I need to know something, Wolf," she said desperately. She moistened her lips, obviously distressed, and distracted by the magnetic power of his gaze. "What happened last night?"

"You talked a lot."

She swallowed. "About the mine? And what else?"

He slid a finger along the curve of her delicate jaw, watching the violet of her eyes darken. She was like a sparking electric wire beneath his touch. He debated telling her what she'd revealed about her dreams of kissing him and all her girlhood yearnings. He wanted to see that adorable blush tint her cheeks and her eyes widen with horror, but somehow he couldn't do that to her. Besides, it was more fun to let her squirm and wonder.

"Nothing too important," he replied casually with a wicked grin that made her wrench free of him with a shriek.

"You said you'd tell me everything!"

"I might—in time."

"Oh!"

She lifted a hand to slap him, but Wolf caught her wrist, holding it just tight enough to restrain her killer instincts, not tight enough to cause any pain. "Simmer down." He grinned. "I'm just trying to get a rise out of you. And you always seem to oblige. But if you're so set on knowing everything you said last night, here goes," he added, suddenly conscience-stricken by the real anxiety in her face. "Aside from mentioning the mine, you said you were afraid of your father's old pards."

"Oh," she murmured faintly.

"And you told me about Neely Stoner."

"I . . . told you?"

His voice softened as she took in several deep breaths. "Not in so many words, but I figured it out. He raped you, didn't he, Rebeccah?"

She gasped, tried to jerk back, was held taut where she was, and at last her head drooped forward in a defeated nod. "Yes," she whispered.

He'd known it was true, but somehow her confirmation of it was like a fist in his gut. "How old were you?" Somehow he managed to keep his voice calm.

"Tw-twelve. It was . . . not long after that day you found me in the shack. Bear . . . nearly killed him. I wished he had."

Twelve. *Twelve.* He released her abruptly, his hands coiling into taut fists that he forced down to his sides. Wolf feared that the whipcord fury flowing through every fiber of bone and muscle in his body would somehow bolt out to hurt her. And the last thing he wanted to do was hurt her.

"I'm sorry, Rebeccah." The words were woefully inadequate, particularly in view of the pain shadowing her eyes. But he said them anyway, needing to say them, his tone low and hard. "I promise you, if he ever comes near you, I'll kill him."

"I don't n-need your protection. I'm a crack shot, and I'm not afraid to use a g-gun. I'm not a defenseless child anymore."

"I know that. But . . ."

"Don't feel sorry for me!" she cried, unable to

bear the sympathy in his eyes. "I don't want your pity or your help or . . . anything!"

She shoved at his chest as hard as she could, but she didn't budge him an inch.

"Rebeccah—"

"Leave me alone," she shouted, and in frustration she spun toward the door. She needed to run, to flee from the furious emotions he aroused in her, from the memories he was forcing her to confront. She flung open the kitchen door and raced outside, her feet pounding across the yard and tears burning at her eyes as her heart ached with the desperate need to escape.

He caught her near the spruce tree. He swung her around and into his arms. "Come on, Rebeccah. Running away won't solve anything."

He was right. But she'd rather die than admit it. "What else did I say last night?" she demanded, needing to change the subject, needing to divert both of their thoughts from what had happened to her long ago. Wildly she cast about for something to distract him, for something to put them back on familiar, fighting ground. "You said you'd tell me everything," she accused suddenly, her eyes lighting. "But I don't think you have. I . . . vaguely remember saying something about . . . you . . . us. I mean, me . . ."

"You mean about how you used to dream about me kissing you?" Wolf retorted.

"I never said that!"

"You sure did."

"Liar!" Pure mortification surged through her,

making her strike out at him with feverish desperation. "For a lawman you're damned close to dishonest!" she cried. "You make up ridiculous tales just because it suits you, so that you can embarrass me, or confuse me. And," she added, struggling futilely against him, "that's twice now you've broken your word—you were supposed to tell me what happened, not what you *wish* had happened," she finished triumphantly, hit by a stroke of genius. "And another thing, Sheriff Bodine—I wish you'd stop chasing me—and kissing me. Why you keep doing that when it's clear we detest each other, I simply don't understand!"

"For an intelligent woman you're damned close to stupid," he said, echoing her words with light mockery. But there was a gentleness in his tone and in the hands that held her that made her forget about struggling. She froze and glared up at him, uncertainty holding her motionless beneath the shimmering blue sky.

Against all reason, against all of his good intentions, Wolf felt desire quickening in his blood. She was as wild as a mustang caught fresh from the hills—untamed, wary, and spooked. Wolf wanted inexplicably to gentle her.

Suddenly his mouth quirked upward at the absurdity of comparing this lovely, sensuous Rebeccah Rawlings to a horse.

"What're you smiling at?" she demanded, suspicion once more darkening her eyes.

"I'm thinking about—"

"Liar."

"Now you're hurting my feelings."

His wounded air sent a wave of irritation through her. "Oh, I forgot," she said acidly, yanking free of his arms. "Lawmen don't lie. Lawmen are good, pure, honest, upright—"

"Lawmen are men, Rebeccah," Wolf said tautly, his arms flashing out to snare her tight against him once more. Her glowing, sunlit face upturned toward him sent his blood pounding and turned his voice husky. "Flesh-and-blood men. Don't ever forget that."

How could I? Rebeccah wondered dazedly, when he was kissing her with such succulent, demanding kisses, again and again, holding her so tightly within those corded arms, she might have felt trapped but instead felt oddly, gloriously free.

Wolf was touching her breasts, cupping them in his hands, freeing them from the confines of her scooped-neck blouse while all the while his mouth sent flames of heat searing through her to the very depths of her soul. The autumn air whistling down from the mountains was cool, but there in her open, isolated yard Rebeccah felt herself burning up, like a candle set aflame. Her fingers flew to the buttons of his shirt, flinging them apart. She pressed wild kisses against his bare skin, closing her eyes as he tugged at her skirt.

Then the pounding of approaching hoofbeats startled them both out of the fever engulfing them.

"Who is it?" Rebeccah gasped, yanking her blouse frantically into place.

Wolf was already squinting out toward the road.

"Navarro." There was an edge of grimness in his tone and in the gray depths of his eyes as he started buttoning his shirt.

Chance Navarro. Oddly enough, with all she'd forgotten from the previous evening, she vividly recalled her engaging, wavy-haired dancing partner. As Rebeccah hastily smoothed her hair, shook out her skirt, and then, her cheeks still burning, put several yards between herself and Wolf, she cast a fleeting glance at his taut, flushed face. Was he jealous? Or merely annoyed with Navarro because he'd interrupted them?

Rebeccah could only be grateful that someone had brought an end to her mad sojourn into passion. Being alone with Wolf Bodine destroyed all her good sense and reason, and melted her defenses. *Defenses?* she asked herself bitterly, taking deep breaths of cool air. *What defenses?* When it came to Wolf Bodine, she had no defenses at all.

"Good morning, Miss Rawlings," Chance called out as he reined in his big bay before them. Today he wore an elegant broadcloth suit, string tie, and brocade vest, with his derby set at a jaunty angle upon his head. "I just wanted to see if you were all right," he drawled, "but I see that you've still got the deadliest sheriff in the West to protect you."

Wolf regarded him through narrowed eyes. "I reckon I'm here to do whatever Miss Rawlings needs me to do," he returned cryptically, hooking his thumbs in his gunbelt.

Rebeccah tried to blot out everything that had happened a few moments ago. She tried to think about this very handsome and very appealing Chance Navarro. But she was intensely conscious of Wolf's virile presence, of the way he had touched her, aroused her, and brought her to a point of such heated desire that she had nearly made love to him a scant few moments ago. She quivered like a drawn bowstring when he sauntered to her side and draped an arm across her shoulders.

"Would you like a cup of coffee, Mr. Navarro?" she offered weakly, hoping he wouldn't notice how rapidly she was breathing, or how her cheeks burned.

But Wolf answered before Chance could get out a single word.

"Don't trouble yourself, Rebeccah. He's leaving. He only came out to make sure you were all right. Well, any fool can see that you are, so . . ." He threw a meaningful glance at the other man, still seated on his horse. "Adios, Navarro."

Chance chuckled, and swung down from his bay with the same smooth grace he'd exhibited while dancing. "But there was something else I wanted to talk to Miss Rawlings about, Sheriff. That can wait until we're alone, though. Meantime, Rebeccah—I can call you Rebeccah, can't I? I've got to say you look right pretty this morning. Doesn't she, Sheriff? Have you ever in all your days seen a prettier woman?"

Rebeccah held her breath as she waited for Wolf's reply.

She is the most beautiful, complicated, and extraordinary woman I've ever laid eyes on. And if you value your hide, Navarro, you'll stay away from her.

Aloud, Wolf said, without once glancing in Rebeccah's direction, "I'm in no mood to engage in a flattery contest with you, Navarro. Miss Rawlings and I have some important business to discuss. Come back another time and try to turn her head, if you reckon it'll do you any good, but right now we're busy."

"I don't think I like your tone, Bodine," Chance growled, the genial smile fading from his face and an indignant flush replacing it. "Maybe we should just ask Miss Rawlings whose company she prefers at this moment. . . ."

"Gentlemen, this is a fascinating exchange, and I'm honored to be the subject of such attention, but I have too many chores to attend to this morning to stand around jabbering with a couple of roosters both trying to ruffle the other's tailfeathers. Good day to both of you."

And without another glance at either one of them she turned on her heel and stalked into the house. Slamming the door, Rebeccah leaned against it, listening for sounds of retreating hoofbeats. Part of her wanted Wolf to stay, to continue where they'd left off, and another part of her prayed he would leave and give her time to *think*.

When she heard hoofbeats, she went to the window and saw Wolf Bodine riding toward his own property, and Chance Navarro headed back in the direction of town. Her gaze followed Wolf, and she swallowed back the urge to race, shouting, after him. But as she watched, Navarro reined in his horse and turned around. To her astonishment he galloped right back the way he had come, halting the bay in her front yard.

"What is it?" she demanded, coming out onto the porch again, staring at him in bewilderment.

"I don't give up that easily." He dismounted with a soft thud, his boots scattering dust as he walked toward her. "Bodine never would have left us alone if he'd thought I was staying, so I let him believe I was leaving." He came up the steps of the porch and seized her hands. "Rebeccah, are you sure you're all right? I was worried about you last night."

"I'm fine." She spoke quickly, hoping he wouldn't notice how distracted she was. "I'm horribly embarrassed that I got drunk on two glasses of huckleberry wine, but other than that I'm fine."

He was very handsome. It was his dancing green eyes and his earnest grin that made him so disarmingly appealing, she decided. That and the smooth, wiry way he moved, the quick flash of intelligence in his eyes. *That's right, think about him. Don't think about Wolf.* "I've never before made a fool of myself like that, Mr. Navarro, so please don't fancy I make a habit of it."

"I'd never think such a thing. Besides, you didn't make a fool of yourself at all. You were downright adorable." That quick, lightning grin again that seemed to flash a hole clear through her. "I wanted to make sure the sheriff didn't take advantage of you. He insisted on bringing you home, despite the fact that Mr. Pritchard offered and so did I."

"He did? I mean, *you* did? How kind."

"I'm not kind at all," he told her softly. He

reached out a strong, slender white hand to cup her face very gently, as if her chin was made of spun glass. "I did it for selfish reasons."

For a moment Rebeccah found herself lost in those provocative moss-green eyes. Then she coolly removed his hand and stepped back a pace. "You're being rather forward, Mr. Navarro," she said steadily, but she couldn't help smiling at him.

"That's a fault of mine," he admitted. "When I see a beautiful woman, a woman of great charm and intelligence, I just have to let her know that I'm loco about her."

"When I hear a man say flattering things like that, I just can't help but wonder exactly what he's after," she returned sweetly.

Chance laughed. "Well, for one thing, I'd like you to call me Chance. Most everybody does. For another I'd like to get to know you better. And if you have doubts about my reputation, Rebeccah, you're a smart gal. And you're on the right track. I'm no good. Let me say that straight off. I like to move around, I hate ordinary chores and timetables and talking about the weather. I like riding fast and hard, staying up all night gambling, dancing with a pretty girl, doing something different and meeting someone new every day. I also have a past. Right now I'm a gambler. But I've been a lot of things—a cowboy, trail guide, prospector. Never any one thing for long. The good part is I found out along the way that my luck didn't revolve around discovering gold but in winning it. Every time I take a chance in a poker game or at a roulette wheel"—

he shrugged, the smile still playing around the corners of his mouth—"well, let's just say fortune smiles on me again and again. My lucky chances pay off. That's why I picked my name." He suddenly swept his hat off his head and crushed it to his chest. "I never stay too long in any one town— it's in my nature to drift, I reckon, but I've been in Powder Creek for weeks now, ever since I heard about you at that town meeting. You had the whole town in an uproar. It made me curious to meet you. I had a hunch you were someone I should meet, someone different from everyone else, not just an *ordinary* woman. And Rebeccah," he added, chuckling, "you should know that my hunches nearly always pay off."

The magpie chattered from the tree again. The autumn sun dappled shadows across the yard and glinted upon Chance Navarro's neat black hair.

"I don't know if it's luck or fate or chance or *what* that brought me to Powder Creek in the first place," he finished, "but I've been enjoying my stay. And I think I'd enjoy it a lot more if you'd have supper with me in town tomorrow night."

Rebeccah could only stare at him, overwhelmed by his lengthy speech. She knew she shouldn't trust him—the things he had told her hardly revealed a steady character—and yet there was something so disarmingly open about him, so delightfully breezy and unpredictable, that she found herself liking him despite it all. And above all, it was easy to be with him. Her feelings for Chance Navarro were so much less complicated than those for Wolf.

"All right—under one condition," she said. "Over supper you must tell me everything that happened at the schoolhouse last night—from the moment I began to dance with Sheriff Bodine until I left with him later. All that I said, all that I did, as far as you know. Deal?"

"Deal." Chance squeezed her hands and chuckled. He backed down the steps. "You worry too much, honey. I can tell you're wondering what people thought when you had a bit too much to drink. Well, why should you care a hoot about that? A woman as lovely and full of life as you are should be able to do anything she pleases and to hell with anyone who doesn't like it."

He made it sound so easy, Rebeccah reflected wryly, watching him ride off with a wave and a grin. She waited until his dark-clad figure had disappeared across the golden-gray buffalo grass, which rose like a sea for miles around, before returning to the kitchen to scrape and wash the breakfast plates. For some reason she was drawn to Chance Navarro.

He reminds me of Bear. In some strange way the same philosophy expressed by Chance had guided her father as well. He, too, had never stayed in one place for long, had never thought rules or chores or ordinary, everyday living applied to him. Something in her responded to this free-spirited philosophy. Of course she didn't think it applied to committing crimes, to stealing other people's gold or money, but why *should* she be so worried about what anyone thought here in Powder Creek?

Especially Wolf Bodine. He meant nothing to her. Didn't he?

Yet he had brought her home from the dance, watched over her through the night, chopped her wood, and promised to protect her from Neely Stoner and the others. And something else.

He had very nearly made love to her out in the yard a short time ago.

Rebeccah paused, his plate in her hand. The strangest part of it all was that she had wanted him to make love to her.

She hadn't been afraid. She hadn't wanted to stop. The icy panic and nausea had not risen up to blot out all of the pleasure that she was feeling.

Even in her girlhood dreams Rebeccah had never wanted Wolf to undress her or touch the intimate parts of her body or do the things with her that a man and woman in love normally did. She'd dreamed of him kissing her, yes. Of him telling her she was beautiful and that he loved her, yes. But somehow or other the dreams had always faded to a blurry end before anything else had happened, anything remotely similar to what Neely Stoner had done.

But when Wolf had caressed her with those fierce, knowing hands, when he had reached for her, taken over her senses with his kisses and commanded her body with his passionate need, she had known only sweet, hot yearning—not fear, not revulsion.

The soapy plate slipped from her fingers and clattered to the floor. Rebeccah bent to gather up the shards, lost in thought.

If only he loved me, she thought miserably, rising and placing the broken pieces of crockery on a towel. *Then there might be some hope.* . . .

She could no longer deny that she loved Wolf. She loved him with all of her poor, stubborn heart. And she knew that she loved him as he was now, here, in Powder Creek. It was not the memories of that decent young lawman in Arizona that haunted her thoughts and dreams of late, but of Wolf, the tall, rugged sheriff who'd tried to scare her out of town. She loved this man who was so difficult to know, who teased her and protected her and looked out for his mother and his son, who stomped off when she came to dinner and saved her from waltzing with Waylon Pritchard, who drove her home when she was drunk and chopped her wood while she slept and kissed her in the open yard until she was ready to swoon. . . .

Wolf.

Could a man like Wolf Bodine ever love an outlaw's daughter? Could his intentions be honorable toward her, his feelings any deeper than base, physical lust?

How am I to know? she wondered in despair as she pressed her eyes closed. *I understand so little about men when it comes to love, and certainly nothing about Wolf Bodine. For all I know, he will never love any woman the way he loved his dead wife.*

But she did know some things about him, Rebeccah realized slowly, her hands dropping to her sides. *I know that he is decent and good, that he cares for his family and his town, that he despises dishonesty, and values justice and law.*

Maybe that is enough, a voice whispered inside of
her. *Maybe you know enough to understand him,
enough to make him love you in return.*

But Rebeccah, feeling weary and confused,
wasn't at all sure that it was.

16 "Mountain," Rebeccah repeated in a clear, ringing voice. She nodded at Evan Kramer, seated in the third row. "Try," she said encouragingly, as a panicked look flitted across the boy's face.

"M-o-n-t-a-n," he mumbled, a scarlet flush crawling up his neck.

Rebeccah gave him a heartening smile. "Not quite, but you were close. You did spell almost all of *Montana*. Cara Sue, can you spell *mountain* for us?"

"M-o-u-n-t-a-i-n," the pigtailed child recited proudly.

"Excellent. Now, who can tell me the names of our two largest rivers here in the Montana Territory? They run along right here on the map," she added, tracing the pointer along two different winding routes. "Does anyone know? Billy?"

"The Missouri River and the Yellowstone," Billy Bodine replied in a subdued tone, and Mary Brady, who'd been waving her hand in the air, nodded agreement.

"Good. All right, class, there are ten more spelling words to copy down this week, all having to do with geography. I've written them on the blackboard, and I want you all to write them five times each. You may begin."

Outside the schoolhouse window the first snowflakes of the year tumbled down from an ash-gray sky. It was only the middle of October, yet crunchy frost covered the landscape, and the air rushed bitter cold through the foothills and valleys, soaring over the mountain lakes and buffeting the open plains.

When the school day ended, Rebeccah watched the children tug on their woolen coats and scarves and mittens with an odd tightness in her throat. How had they become so dear to her, these varied faces? Large and small, homely and charming, quick-witted and dull. She knew them all, cared for them all. How had it happened in only a few short weeks?

"Good day, Toby. Button your coat, Joey. Thank you for the apples, Cara Sue," she called as she stood at the door and watched them file quickly past her. "Don't forget, Friday is the spelling bee!"

As she turned from the door, she saw that, as usual, Billy Bodine had lingered behind. He was studying the map of the United States displayed at the front of the classroom, waiting for her to see the other children off.

"Yes, Billy, what can I do for you?" Rebeccah asked. She strolled back to her desk and began gathering up her books and papers.

"I have a question, Miss Rawlings."

"Go ahead."

She expected him to ask her something about the arithmetic assignment or the Yellowstone River or to give him her opinion of last week's essay—any one of the typical questions that he posed to her most days after school, when he really only wanted a few extra minutes of her time and attention. But instead he caught her completely off guard.

"Why do people have to die?"

Stunned, she could only stare at him. "What makes you ask that, Billy?" she asked gently, and wondered if he was thinking about his mother.

"It's my gramma."

"Caitlin? Is something wrong?" Rebeccah's stomach clenched when Billy nodded.

"She took sick yesterday—real sick. Doc Wilson said she might die. Pa doesn't know I heard, but I did. And I'm scared."

A cold chill pierced Rebeccah. She sank weakly upon her chair. "But she was perfectly fine a few days ago. She gave me the recipe for vinegar pie and helped me pick out a pattern for new slipcovers. What happened?"

"The fever came on her all of a sudden. Joey's ma brought her soup, but it didn't help. Mrs. Adams has been nursing her, and last night I heard her telling Pa that Gramma was no better. Doc Wilson said the same. Then later . . ."

"What, Billy? What has scared you so?"

"Gramma called Pa in and she told him that she wasn't going to get well. And she said he'd better start planning to take himself a wife, because she didn't want to die knowing the two of us were going to be left all alone in that big house."

Stunned, Rebeccah swallowed back her dismay.

She couldn't bear the thought of losing Caitlin. Billy's words alarmed her considerably, but she spoke as cheerfully as she could. "Don't give up hope, Billy. She might get well. We must pray and hope and take good care of her."

"I'm scared, Miss Rawlings! I don't want to lose Gramma. First my ma died when I was a baby and now if Gramma dies . . ." His voice cracked. Tears welled in his eyes. He swiped at them with a grimy hand and sniffed. "There's something else. I'm worried my pa will marry Miss Westerly or Mrs. Simpson. I don't want either of them coming to live with us in our house—trying to be my ma or to take Gramma's place. If they do, everything is going to change."

He began to sob—small, frightened sobs that shook his narrow shoulders and brought anguished tears coursing down his cheeks. Rebeccah's heart went out to him. She drew him into her arms without even thinking, hugging him and stroking the fine, dark silk of his hair.

"Billy, I know just how you feel," she murmured. "Change is frightening. I know all about that. When I was little, I used to ride with my father's gang all over the West. We were always together. And then one day he sent me away. To boarding school all the way in Boston. Look, this far away." She pointed on the United States map. "I hardly ever saw my father after that. And my life was completely different. I used to lie awake every night wishing things could go back to the way they were. I hated all those changes. I was scared—as scared as you are now. But you don't have to be afraid,

Billy. You'll still be with your father, no matter what else happens."

He was sniffling now, watching her. She continued in a soothing tone.

"Your father will always take care of you. He'll help you handle things no matter what happens. That's something you can always count on."

"She's right, Billy."

Wolf's voice came quietly from the doorway. Both Rebeccah and Billy jumped, twisting around to gape at him.

"Pa!" Billy pulled free of Rebeccah's arms and ran to his father. "What are you doing here? Is Gramma . . . did she . . . ?"

Rebeccah's heart slammed into her throat until Wolf's next words brought a modicum of relief. "No, son, she's holding on. But I'm here because she made a request. I came by to talk about it with Miss Rawlings."

He strode toward the front of the room, seeming to fill the schoolhouse with his tall form, with the quiet, iron strength that characterized him. But he looked tired, Rebeccah noted, and there were grim lines around his mouth.

"Caitlin asked for you to come. She didn't say why. But I rode home to check on her a while ago, and Emily Brady said she'd been fretting for you." He took a deep breath. "Will you go to her?"

Rebeccah jumped up. "Of course. Let's go right now. Wolf, I'm so sorry Caitlin is ill. What can I do to help?"

"A visit from you will help a lot." He reached for the armload of books and papers she'd quickly scooped off the desk. "Let me carry these. Billy, do you want to ride with Miss Rawlings or come with me?"

"I think you should go with your pa," Rebeccah said quickly, seeing that the boy was ready to speak her name. "You two need a chance to talk. You'll have to rely on each other now until your gramma is well again."

His gaze locked on hers. She read the truth in his eyes and felt her knees tremble. Oh, God. Wolf didn't believe Caitlin was going to get well.

She wanted to ask questions, for she couldn't understand how things had reached such a bad pass so quickly, but she couldn't question him in front of Billy. She reached for her dark blue cloak, choking back tears.

When they reached the Double B, Wolf came to help her down from the buckboard while Billy ran inside. She put a hand on his sleeve and searched his weary face.

"Wolf, is it really that bad?"

"It's bad." He glanced around to be certain Billy wasn't within earshot. "She'd been nursing Sally Ralston—Sally'd come down with influenza, along with her whole family. Caitlin worked around the clock trying to get Sally and the others well. Doc Wilson warned her that at her age she might be susceptible to catching it bad herself, but she's never been one to flinch from helping someone in need." He sighed. "She's upstairs, waiting to see you. Come on."

Caitlin looked like a tiny, gray-headed doll tucked up in her bed. The windows were shut fast against the early snow and the groaning wind, and a small fire burned in the hearth, but she seemed unaware of either warmth or light, staring sightlessly toward the wall. Her lined cheeks blazed feverishly, looking brighter than peonies against the white bedsheets drawn up across her frail chest. Her breathing sounded labored, raspy, and uneven.

Beside her Billy huddled in a rocking chair, his hands tautly gripping the carved arms. Rebeccah threw him an encouraging smile, though her own heart sank as she saw the shriveled figure lying on the bed.

"Caitlin, it's Rebeccah." She knelt beside the bed and sought the blue-veined hand that clutched at the folds of the patchwork quilt. Rebeccah reassuringly clasped the hot fingers in her own. Even Caitlin's hand, once strong and firm despite her years, now felt thin and crumpled as paper.

"You . . . came."

"Yes, of course I came. What would you like me to do for you? Please tell me how I can help."

"Piano."

"I beg your pardon?"

"Play . . . the piano. Would you play . . . my favorite song."

"With pleasure. Which song, Caitlin?"

A cough bubbled out of her gray lips. Then she formed the words with difficulty. "My mother always used to sing me 'Oh, Susannah.' I loved it. It was . . . Jimmy's favorite too. When he broke his leg falling out of the tree . . . and we had to wait all night for the doctor to come, I sang him that song, and it kept him calm. Remember, Wolf?"

"I remember."

Rebeccah heard only calm in Wolf's voice. None of the pain or anxiety he must be feeling. Glancing up at him, standing only a few feet away, she saw the stoic expression on his face, but she also saw something else. Beneath his calm a deep anguish burned, apparent only in the very depths of his eyes.

"I'll play it right now if you like," she said, turning back to Caitlin with a forced smile. The dim blue eyes blazed with the fever, and she looked completely bereft of strength.

"Do, please, dear," she whispered, and somehow managed to pat Rebeccah's hand.

So Rebeccah left the sickroom, with Billy's anxious face imprinted on her mind and Wolf's strong one helping to keep her own emotions at bay. She hastened downstairs to the piano.

With the door upstairs left ajar, she knew the notes would carry up the stairs and along to Caitlin's bedroom. Her hands shook as she raised them over the keys. Dear God, it terrified her to see Caitlin so ill. Surely she would recover. With good care and Doc Wilson's skill there must be a chance.

Her fingers skimmed across the keys with deft precision, and the tune rolled out with a hearty festiveness totally at odds with Rebeccah's spirits. She played the song through twice and then rose from the bench, her knees trembling. But before she reached the stairs, Wolf appeared at the landing, with Billy trailing behind.

"She fell asleep halfway through the second time

you played it. Maybe she'll rest more easily for a while."

She wanted to reach out and caress his cheek, to put her arms around him and tell him everything would be all right. But instead she offered to cook supper.

"We'd appreciate that." Wolf rumpled Billy's hair. "Wouldn't we, son? If it's not too much trouble," he added politely.

"No trouble at all. It will give me a chance to try some of the recipes Caitlin has given me on some-one other than myself."

But then she saw that Wolf was no longer paying attention to her. His gaze had swung beyond her, to the front window.

Rebeccah turned to follow it. Her lips tightened.

Nel Westerly was trodding gracefully across the porch, a large wicker basket slung over her arm, and as all three of them watched, she gave a quick knock and pushed open the front door.

17

"Yoo-hoo. May I come in? Wolf, tell me, please, how is Caitlin? I brought her some of Mama's special chicken broth and also a sweet potato pie. And Billy, I brought you a whole batch of my very own shortbread cookies!" She sparkled her famous smile at the ten-year-old regarding her darkly from beneath his lashes, flipped her fair hair over her shoulder, and turned brightly to Rebeccah.

"Why, hello, Miss Rawlings. What brings you here? Did you bring sustenance to these big hungry men too?"

Something in that gooey-sweet voice jarred Rebeccah as much as fingernails scratching down a blackboard. She longed to slap that smug grin off Nel's pretty, lightly freckled face, but she reminded herself that she'd be setting a very poor example for Billy and that Wolf would probably arrest her for public brawling. "Not exactly," she countered, meeting the other woman's cloying gaze with a cool, direct glance. "But I've just offered to fix supper for them, so—"

"Well, aren't you sweet, but I reckon that won't be necessary. I'm here now and I'd be glad to do it. What would you like for supper, Billy—fried chicken and dumplings? I can whip up a batch faster than you can spell *Mississippi.*"

The boy glared at her. "I want Miss Rawlings to cook us supper. She was here first."

Rebeccah wanted to kiss him. Wolf's expression was suspiciously unreadable, but he did say in a flat tone, "Billy, that's not polite."

"Oh, I don't mind!" Nel let out a light laugh. She stooped gracefully before the boy and appealed to him. "Billy, you don't exactly understand. Miss Rawlings is trying to be nice, but she's probably not used to cooking for two great big hungry men, while I have three big brothers and know exactly what hardworking, fast-eating men like."

"I believe I'll manage somehow. When I was eleven, I cooked for an entire gang of ravenous outlaws," Rebeccah tossed out casually. She allowed the tiniest of smiles to touch her lips. Turning her head so that only Billy could see, she winked at him. Then she reached for Nel's basket. "Let me put this away in the kitchen, and then I'd best get started on supper. Wolf, you go right ahead and visit with Miss Westerly. I'll call when I'm ready to serve."

"She's leaving!" Billy whispered a short while later, peering from the kitchen into the parlor. "Pa's walking her outside!"

"It's bad manners to spy on people," Rebeccah said primly, rummaging through the pantry to assess the kitchen's provisions. But she was pleased when Billy reported that Nel had ridden off.

"Pa's going back upstairs," he added.

"Fine." She set a sack of flour on the counter and then knelt beside him. "Why don't you go see to your chores for a spell and let me get busy in here fixing you a scrumptious supper?" she urged. "Your gramma will probably sleep for a while, and I'm sure your father is counting on you to keep up with your responsibilities. He needs your help now, Billy, to keep things running smoothly around here —and he needs you to be a strong young man."

Outside, Sam began barking, and Billy glanced eagerly toward the door.

"Go on, shoo. See what Sam is all fired up about —but don't forget your chores," she called, smiling after him.

Children needed to play, she reflected as she tied on one of Caitlin's starched cotton aprons. It wasn't good for them to fret and worry over things beyond their control. She hated seeing Billy so sad and so scared. The best thing for him to do right now would be to get his mind off Caitlin's illness for a while and to put his cares aside. But what about Wolf?

Rebeccah sensed his frustration at being helpless. A man like Wolf Bodine was accustomed to solving problems, to taking action. But in this circumstance there was little he could do except pray, hope, and wait.

That would be hard for him to swallow. But he would do it. There was an inner as well as an outer toughness about him that would enable him to handle just about anything—even death—with steady strength.

Death. She closed her eyes, praying it would not

come to this house, praying that Caitlin would find the strength to fight off the ravaging fever.

But deep inside, the fear was there, and her heart was leaden as she set a kettle of water on the stove to boil for stew and sliced up beef, potatoes, and onions to simmer.

It was a simple meal, in the end, but to Rebeccah's relief both Wolf and Billy thoroughly enjoyed it. In addition to the stew she fried chicken and baked cornbread biscuits and even served Nel Westerly's sweet potato pie. Wolf ate two servings, she noted, but Billy avoided it and stuffed himself with half a dozen biscuits instead.

It felt strange to sit at the table in the pleasant kitchen without Caitlin there. Just as they finished, Doc Wilson stopped by for the second time that day to check on her.

Rebeccah had finished washing the dishes and Billy was drying them when Wolf and the doctor came down the stairs.

From their grim expressions she knew the outlook was not good.

"Do you think she could take some soup?" she asked the doctor as he shuffled wearily toward the door.

"You could try, but I don't know if she has the strength for it." His gaze settled briefly on Billy's anxious face, and he forced a wan smile. "Hey, there, young man, you're sure shooting up fast. One of these days you're going to be as tall as your pa."

That was all. No words of encouragement, no offering of hope. Rebeccah fought back tears as she hurried into the kitchen to dip Caitlin a bowl of soup.

But the woman in the bed appeared to have withered even since the afternoon. And the fever had not yet broken. Despite cool compresses, her papery skin was hot to the touch, and sticky perspiration filmed her face and neck.

After failing to coax her into swallowing more than a mouthful or two of soup, Rebeccah took to sponging her skin with a cool cloth. A cold autumn darkness was falling, a darkness mixed with bits of swirling snow, when Caitlin opened her eyes and seemed to focus her attention with great effort.

"Who is here?" she asked weakly. "Billy? Wolf?"

"It's Rebeccah." Leaning closer, Rebeccah caressed the frail hand lying limply on the sheet, and kept her tone soothing. "I'll get them for you. . . ."

"Wait." Caitlin's breaths came in short, painful wheezes that made Rebeccah wince. Her faded eyes struggled valiantly to make out the figure of the young woman sitting by her bedside. "Promise me . . ."

"Yes, Caitlin, anything. What can I do?"

"Take care of Wolf. He . . . needs you."

For a moment Rebeccah was speechless. She moistened her lips. "Your son is quite self-sufficient, Caitlin," she responded at last with a note of rueful humor. "Other than needing for you to get well, he really doesn't—"

"Yes, he does," Caitlin insisted, sounding crotchety for the first time since Rebeccah had known her. Suddenly she began struggling to sit up. "He needs . . . *you*."

Alarmed by her patient's restless distress, Rebeccah eased her back against the pillows. "There, now, Caitlin, you must lie still. Please, don't upset yourself. Let me sponge your face. There's no cause for being so troubled. Wolf is fine."

The brief burst of agitation had already taken its toll. Caitlin's chest heaved with the effort of breathing, and her skin looked ashy gray beneath its flush of fever. Still she would not be silent.

"Ever since Clarissa, Wolf has been alone." Her lips struggled to form the words. "He was so hurt. . . . I thought he'd never let himself love anyone again. . . . But when he talks about you . . . or listens to Billy talk about you . . . he gets this look on his face. . . ."

Sharp wheezes burst from her. Rebeccah's fear grew, her eyes darkening with concern. "Don't talk anymore, Caitlin, please."

But the old woman went doggedly on, her voice no more than a whisper. "Rebeccah, he doesn't look like that when he talks about that Westerly girl or . . . Lorelie Simpson . . . only when your name comes into the conversation. . . . He cares for you, I tell you. Don't hurt him," Caitlin begged.

Hurt Wolf? Rebeccah shook her head, confused by Caitlin's words. *He cares for you.* Could it be?

"Rest easy, Caitlin. I would never hurt Wolf."

"Do you . . . promise?"

"I would sooner hurt myself," Rebeccah whispered fiercely, her voice breaking. Then, gazing at that dear face so wracked in misery, the next words poured out of her before she realized what she was saying.

"I love him, Caitlin. I love him so much, it hurts *me* every time I think of it. I'd never hurt him. Never."

A wan smile broke across the seamed features. Her sparse eyelashes fluttered wearily closed. "I'm . . . glad. You're a fine young woman," she murmured. "You're special, Rebeccah. And good. You have a . . . sensitive heart. I knew that from the very first. Not at all like Clarissa. . . ."

What did that mean? Startled, Rebeccah could only gaze at Caitlin's shuttered eyes. *Not at all like Clarissa.*

She didn't understand. But it was late, and Caitlin was too exhausted to endure even a single question. Noting the darkness that had come over the mountains, Rebeccah realized it was past time to be headed home.

She found Wolf downstairs talking in low tones with Emily Brady. Billy had fallen asleep across the sofa.

"I'm going to sit up with Caitlin tonight so Wolf can get some sleep. Billy needs to sleep too," Emily commented with a worried glance at the boy. "He's plumb tuckered out from worrying about Caitlin all last night. They were both up until dawn."

"She's sleeping at the moment." Rebeccah noted the chill that had seeped into the room and immediately took the Indian blanket folded across the back of the sofa and draped it across Billy's inert form. She wanted to reach out and smooth the hair back from his brow, but, conscious of both Wolf and Emily watching her, she refrained. Instead she went to the fire and poked at it until the embers stirred to a brighter blaze.

"I'll be going now," she said, reflecting with sudden self-consciousness that she had betrayed enough motherly instincts for one night. If she wasn't careful, they would all see how concerned for Billy she was.

"I'll take you home," Wolf said, rising and striding toward the door.

"That's not necessary."

"Don't argue. Emily, I'll be back within the hour."

He took Rebeccah by the arm before she could protest further and propelled her out to her buckboard. "Look, I need to talk to you anyway. I've been sending wires all over the west, but no one seems to have a handle on where this Neely Stoner might be," he told her as he lifted her onto the seat. He deftly tied Dusty behind the buckboard, then sprang up on the seat beside her with an agile leap. "I've got a hunch he's close by. If you think I'm going to let you traipse around at night alone with him and those other varmints gunning for you, you're dead wrong, Rebeccah. And if you say one word about not wanting to be beholden to me, I'll personally wring your neck," he promised.

But his tone was almost caressing, and she gazed at him in surprise. "I'm . . . very pleased for the company," she said meekly. "I only wanted to spare you any inconvenience, since I know how worried you are about Caitlin," she explained.

"You're not an inconvenience, Rebeccah."

Snowflakes danced across her cheeks, but a tiny warm flame shot through her at his words.

Suddenly the wind howled across the open land with an icy blast that made her shiver. Wolf's strong arm slipped around her shoulders and pulled her close against the warmth of his body.

"Better?"

"Yes . . . much better."

They rode in silence. It was almost unbearably wonderful to sit like that, with his arm around her, feeling cared for, protected. A longing grew deep inside of her. Sweetly hopeful emotions that she had never experienced before sprouted within, like warm, fertile seeds blooming in a barren garden.

"I overheard what you said to Billy at the school-house today. About change. I want you to know that I appreciate your talking to him like that. It won't be easy for him if Caitlin—"

"She'll get well," Rebeccah said quickly. "She must."

"I don't make it a habit to lie to myself, Rebeccah, or to anyone else," he said quietly. "I've faced some hard things in my life, and this is one of the hardest, but Doc Wilson doesn't hold out much hope. He thinks it's only a matter of a day or two."

"Oh, no!"

He halted the horses as she began to cry. Both arms wrapped around her, and she was pressed up hard against the roughness of his coat, inhaling both his warm, comforting scent and his reassuring strength. "You're a baffling woman, Rebeccah Rawlings," Wolf muttered.

He was stroking her hair with gentle fingers, comforting her in her grief, when she knew she ought to be comforting him.

"You're so calm," she blurted. "So strong." She leaned her head against his chest. "Were you this strong when Clarissa died, Wolf?"

She felt him tense. Every muscle went taut, and his sharply indrawn breath sounded loud as a drum roll in her ears.

"Haven't you learned by now that I don't care to discuss my wife?" He released her abruptly, turning away.

Rebeccah, her face still streaked with tears, realized she had again made a terrible mistake. Of course she knew that every time she mentioned his wife, Wolf either pulled away or worked himself into a fury. But she'd hoped by now, based on what Caitlin had said, that he was beginning to recover from her death, that he was starting to fall in love again.

"I'm sorry," she said miserably, feeling a weight like an anchor in her chest. "I know you must have loved her to distraction if even the mention of her name causes you such pain."

"Loved her to distraction?" He cracked out a hoarse, bitter laugh. "I hated her more than any human being I've ever known."

Blood pounded in Rebeccah's ears. She swung around to stare at him incredulously. *"Hated* her?"

It didn't make sense. It seemed impossible to believe, based on the assumptions she'd been making ever since she'd heard about his marriage—but the harsh expression on his face and the banked fury in his eyes told her it was true.

"I thought you were still grieving for her. I thought no one would ever replace her."

"Rebeccah, it's wrong to speak ill of the dead, so I won't say much about Clarissa. But what would you say about a woman who gives birth to a child and then decides she's bored taking care of it, is tired of staying home every night tending to her family, and wants only to go out dancing and drinking whiskey with any cowpoke who winks at her? What would you say about a woman who took to lying to her husband, sneaking out behind his back with gamblers and drifters and riffraff, who left her own baby home all alone?"

"She did that—to you and Billy?"

He nodded grimly, his breath coming out in short white puffs as he spoke. "I knew the marriage was a mistake almost immediately. I met Clarissa only a few months after I met you that first time in Arizona. She was eighteen years old, beautiful and full of life, always laughing, restless for fun. Oh, we had fun together, that's one thing I can say. I was never bored in those days with Clarissa. She enchanted me." He paused, staring out at the vast expanse of glittering stars as if searching for answers to questions beyond comprehension. "I think there was always something restless and discontented in Clarissa, a coldness and an almost defiant wildness, but I was too much of a lovesick fool to see it. Maybe I just didn't want to see it. Or maybe I thought that if she loved me enough, I could change her, make her happy. I knew I wanted her more than I'd wanted any other woman I'd ever met."

Rebeccah watched his face, her heart aching. All those nights on the run with Bear in Arizona after she'd met Wolf at the hideout, when she'd been thinking of him, dreaming her foolish little-girl dreams, he'd been pursuing and marrying Clarissa. And starting his family with her. Within months, Wolf told her, Billy had been conceived.

"She was excited about having a baby at first, but she hated it when she started getting larger. Clarissa was so proud of her figure. I thought she'd be fine once the baby was born and she went back to her normal size and shape, but it soon became obvious that something was wrong. She didn't seem interested in Billy. I mean, she fed him and changed him, but she didn't like rocking him to sleep, she never sang to him or seemed to want to hold him—or even talked to him much. She told me she was going loco staying home with a crying baby all day.

"I had taken a job as a deputy in Texas." Wolf's voice was flat, almost emotionless, but his eyes shone with remembered pain. "The pay wasn't much, but I managed to scrape together enough money to pay a local Mexican woman to come help out with the chores and the cooking—and with Billy—so that Clarissa would be happy. But she wasn't happy. One time I came home to supper and she was drinking whiskey. Entertaining a gambler named Stone Dillon. Right in my front parlor." His eyes narrowed with anger, and he clenched the reins until his knuckles whitened. "And Billy was squalling upstairs, hungry, his swaddling clothes sodden, but she was too busy to go to him. I went crazy. We had a terrible argument, and I nearly killed Dillon on the spot. Clarissa cried. She begged my forgiveness. She could do that mighty prettily too," he said with a short bitter laugh. "She swore upside and down it would never happen again; she picked up Billy and started cooing to him and covering him with kisses. I thought maybe she'd realized she had to change her ways. But then I got called away to Waco to testify at a trial, and when I got back a few days later, the worst thing of all had happened."

"What could be worse?" Rebeccah whispered, her heart going out to him. The painful memories were etched deep within his eyes, and she longed to gently kiss away the grim, tormented set of his mouth. "Tell me, Wolf," she said in a low tone, sensing it would be healing for him to talk about it, to purge such awful memories from his mind.

"I came back from Waco a day early. It was late at night, but I'd ridden straight through the day and evening to reach home—to be with Clarissa, to see my wife and son."

"And?" Rebeccah breathed, feeling a prickly dread begin to grow.

He stared straight ahead. "And I found Billy in his crib, covered with flies, burning up with fever. And no Clarissa."

"Wolf!"

"He was screaming, sobbing loud enough to wake the devil—as ill as I've ever seen a child, Rebeccah—and he was all alone. *Alone,* damn it. Clarissa, it turned out, was in some saloon in town, hanging all over Stone Dillon while he cleaned up at five-card stud."

"How could she do a thing like that?"

"She claimed Billy wasn't sick when she left, that he was only asleep. As if that made everything right."

Wolf turned to meet her gaze. "After that I knew I couldn't trust her to care for Billy," he said heavily. "Something was missing inside her, some bond between her and the boy—between her and me too. I wrote to Caitlin and asked her to come live with us so that I would know Billy would be looked after whenever I wasn't there. But Clarissa didn't wait for Caitlin to come. She up and left one morning, ran off with Dillon and didn't even leave a note."

"What did you do?"

"I let her go. I was relieved, if you want the truth. It hit me hard, how wrong I was about her, the weakness of my own judgment. It shook me badly. That she could run off and leave her child like that and never even write to ask how he was—" He broke off, as if aware of the heavy bitterness in his voice. When he spoke again, his tone was clearer, calmer, but just as solemn. "She died three months later—caught in the cross fire in some saloon fight in 'Frisco. She was with another gambler by then, I don't even remember his name. Larson, maybe. Earl Larson. Not that it matters worth a damn."

Rebeccah sat beside him in stunned silence as the horses restively pawed the ground and a frigid gust of wind sent the ends of her hair flying. Shyly her hand stole out to clasp Wolf's, still taut on the reins.

"I'm sorry."

The words sounded hopelessly inadequate, and she immediately cringed at having uttered them, but to her surprise Wolf suddenly turned and swept her into his arms.

"I've never told a soul that story except for Caitlin. We left Texas and moved here, and as far as anyone else knows, Billy's mother died of cholera in her own bed. My son will never know that his mother abandoned him. He keeps a picture of her by his bed—but I'll be damned if I'll keep one on the mantel and look at it every day."

Fury suffused him again, but as he stared into Rebeccah's wide, worried eyes, the tension evaporated from his body and the anger died out of his face.

"I'm not sure why I told you all this."

"Perhaps so I'd have sense enough to stop bringing up her name," she muttered ruefully.

At this he laughed. His eyes softened, and his spirit suddenly seemed to grow lighter. She had that effect on him. "That'd be a pleasant change, Rebeccah," he teased.

"When I think how many times I've thrown her in your face!"

"Maybe you can make it up to me," he suggested with a hint of a smile, watching her eyes widen and glow in the moonlight.

"Do you have any suggestions how I might do that, Sheriff Bodine?" she questioned softly, amazed at her own boldness.

His deepening grin was her reward. "Matter of fact I do."

But as he pulled her up against him on the cold seat of the wagon and Rebeccah felt her limbs go soft as candle wax and her heart flutter like a mad, wild bird, there came the quick clatter of hooves and rustling of brush on the road behind them.

Whoever was coming was riding fast up the trail. In an instant Wolf had thrust her from him and drawn his gun.

Twisting on the seat, Rebeccah peered through the darkness and saw Chance Navarro riding over the gray-shadowed ridge directly toward them. She recognized his wiry build and jauntily set derby, illuminated in starlight as his bay bore down on them.

"Whoa," Chance called, and reined in smartly beside the buckboard.

It sounded to Rebeccah as if Wolf was grinding his teeth.

"What a lucky chance running into you here, Rebeccah. I was just on my way to your place to see if something was wrong."

"Wrong? Why would you think . . . oh!"

Her hands flew to her throat. "I was supposed to meet you for supper at the hotel tonight! Oh, Chance, I clean forgot. I'm so sorry. Caitlin Bodine took ill, and I was helping out at the Double B. Everything else completely slipped my mind."

Chance was no longer looking at her. He and Wolf were glaring at each other, sizing each other up like two hound dogs ready to do battle over a slab of raw meat.

"I'm real sorry to hear about Mrs. Bodine," Chance said, turning back to Rebeccah at last.

No, you're not. You couldn't care less about Caitlin, she realized with a flash of insight. *You only care about being cheated out of time with me.* She had been meeting Chance in town for supper once a week since the schoolhouse dance and had even cooked Sunday dinner for him once out at the cabin. And then there had been their picnic. They'd brought a basket of food down to the stream, and he'd played the mouth harp and later carved a rose from a block of wood and given it to her.

He was good company—lighthearted, attentive, and charming. But he didn't care much about most people, she'd learned. There was a coldness beneath his lively attitude, a curious purposefulness that led him to mock those people and events that didn't fit in with whatever amusement or game he had in store for himself. He cared about gambling—and winning—and about pursuing her, Rebeccah knew. She also knew that for a man like Chance Navarro the chase was everything. If she allowed herself to be easily caught in that web of charm, he'd quickly lose interest.

But much as she enjoyed his lighthearted company and his gallant compliments, Rebeccah was in no danger of losing her heart to Chance Navarro. Even on the picnic, when Chance had surprised her by dancing wildly with her up and down the stream bank and lavishly praising her chicken sandwiches and strawberry tarts, she had rebuffed his attempts to kiss her, feeling complete disinterest.

There was only one man whose kisses she sought. Considering the torment she'd suffered at the hands of Neely Stoner, she'd never expected to experience anything close to soaring physical desire, but when Wolf kissed her, her entire body burst alive.

With Wolf everything was different from what she would normally expect.

Even now. His response to Chance's arrival and the discovery that her original plans for the evening had included supper with another man prompted him immediately to climb out of the wagon and begin untying his horse.

"I reckon Navarro will be glad to see you the rest of the way home. I've got to get back."

"My pleasure," Chance agreed, and winked at Rebeccah.

Wolf saw the wink, and an iron hardness settled over his face as he swung into the saddle.

Rebeccah bit her lip in frustration. She wanted to cry, *I want you to take me home! Chance Navarro means nothing to me—but you do! You mean everything!*

But of course she couldn't say anything so foolish. Chance was watching her, watching and listening. And besides, she and Wolf had already spent a long time talking—she knew he had to get back to Billy and Caitlin.

"I hope Caitlin is better tomorrow," she said instead, feeling a curious hollowness inside.

His only reply was a curt nod. Then, without another word to either her or Chance Navarro, Wolf headed Dusty at a gallop back the way they had come.

"You've had a mighty long day, Rebeccah. Come on, I've got a flask of brandy in my saddlebag. A shot of that will soothe your nerves. And warm you up. It's damned cold out here, and I can see you're shivering."

She picked up the reins and glanced at him
numbly. He gave her an encouraging smile. "Let old
Chance take care of you," he urged, moving his bay
close alongside the buckboard. "When it comes to
building up a good fire, there's no one better than
old Chance." He gave a funny kind of laugh, as if
amused at some secret joke he shared with only
himself. When she gazed at him uncomprehend-
ingly, he cocked his slender head to one side.
"Come on, Rebeccah, let's get back to the cabin.
Trust me, honey. I know exactly how to get you
warm."

I'll wager you do, Rebeccah thought wearily, not
answering as she started the team across the uneven ground, past the copse of alders sloping down
toward the stream. But she wasn't interested in
Chance Navarro or his flirtations—nor in getting
warm or even in eventually going to sleep. Her
thoughts were centered on Wolf Bodine, riding
back alone toward the Double B Ranch with Caitlin
in the grips of a deadly fever and Billy sleeping,
exhausted, on the parlor couch.

18 Rebeccah peeled potatoes in silence, working numbly alongside of the other women filling the Bodine kitchen. Only two days ago Caitlin Bodine had yearned to hear "Oh, Susannah," had begged Rebeccah not to hurt Wolf, and had smiled through her pain. Now she lay in the cold, hard ground—like Bear, Rebeccah thought miserably—never to be seen or smiled at or sung to again.

"She'll be sorely missed," Myrtle Lee Anderson sniffed into her handkerchief as Emily Brady heaped sliced beef on a platter and young Mary Adams shelled peas for the Bodines' dinner.

"She will be, that's for sure." Emily sighed quietly, fighting a new flood of tears.

In the parlor Lorelie Simpson was serving steaming cups of coffee to Wolf and Culley Pritchard. Nel Westerly set out a plate of cookies alongside slices of her famous chocolate cake. The whole town had attended the funeral this morning, and they were now rallying around the sheriff and his son, consoling them in their grief, as the leaden rain fell from the sky and everyone tried not to think about how strange the house felt without Caitlin's brisk, cheery presence.

Joey Brady popped suddenly into the kitchen. "Billy's crying in the barn and he won't come out. He won't even talk to me."

Rebeccah and Emily Brady exchanged glances. "I'll go to him," Rebeccah said in a low tone, and hastily threw on her cloak.

As she hurried across the sodden yard with raindrops pelting her face and soaking into the wool of her cloak, she wondered what she would say to him. How could one begin to heal the pain of such a fresh, raw, and devastating wound? Somehow she must try.

Inside the barn it was quiet, except for the soothing sounds of the horses munching their oats and whickering softly at her arrival.

"Billy?"

There was no answer.

Rebeccah walked past the first few stalls, letting her eyes adjust to the shadowy dimness. "Billy—Sam—are you here?"

Then she heard the dog's low whine and something else—a child's muffled sobs. She found them huddled in the farthest stall among piles of clean, sweet-smelling hay.

Sam's tail thumped the floor as Rebeccah paused in the entrance to the stall. Billy didn't look up.

"It's all right," she said softly. "It's good to cry."

As if released by her words, the sobs wracked out of him then, convulsing his narrow shoulders and hunched back. The tears flowed without restraint. "I'll . . . never see her again. . . ." He gasped once and buried his face in Sam's neck. Little hiccupping coughs came in between the sobs. "I don't want her to be dead! I want her to be back with us just like always!"

"Yes, yes, Billy. Of course you do. So do I. She was my best friend in Powder Creek—the only woman friend I've ever known. I'll miss her terribly, and so will you and so will your pa. But she'll always live in our hearts. Even death can't take a person we love out of our hearts."

"It c-can't?"

He looked up at last, the gray eyes swimming with tears. His face was blotchy and red, and his nose was running. Rebeccah knelt beside him as she handed him the handkerchief from her pocket. "No, of course it can't. Why, my father is still in my heart every single day. I think about the way he used to brush his horse so carefully and sing to him sometimes . . . and the way he'd listen to me with both eyes wide whenever I told him a joke or showed him a card trick. And the way he used to admire the sunset—he wore this expression of pure awe sometimes when he looked out over a canyon at the setting sun. Oh, I remember everything . . . and those memories keep him close to me." She settled down in the straw beside him and ventured a light hand on his arm. "Caitlin can stay close to us too. We can talk about her and think about her and remember her as much as we want. Every time I bake her strawberry pie—the one she taught me how to fix so that the crust was just right—I'll remember her and smile. And every time you look at her sewing box under the tea table, or the chair where she used to sit and test you at your spelling, you'll remember her. And you'll smile, too,

Billy. You'll feel all of your love for her and her love
for you. Caitlin will never really go away."

He had grown calmer while she talked. With one
last sniffle he leaned his head against Rebeccah's
shoulder. They sat like that for a while in the
sweet-smelling dusk of the barn, with the rain pat-
tering on the roof and Sam stretched out beside
them, his shaggy head resting on Billy's knee.

That night Rebeccah dreamed of Bear and of
Caitlin, square dancing together in what might
have been the schoolhouse, but there were no fiddlers, no music or bright frontier garb or any other
dancers at all, only the two of them, dim, shadowy
forms with bright light illuminating their solemn
faces as they did a *do-si-do* down a wide tunnel of
blackness.

A week passed. Life went on in Powder Creek.
But Rebeccah still found it difficult to believe Caitlin was really gone. *Don't hurt him,* Caitlin had
pleaded, almost her last words spoken on earth.
Now that Rebeccah knew what had transpired with
Clarissa, Caitlin's concern made a bit more sense
to her, but she could still scarcely believe what
else Caitlin had said: that Wolf cared for her more
than for Lorelie Simpson or Nel Westerly—that she,
Rebeccah Rawlings, had the power to hurt him—or
possibly, she reasoned with a sense of wonder, to
heal.

Rebeccah hadn't seen Wolf since the day of the
funeral, though she had brought over a kettle of
stew and a batch of cornbread muffins one night,
and on another a mess of fried chicken and boiled
carrots. Both times women from the surrounding

area had been at the house to accept the offerings, for it seemed the town was banding together to help Wolf in his time of grief. Mary Adams helped with the wash and the household chores, and the women of the community took turns keeping an eye on Billy and making sure the Double B larder was stocked with food, not to mention providing a good quantity of freshly prepared meals.

When she brought the chicken and carrots over just before supper one night, she was surprised to find Abigail Pritchard and Coral Mae Taggett working side by side in Caitlin's kitchen. Coral was removing a batch of cinnamon rolls from the oven as Abigail tossed onions and turnips into a frying pan sizzling with butter.

Neither woman appeared to be speaking much to the other, but they both forced tense smiles when Rebeccah came in. She soon learned that since the schoolhouse dance they'd been trying to become better acquainted.

"I reckon if Waylon's so set on her, there must be something to recommend her," Abigail muttered after summoning Rebeccah to a private conference in the parlor. "She's coming to supper tomorrow night, and then we'll see. But I can't help wishing Waylon had picked someone more like you, Miss Rawlings. Or like Nel Westerly. She's a sensible, respectable young woman, and her father's property adjoins ours. Why, a union between those two would be downright convenient. Still," she added regretfully, "I've a hunch Nel's already spoken for —or will be soon." She smiled confidentially at Rebeccah. "Rumor has it that Wolf proposed to her the day after Caitlin's funeral, and she accepted, but they don't want to announce it until a decent mourning period has passed."

Before Rebeccah could react to this startling pronouncement, Coral Mae Taggett, who'd obviously been eavesdropping, stuck her head out the kitchen doorway. "Don't believe everything you hear, Mrs. Pritchard!" she informed Abigail tartly. "Molly Duke has been seeing a lot of Wolf lately, and she told Hank Boswell, who in turn told me, that Wolf is planning to propose to Lorelie Simpson within the week."

Coral noticed Rebeccah's sudden pallor. "Miss Rawlings, what in heaven's name is the matter with you?" she cried in alarm, and then let out a muffled oath as she recalled the way the very drunk Miss Rawlings had looked at Wolf Bodine the night of the schoolhouse dance.

"N-nothing. I'd better be going," Rebeccah said faintly, trying not to think about Wolf with either Molly Duke, Lorelie Simpson, or Nel Westerly. She made her excuses and fled the Double B as quickly as she could.

Yet she lingered for several moments in the buckboard before starting the team toward home, pretending to settle her cloak more comfortably around her while she struggled to contain her inner turmoil.

Could those rumors be true—any of them? Most likely not, she reasoned, trying to stop her hands from trembling as she picked up the reins. Rebeccah had already learned that towns like Powder Creek thrived on gossip, much of it untrue. But she would have dearly loved to see Wolf Bodine come riding up at that moment so that she could ask him straight out if they were true. It would be embarrassing—no, *humiliating*—to show such interest in his affairs, but Rebeccah would rather at that moment have known humiliation than the frantic uncertainty churning inside of her after hearing what Abigail and Coral had to say.

But the trail from town was deserted, and there was no sign of Wolf returning home, so she clucked to the horses and went on her way, telling herself that Wolf could not be planning marriage to either of those women because Caitlin had said he cared for *her*.

And hadn't he confided in her about Clarissa, admitting that no one else in Powder Creek knew the truth? That counted for something—it must. It showed trust, didn't it? And the way that he kissed her. . . .

A strangled sob rose in her throat. Did he kiss *them* with the same hungry, urgent intensity? Did he hold them in his arms and make them feel that what they thought and felt mattered to him deeply and that he'd rather be there kissing them and touching them than be anywhere else?

She spent a sleepless night, listening to the coyotes howl in the windswept darkness, pacing the cabin, trying to lose herself to no avail in the poetry of Byron, but the knots in her stomach seemed to be closing off her lungs, making it difficult to breathe. At last, just as a delicate peach-colored dawn was painting the sky, she wrapped herself in the eiderdown quilt, flung herself onto her front porch, and gulped in great deep breaths of crystal-sharp air. Gazing out at the jade glitter of the distant lakes tucked in the steep ridges of the mountains and scanning the high, magnificently forested horizon in every direction, she wondered if she would not have been better off remaining in Boston, in that cold, stifling life she had known before she'd come to Powder Creek. She may not have been happy there, but now the grief and heartbreak and love and despair that enveloped her seemed too much to bear. Gazing out at the vast, breathtaking beauty of mountains, forests, lakes, and prairies, of soaring eagles above the firs and the solitary elk she spied on a distant butte, she felt tiny, insignificant, and powerless. She had come to Montana for peace and solitude, and instead she had found bursting, confusing Life: rambunctious children, kind friends, lonely danger, death, isolation, a sense of community, hope, desire, love—and uncertainty.

Life.

Later that day, still in a troubled mood, Rebeccah felt a flicker of irritation when Chance Navarro arrived at the schoolhouse just as the last of the children trudged off for home.

"Something's wrong," he said at once, following her back toward her desk at the front of the classroom. "It's Mrs. Bodine's death, isn't it, honey? You're missing her?"

"I didn't think it showed." She wasn't about to tell Chance the other reasons for her low spirits. "I've been trying to put on a cheerful front for the children, especially Billy. I know how hard it is to lose someone so important to you. He must feel as if he'll never recover from the pain." She picked up the apple Evan Kramer had brought her that morning and studied its glowing red skin.

"You know, Chance, when my father died, I felt as if I'd lost the only person who had ever cared about me, the only person who ever *would* care about me. He was all I had, all I had ever had. I loved him so very much that for a long time after he died, the pain was like a great weight pressing on me, crushing me."

"You've never mentioned your father to me before, Rebeccah."

Startled, her eyes flew to his face. "Haven't I? Well, I don't usually talk about him, I suppose. You . . . know about him, I'm sure. Everybody does."

"That he was Bear Rawlings, the famous outlaw? I sure do, honey. But I'm the last one in the world who would ever hold that against you." Chance covered her hand with his. "You see, my daddy was an outlaw too."

She let the apple slip from her fingers and thud onto the desk, her eyes mirroring her astonishment. "Who . . . was he?"

"Oh, no one as famous as Bear Rawlings, but he had a bad reputation throughout Missouri. Why do you think I changed my name? Rebeccah," Chance said softly, "I told you all along that we have a lot in common."

"Yes, but I never realized . . . Chance, it's strange isn't it? To love someone so much and yet the person you love is someone others despise? To know that they've done wrong and yet . . . ."

Seeing her distress, he clasped her hand and held it firmly. "I know, honey. My daddy was a good man—at least to me. My ma brought me up, and we didn't see much of him, but he sent money regularly, and Ma was so grateful, she didn't even bother to ask where it came from. I guess she figured we were better off not knowing."

Rebeccah nodded. Bear's exploits had kept her in elegant gowns, jewels, and fripperies, and enrolled at Miss Wright's Academy for years. She didn't like to think about that.

"Did your father leave you pretty well taken care of?" Chance asked, studying the slender hand cradled in his. "I reckon he must have, with all the bank jobs he got away with. I'll wager you just haven't had time yet to build up your ranch, but surely come spring you'll be buying yourself a whole big herd of cattle and cashing in on the beef market in the East."

"I don't know what will happen come spring." Rebeccah shrugged. She slid her hand free of his and straightened a pile of papers on her desk. "I donated the stock holdings and money Bear left me to some far-worthier causes and only kept the ranch because he won it honestly—but as you can see, it's not much. I plan to buy some cattle, a little at a time, and to build a corral and try to make a go of ranching—but it'll take time. Right now I'm trying to save up enough money to start with a small herd of longhorns and a part-time ranch hand to do the branding."

Chance fingered the brim of his derby, his green eyes jewel-bright against his leather-brown skin.

"Donated the stock holdings? And the money? You're downright noble, honey."

Rebeccah retrieved her dark blue cloak from its peg by the door. "Noble, my foot. I accepted Bear's ill-gotten gains for years and enjoyed the luxuries they bought me. But at some point while I was at school, I started thinking about the suffering that was caused by his stealing that money, about the innocent people who might have needed it, needed it far more than Bear or I did, and then . . . well, I couldn't benefit from it anymore."

"You've got an honest soul, honey." Chance sounded almost amused. "What about the rest of what Bear left you?"

"The rest? That was all—except for a few jewels and keepsakes, and I'm going to try to hang on to those . . . for sentimental reasons. It might not be exactly right, but . . ."

"There must have been more—he acquired a lot of loot in his life, from what I heard. . . ."

Rebeccah stared at him, and abruptly Chance broke off. Color flooded his cheeks. "Sorry, Rebeccah. It's sure none of my business. But this is the first time you've opened up to me about your pa, and since we have so much in common, I thought . . . well, I'm curious, you see. I thought for sure he'd have left you rolling in gold, or silver. . . ."

"You thought wrong," Rebeccah said. But she was staring at him, really staring at him, and a faint prickle of uneasiness slid down her spine. She suddenly became aware of how isolated she was, here in the schoolhouse with Chance Navarro. Strange, she had never been uneasy being alone with him before, but suddenly all of his questions disturbed her. The eager glow in his eyes disturbed her. She must be loco, she told herself, unconsciously squaring her shoulders as she turned away toward the schoolhouse door. What she was thinking was ridiculous. Just because Chance had asked her a lot of questions . . .

"I have to go now," she said, forcing a smile. "The Moseleys have invited me to supper with them, and I promised to tutor Cara Sue in her mathematical tables, so I mustn't be late."

"I'll ride over with you," Chance offered, following her out of the schoolhouse into the chill, clear air, but Rebeccah shook her head and kept the smile pasted on her face.

"There's no need. It's not far. Good day!"

She'd been rude, she realized as she clambered into her buckboard before he could assist her, and then wondered with a stab of conscience, as she saw the chagrin tighten his face, if she had been wrong. Maybe Chance was not unduly interested in Bear and his ill-gotten gains, and in her own acquisition of them, but she couldn't shake the suspicion that there was something besides innocent curiosity underlying all of his questions. She felt unaccountably relieved when he mounted his horse without pressing her further, and simply lifted a hand in parting.

In light of his odd behavior this afternoon she needed time to think. To be alone and to think. She waited until Chance had ridden off toward Powder Creek and then she turned the team east toward the Moseley ranch, her mind full of unwelcome suspicion.

She didn't see the cluster of riders watching her from the butte behind the schoolhouse.

And she didn't see them disappear one by one over the bluff as she headed alone along the deserted trail.

19 "Heard something today. Thought it might interest you," Molly Duke murmured over the rim of her whiskey glass. She was stretched languorously across the crimson velvet coverlet of her bed, hoping Wolf would be so overcome by the sight of her voluptuous breasts peeping naughtily out of her purple satin dressing gown that he would swoop down and take her there and then. But Wolf, damn it, seemed perfectly comfortable right where he was, leaning back against the cushions of the overstuffed velvet chair, his big boots planted firmly on the floor.

So Molly sighed and continued, running a finger absently around the rim of her glass. "It's about the Rawlings gang."

Immediately she had his attention. His eyes razored in on her, and she saw his shoulders tense.

"What about them?"

"Fellow came in a while ago and got to talking to Pokey at the bar. Mentioned a name—the same name you asked me about not too long ago—Russ Gaglin. Wasn't that one of the hombres you wanted me to watch out for?"

"Yes. Go on."

"Seems this fellow talking to Pokey met a man by that very name over in Jefferson City a day or two ago. They got to playing cards, and the fellow asked him how far it was to Powder Creek. The reason he mentioned it was because this Gaglin hombre later sneaked out of the saloon without paying up his debts, so this man came to Powder Creek looking for him—said Gaglin owed him fifty dollars. What do you think of that?"

"I think Gaglin's mighty stupid or mighty cocky to be using his own name like that," Wolf replied, getting to his feet. "But it's sure a break for me." He regarded her a moment, breathing in the heavy, cloying but sensuous smell of her perfume as, with her dressing gown open, she lounged across the bed. He bent and kissed Molly's fragrant cheek. "Thanks for the tip. Let me know if you get wind of Gaglin or if you happen to hear anything about Homer Bell or Fred Baker from that Rawlings outfit— pronto."

And he was gone quick and light as an Indian, vanishing through the door and down the stairs like a ghost in the night. Molly sighed and fell back against the fringed velvet pillows. She hoped that skinny, tart-tongued, black-haired schoolteacher knew how lucky she was.

Wolf mounted Dusty and turned the horse toward Rebeccah's property. The sun was sinking, and the vast Montana sky was turning into a rainbow of rose and orange and gold. He told himself there might not be any immediate danger—Russ Gaglin might have no idea that Rebeccah was in

Powder Creek—but every instinct told him that the buzzards were swarming in for the kill.

But was Gaglin alone? Or were one or two of his former pards—maybe even his long-lost pard, Neely Stoner—closing in on Rebeccah too?

That does it, Wolf decided, his fingers tightening on the reins as he spurred Dusty to an all-out gallop. *Rebeccah is not spending one more night alone on that ranch until this business of the silver mine is settled. I don't give a damn how good a shot she is or how many derringers she keeps hidden on the place, she's coming to the Double B until these hombres are either all locked up or dead.*

For the hundredth time since Rebeccah had confided her danger to him, Wolf damned Bear Rawlings for leaving her in this mess. Wolf didn't know if there was or wasn't a mine, but either way it meant trouble for Rebeccah.

There was no sign of her at the ranch. She must not have returned from the schoolhouse yet—maybe she was keeping one of the students after school. Wolf headed toward the schoolhouse, a prickle of apprehension growing inside him. He didn't like the looks of the sky. More snow was coming. A storm maybe. He'd better get Rebeccah Rawlings all packed up and moved someplace safe before it hit. Yet when he reached the schoolhouse, he found the little building closed up and empty.

Now what?

Wolf didn't like the feel of this. He told himself there could be an explanation—that maybe she had gone to one of the nearby ranches for supper —it was customary for families to take turns having the schoolteacher to supper. But a sixth sense warned him that something was wrong. Calling on his training and experience to keep his sudden fear for her at bay, he counted with cool precision the ranches within a five-mile radius.

He decided to try the Moseley place first.

Wolf spurred Dusty forward as the first heavy snowflakes began to fall.

They surrounded her before Rebeccah even had a chance to scream.

One moment she was headed at a fast trot toward the Moseley ranch, admiring the sunset sky while uneasily sifting through her thoughts about Chance Navarro, and the next she was ringed by three dark-garbed, weather-beaten riders, who left her no space in which to escape.

"Howdy, Reb. I wonder if you remember me?" The man on the dun horse edged closer as Rebeccah glared at them. Her team was tossing their heads and pawing the ground nervously—sensing trouble every bit as much as Rebeccah did.

"I'd never forget you, Russ!" she replied evenly, trying to look more nonchalant than she felt. Her swift gaze had taken in the faces of all three men, and she recognized the other two as well.

Fred Baker and Homer Bell. The three surviving members of the Rawlings gang. She didn't have to wonder what they wanted now.

If Bear were alive, not a single one of them would have had the courage to look sideways at his daughter, much less accost her like this on the road. But now that he was dead, Rebeccah realized grimly, their greed was too much for them. They thought they'd get that silver mine from her and then live high on the hog for the rest of their days. And it didn't matter that they'd be stealing from their former leader's daughter to do it.

"I know what you want, Russ, and I can't help you—any of you. Homer, Fred—I don't have the deed to any mine—or a map. The mine doesn't even exist!"

"Well, we know for a fact it does," Homer Bell retorted. He scratched the blond stubble covering his long chin. "So you're lying, Reb. Can't say I blame you. Bear taught you real good, didn't he? But it won't get you nowhere. Bear promised us all a piece of that silver mine one night when he was drunk as a skunk and feeling grateful because we saved his hide from getting shot by a Pinkerton detective who had him trapped upstairs in a fancy house. We killed the hombre and got Bear out the window. He told us we would all be rich men."

"And then he died," Fred Baker continued, his prune-black eyes boring into her, "died without leaving us a clue as to how to get our hands on that silver. But we knew he'd leave it to his little gal. He sure was fond of you—talked about you all the time, Reb."

Russ cut in. "Bear promised to share that silver mine with all of us, and I think out of respect for his memory, Reb honey, you ought to fork over the deed and do the same."

"There is no mine!"

"Don't be greedy, Reb," Homer warned, his milky

blue eyes peering out from beneath a filthy mop of pale hair. "It'll only get you buried."

"Are you working with Neely Stoner?" she asked in a sharp tone. Snow had begun to fall thickly around them. It dusted her cheeks and eyelashes. It slid down the back of her neck, inside her cloak, chilling her.

Or was she shivering from fear—fear of these men she had once ridden with and lived with on a daily basis, men she'd cooked for and played cards with around a campfire and from whom she'd learned how to lie, steal, and run? She'd never been afraid of them before—but then, Bear had always been there, and no one had dared cross Bear.

Except Neely Stoner.

"Stoner?" It was Fred who answered her, his thin mouth forming a sneer. Those black eyes seemed to burn with malice in the last quickly fading rays of daylight. "We ain't seen him in years. But we heerd that he wanted that silver mine too. Thought Bear owed him something, after kicking him out of the gang all those years ago and nearly killing him."

"But the way we figure it, Reb," Russ said, leaning forward in his greasy gray duster, "Stoner was clean out of the gang when we helped Bear out of that tight spot—he had no part in it—so he don't deserve to get chicken shit."

Neither do you, Rebeccah thought, but she didn't bother saying it. These men understood only one thing, so she'd better give it to them.

With one smooth, rapid movement she scooped

the rifle from the floor of the buckboard and cocked it straight at Russ Gaglin's egg-shaped face.

"Anybody moves a muscle, Russ, and you get it right between the eyes," she said coolly. Somehow she managed to keep the arm that was steadying the rifle from shaking.

She heard their sharp intake of breath, saw the surprise register in their eyes and something else, the sneaky look of men planning an attack. "Russ!" she bit out sharply, "Tell them to drop their guns, or you're a dead man!"

"Now, Reb, no one's goin' to end up dead," he began in a wheedling tone, but she could see that he was nervous. "Maybe you should just put that thing away and—"

"Drop your guns!" she ordered. "I'll kill Russ and at least one other of you before you can drop me, and you know I can do it too!"

It might have worked if not for a deep voice shouting suddenly from the edge of the woods that bordered the trail.

"Miss Rawlings? What's wrong?"

Toby Pritchard and Louisa Moseley, arm in arm, had emerged from the clump of winter-bare trees. Rebeccah knew that the strapping, gentle Toby had been carrying fifteen-year-old Louisa's books home for her every day the past two weeks. They must have been walking in the woods together, holding hands, maybe even kissing, when they'd seen her surrounded by the three men, pointing her rifle at one of them. In a flash she realized they must have been alarmed and called out to her without thinking. But it was as far as they got.

Fred drew his heavy Remington revolver and spun automatically in the saddle to fire at the masculine voice.

"No!" Rebeccah screamed as he pulled the trigger.

She jerked the rifle toward him and fired, knocking him out of the saddle. Homer yelled something she couldn't understand, and then he and Russ both charged her at once. Before she could fire again, Russ yanked the rifle from her and backhanded her so hard, she nearly fell out of the buckboard.

"You'll pay for this, Reb," he was shouting at her through the pain drumming between her ears. "We could have done this nice and easy, but now. . . . Look it, you've killed Fred! Damn it, Homer, grab her onto your horse and let's get out of here!"

"What about those kids?" Homer Bell rasped, pointing toward the woods, where Toby had collapsed on one knee and Louisa was crouched in frozen terror beside him.

"Toby, Louisa! Run!" Rebeccah screamed.

Russ cursed her and tried to hit her again, but she ducked aside just in time. To her immense relief she saw Louisa and Toby scurrying back into the copse of trees from which they'd come.

"Son of a bitch! I'll get 'em," Homer muttered, but Russ stopped him with a shout.

"Let them go! They don't matter. Take Reb and let's get the hell out of here!"

She clutched at the reins and tried to urge the frightened team forward, but Homer Bell plucked her off the seat before she could manage it and plunked her down hard in the saddle before him.

"Don't say a word, or cry, or cause one bit of trouble, Reb, or you'll be sorry—and I don't care if you *are* Bear's daughter! Ride, Gaglin, ride!"

The last thing she saw was Fred's inert form bleeding into the snow in the road. Then they were galloping hard away from everything familiar, riding hell-bent toward the snow-dusted foothills that rose to the north, looming gray and white and purple against the darkening winter sky.

20

"Calm down, Toby, and tell me everything you saw."

Wolf placed both hands on Toby Pritchard's shoulders and studied the young man's desperate face. A few feet away, in the rapidly falling darkness, a dead man sprawled in a bloody heap across the trail.

"Those men won't kill Miss Rawlings, not until they get what they want from her, so don't worry. I'll find her before then. But you have to tell me everything that happened. How many were there? Did you see which direction they headed? What did their horses look like?"

Wolf had come upon the dead man just as Culley Pritchard, Waylon, and Toby had ridden up. Rebeccah's team and buckboard stood over to the side of the road, the horses foraging in the snow-dusted winter grass, and at the sight of them an iron band had tightened around his lungs. He was too late!

But he remained deadly calm as Toby told him what he and Louisa had seen and how they had come tearing back to the Pritchard ranch after Toby had been shot at, alerting his father and brother that Miss Rawlings was in trouble. With every word the boy spoke, Wolf's grimmest fears were confirmed. It took every ounce of his self-control to think clearly, to put aside his fears for her and the dread that filled him when he thought of all the ways they might hurt her, and to concentrate on what must be done to find her. *Stay calm. Think. You can catch them in time.*

If they hurt her . . .

No. Don't let yourself think that way. You'll find her.

"And then this hombre shot at me, and then Miss Rawlings shot him. The other man hit her, and then they dragged her onto one of the horses and rode off. Damn it, if I'd had my six-shooter on me none of this would've happened," Toby exclaimed, running a hand in frustration through his sandy hair. "Miss Rawlings would be safe, and Louisa wouldn't have had to be scared to death!"

"Do you think you can find them, Wolf?" Culley Pritchard interrupted, casting a worried glance at the densely falling snow.

Wolf nodded, his face coldly set.

"Want some company?" Waylon offered.

"No. I don't know how long this will take. But you could help. Will you take care of that hombre over there? And then there's Miss Rawlings's horses and her buckboard."

"Consider it done," Waylon said.

"There's something else. Billy."

Culley cleared his throat. "What do you want us to tell him?"

"Tell him everything will be all right, but I want him to stay with the Bradys until I get back. He's there right now, matter of fact. I sure hope Emily doesn't mind if this visit is extended for a day or so," Wolf muttered.

"He's welcome to stay at our place if it's not convenient for her," Culley said, clapping a hand on Wolf's shoulder. "Don't worry about the boy, he'll be well taken care of while you're gone."

"How long do you think it's going to take?" Toby asked. He appeared now more angry and frustrated than frightened—his "wound" was only a slight grazing above the knee, already bound up and hurting him hardly at all. His concern for Rebeccah, and for Louisa, badly shaken, overshadowed whatever discomfort he'd endured from his injury.

Wolf shook his head. "We'll see. They don't have too much of a head start on me, I'd reckon, but it's getting dark fast. I may not catch up with them until tomorrow."

"Give those low-down bastards hell!" Culley Pritchard growled as he glared over at the dead man in the trail.

"I intend to," Wolf answered softly. Then he mounted again with easy grace and turned Dusty toward the foothills to the north.

"Tell Billy not to worry!" he shouted over his shoulder, and then he was riding as hard as he could across the sloping land, cursing the late hour, the clouds and whirling snow—and the approaching darkness.

The snow fell faster and ever more frenziedly as inky blackness clamped down over the hills. Russ and Homer never slowed their mounts, instead riding at the breakneck pace of outlaws on the run.

Hunched in the saddle before Homer's thin, muscular frame, Rebeccah tried to keep track of her surroundings, but the land was unfamiliar to her, and after a while she gave up trying to find a landmark in the endless clumps of woods, the twisting ravines, and the narrow, coiling trails her captors followed.

When she felt certain that she would surely freeze or faint from weariness if they traveled another mile, they halted before a rambling log shack set on a high bluff. Below was a frozen stream. In the distance rose the gray-and-purple mountains, their sharp peaks frosted in snow.

Rebeccah glanced about as Homer yanked her down from the saddle. The rickety wooden building he was dragging her toward appeared to be in even worse shape than her cabin had been when she'd first seen it. There were huge chinks in the walls and roof, which must let in a good deal of rain and sleet and wind, and the weeds surrounding the place were waist high.

The moment she stepped through the scarred wooden door and saw the thick smoke curling through the air, the long knotted-pine bar along the far wall, the scattered tables and chairs, and the profusion of glasses and whiskey bottles, Rebeccah recognized what kind of a place it was—she had been in many such as this one in her lifetime. A hideout saloon, frequented solely by outlaws, rustlers, gunfighters, and their ilk, a place where men who flouted and fled the law could meet, drink, and rest—or count their loot—while they planned their next move.

"Come on into the back room and have a drink,
Reb," Homer invited coldly, dragging her by the
arm across the dirt floor. A few seedy-looking men
glanced up from their whiskey and cards to stare
as he propelled her past their tables and pushed
her into a dim hallway, but as Russ followed, yelling for Redeye, no one said a word or even showed
much interest. Rebeccah knew better than to seek
help from any of the men in this place. No one
would pay her any attention, at least not the kind
of attention that would help. Minding your own
business was the way an outlaw stayed alive. Only
a fool would risk his neck to save a stranger.

She would have to save herself. But at the moment she wasn't sure exactly how she would do it.
The knowledge that she still had a derringer tucked
inside her right boot gave her only a small measure
of reassurance. One little hideout gun against her
captors' powerful revolvers wouldn't necessarily
get her out of this alive. And even if she killed
them, how did she know that the other men in this
place would let her leave?

Rebeccah had no choice but to bide her time and
watch for a chance—but a chance to do what? She
would just have to see when the time came, move
quickly, and pray her reactions were quick and
sure enough to guarantee her survival.

Russ Gaglin pushed her into a dingy back room
furnished with a lumpy bed, a three-legged chair,
and an oil lamp set on a small table. The table was
littered with whiskey bottles and tin cups. A greasy
burlap curtain hung lopsided across the window.

"Have a seat, Reb." Russ shoved her backward

so that she stumbled down onto the bed. It was crawling with ants. And probably fleas as well, Rebeccah thought in disgust. She sprang up again.

Russ chuckled meanly and shook his finger in her face. "Kid, it's damn lucky for you that you're Bear's daughter, or I'd give you a whipping right now that you wouldn't soon forget. Pulling a gun on me, yore old pard. That's no way to act. And killing Fred. What's got into you?"

"I don't exactly take kindly to being held up on the road by three of my old 'pards,'" Rebeccah retorted. She flashed a furious glance at Homer, who was standing with his feet planted apart and his thumbs curled around his gunbelt. "And there was no need to shoot at that boy in the woods—he's only sixteen, he didn't have a gun, and he's one of my students! Besides that, he has nothing to do with any of this!"

But Homer had latched onto her words with contemptuous disbelief. "Students! We heard you was a schoolteacher! If that don't beat all! Little scruffy Reb Rawlings teachin' school!"

"Well, you've sure growed up real pretty—and you must be smart too. Bear was right proud, you know." Russ leered at her and tossed his lank reddish hair back from his brow.

Rebeccah met his appraisal coldly, though she shuddered inwardly at the filth of these two men, at their unkempt, desperate appearance and at the queer, vicious lights in both of their eyes. "What do you think Bear would say about your grabbing me and bringing me here like a sack of loot?" she demanded, hoping to cow them by the mere mention of her father's name, but as she suspected, their fear of Bear's wrath had only endured until he was set in his grave.

"He wouldn't like it much, but there ain't a hell of a lot he can do about it now," Homer pointed out, his milky blue eyes shining.

Russ went to the table where a bottle of whiskey sat amid a clutter of tin cups. "Here, Reb, reckon you could do with a bit of refreshment after all that riding. You're not used to it, no more, I'll wager. See, we can still take good care of you. Just like Bear would want. Only thing is, you got to cooperate. When you're part of a gang, everyone looks out for the others. But it works both ways—you've got to look out for us too."

"That means sharing the profits from that silver mine," Homer muttered darkly.

Russ held up a grimy, nail-bitten hand. "Maybe Reb here got the idea we wanted the whole thing for ourselves. Hell, kid, that's not it at all. We'll be happy to split with you, Reb. 'Specially now that Fred ain't in on the deal no more, there's plenty to go around."

He held out a cup of whiskey to her, regarding her with what she gathered was an avuncular expression. She wanted to hurl the contents in his face, but thought better of it. Instead she accepted the cup without a word, took a tiny sip to quench the painful dryness of her throat, and decided that was enough. She was unaccustomed to liquor, and if two glasses of wine had made her drunk as a skunk, she shuddered to think what a single glass of whiskey would do to her. No, she needed quick wits and luck to extricate herself from this situation.

If it was possible to extricate herself from this situation.

During the entire time they'd been riding through the foothills, Rebeccah had been thinking. No doubt Toby and Louisa had run to the Pritchard ranch, which was closest, for help. Word would have been sent right away to Wolf in town, and when he heard what had happened, he would follow her. Wouldn't he?

A tiny sliver of hope pierced her heart. Yes, he would. He would never abandon her, or anyone else, to face trouble alone—no matter how bad it was, how dangerous or difficult. That was not in his nature. It would violate the stringent code of honor by which he lived.

She thought briefly of how she had once scorned him for being a lawman—yet coming to know Wolf Bodine, really know him, she had learned that being a lawman meant far more to him than just wearing a badge and locking people up in jail. His dedication to protecting honest citizens was deeply ingrained in him. It governed him more strictly than any written law or rule or official code of behavior ever could. Perhaps it was because of that crooked sheriff, the one who had killed his brother, Jimmy. Or maybe it was the memory and influence of his father, the Texas Ranger, who had died when Wolf was young. Or maybe it was just the way he'd been born. But he was a man of courage and honor, who would not desert her when she needed him.

And she needed him now.

Russ and Homer were getting restless with her continued silence. They paced the room, drinking cup after cup of whiskey, muttering between themselves and casting her dark looks. Well, she would have to stall them until Wolf got there and could help her. Probably it would be dark before the Pritchards even reached him, and he'd have to wait until morning to start.

Suddenly the brief flicker of hope in her snuffed out, and in its place flared a new fear.

What if something happened to Wolf when he tried to rescue her? What if Homer and Russ and the outlaws in the saloon killed him? He could hardly take on every single one of them at once— and all alone.

Dread clawed through her. *There has to be a way to better the odds,* Rebeccah thought frantically. *It's up to you.*

"Russ." She slanted him a friendly smile. "How about some food? Maybe we can talk business over a good meal. I don't know about you and Homer, but I'm hungry enough to eat a horse."

The two men exchanged glances. Then Russ fingered his rust-colored beard. "Sure, Reb, sure. We'll eat. And talk. We're all friends, right? Come on outside and we'll see what Zack can rustle up."

A short while later she chewed tasteless dried beef, hardtack, and burned slabs of salt pork, washing it down with several cups of strong black coffee. She kept her cloak wrapped tightly around her, for the shack was cold. Outside, snow tumbled from the heavens in a froth of white. No one could follow tracks in such a blizzard, she realized dismally, yet against all reason a part of her still clung to hope.

Russ and Homer ate ravenously and chewed their food as if they were in a race to see who swallowed each mouthful first.

Rebeccah had an opportunity to survey the saloon.

There were only three other men here, besides the stout, graying bartender. They all seemed to be keeping pretty much to themselves. But who knew what would happen when a lawman burst in and everyone reached in panic for their guns?

"Russ," she said suddenly, "I'm going to be honest with you. I do know something about that mine. But not enough. Otherwise don't you think I'd have claimed it by now and be living rich as a queen in San Francisco or New Orleans or somewhere else nice and fancy instead of teaching school in a one-horse town like Powder Creek?"

"We did kind of wonder about that," Russ nodded, leaning forward on his elbows.

Homer smeared his napkin across the grease dripping from his lips and all the way down his blond, stubbled chin. "Fred figured you was just biding your time, waiting to cash in on the mine so that you could throw us off the scent."

"No, that's not it at all. I'm more than happy to share with you. The only problem is"—Rebeccah set her fork down carefully on her plate and regarded them with a helpless shrug—"I've misplaced the deed and map."

"You . . . *what?*" Both men shouted at her.

The outlaws at the other tables glanced up, stared hard, then quickly turned away.

Rebeccah lifted her hands imploringly. "I was afraid you'd be angry," she murmured. "But it wasn't my fault. It was Neely Stoner."

"Stoner?"

"That's right. He sent a man—a horrible man—to try to get the deed and the map from me when I was still in Boston. Fortunately I was able to chase him off. You must know, I'd rather eat nails than share one cent with Neely Stoner!"

They both nodded at this, remembering how Bear had beaten the man to a bloody pulp over some slight that he'd offered Reb when she was just a kid—but no one ever knew exactly what had happened. There was bad blood left over, that's all they knew. And Stoner was kicked out of the gang for good. Everyone had considered him lucky to get away with his life.

"Well, I packed up all my belongings and my papers quick as could be and left Boston, because obviously Neely Stoner knew where I was and might come after me again! That's when I went to Powder Creek," she explained, smiling confidingly at each of the men in turn, "to live on the ranch Bear left me."

"The mine, Reb. Get to the mine," Homer growled. He banged both fists on the table before him.

Rebeccah hurried on with her tale, her brain racing to concoct it a split second before the words tripped from her tongue. "Of course I meant to claim the silver mine right away, but when I unpacked my belongings, I found that there was no map or deed. All I had to go on was a little paragraph in Bear's will, mentioning them both."

"What did that will say?" Russ inquired, scratching his jaw.

"Only that the mine was in the Nevada Territory."

"Mighty big territory. Are you sure, Reb, that the deed and map weren't there?" Homer demanded suspiciously.

"If they ever were among Bear's papers, they were gone by then, lost or misplaced in my haste to get out of Boston."

Russ's eyes flashed. "Did you see a map or didn't you?"

"I can't remember, and that's the truth." She sighed. "There were so many papers from Bear's solicitor. I don't seem to recall a map or a deed. So maybe I haven't misplaced them at all—maybe the solicitor missed them when he collected everything Bear had tucked away. As a matter of fact he did tell me that he had to collect a great many papers and stock certificates and cash and other assets Bear had accumulated, all deposited in various banks across the West. It was quite tiresome for him, but Bear had given him a list of, oh, two or three different banks and the aliases under which he'd left accounts. If there was a map, it would have been in one of those, wouldn't it? So maybe the solicitor missed something—or maybe I had the map and the deed at one time, but they're missing now. And without them I can't find the mine any easier than you can. Believe me, I wish I could."

"Son of a bitch. They have to be there some-where." Russ ground his teeth in frustration and gulped down another cup of whiskey. "You wouldn't have lost something so important, Reb."

"Not intentionally, of course, but I was pretty scared when that fellow showed up in Boston."

"Hmmm. Like you were scared of us, right?" Ho-mer asked slowly, his strange pale eyes taking shrewd stock of her, despite the quantity of whis-key he'd imbibed. "You don't seem to scare that easy, kid."

"I got an idea." Russ peered over his shoulder to make certain no one else in the saloon could hear what he was about to say. "Let's say that maybe that there solicitor did miss finding one of Bear's secret bank accounts. And maybe that's why you never got 'em, Reb. Maybe there was one stash, say, that Bear forgot to tell him about, or that he never had a chance to tell him about."

They'd swallowed it, Rebeccah thought trium-phantly, keeping her gaze downcast so they could not read the satisfaction in her eyes. They'd bought the entire fabricated story. And what was even better, they were starting out on a wild goose chase of her design, one that should easily draw them away from this place by tomorrow, when Wolf might be expected to catch up with them. If she could arrange it so that he caught them out in the open, taking them by surprise with no one else around to interfere, the odds of both she and Wolf coming out of this alive zoomed upward.

Only too eager to entice them along the path she'd chosen, Rebeccah nodded. "That could be it," she said slowly, bobbing her head up and down, letting eagerness creep into her voice. "That would explain everything."

"Let me think," Russ mumbled, scraping back his chair. His eyes were bleary from the whiskey he'd drunk as he stretched his bow-kneed legs before him and squinted with concentration. "Now, Bear had a bunch of aliases, and I knew 'em all. Let's see, there was Jonah White—that was the one he used in Texas. He went by the same handle down in Arizona and New Mexico. But in Abilene, at the First Main Bank, he liked to go by Edward Tatley. Remember, Homer?"

"Shore do. Took it from a young feller who tried to join the gang years back and got shot by a marshal first time he pulled a job with us. Edward Tatley, that was his name. Bear thought it had a nice ring to it."

Rebeccah shuddered inwardly and changed the subject. "The solicitor showed me the list. Both of those names were on it."

She didn't want to make it too easy for them. Her father's third alias, Bill Watson, was the one she would claim not to know. She knew he had used that name frequently when traveling through the Montana Territory, particularly when doing business with the Independence Bank of Butte, where he'd kept his stock certificates. But if she pretended that papers from the Butte account weren't included among those in the solicitor's possession, Russ and Homer would assume that the deed and map might be there. If she could lead them toward Butte first thing in the morning, away from this outlaw den, Wolf would have a better chance of surprising them in the open.

And before that even happened, she thought with a flutter of hope, she might find a chance to escape.

So when they mentioned Bill Watson, she feigned ignorance.

"That name wasn't on the list I saw! That could be it!"

Russ and Homer sat up straighter in their chairs. Russ gave a squeal of triumph. "Last few years Bear spent a lot of time down in Butte. He'd disguise himself and head into town—did a pretty good job of it, too, remember, Homer? Did some business down there with the Independence Bank. Always went by the handle of Bill Watson."

"Yep, we never could tell if it was Crystal McCoy who kept him coming back to Butte or that there bank business he was always tending to—I used to think it was Crystal, but now . . . hell, we won't know until we get our hands on whatever he'd got hidden in that there vault."

"Crystal?" Now Rebeccah was genuinely surprised. She'd never heard the name Crystal McCoy. "Was she a dance-hall girl or something?"

Russ and Homer chortled. "Crystal McCoy is a lady," Russ said, tipping back another cup. "Owns the Double Barrel Saloon. And the sawmill. Rich as hell. First we thought Bear might have left the mine to her, but that wouldn't have made no sense. Crystal didn't need a mine—she's about the richest gal in the Territory. And she didn't want nothing from him nohow. So we figgered pretty quick that

Bear would only have left it to you—his pretty little schoolgal, the apple of his eye."

Homer belched and then squinted at Rebeccah over the rim of his cup. "Bear and her were thinking about gettin' married. . . ."

"Married!"

Homer guffawed at the stunned look on her face. "You mean Bear never once said nothin' about her to you? Well, he sure made a point of getting himself into Butte right regular. Even thought about giving up some of our stage jobs just so he could stay close by Crystal McCoy."

"He was jest about ready to go straight for her," Russ snorted, "but before he could make up his mind to it, that posse plugged him."

"That settles it," Homer grinned, leaning back in his chair. "That deed and the map leading to the mine have gotta be in the bank vault in Butte, waiting for Mr. Bill Watson. First thing in the morning we pay that Independence Bank a little visit."

"And we'll split the proceeds of the mine three ways?" Rebeccah asked sternly. They would expect that of Bear's daughter. "Fair and square?" she demanded.

"You bet, Reb. We wouldn't cheat Bear's daughter out of nothin'—'specially since she's growed up to be such a looker."

Russ winked at the other outlaw and then playfully pinched Rebeccah's cheek. "Ain't that right, Homer?"

Bell snickered. "Sure is. Everything equal—fair and square."

They're probably planning to shoot me the moment

they get their greasy paws on those documents,
Rebeccah concluded. But she was counting on
things never getting near that point.

"Come on, Reb, ain't you beat after that long
ride? You come get some shut-eye in the back room
with us. Don't worry, we got bedrolls. You kin have
that nice bed all to your lonesome. Unless you
want some company?"

"Isn't there another room where I can stay in this
hovel—alone?" she fired back.

Russ shook his head, barely able to suppress his
drunken excitement. "Even if there was, do you
think we're going to let you out of our sight? Bear
taught us a few things over the years, kid, and one
of 'em was, don't trust no one."

"And that means even a pretty little thing like
you," Homer added softly, and this time Rebeccah
didn't at all like the way his strange milky eyes
roamed appreciatively over her.

"What's the matter, honey, don't you like us no
more?" he continued, seeing the apprehension in
her face. "When you was a little girl, we were the
ones who taught you how to cheat at poker, and
how to spit, and all sorts of useful things. Don't tell
me you forgot."

"Don't *you* forget that if either one of you comes
near me tonight, I'll find a way to kill you before
you touch me—and you know I'll do it," she said
coldly, and the icy glint in her eyes left no doubt of
her determination.

That threat, the dead-serious resolve behind it,
and the derringer still hidden in her boot, were all
that stood between her and those two mangy ani-

mals, Rebeccah knew. She prayed it would be
enough. Still, her knees trembled as she rose, and
Russ took her arm to lead her toward the hallway
at the rear of the saloon.

Suddenly the door to the hideout saloon crashed
open. A man burst in without warning.

He had a silver-handled Colt .45 gripped purposefully in each fist.

"Nobody move!" he ordered in a tone of such
iron command that nobody did.

Wolf! Rebeccah froze between Russ and Homer.
The outlaw den was a marble tableau of silent, motionless shock. No one appeared to breathe as every man there assessed the situation and swiftly
debated the wisdom of holding still versus that of
trying to draw on the heavily armed, tough-looking
stranger commanding them to obey his shouted order.

Wolf smiled thinly, and now that he had their
undivided attention he continued in that same
deadly-chilling tone, his ghost-gray eyes scanning
each man and seeming instantaneously to take his
measure. "I want the woman—and the two men
that brought her. No outsiders have to die tonight
—unless they want to," he added coldly.

Rebeccah didn't even dare to breathe. Wolf was
either very sure of himself or very foolish. How
cool he was, she marveled in awe, even as her
heart hammered with sick fear. If he didn't succeed
in facing them all down, he'd have to take them all
on—all six of them. One man against six?

She felt her throat closing in terror.

Suddenly there was no more time for fear or

wondering or even hope. Homer Bell, cussing, went for his gun.

Wolf yelled, "Rebeccah, get down!" and at the same moment, with cold purpose, he fired.

Blood bloomed across Homer's chest, bubbled from his lips, and he crashed to the floor, twitching. Biting back her screams, Rebeccah dove under the table. She was never sure later exactly what happened next.

Another outlaw in the saloon opened fire; there was an explosion of deafening gunshots, the stink of gunsmoke, the thud of another body. And a death scream.

Rebeccah had her derringer out. She saw Russ go for his gun, drawing on Wolf, who had leaped forward in a half crouch, then a spin, firing and dodging bullets with a cool, astonishing agility beyond her comprehension. In a flash she aimed the derringer, but even before she could fire, Wolf wheeled toward Russ and shot first. Gaglin slumped to the floor right beside her, blood spouting in a crimson fountain from his temple.

On her hands and knees, staring into his sightless eyes, Rebeccah bit her lips against rising hysteria.

She heard someone—the bartender? one of the other outlaws?—say in a low tone, "Don't try anything, Huff, that's Wolf Bodine!"

Then she heard Wolf's voice, just as purposeful, drawling, "Mighty wise of you, fellows."

He edged toward her table, still with his gun trained on the remaining three men. With a sudden movement he tossed aside the table under which she crouched and, still training one of his revolvers on the bartender and the remaining two outlaws, he reached down a hand.

"Come on, we're getting out of here."

Somehow, then, they were out in the blizzarding night and Wolf was lifting her into the saddle. In one quick motion he had untethered Russ's horse and was holding its reins, and then he vaulted up behind Rebeccah and spurred Dusty to a gallop.

"Did they hurt you?" he shouted into the wind, as the sorrel's long legs gathered speed and the whirling snow blanketed their shoulders and whipped against their eyes and cheeks.

She shook her head, nestling deeper into his arms, letting herself go limp with relief and weariness.

"We're not going far," Wolf yelled. "I know a place where we can spend the night!"

"Wolf." She stirred suddenly, and raised her voice, calling to him over her shoulder. "Is Toby all right?"

"Toby's fine," he yelled back, and they both leaned low over Dusty's mane as they swung under a cluster of low-hanging branches as the horse veered onto a twisting, wooded track.

They rode in silence then through a belt of forest, emerged to follow a short burst of rolling land, then twisted their way along a steep, treacherously snow-covered ravine. Then once more they were flying along beneath slender silver birches. A rabbit bolted through the white night, its tracks quickly swallowed up by the endlessly twirling snow. At last they snaked their way through a convoluted trail that led between two walls of rocks, then rode downward into a hidden gully. There, tucked behind a copse of pine, sheltered on all sides by rock, was a small cabin, barely noticeable in the dimness, blending into the trees that surrounded it.

Wolf rode to the rear of the cabin. He halted Dusty before a half-hidden lean-to amid the brush. With her help he tethered both horses in the lean-to, then paused a moment, listening. When he was satisfied that there was no pursuit, he turned back to Rebeccah.

She looked half frozen and utterly exhausted, her normally pale skin bright from the cold. Shivering, her sable hair glistening with snow, she looked as if she would sink down to the earth at any moment with exhaustion.

Wolf slipped a strong arm around her waist, alarmed as she sagged against him.

"Are you sure you're all right?"

Looking up into his strong, dearly handsome face, so filled with concern, she felt a surge of powerful love bursting through her. She didn't know how much longer she could hold it back. He had rescued her—again. He had risked his life to save her. He must have ridden for hours through the dark and the snow, despite all weariness, doubt, and the battering of the elements, tracking Russ and Homer somehow, with relentless determination and skills she could not even begin to imagine. He had found her, killed for her, and brought her to safety.

"I'm fine—no, I'm perfect—now that I'm with

you," she heard herself whispering, a catch in her voice, and with a sweet ache inside of her she reached up shaking fingers to touch his cheek.

She felt his body tense with some powerful emotion—a reaction to her words, or her touch, or both. His eyes lit with a vivid silvery-gray intensity, pinning hers so powerfully, she could not look away. Then Wolf swept her into his arms and carried her with no apparent effort and a great deal of lithe grace into the hidden cabin.

21 Wolf set her down on the floor of the pitch-black cabin, but his hands lingered around her waist, as if he was reluctant to let her go. His eyes quickly accustomed themselves to the darkness of the cabin. Moving away from her at last, he busied himself with matches and a kerosene lamp, which sat on a long table near the stove. He turned up the wick until the cabin was flooded by a soft yellow glow.

It was only one tiny, square room, but to her weary eyes it was a beautiful, snug haven. It needed a good sweeping, but otherwise it was surprisingly clean and neat. Besides the table there was a wooden bench, a pile of logs in a crate beside a blackened hearth, and an old cast-iron stove over in one corner.

But she noticed there wasn't a bed.

The wind wailed mournfully against the cabin's two small rawhide windows. The log walls creaked beneath the force of it.

"I'll get my saddlebags and start a fire." Wolf studied her lovely, cold-reddened face. "You look like you could use some brandy, Miss Rawlings. As luck would have it, I've got a flask in my pack."

"You certainly come prepared for everything, don't you?" she said lightly, for now, more than the ordeal she'd gone through with Russ and Homer, it was the idea of being alone here in the dark woods with him all night that made her tremble. She tried to keep the conversation casual. "And I suppose you've forgotten my high susceptibility to spirits?"

"I haven't forgotten anything about you," he returned with a cool grin that made her eyes widen and her heart spin like a top. "I have every intention of taking full advantage of your 'high susceptibility to spirits'—so consider yourself warned."

He disappeared into the bitter night.

A short time later they spread a heavy woven Indian blanket before the blazing fire and sat side by side a few feet from the flames. They sipped from steaming mugs of coffee generously laced with brandy. As the snowfall tapered to a gentle tumbling of lacy white bits and the brandy-flavored coffee tingled down her throat hot and potent and comforting, Rebeccah felt her cares slide from her shoulders.

He's doing this on purpose, she thought, feeling her body grow warm and relaxed, her skin begin to glow, and all the remaining tension melting from her limbs. *He's trying to make me forget about those other women forever hanging around him, trying to make me forget about all the reasons we do not suit each other, trying to make me forget that whenever we are together, one of us always ends up angry with the other.*

It was working. Whatever his plan, whatever his intentions, as she sat there beside him in that tiny firelit cabin hidden away in the woods, protected by rocks, trees, and a secret gully, she felt herself growing increasingly warm, felt every worry and objection and doubt rinsing away as though she stood with dust-caked skin beneath a softly sparkling waterfall.

She turned her head to gaze at him. He was looking into the flames, his eyes narrowed thoughtfully, the thick, burnished hair so like the color of fine mahogany tumbling carelessly over his brow.

He was so different from that carefree young man who had discovered her under the bed in that hideout cabin so many years ago—so much had befallen him since. His brother's death, the hard years as a lawman battling the worst savagery of the West, Clarissa's desertion . . . and now Caitlin's death.

Rebeccah didn't know if it was the brandy warming her and stimulating her blood or the rush of feelings long kept dammed, but she suddenly wanted Wolf Bodine more than she had ever wanted anything before: she wanted to reach out to him, to chase his demons away, to soothe his troubled soul. For she knew once and for all that beneath the steely veneer of the professional lawman, beneath the hard set of his features and the keen flintiness of his gray eyes, there lurked a lonely man.

A strong, courageous, decent, and ultimately lonely man—a man who would risk his own life for others, who would be strong for them and brave when no one else would be. But she knew a secret about him, something she felt certain he did not suspect she knew. Beneath the steady strength and courage of his everyday life, he felt an emptiness, a long-standing sense of pained betrayal that was all Clarissa's doing.

Rebeccah wanted suddenly, yearningly, to pervade that emptiness, to fill that void. But there was something she needed to discover first.

"Wolf?"

At the husky note in her voice he turned his head. She nearly took his breath away, she was so beautiful. Her delicate face aglow in firelight, her hair shining blue black, like the finest, glossiest sable. But it was the expression in her brilliant violet eyes that was his undoing. Soft, rapt, glistening with something that could only be tenderness.

It seemed impossible that the cold and haughty young woman who had stepped off the stagecoach a few short months ago with a chip on her shoulder and a grudge against lawmen could be looking at him this way now . . . her eyes begging him to kiss her, her lips seeming to beckon and summon his to taste of their sweetness.

Memories flooded over him. He remembered how gentle she had been with Caitlin at the end, how she had soothed her with music, and how openly and understandingly she had talked with Billy. She was not the same brittle girl who had come to Powder Creek—or was it he who had changed, he who now saw beneath the stony pretense she paraded for the world, he who now recognized her softness, her goodness, her inner beauty. . . .

"Wolf," she breathed again, as he continued to

stare at her, drinking in the sight of her, a sight warmer and more potent than a gallon of brandy-laced coffee.

He couldn't drag his gaze from those bewitching eyes.

"What, Rebeccah?"

"Can I ask you a question?"

"You just did."

The bewitching eyes smiled. "Tell me if the rumors are true," she murmured, trying to sound casual, trying to disguise how much depended on his answer, how the direction of her life, her dreams, all hinged on what he replied.

"Rumors are almost never true," Wolf commented ruefully. He lifted one brow. "Which rumors do you mean?"

"That you are either already betrothed or about to become betrothed to—"

"False."

"False?" Rebeccah's normally dulcet, low-pitched voice actually squeaked with excitement. The rapt sparkle suddenly returned to her eyes.

Wolf stared at her in disbelief, wondering who had filled her head with such stories. "False," he reiterated firmly. "No way. Anything else?"

She nodded, so relieved and overjoyed by this abrupt dismissal of her worst fears that she said the next thing that popped into her mind.

"Make love to me."

Wolf reached out and gently touched his finger to her lips, tracing the tender shape of her mouth as lightly as a butterfly. "Rebeccah, you shouldn't say a thing like that to a man if you don't mean it."

"I mean it."

Damn it, he thought, every muscle heating, his loins growing hard and heavy at her words and at the eager invitation in her eyes.

Was she drunk? Despite what he'd said earlier, he couldn't take advantage of that. One man had already taken advantage of her in the cruelest way imaginable and he couldn't add to her pain. . . .

But she was leaning toward him, sliding her delicate hands around his neck, murmuring against his lips as she closed the distance between them with a little wriggle. "I'm not drunk, if that's what you're thinking. And I'm not going to change my mind. I love you, Wolf. I want you. I hoped you wanted me too. Maybe I was wrong."

"You loco little she-devil, I do want you—more than I ever wanted any woman—more than I ever wanted Clarissa." He gripped her wrists. "You're in my blood, woman, like gold fever or whiskey—only worse. Hell, much worse. I can't think of anything but you. The other women I know—women I thought I could care for—can't hold a candle to you. When I'm with them, I think of you. When I'm alone, I think of you. And when I'm with you, God help me, I think about the things I'd like to do to you."

"Do them," she urged breathlessly, and ignited his mouth with hers.

The kiss was soft, dazzlingly sweet, but after a few moments it became heatedly intense. His lips seared and tormented hers with a devouring urgency that left her moaning and gasping for more. Holding her head firmly between his hands, he

deepened the kiss still more. His tongue touched
hers, caressingly at first, then more boldly, posses-
sively. Rebeccah felt her senses spinning out of
control.

"I love you, Rebeccah, every single beautiful
thing about you," Wolf breathed, his voice low and
husky. Rebeccah could feel the heat and hardness
and strength of him, she felt also the whipcord tension vibrating through his broad shoulders, his
muscled arms and legs.

"I love you, Wolf. I want you. Need . . . you."

She murmured incoherently as his hands found
her breasts and cupped them through the layers of
her garments, sending delicious spirals of delight
straight down to her knees. Desire sprang eagerly
through her, soft as sunshine, intense as flame.
While he kneaded her breasts, his fingers moving
ever more arousingly as little squirms and moans
of pleasure came from her, his lips, warm and sensuous, seared kisses down the side of her neck.

Sweet, sweet torture. Rebeccah gave a low moan
deep in her throat as he lowered her onto the blanket. He straddled her, gazing with glinting purposefulness into her passion-glowing eyes. Slowly,
letting the tension and suspense build between
them, he began unbuttoning her blouse. His fingers
were sure and knowing, his eyes full of determined
promise, while all the while he brushed kisses
across her eyelids, her cheeks, and inside the fragile, exquisitely sensitive hollow of her throat.

Dizzying sensations electrified her everywhere
he touched. His mouth was heat lightning, his fingertips pure fire. And what she saw in his eyes

filled her with a half-joyous, half-fearful anticipation. When he at last tugged the blouse free from the waistband of her serviceable navy wool skirt and tossed it aside, leaving her soft, rose-peaked breasts all but exposed except for the dainty lace camisole, Rebeccah's pulse quickened painfully. Her heart was beating so rapidly, she thought it would explode through the wall of her chest.

Wolf's keen gray eyes gleamed with pure sensual appreciation as they roamed over her, seeming to drink in the exposed sight of her beneath him.

He smiled down at her, a hard, yet oddly tender smile, as he noted the glowing sheen of her skin, hot to his touch, the quickness of her breathing, and the delectable rise and fall of her breasts as she reached up to pull him down to her.

She was so lovely. So warm and giving and innocent, he thought he would die with the wanting of her. He inhaled the sweetness of her hair, letting the dark, satiny strands trail through his fingers. He lowered his head and licked at one impudent, hard-peaked breast, his own excitement growing as she gave a startled gasp. His mouth closed over the nipple even as his hand firmly captured its twin and began a deliberate torment.

Her body was so hot and soft and willing. Passion ruled this dark-haired angel, however cool and starched a facade she might present to the world. Whatever Neely Stoner had done to her, at least it hadn't destroyed this part of her, the capacity to feel passion and love. As Rebeccah's body arced and writhed beneath the expert torment of his lips

and hands, Wolf knew that he would never get
enough of her, not until the end of his days.

Moaning softly, Rebeccah wrapped her fingers in
the silk of his hair even as her mouth demanded
attention from his. His body pressed upon hers felt
as much on fire as hers did, and his manhood felt
huge and powerful. Her effect on him filled her with
a curious, surging sense of power. Without thinking, acting only on need and instinct, she arced to
meet the hard angles of his form and, with insistent
arms, entwined him ever closer.

"You're beautiful, Rebeccah. You're so unbeliev-
ably beautiful," he whispered, his breath warm
against her lips. "I promise you I won't hurt you,
sweetheart. I'll never let anything hurt you again."

What followed between them was a blur of taut,
sweet sensation. Rebeccah only knew that she
wanted him with a fierceness that would not be
denied, and she sought to give him the same savage pleasure he was raining ruthlessly down on
her. They were naked before the firelight, their garments flung in little careless heaps, and the woven
blanket rough against their burning skin as they
thrashed together on the floor of the cabin.

She wrapped her legs around him and fluttered
kisses across his shoulders and his chest. Lively
hands played with the muscles that rippled across
his supple back. With her head flung back, she
found herself clinging to him, submitting to the
pleasures of his hands, his tongue, and his teeth,
which stopped just short of inflicting pain as he
kissed the satiny length of her body and gently,

surely, probed the moist, sweet depths of her womanhood.

When he spread her legs and lowered himself upon her, she instinctively welcomed him, but as he eased his manhood into her, she tensed. Her eyes flew open, wide with apprehension in the flickering firelight, and Wolf could only guess at the ugly memories crowding to intrude.

Damn Neely Stoner. Damn him to hell.

"Don't be afraid, sweetheart. Trust me."

Trust. Staring up at his flushed, leanly handsome face poised above her, Rebeccah nodded. She did trust Wolf, she trusted him completely. Only . . . panting, she braced herself for pain. But Wolf soothed her with kisses, and touches, and with seemingly infinite patience he eased into her, inch by careful inch, until at last the muscles of her body relaxed, and the aching need returned to her, and he slid into her fully, watching her eyes. The fear had gone from them, and now they were magnificent violet stars burning up into his with love and wondrous eagerness, and at last he allowed his terrible restraint to loosen. Pressing his hungry mouth to hers, to soothe and reassure her, he began to move and thrust.

Rebeccah cried out at the throbbing fullness that filled her as he plunged deeply into her, again and again. Joy burst through her, a wild, swiftly gliding joy. She felt as if she were racing down a steep canyon at breakneck speed, spinning into whirling space, out of control, and yet brilliantly, torturously alive and aware and *knowing*.

At last, deliciously spent, cozily entwined, they

lay together as the flames of the fire dwindled and darkness cocooned the room.

"Sweet Rebeccah," Wolf murmured, holding her close against his naked side. He leaned down to drop a kiss upon the peak of her breast. "Don't ever leave me."

"Leave you?" Like Clarissa? Even after tonight, with the glory of their lovemaking, was there a seed of worry inside him? She pulled free and stared at him. "I would sooner ride off a cliff at the top of Bull Mountain than ever leave you," she told him fiercely and sealed it with a long, giving, fervent kiss. "Wolf," she said shakily at last, coming up for air. "Don't ever, ever doubt my love."

"I won't," he said, and the slow, heated grin she loved spread across his face. "On one condition."

"What condition?"

"Snuggle back down here and demonstrate it for me all over again."

He gave her no time for any spoken reply, but reading only the delighted gleam in her eyes, he yanked her back into his arms and they began all over again.

22 "I have an idea," Rebeccah said the next morning as she sat up naked on the bedroll and stretched her arms luxuriously above her head.

Wolf immediately tugged her down atop him, holding her there facing him, with her breasts pressed against his chest and her hips molded against him, and grinned.

"So do I."

A laugh bubbled from her lips. She felt beautiful, and deliciously satisfied. Cool, wintry sunshine filled the Montana sky outside the window, the snow was melting, and life tasted incredibly sweet. "I'm serious."

"So am I."

The hand that cradled her buttocks slid languorously up her spine until it touched the long, thick curtain of her hair. He twisted his fingers in the ebony strands and kissed her with gently nibbling kisses until she forgot what she was going to say.

As her breathing quickened, Wolf rolled her onto her back and moved his body atop hers. His tongue found her breast and began to lick the taut, achingly sensitive nipple.

"I must admit, I like your ideas," she gasped, and it was his turn to laugh.

"I've got lots more ideas to show you, Rebeccah," he promised as he slid his hand between her legs.

Much later they raced out of the cabin to the tiny creek trickling through smooth gray rocks, and, yelling and splashing, they bathed quickly in the icy water. Their fingers shook afterward as they pulled on their clothes and then scurried back to the house and the heat of the stove for a makeshift breakfast of jerky and hardtack, which Wolf kept stored in his pack.

"So," Wolf said, swallowing a mouthful of the jerky and admiring the lovely way her skin glowed in the clear winter sunshine streaming through the window. "What's your idea?"

"Now he wants to know," Rebeccah murmured to no one in particular, throwing up her hands. "It would serve you right if I couldn't remember it at all."

"But you do."

"Of course I do." She poured them each another cup of coffee. "I think we should go to Butte right away and see Crystal McCoy."

"Who the hell is Crystal McCoy?"

"My father's mistress." At his raised brows she hurried on. "I didn't know anything about her until Russ and Homer told me yesterday, but it seems to me that if anybody knows anything about some papers relating to this mine, it would be her. I certainly don't, and she seems to be the only other person my father cared for." Quickly she told him what Russ had said about Bear's visits to Butte.

"It's worth a try. Maybe she can shed a little light on this whole thing. But I'll tell you this, Rebeccah. I'm going to get to the bottom of this mine business once and for all—even if it means rounding up any and all of the hombres who think you've got possession of these mine papers and throwing them in jail—or killing them. No more waiting around until the next varmint comes after you. Next time we might not be so lucky."

We. He said we, Rebeccah thought with a joyous lift of the heart. "Yes, Wolf," she said meekly, too happy for the moment even to think about reminding him that going around killing people without cause was against the law. He wouldn't do it, she knew, not unless it was self-defense or to actually protect her, but she enjoyed the sentiment. Wolf finished his breakfast in deep thoughtfulness, obviously still troubled by how to extricate her from danger before it struck again, and Rebeccah feasted her eyes on him and wondered at her own fortune in having won the love of this incredibly splendid man.

They started toward Butte at mid-morning, traveling in easy stages throughout the day, the pristine banks of snow glistening and melting all around them. After a short stop in the small town of Serenity, where they consumed a quick dinner in the tiny hotel dining room, which smelled like grease and burned ham, they then pressed on for Butte, reaching the town just as daylight was fading. The sky burned a fiery amber-red as Wolf and

Rebeccah reined in before the Double Barrel Saloon.

Rebeccah felt the stares of the cowboys, miners, gamblers, and drifters clustered throughout the wide, opulent room as Wolf escorted her through the swinging double doors and over to the gleaming mahogany bar. She tried to ignore the glances she received, but one cowboy in a gray wide-brimmed hat and fringed vest actually let out a low whoop as she passed by him, and Wolf spun quickly about to grab him by his shirt.

"Down, boy!" Wolf growled softly. His eyes flashed an ominous warning that the cowboy couldn't mistake.

"No offense meant, ma'am," he stammered quickly with a pleading glance at Rebeccah.

"None taken," Rebeccah murmured. And then she put a hand lightly on Wolf's arm. "Wolf, it's *all right*. Let him *go.*"

A balding piano player with a gray handlebar mustache banged on tinny keys in the duskily lit corner of the bar. There were paintings of women in various states of dishabille adorning the gold-flecked walls, and smoke hung everywhere. Men played cards at most of the tables, but occasionally two or three sat in groups, talking in low voices, or watching the saloon girls, who pranced back and forth in their black silk stockings, high kid boots, and bright velvet dresses, the latter gaudily low-cut and spangled with sequins and baubles, flowers and feathers. Rebeccah had been in such places in her youth, but it was a long time ago. She wanted to stare about curiously and marvel at this strange, wild, decadent atmosphere, but she had business to conduct, and it was far more important than indulging idle curiosity.

At the bar Wolf asked for Crystal McCoy.

"Who wants to see her?" the potbellied bartender asked, peering shrewdly at them from beneath shaggy black brows.

Rebeccah put both palms facedown on the gleaming surface of the bar. "Rebeccah Rawlings," she said crisply.

The bartender started, and focused his small, mud-colored eyes on her for a long moment. He swore under his breath.

"Rebeccah Rawlings, are you, now? If that don't beat all. Come with me, lass. Crystal will sure want to see you."

He left his post and lumbered like a grizzly around the bar, leading them into a murky corridor off the main saloon and then up a short flight of stairs to a closed door.

The sign on the door read PRIVATE.

He rapped on the paneled wood. "Visitors."

"Who is it?" called a tired-sounding voice.

The bartender grinned and pushed open the door. "Rebeccah Rawlings!" he announced.

Wolf and Rebeccah stepped inside.

Two men rode from opposite directions and met at a bald knoll ten miles outside of Powder Creek. They dismounted and walked toward each other, their breaths coming in white puffs in the chill air of dusk.

"Why'd you let her out of your sight?" the larger

man demanded, looking as if he'd like to shoot his slimmer companion between the eyes.

The other man cupped his hands and lit up one of his homemade smokes, calm as dawn. "What did you expect me to do—blow the whole plan to smithereens by making a nuisance out of myself? She was getting damned suspicious as it was. That's one filly who's too shrewd for her own good." He drew in deeply on the tobacco, a scowl darkening his handsome features. "I've got a funny feeling she trusts that damned sheriff a hell of a lot more than she trusts me."

"Good work!" the other man exclaimed sarcastically. "This whole plan is collapsing under our noses, Navarro! We should've just grabbed the girl, taken her somewhere where Bodine can't find her, and made her talk!"

"That's what your old pards tried to do, and now they've got Bodine breathing down their necks, you damned fool," Chance Navarro said coldly.

"Look here, maybe you're scared of him, but I'm not," Neely Stoner flashed back. "This business is taking much too long—and it's not the way I usually get things done. I've had my fill of your trying to sweet-talk her into trusting you and telling you about the mine. I've had enough of waitin' and spyin'. I say we grab her as soon as she and that infernal sheriff get back."

"Your problem, Stoner," Chance said, his green eyes shining, "is that you don't have any imagination. Reb Rawlings will squawk her head off about that mine and beg us to take that deed and map off her hands when I'm finished with her. And we won't have to harm a single hair on that pretty little head of hers."

"Since when are you squeamish about hurtin' hairs on a woman's head? You don't seem to have any problem burning 'em up alive—"

Chance lunged at him before his words were done. Navarro's eyes were now evil slits, his voice low and chilling. "Keep your damned mouth shut, Stoner, or I'll shut it for you—savvy? Don't ever say that again."

"Son of a bitch! Navarro—let me go." Stoner shoved him away, but his weathered, pockmarked skin had paled. There was something about the handsome young gambler that made him feel queasy—like he'd eaten too much bacon fried in its own grease. "Hell, I don't care what you've done, so long as you come up with a way to make the girl talk."

"I have. It's easy."

"Well?"

Navarro regarded him with a tight little smile. "It's been my experience that most women will do anything—anything—to protect the folks they love. And Rebeccah Rawlings thinks she loves Bodine—and his kid, Billy."

"So?" Then it hit him. Stoner started to grin. Navarro nodded, his own smirk widening.

"That's it, Stoner. You're pretty quick. We can get Reb Rawlings to do whatever we want. All we have to do is snatch the kid."

"What about Bodine? He'll come after us with both barrels blazing if we—"

"Leave Bodine to me," Chance Navarro said

softly. There was a curious anticipatory light in his moss-green eyes. He started toward his horse. "He won't be a problem."

Crystal McCoy was not at all what Rebeccah had expected. She had thought the saloon owner would be a woman like Molly Duke, tall, voluptuous, crude, and sultry. Instead she found a silvery blond-haired woman of medium height and build. Crystal McCoy had a pert, intelligent face, lovely cheekbones and ivory skin, and clear hazel eyes set beneath slanting, forceful brows. She was perhaps forty. She wore a businesslike white shirtwaist and severe gray wool skirt, no rings or brooches or other jewelry, and kept her fair hair piled in a dainty chignon at the nape of her neck, tied with a black velvet ribbon.

"Come in, Rebeccah," she said warmly, rising and holding out her hand as she saw the dark-haired girl enter the room. "Please, make yourselves comfortable. This is a wonderful surprise."

Rebeccah, astonished as much by the low, cultured voice as by the friendly greeting, found herself gripping cool, slender fingers.

Quickly she introduced Wolf and then glanced around the small, simple office, where sheaves of papers covered an old desk and wooden shutters had not yet been closed against the encroaching nightfall. Already, though, a kerosene lamp glowed on the desk.

"What brings you here?" Crystal asked, after offering them drinks, which they both refused, and then settling back into her well-worn green leather chair.

"I need some information," Rebeccah told her, meeting that inquisitive, polite gaze with a searching one of her own. She took a deep breath. "Russ Gaglin and Homer Bell told me about your relationship with my father. I never knew of your existence before then. But I suddenly realized that you might be able to shed some light on a certain matter for me. If you will."

"Anything I can do for Bear's daughter, I will certainly be happy to do," Crystal McCoy said quietly.

She loved him, Rebeccah realized, gripping the arms of her chair. This had been no tawdry, shallow coupling, arranged as a matter of convenience whenever Bear was in the vicinity. There was a sadness in Crystal McCoy's eyes, which Rebeccah recognized as one of genuine grief. She remembered what Homer had said about Bear and Crystal's plans to marry, a statement she had not put much faith in before now. But her heart lifted suddenly at the knowledge that Bear, too, had found love, that he had not been all alone these past years, that he had shared a part of his life with someone who cared for him in return.

"Tell me," Crystal went on, "what it is you need to know."

So she explained about the mine—about Neely Stoner, Fred Baker, Russ, and Homer. "Bear never mentioned anything about it during his visits to me, or in any letters—that's the strange part," Rebeccah concluded. "I have no deed, no map, no reason at all to believe that there even is such a fabulous find—but I can't convince any one of these outlaws that it doesn't exist."

"Do you know anything about it?" Wolf inquired, studying Crystal's startled expression. "We'd appreciate any information you can give us, no matter how unimportant it seems."

"Oh, I can do better than that, Sheriff Bodine." Crystal rose and hastened toward a gilt-framed seascape hanging on the wall. She suddenly swung the painting outward away from the wall to reveal a safe behind it. From the pocket of her skirt she drew a key. "I've kept all of your father's letters to me these past few years. One in particular will be of interest to you."

Wolf and Rebeccah exchanged glances. Crystal withdrew a packet of letters tied with blue ribbon. She brought them to her desk with slow steps and began riffling through them. "Here it is," she exclaimed at last, and held out a sheet of plain paper. "Rebeccah, read this. He wrote it about a year ago. This page here is all about the mine."

Rebeccah's heart twisted painfully as she glanced down at the bold, rather awkward script that was her father's handwriting. Her breathing quickened as she read the words.

The boys helped me out of a bad spot last week, and I was mighty grateful to them. I don't want to scare you none, Crystal honey, but if they hadn't come through for me when they did, I wouldn't be here to tell you all about it, and wouldn't be coming to see you soon neither. I told them a tall tale, though, when we'd all made good our escape, and I feel right bad about it. I told them that I had the deed to a big silver mine, that I'd won it at cards like I won the ranch, and that they'd all get a piece of it one day. Russ pressed me to say where it was, and all the boys wanted to go straight off and claim it, but I told them we'd cash in our chips when the time was right. Well, Crystal honey, the truth of the matter is, there ain't no silver mine at all. But I got to thinking after they helped me out of that tight spot that next time they might not want to risk their necks for old Bear—unless they thought there was something in it for them. If they think I've got something that's going to make rich, fat men out of all of 'em one of these days, they'll make a damned sight sure I live long enough to spread that wealth around. It seemed like a mighty good idea at the time, but somehow or other, rumors have started flying about that mine—folks I never even met are whispering about it. And I realize that if I 'fess up, the boys'll be mighty riled at me for getting their hopes up and making them look like damned fools. So I reckon I'd better keep my mouth shut and hope they forget all about it and the talk dies down, or else things might get pretty ugly. I reckon if I would have thought it out before I started the story, I'd have thought better of it, but these days I'm not thinking about much but being with you, my sweet pretty little Crystal. Well, I reckon it's no harm having them think they've got a silver boon coming if I stay healthy. Maybe sometime I'll tell them the truth and see if they know how to laugh at themselves. Meanwhile I'm going to visit my darlin' Reb in a week or two, and I can't hardly wait. She's

*turned into a beauty, and a young lady to boot, and
I hope one day the two of you will get to meet each
other. I figure you'd get along real good—my two
favorite gals.*

Rebeccah bit her lip. She found that her hands
were shaking. He sounded so happy, so filled with
affection for this woman who stood across from
her, her gaze turned toward the window while
Rebeccah read. Wordlessly Rebeccah handed the
letter to Wolf and waited as he read it. She was
struggling with her emotions. Fresh grief welled up
in her for her father. Bear Rawlings had been many
things, not all of them good, but to her he had always been the kindest, strongest, smartest, and
most bighearted of fathers.

She saw Crystal McCoy wipe away a tear and
knew instinctively that this demure, elegant woman
missed him as much as she did.

"Well, that explains it," Wolf muttered, handing
the letter back to Crystal. He threw a hard glance at
Rebeccah. "Some little joke. Too bad he never fore-
saw that it could cost his daughter her life."

"Bear would never have done anything to endan-
ger Rebeccah," Crystal said quickly.

Rebeccah liked how she sprang to his defense.

"He thought of her in Boston as being so completely safe and far away and removed from everything wild and rough—I'm certain he never, ever
dreamed this silly rumor would grow and become a
threat to her. Or he would have ended it immediately."

"Well, we have to end it now—somehow," Wolf

said grimly. "Mind if we take this letter with us, Miss McCoy?"

"Call me Crystal. And yes, please take it and use it however you can to put an end to all this. What else can I do to help?"

"You've done so much already." Rebeccah smiled. "I don't know how to thank you."

"Stay in town and have supper with me," Crystal implored, her velvety smile embracing them both. "The Emerson Hotel has the finest steak and potatoes in cattle country. Say you'll join me."

Rebeccah threw Wolf a hopeful, questioning glance.

"We have to eat." He shrugged, still pondering how he could protect her from a lying boast that was bringing the worst scoundrels in the territory to her door. How the hell would he do it?

"You heard what the man said. We have to eat," Rebeccah told Crystal and then grinned. "We'd be pleased and honored to join you."

"You gotta eat," Neely Stoner told Billy. He gave a mocking guffaw at the boy's curt shake of the head. "What's the matter—campfire grub not good enough for you? Well, you'll get used to it."

Billy only glared at him, trying to look as if he wasn't afraid. But he was afraid. He was afraid of both of these men who had sprung out at him and Joey while they were hunting squirrels with Sam. The taller man had knocked Joey to the ground with one powerful blow, while the other one, the one who was always hanging around the saloon and visiting Miss Rawlings, shot Sam.

Billy tried not to think about Sam being dead. Sam had tried to protect him when Chance Navarro had scooped him up onto his horse and started riding off with him. But it had all happened so quickly, Sam couldn't have stopped any of it. Why did Navarro have to shoot him?

Billy knew the answer to his own question. Because both Navarro and this tall, long-faced hombre with the curly tobacco-colored mustache were badmen. Evil men. The kind of men his father was sworn to go after to keep ordinary citizens safe.

Billy knew he wasn't safe with men like these. They thought no more of snuffing out a human life than a dog's—or a mosquito's for that matter. Tears started behind his eyes. He was thinking about Sam.

Don't, he ordered himself. *Don't cry. They'll like that. You can't let them see that you're scared.*

But he was too late. The one called Chance was grinning at him over his coffee cup, stretched out leisurely on the opposite side of the campfire.

"Don't cry, boy," he taunted in a soft voice. "You'll come out of this all right. We're not interested in you at all. We're only hankering to get a certain lady's attention."

"Miss Rawlings? You've tried to do that—but she doesn't pay much attention to you, does she? She likes me and my pa better."

"You'd best hope she likes you well enough, kid," the tall man warned, sitting down next to Billy and taking out his gun. He began to polish it with a cloth from his saddle pack, studying every angle and line of the Colt with a loving eye. "Or else you can say adios to your pa and Miss Rawlings and Powder Creek—forever. If Miss Rawlings don't do exactly as we tell her, we're going to shoot you full of holes and drop you down that ravine over there and let the buzzards eat you."

He broke into raucous laughter, and Navarro let out an answering chuckle. Billy clenched his teeth.

"Go to hell," he muttered, too angry to be scared anymore. "My pa is going to kill you both. And the buzzards'll eat *you.*"

Both men sobered suddenly and regarded him with hard, stoic expressions. "Could be," the tall man said slowly, and nodded. "But don't bet on it, boy."

Chance Navarro smiled coldly at him across the fire.

"Pray tonight, boy. Pray real hard. And maybe you'll live to see your pretty Miss Rawlings again."

He didn't say I'd see Pa, Billy thought with a little choke of fear. He stared at Navarro, who was watching him smugly. *Why doesn't he think I'm going to see Pa?*

Billy inched closer to the fire and closed his eyes. He hoped his gramma was watching over them. He and Pa and Miss Rawlings were going to need all the help they could get.

23 It was suppertime the next evening when Rebeccah and Wolf rode up the trail to her ranch. The quiet of early evening was descending. Barely a twig rustled or bird chirped as they dismounted before the little cabin and went inside.

Everything was just as neat and orderly as she had left it two days ago when she'd set out in the morning for the schoolhouse. Rebeccah could scarcely believe that so much had happened in the space of two days.

"Pack what you'll need, and then we'll go find Billy," Wolf said after making a quick inspection of the bedroom to make certain no one had been inside. "You're not spending one more night alone here."

"What will the townsfolk say about my staying with you, Sheriff Bodine?" she teased, too happy with all that had happened between them to share his grim concern. "Honestly I do think you're worrying more than is necessary. Russ, Homer, and Fred were the last members of the Rawlings gang. The only other person who seems to be after this imaginary mine is Neely Stoner."

So safe did she feel now with Wolf that she even

managed to speak the name without a tremor in her voice. But Wolf took her by the shoulders. "He's the last man on earth I want you to have to tangle with. I've been making inquiries, and there's no word yet on him passing through any towns in these parts. But I haven't given up. He's probably using a different handle these days. I'm going to find him, Rebeccah, and put an end to this once and for all. In the meantime I'm not taking no for an answer. You're coming back to the Double B tonight."

His kiss was rough and urgent, yet tender for all that. "Go pack," he ordered softly, tracing her lips with his tongue.

"But I have a better idea," she coaxed, her fingers sliding over the hard muscles of his back.

Wolf chuckled. "I'll bet you do, sweetheart."

"No, that's not what I meant. Why don't you go and find Billy and bring him back here for supper? That will give me time to get my things together, and afterward we'll all go back to the Double B together."

Wolf glanced out the window. It was quiet. Too quiet. He had a strange feeling in his gut, but he couldn't identify the cause. He felt a sudden urgency to see his son.

"All right, Rebeccah." He kissed her quickly on the lips, wanting to linger, to hold her, and indeed to make love to her right here in this very parlor, on that horsehair sofa where she had bandaged his wound that first night and served him coffee. But he couldn't stay now. He needed to find Billy.

"I'll check at the Double B first to see if he's

there doing his chores. If not, I'll try the Pritchards' and the Bradys'. We'll be back before you know it."

"By then I'll have fixed us all a special celebration supper. It might help break the news to him that he's going to have a houseguest."

"Not just a houseguest. A new mother." Wolf's arms felt deliciously strong as he wrapped them lovingly around her. He spoke against the fragrant cloud of her hair. "Someone more like a real mother to him than his own mother could ever have hoped to be. He's one lucky hombre. We both are. And you and I, Miss Rawlings, are going to make it official just as soon as you can get yourself the prettiest wedding dress you ever imagined."

"I'd happily marry you in this," Rebeccah assured him, indicating her much-crumpled wool skirt and blouse, "but since you mentioned it, I did happen to spy the most heavenly mauve satin. It was in a mail-order catalog at Koppel's, and—"

Rebeccah abruptly broke off. She threw herself joyously into his arms. "Oh, Wolf, I'm so happy!"

Never before had she even dreamed of happiness like this. Never before had the notion of settling down in one place with one man and his one young child sounded so delightfully wonderful to her.

"When I was a little girl," she said slowly, "I moved around all the time. And every time that moment came for us to ride on, to run and rob and hide somewhere new, Bear used to tell me that I was like his little daisy—a hardy wild flower, he said, meant to be plucked from the earth and cast anyhow into the wind. 'See where the wind takes you, Reb,' he would tell me as he'd put me up in the saddle. It was a virtue in his mind—a strength—to be able to let the wind take you this way or that, never putting down roots or getting tied to an ordinary life. But now I see that he was as wrong about that as he was about other things," she told Wolf quietly, her hands gently cupping his face. "I want to put down my roots, I want to be connected deeply and firmly to a life with you and Billy, here in Powder Creek. I don't want to be blown this way or that anymore or ever to know that kind of 'freedom' again."

"You never will. I'd never let you blow away," Wolf told her, his arms tightening around her. "You're far too precious."

Their kiss lasted long, yearning moments. Finally, remembering about Billy, Rebeccah laughingly pushed him away. "Bring Billy back soon," she urged. "Tell him I'm going to whip up some of those cheese biscuits he likes so well."

She waited until Wolf had disappeared over the rise before she went to work in the kitchen mixing flour and milk and butter into a soft dough, humming a little and thinking about the chicken dumplings she would prepare while the biscuits were baking. . . .

Then she saw the kitchen door opening.

"Wolf . . . ?" Rebeccah began, startled, her heart jumping into her throat, but when she saw who it was, her heart completely stopped.

"Howdy, Reb," Neely Stoner said amiably, leering at her from beneath his grimy black Stetson. "No need to look so surprised. You knew I'd be here someday. I always come fer what I want—don't you remember that?"

She went for the gun in her boot, but there was too little distance between them. Stoner dove at her and grabbed the derringer, twisting it easily from her grasp.

"You won't be needing this, Reb," he snarled, no longer even bothering with the sickening, subtle facade. The animal that he was had sprung out even as he leaped for her. He gave a mean, low laugh as he pocketed the derringer and pinned her arms to her sides. "Come on out to the barn," he invited, panting into her ear. "I have something to show you, something you jest have to see."

Gripped by terror, Rebeccah struggled wildly, but she was no match for Stoner's strength. He locked an arm across her throat and tightened it until red dots quivered before her eyes. At the same time he forced her toward the kitchen door, out onto the porch, then across the yard to the barn.

It took a few moments for her eyes to adjust to the darkness. Stoner suddenly released her and shoved her into a bale of hay. She heard her horses whickering nervously from their stalls.

Then came the scratch of a match, and a lantern was lit. A murky light swam out through the blackness, and Rebeccah saw Stoner only a few feet away wearing a wicked grin. He set the lantern down and came toward her. As Rebeccah shrunk back, he grabbed her arm, twisting it harder the more she tried to flinch away.

"Lookee over here, Reb. You've got company. Say hello to the kid."

And looking, she saw Billy, trussed up with heavy rope in the back of an empty stall, with a silk neckerchief bound tightly across his mouth and an expression of hopeless fear in his wide, gray eyes.

"Billy!" With a strength she didn't know she possessed, she wrenched free of Neely Stoner and shoved him backward. He fell over a crate of tools and went down with a crash. Rebeccah didn't even bother to glance at him. She was already at Billy's side, tearing the gag from his mouth.

"Billy, did he hurt you?" Horror choked her as the wet neckerchief fell away. Immediately she started struggling with the knotted rope at his wrists, but before she could budge them, a sharp blow knocked her backward.

"That wasn't smart, Reb. Not smart at all. The kid stays jest like this until I say he can go. If you want to see him safe and take care of him—get him some grub, bandage his hurts, anything like that— there's only one thing you have to do: Hand over those papers for that mine. If you don't, you and the kid won't leave this here barn alive."

"His father will kill you for what you've done to him, you stupid bastard! Do you remember what Bear did to you that day? Wolf Bodine will make that beating look like a Sunday-school picnic in comparison when he gets hold of you, Stoner."

He shook his head. "Your fancy sheriff won't find me—or either of you," he said, laughing softly again. "He's got other things on his mind right now, Reb. My pard is making sure of that. Bodine's going to be too busy to come looking for either of you for a while—and by then our business will be all settled."

He suddenly drew his gun, pointed it at Billy's head, and put his finger on the trigger. "Spill your guts, Reb. Or I'll spill the kid's brains all over this here damned barn."

Chance Navarro had watched Wolf and Rebeccah ride back toward Powder Creek from a hidden ledge on Elk Hill. He waited until he saw that they were both headed toward the Rawlings ranch, and then, when they were safely past, he rode like hell for the Double B.

His palms itched with the fervent desire to carry out his plan. In fact he itched all over. It had been a long time since he'd done anything like this—too long. He could hardly wait to do it and watch it. But he couldn't stay around for too long, Chance knew. He'd have to get out of sight and back to Rebeccah's barn before all hell broke loose and people started coming from miles around. Damn, he wished he could watch it from beginning to end!

Chance no longer wore the dapper broadcloth suit, narrow black tie, and elegant derby that were familiar sights to the residents of Powder Creek. What good would it have done wearing that mask when he and Stoner grabbed the kid if he still had on his trademark gambler's garb, a dead giveaway that that other kid might have recognized? No, since yesterday he'd shed his fine clothes for a red woolen shirt, plain trousers, a thick gray duster, gray sombrero, and black silk scarf. No one seeing him at a distance would recognize him as Chance Navarro, gambler dandy. He had thought of everything.

He rode right up to the Double B ranch house and went inside, smiling to himself.

As expected, no one was about. Every man in the area had joined the posse organized by the deputy, Ace Johnson, and Culley Pritchard to hunt down the men who'd taken the sheriff's boy. There was a note nailed to the front door for Wolf Bodine. Telling him there was trouble—telling him to come to the Pritchards' or the Bradys' or Mayor Duke's house when he got home and find out what had happened while he was gone.

Navarro whistled as he strolled into Bodine's house.

Nice place. Everything clean and cozy and pleasant.

Too bad it was going to burn.

He went up the stairs, glanced in at the boy's bedroom, and then the one that had belonged to the old lady. He went at last to the room that belonged to Wolf Bodine.

He stared at the oak-framed bed and wondered if Rebeccah Rawlings had ever lain in it.

His eyes shone with scorn. The woman was a fool. She had chosen to place her trust in a dull small-town sheriff instead of hooking up with the gaiety and excitement he would have offered her. She had chosen Wolf Bodine over him. She didn't deserve a silver mine. She didn't deserve to breathe. She was just as stupid and ignorant as all the others.

Chance went over to that bed and closed his eyes, trying to summon up the image of Rebeccah Rawlings lying there with Wolf Bodine. Oh, yes, he could see it. He could see them together in this very bed, the springs creaking as she laughed about how she had spurned him, keeping her little secrets from him, sending him away night after night with nothing but an occasional good-night peck, while she let Wolf Bodine do whatever he wanted. . . .

"You made a mistake, Miss Rebeccah Rawlings," Chance whispered to the silent, empty room. "A very big mistake."

He took the box of safety matches out of his pocket and, smiling, set to work. The magical fire sprang to life before his glowing eyes, and he threw the box of matches onto the bed.

He watched for a few precious moments as the sparks caught, grew, burst into beautiful shooting orange flames.

A glorious shudder went through him, and he laughed aloud.

Lovely. Prettier than any sunset he'd ever seen. Prettier than any woman he'd ever known. A fine, beautiful fire.

The sight of it took his breath away.

He turned and ran lightly down the stairs and out the door, hoping Bodine came home in time to see it. With any luck the sheriff would try to rush inside and save some of his possessions—family photographs maybe, or the old lady's jewels—would get trapped . . . and die.

Navarro whistled as he sprang into the saddle

and turned his horse toward the woods. He looked back once and saw smoke shooting through the roof and out the upstairs windows, and flames sparkling against the darkening sky.

A fine, beautiful fire.

24 Wolf heard hoofbeats approaching when he was half a mile from the Double B. When he saw Culley Pritchard riding hard toward him, he started to call a greeting, but the friendly words froze on his lips as he observed the flushed tension in the rancher's face.

"Thank the Lord you're back, Wolf," Culley exclaimed as he drew up alongside.

"What's wrong, Pritchard?"

"It's Billy. Sorry to tell you this, but two men grabbed him yesterday while you were chasing after Miss Rawlings."

The color drained from Wolf's face. At the same time, his blood seemed to chill, the iciness seeping into his bones.

"Go on," he said harshly as the rancher watched him with sympathetic eyes. "Tell me all of it."

"We're looking for him, Wolf, but damn it, he hasn't been seen since. The bastards knocked down Joey Brady and they shot Sam—but Toby patched him up. Anyway, Joey went for help. Ace and me formed a posse, and we've been trying to follow their trail, but they lost us last night. These hombres are wily. The other boys camped out down by Squirrel Lake and hope to pick up their tracks again today, but I came back thinking I might hook up with you. Why the hell would someone grab Billy? What for? Do you have any idea what's going on here?"

"I just might," Wolf muttered grimly. *Damn Bear Rawlings and his phony silver mine.* "Two men, you said? Any idea who they were?"

Culley shook his head. "They were wearing masks. Joey couldn't recognize them. Did you find Miss Rawlings?"

"She's home, safe for the moment."

Safe. Was she really safe? Was anyone in Powder Creek really safe until this silver-mine mess was cleaned up? First it was Rebeccah who was carried off by those no-good desperadoes and now Billy. Wolf felt certain that whoever took Billy had to be after the mine. Someone knew they could get to Rebeccah through him. Someone in town, listening, watching—someone who'd heard talk, or observed without being noticed.

"Do you smell smoke?" Wolf asked suddenly, and Culley started.

"Damn right I do. Look!"

Wolf followed the direction of his pointed finger and saw the black plumes of smoke surging up above the trees ahead. "It looks like it's coming from the Double B. Culley, you ride to the Moseleys' and bring help. Leave someone to spread the word—and hurry!"

As Culley Pritchard wheeled his horse toward the Moseley ranch, Wolf veered off the trail and straight into the woods. He knew a shortcut to the

Double B. It was a rougher road, full of treacherous
low-hanging branches, but it would take less time
than the main trail. He was about to spur Dusty to a
roaring gallop when he heard the steady thud of
another horse's hooves and the crunching of
brush. Some instinct caused him to swerve behind
a stand of cedar and rein Dusty to a standstill.

A blur of a figure flashed past him, headed
toward Rebeccah's ranch. Wolf caught a glimpse of
a dark duster and hat, but didn't recognize the
rider crouched low over his horse's mane. But he
knew it wasn't one of the ranchers or cowboys
from town, and sensed it wasn't a friend who had
spotted the fire and was riding for help. There was
something furtive about the man who'd come tearing through the forest, something he couldn't de-
fine or explain. Wolf hesitated. He ought to get to
the Double B pronto and save what he could of
whatever building was on fire. He could at least
begin throwing buckets of water at the fire until
help arrived to put it out. But something told him
to follow the man racing away from the ranch. He
felt in his bones that the rider was connected
somehow, that all of this was connected somehow.
Billy missing, the ranch on fire—disaster was strik-
ing everywhere he looked, and he had a feeling it
all revolved around those papers certain folks
thought Rebeccah held. Rebeccah . . .

Fear brushed his spine. Why had he left her
alone?

Without another glance toward the fire, Wolf
urged Dusty along the wooded trail in pursuit of
the rider.

* * *

"It's done," Chance announced, his gun drawn as he stepped into the barn to meet Neely Stoner's questioning gaze. Stoner let out a grunt of approval.

"What about her? Did she talk?"

"First she claimed there was no mine," Neely Stoner sneered. "Claimed Bear made the whole thing up. Said she had a letter to prove it, but Bodine is carrying the letter on him. Convenient, right? She must think I'm a damned fool."

"Did you threaten the kid?"

"Yep. Then she swore there was a mine, but she wouldn't say a word until we let Billy boy go."

"Let me handle her," Chance urged.

Stoner nodded. He smiled with anticipation. "Don't mess her up too bad, whatever you do. I want a go at her before we hightail it out of here. And I want her still lookin' pretty. It's more fun that way. You savvy?"

"You'll have to wait your turn for her, my friend." Chance fingered the holster of his gun. "If I get the information we need from her, I get her first. And by the way, her cabin's on fire."

"Already?" His mouth dropped open. "You damn fool! Son of a bitch, Navarro! Couldn't you wait until we were finished here?"

"It's more exciting this way," Chance murmured, his eyes very bright in the dimness of the barn.

Stoner yanked the barn door open again and saw the black ribbon of smoke streaming up toward the sky. He couldn't see any flames yet.

"I started it small," Chance explained smugly.

"But we don't have too much time." He lowered his voice so that it would not carry. "We'll finish with them and leave the boy's body in here. The fire'll spread soon enough. But I say we take the girl along for fun. That way we'll both have plenty of time to enjoy her."

Straining to hear the soft, muffled words, Rebeccah's blood curdled. Her cabin was on fire! She knew then without a doubt that neither of these men intended for her or Billy to survive. Before they'd lowered their voices, she'd recognized the man who'd entered the barn, the one helping Neely Stoner. Chance Navarro! Her breath hissed out of her as he approached the entrance to the stall.

"I should have known," she cried contemptuously, her hands clenched so tightly, her nails dug into her palms. "You're about as low as a worm, aren't you, Navarro? But then, you told me, that's not your real name, is it? Nothing about you is real. Not your name, not your fine words or pretty manners. You're just a cheap fake."

"Careful, Rebeccah." Chance regarded her soberly. "You don't want to make me angry."

No, she didn't. Furious as she was, Rebeccah decided that she'd best hold her tongue. She had Billy to protect somehow, though how she was going to keep these two animals from hurting him was a mystery to her at the moment. And how they were going to escape these men before the fire spread to the barn, she couldn't imagine. She must manage it somehow.

Why hadn't she seen through Chance Navarro sooner? That day, when he'd begun asking her all

those questions, she'd had a feeling about him—
but nothing more than that. She hadn't even really
had time to ponder it and see where that feeling
led, whether or not it formed an actual suspicion,
because Russ and Homer had grabbed her before
she'd had the opportunity to reflect. But now, seeing him here with Neely Stoner, everything fell into
place. Chance, the happy-go-lucky, charming gambler who'd tried so hard to win her friendship and
her trust, was in cahoots with Neely Stoner—he
was part of this evil plan that put Billy's life and her
own in danger. He was no friend to anyone, only a
low-down snake obsessed with his own greed.

"Don't worry, Billy, everything will be all right,"
she whispered to the boy huddled beside her, and
put an arm across his thin shoulders.

She had convinced Neely to remove the gag at
least, but the monster had not allowed her to untie
the ropes binding Billy's wrists and ankles. The boy
moistened his lips and whispered back, "I know."

But he sounded scared—as scared as Rebeccah
felt.

Rebeccah's eyes narrowed as Chance, overhear-
ing the boy's brave words, laughed out loud.

"Did you hear that, Stoner? These two think everything's going to be all right."

Neely, coming up behind him, gave an answering
grin. "Sure it will—if Reb here decides to talk."

"You'd better speak up real soon, too, Rebeccah,
because we don't have any more time," Chance
said. Suddenly he reached down and yanked her to
her feet. "If you think that small-time sheriff is going to rescue you, you can just put that thought

right out of your mind. He's got other things to think about right now. Like his boy having disappeared—and his ranch burning down."

Chance's green eyes shone with pleasure as he saw the horror transfix her face and heard Billy's cry of despair.

"Want to know my real name, boy?" he asked suddenly, keeping his glance pinned to Rebeccah's paper-white countenance. "It's Larson. Earl Larson. Maybe your pa mentioned it to you sometime."

Larson. Even as the first whiff of smoke reached her nostrils, a memory stirred inside Rebeccah— Earl Larson was the name of the gambler Clarissa had been with when she'd been killed, caught in cross fire.

"There was this woman, you see, kid, and she left her weak, sniveling husband and squalling bambino and went traveling—she met up with me and brought me luck—for a while. And then one night I had an ace up my sleeve and got caught—and this hombre wanted to kill me, so I pulled this woman in front of me and used her as a shield while I drew my gun—"

"Oh, no," Rebeccah breathed.

"—and she got the bullet that was meant for me, and saved my life, and I managed to shoot that dirty hombre before he could get off a second shot. Pretty clever, eh, kid? You want to know that woman's name? It was a real pretty name. . . ."

"No!" Rebeccah cried, and struck him across the face with all her strength. "Shut up!" she shrieked.

Chance grabbed her, his fingers digging into the flesh of her arms with brutal force.

"You're not in charge here, Reb," Neely Stoner shouted, leering at her, his rancid breath hot in her face. "And there's no Bear Rawlings to save you now. It's just you, the kid, and us. So tell us what we want to know, because we're running out of time."

"Let Billy go and I'll tell you! I swear I will. But not until he's safely away from here."

"I told you, girl, you're not in charge!"

As Chance spun her around so that she faced the other man while he still held her helpless, Stoner raised his arm, swung it back, and smacked her across the jaw. Reeling pain tugged her into blackness for a second, then the world returned, blurred, edged with agony, making her knees buckle and her eyes smart.

The smell of smoke seemed stronger, seemed to infuse her lungs.

"Hit her again," Chance ordered. "That should knock some quick answers out of her."

"No! Let her go!" Billy shouted, twisting frantically against his ropes.

Stoner threw him a contemptuous glance. "Who's going to make us, kid? You?" he jeered, and lifted his booted foot to kick the boy.

"No. I am," Wolf snarled behind him, and with furious strength slammed the butt of his gun against the back of Neely Stoner's head. Stoner pitched to the ground like a load of pine logs rolled down a hill.

Chance Navarro yanked Rebeccah across him as a shield and went for his gun. But Wolf was faster, already lunging for Chance's gun hand. As they struggled over the weapon, grunting and twisting in a deadly contest, Rebeccah wrenched free and fell to her knees beside Billy.

"Pa!" Billy yelled, biting back tears as for a moment the gun veered toward Wolf's face.

Then, with a satisfied grunt, Wolf wrested the revolver away. And in the next instant he landed a staggering right hook to Navarro's jaw.

Chance staggered back, shook the dizziness away, and flashed his hand down for his second revolver. But a shot rang out before he or Wolf could draw.

For a moment Navarro stood, his face blank with surprise. Then the bright stain bloomed across his chest, and he went down with a grisly thud.

Wolf met Rebeccah's gaze across the barn. A tiny curl of smoke rose from her derringer.

"Nice shot."

"I couldn't let you have all the fun," she whispered.

She wanted to rush to him, to hold him close and thank God that he was safe. But there was no time for celebrating yet—the smell of smoke now pervaded the barn, and they heard the crackling hiss of the fire. And there was Billy.

His freckles stood out against his ashen skin, and the taut fear still stamped his face as Wolf cut the ropes with his knife.

"It's all right," Rebeccah soothed him in a steady tone. "Everything is going to be all right."

"Listen to the woman," Wolf added as he lifted the boy in his arms. "She's a force to be reckoned with."

Then he and Rebeccah, side by side, with Billy in his arms, ran from the barn.

The fire was rapidly engulfing the little cabin. Flames shot out the windows and the chimney, and even as they watched, chunks of the roof collapsed with a muffled roar.

The three of them held each other.

"It's all over now," Wolf said soothingly, as Billy, despite all his efforts, started to cry.

"Yes, you're safe now," Rebeccah told him, stroking his hair, watching with anxious eyes as Billy fought the tide of his emotions.

"They shot Sam," he gasped.

"Sam is fine." Wolf found it was a relief to smile again in the midst of this devastation. "Toby Pritchard patched him up good as new."

Billy's face lit with sudden joy, cleanly wiping away all traces of the ordeal he'd been through. He smeared a hand across his teary eyes. "Sam! Really? That's great. . . . Pa, is the Double B on fire too?" he asked more steadily. "That man said it was burning down. Is it true?"

"I think so, Billy. But Culley Pritchard and our neighbors are working to put it out. Just like we're going to work to put this fire out."

Rebeccah turned back to the fiery shambles of her cabin. With a heavy heart she thought of all her belongings, of her books, her new lace curtains, the pretty paintings on the walls.

"It's all right," she told herself and Wolf, as he set Billy down and swung a bracing arm around her. And she meant each word as she spoke them.

"They're only possessions. We're all safe. That's all that matters."

"This woman here is wise beyond her years," Wolf told Billy. "Pay attention to her." But his eyes lingered intently on Rebeccah's drawn face. "I love you," he told her roughly as he watched the various emotions flit across her vividly expressive countenance and saw her come to grips with each of them. His arm tightened, solid and strong, around her. "Damn it, Rebeccah, I love you. And I want to stand here and take you in my arms and make you feel better somehow, but there's no time. I've got to get the horses and that varmint Stoner out of there before the barn catches fire."

"Stoner!" Billy's eyes shone wildly. "No! Leave him! Can't you just let him die, Pa? No one would care! He doesn't deserve to live."

"I can't do that, Billy." Wolf threw a measuring look at his son. "That would be murder, not justice." He dropped a firm hand to his son's shoulder and went on quickly. "That man in there is as bad and vicious as they come, but the law will deal with him. He'll get his comeuppance, but it'll be through the courts and the hangman's noose, just like those men who killed Uncle Jimmy. Stoner's punishment is not for you or me to say. All we can do is uphold the law. But the law will get him, son. I'll see to that."

"Your father is right, Billy," Rebeccah added softly, giving the boy an encouraging smile. Hard as it was to accept, she knew that Wolf was right. There had been enough violence, enough hatred and death. Survival was one thing, revenge quite another. Wolf's beliefs, his integrity, his respect for the law, were what set him apart from violent and unscrupulous men like Navarro and Stoner and, yes, even from Bear. She would always love her father, but she knew that Wolf Bodine was a fairer, wiser, stronger man than Bear Rawlings had ever been. At that moment she loved him more than ever.

"It takes a strong man to do what is right," she told the boy, and saw him slowly nod.

The next few moments passed in a blur of frantic activity as Rebeccah and Wolf and Billy hurriedly led the horses from the barn and Wolf dragged Stoner's and Navarro's bodies away from the wooden structure. He tied up Stoner with what was left of the rope, in case the outlaw came to, though there was no sign of that happening.

Wolf sent Billy to ride for help. But the cabin was lost, Rebeccah knew, as she and Wolf futilely tossed countless bucketfuls of stream water on the snapping, hissing flames.

"I'm sorry," Wolf shouted as the roof caved in. He put his bucket down to come to her and waved an arm toward the crumbling cabin. "Too little, too late."

"It doesn't matter." A tremulous smile curved her lips. She gazed into his weary, beloved face and touched the black streaks of soot filming his bronzed skin, tracing her finger lightly along his cheek. "We'll start over, Wolf. You, me, and Billy, we'll start over—together."

The past was dead—for both of them. They could leave the nightmares and the pain of past hurts behind and look ahead to the future. Buildings didn't matter. Curtains and sofas and rugs didn't matter. The trust and the love and the passionate, unbreakably tender bond between them did.

What was more important than that?

Pulling her firmly into his arms, Wolf pressed a fervent kiss against her hair. He'd never thought he'd feel this way about any woman, or expected that he'd have a chance again at this kind of happiness. Rebeccah had healed his emptiness, brought him life, love, hope. Who would have ever thought that Rebeccah Rawlings, the filthy, scrawny kid he dug out from beneath a grimy bed, would turn out to be his own personal miracle?

Rebeccah nestled against him. A blissful contentment stole over her, despite the roar of the fire filling the night.

"You're right," Wolf agreed, tilting her chin up so that she looked directly into his steady, loving eyes. "We will start over. We'll build ourselves a wonderful life, Rebeccah. The three of us. Maybe even more." His eyes gleamed suggestively down into hers. "By the time we're finished, we could be a family of four, maybe five. If you want. . . ."

"Yes! I do want! I want six of us! You, me—and two boys, two girls. Oh, yes!"

A hungry, happy kiss sealed the bargain. As fire claimed the cabin, they started building new dreams—indestructible dreams that they would pursue and fulfill—together.

EPILOGUE

One week after the fires destroyed most of Wolf's and Rebeccah's homes, the citizens of Powder Creek voted unanimously at a town meeting to build a brand-new house for the soon-to-be-wed sheriff and schoolteacher of their town. Mayor Duke entered the motion into the record, suggesting that the town undertake the community effort as a show of appreciation for the outstanding service of these two fine citizens. Myrtle Lee Anderson seconded. She touted the excellent work of both the sheriff, in keeping the community safe, and the new schoolteacher, in inspiring the youngsters of the community and sharing with them her excellent Boston education.

Mrs. Anderson reminded the citizens at the packed meeting that she was the one who had suggested to the late Caitlin Bodine that Miss Rawlings, a newcomer to the town, would be an ideal candidate to fill the open position of schoolteacher. "She is a superior young woman in every way," Mrs. Anderson stated. "I knew that from the first moment I set eyes on her. And it is our duty to help her and our sheriff begin their married life in a comfortable and befitting home."

The motion was passed unanimously.

Ten days later Neely Stoner was hanged by the neck until dead and buried in a shallow snow-covered grave on Boot Hill beside the outlaw gambler Chance Navarro, also known as Earl Larson. Most of the town witnessed the hanging, but only the undertaker and Wolf Bodine attended the burial.

On Thanksgiving Day Wolf Bodine and Rebeccah Rawlings were married. The whole town attended. The bride wore a flowing silk dress of soft mauve, a mauve lace veil, dainty kid slippers, and around her slender neck, a gold locket whose lustrous surface was etched with the shape of a daisy.

It was a wedding gift from her husband, and that night in their honeymoon bed she swore to wear it always and keep it close to her heart.

When they moved at last into the spacious, two-story frame house built for them by the town, a house nestled in a lovely jewel of a valley affording vistas of blue foothills and towering forests of ponderosa pine, situated smack-dab in the center of their previously adjoining properties, Rebeccah and Wolf and Billy celebrated by throwing a grand party for all of their friends and neighbors. During the party they toasted the betrothal of Waylon Pritchard and Coral Mae Taggett, drank huckleberry wine, and danced until their toes throbbed. Rebeccah played the piano, and everybody sang along. Fortunately Culley Pritchard and the neighbors who had rushed to help fight the fire at the Double B had succeeded in putting out the flames before damage was done to Caitlin's rosewood piano. It was one of the few salvageable furnishings rescued from the house, although Culley had heroically dashed inside in time to also save the Bodine family photographs displayed upon the mantel.

Nine months after the fire a splendid event took place in the Bodine household. In the full glory of a brilliant Montana summer, with the golden asters, bitterroot, columbines, poppies, and daisies blooming riotously across the land—Rebeccah Bodine gave birth to a shrieking, red-faced baby girl.

The ecstatic parents named her Caitlin Daisy Bodine.

The next day Billy Bodine sneaked his dog, Sam, up to the nursery to meet his new baby sister, and Rebeccah came in just as the overjoyed Sam gave Caitlin's tiny face a vigorous all-over welcome.

Rebeccah scooped her precious child from Billy's arms and out of the dog's reach and tenderly dried her cheeks. She rolled her eyes at Billy's impishly laughing apologies and debated giving him a lecture on the importance of carefully handling infants, but when Caitlin actually gurgled forgivingly up at her big brother, Rebeccah could only grin at the pair of them. And Billy chuckled with glee, looking so much like his father that Rebeccah could scarcely contain her own laughter.

Wolf watched her suckle Caitlin that evening as the stars bloomed in a purple-velvet sky. Rebeccah sat propped up with pillows in their huge four-poster bed, the infant cuddled to her breast. Despite the weariness of recent childbirth, the slight lilac smudges beneath her eyes, Wolf thought she had never looked more lovely. Her skin glowed, and her eyes radiated pure happiness.

Downstairs, Billy banged on the piano—he was

learning "Oh, Susannah." Sam barked enthusiastically along.

Wolf and Rebeccah grinned at each other. "Practice makes perfect, Sheriff Bodine," Rebeccah murmured, stroking Caitlin's fuzzy head.

"Well, then, Mrs. Bodine, you and I must have been practicing a lot—because this here little girl is the most perfect thing I've ever seen—next to her mother," Wolf said, and leaned down to touch his lips to hers.

Rebeccah clung to his lips. "She *is* perfect," she agreed dreamily, meeting his gaze with loving eyes. "But that's no reason we should give up practicing. We now have one handsome boy and one exquisite girl. Plain arithmetic says there are at least two more to go."

"Maybe three," Wolf grinned, sitting down beside her as the baby fell asleep at the nipple and gave a tiny, contented sigh.

Rebeccah's violet eyes twinkled back at him.

"Maybe three."

"What are we going to name them all?"

"Oh"—she gave a graceful little shrug, but her eyes danced at him—"I'm sure we'll think of something."

"We always do, Mrs. Bodine," Wolf said softly. His cool smile was a caress in the summer night. "We always do."

Joan Johnston

"Joan Johnston continually gives us everything we want… fabulous details and atmosphere, memorable characters, and lots of tension and sensuality."
—Romantic Times

"One of the finest western romance novelists."
—Rave Reviews

☐ 21129-8	THE BAREFOOT BRIDE	$4.99
☐ 21280-4	KID CALHOUN	$4.99
☐ 20561-1	SWEETWATER SEDUCTION	$4.50
☐ 21278-2	OUTLAW'S BRIDE	$4.99